Good Guys Wear Black

By Lizbeth Selvig

Good Guys Wear Black
Beauty and the Brit
Rescued by a Stranger
The Rancher and the Rock Star

Good Guys Wear Black

LIZBETH SELVIG

AVONIMPULSE
An Imprint of HarperCollinsPublishers

Excerpt from *The Rancher and the Rock Star* copyright © 2012 by Lizbeth Selvig.

Excerpt from *Rescued by a Stranger* copyright © 2013 by Lizbeth Selvig.

Excerpt from *Beauty and the Brit* copyright © 2014 by Lizbeth Selvig.

Excerpt from *The Governess Club: Sara* copyright © 2014 by Heather Johnson.

Excerpt from *Caught in the Act* copyright © 2014 by Sara Jane Stone.

Excerpt from *Sinful Rewards 1* copyright © 2014 by Cynthia Sax.

Excerpt from *When the Rancher Came to Town* copyright © 2014 by Gayle Kloecker Callen.

Excerpt from *Learning the Ropes* copyright © 2014 by Tina Klinesmith.

EPub Edition OCTOBER 2014 ISBN: 9780062370143

Print Edition ISBN: 9780062370150

JV 10 9 8 7 6 5 4 3 2 1

For my mom, Grace Feuk.
Actually, all the books I've written so far and will ever write are really for her. She's the most creative person I know—in life and in spirit. The confidence she's given me to attempt all the things I've done in my own life can't be measured. The love she's taught me can only be passed on—I can't possibly pay her back. The way she's modeled romance to me—and her whole family—is without equal.

Acknowledgments

ABOVE ALL, JAN Selvig, there will never ever be enough time to thank you for all your love, pride, support—and macaroni and cheese (among so many other comfort-food meals). I love you, my romance superhero.

A huge thank you to Georgia Storms, Jennifer Schumacher, and Jodi Selvig for graciously sharing and trusting me with the knowledge and experience you've gained from dealing with loved ones who live with Asperger's syndrome. You are three strong women now blessedly part of my extended family, and wonderful examples of how to love cheerfully with the day-to-day challenges autism spectrum disorder (ASD) brings.

My appreciation to The Autism Society for its wealth of help and information. Check out http://www.autism-society.org for more information on Asperger's and autism.

As always thank you to my phenomenal critique partners Naomi Stone, Nancy Holland, and Ellen Lindseth. Oh my gosh, how *do* you catch all those mistakes? Thank heaven you're the ones who have my back.

Jennifer Bernard and Maxine Mansfield—you rock as beta readers. Between the two of you I think, maybe, we nailed this.

Elizabeth Winick Rubinstein—agent, mentor, friend. Thank you for being a fantastic date at an awards ceremony! And thank you most of all for your smarts, your insight, and your amazing words of encouragement. Again.

Tessa Woodward—my dream editor, the person I look up to and always want to write well for, and the person who always promises I do and then boosts my confidence by saying everything right even when suggesting the best fixes for my stories—I can't thank you enough for believing in what's yet to come.

Oh, and GN and CE: Do you love Dewey NOW? I thought so! Love you two, too.

Chapter One

MIDDLE SCHOOL BOYS could be royal pains in a coach's neck, but Dewey Mitchell had liked eighth-grader Jason Peterson for two seasons. The kid didn't whine, he said, "Yes, sir," and he was talented—starting to come out of his uncoordinated shell and become a natural linebacker. Out of the forty-plus wannabe Quad County Middle School Gryphons darting around the football field like randomly sized tropical fish, Jason's early height and bull-like build made him a standout. A raggedy-jerseyed shark among a school of tangs and angelfish. Maybe this year he'd make the top team.

He trotted toward Dewey, his oversized shoulders wildly lopsided.

"Hey, Coach Mitchell," he called. "Coach Miller says I can't keep going today because my shoulder pads are busted. Gotta take 'em and get 'em fixed tonight."

Jason's eyes registered disappointment. But—the kid didn't whine.

"Yeah, he's right, you can't play without pads." Dewey grasped the deformed shoulder and gave it a wiggle. "How 'bout you pull that jersey off? Let's take a look."

After struggling to shuck off his top, Jason turned his undershirt-clad self in a circle. "It feels like they deflated."

"I'd say." Dewey chuckled. "Looks like you lost a rivet. C'mon, unstrap."

The problem was so minor Jason probably could have fixed it himself, given the right piece. Dewey dragged the toolbox he always had with him from under a bench, unsnapped the lid, and dug for a few seconds before pulling out a nylon pop rivet. Another minute later, the shoulder pads were whole again.

"Man, Coach, you can fix anything! Thanks!" Jason yanked the pads over his head and let Dewey tighten the chest strap.

"If you have the right tools, you can fix just about anything. Now listen, from now on you make it your business and your job to check this equipment every time you get done playin'. I'm not sayin' for sure you'd have caught this, but you might have."

Jason nodded somberly.

"Get back out there. Do some blocking."

"Yeah, okay."

You can fix anything, Coach. The compliment never got old. Every time, it reaffirmed the one vanity he maintained—that if there was a toaster on its last legs, a dryer on its last spin, or a power tool on its last job, everyone in town knew he could repair it. He also had a freakishly close rapport with car engines. He hadn't found a motor old or new he hadn't been able to make purr like a woman in love.

Which was an ironic thought on today of all days—a date that still socked him in the gut and turned him testy if he didn't fill it sunrise to sunset with a hundred and one tasks.

August eleventh. His old wedding anniversary. As well as the date his ex-wife had chosen to walk out on him six years later, proving cars were about the only things he could get to purr. The problem was, her bugout had happened ten years ago. It was time to get over August the eleventh.

Keeping busy was his fallback method of doing that. Working with the football program kept him plenty busy this time of year. Jason's praise hadn't hurt, especially since Dewey wasn't known as the world's warmest, fuzziest coach. He tended to be the taskmaster while the middle school and senior high head coaches played the wise and kindly guides. On the other hand, he couldn't be all that awful. He'd been assistant coach for the past ten years, and they kept taking him back. He hadn't made anyone quit the team crying yet. Once in a while a kid like Jason even seemed to like him. Go figure.

He checked his watch and took a mental run through his schedule for the rest of the day. Practice ended in half an hour. He had three deliveries from the co-op to make, and he had the mayor's car in the garage on a special rush job, work he'd guaranteed would be finished by tomorrow. The new exhaust system still lay in pieces not yet installed, but he wasn't worried about that. He'd get it put back together.

None of his customers, mayor or otherwise, went without their work getting done as promised, whether Dewey had a crap day or not. That wasn't their problem.

Loud whooping rose from the kids on the field, and Dewey looked up as they all stampeded in his direction. Gone were the schooling, colorful fish. Adrian Miller, their head coach, followed like a rancher trying to herd motherless calves. Dewey held up his hands to quiet them when they reached the sideline.

"You all worked your butts off out there today, right?" he asked.

The yeses swelled until he chopped his hand across his throat to silence them.

"And you all know what goes down tomorrow, right?"

This time they all murmured or nodded in silence. The next day team placements would be announced. Red Squad and Gold Squad. The colors supposedly signified political correctness. No one was on a B-Squad—to Dewey's disgust. Children these days were coddled for no good reason even though the kids themselves held no delusions. They knew how team sports worked even in middle school. In this case, every eager face who'd been trying out for four days knew the prize they were after was to be a Red Gryphon.

"Yes, the teams will be set for this season." Adrian took over the day's closing pep talk. "But there are no losers. Right, guys?"

"Right!" came the siren chorus.

"So when you come tomorrow you'd better be prepared to work hard." Dewey fixed the group with his toughest middle school stare. "Got it?"

"Got it!"

"So you know," he continued. "Those of you who worked with me on defense today?" They all waited, still calf-eyed. "Good job. Be sure and get water before you head out."

"See you tomorrow," Adrian added. "Ten o'clock sharp."

The players dispersed as parents arrived. Most of the kids filed past Dewey and slapped his raised hand. Jason stopped and slapped it twice. "Thanks again, Coach. I'm real glad I didn't have to miss the end of tryouts."

"No problem. Remember what I said."

"I will."

When they had all passed out of range, Adrian shook his head and laughed. "Another crop of eager little baby football players who adore you. It never ceases to amaze me. You harp on 'em like they're cadets, I'm the nice guy, and you get the thanks."

"Little puntable humans," Dewey groused. Something he'd say only to Adrian. "Tomorrow, once all the wailin' about not making the team happens, see if they still like me after I lecture 'em on tightening up their big-boy jockstraps."

"You need a passel of kids, Dewey. You'd make a great dad."

The arrow pierced and passed through his lungs and heart. Dewey winced and sucked against the pain. What the hell? Adrian had never said such a thing in his life.

"Oh, sure," Dewey managed. "But that takes more than givin' a few high fives to a raft of wannabes."

"Fine. Get yourself a good woman first, then. Have it your way."

It was definitely time to call it a day on the gridiron. "I'll let you know when she shows up, Adrian."

The cell phone in his pocket buzzed. He pulled it out to see the Gas 'n' Garage's number.

"Yeah, Joey?" he answered.

"Dewey?" The young man who worked for him spoke in agitation, like someone with a gun to his head. "You need to come quick. There's a car on fire."

"A car, what? Where?"

"They drove in ten seconds ago. I called 911, but I don't know what else to do."

Dewey waved a "gotta go" to Adrian, grabbed his toolbox, and dashed for his car. "Get the biggest of the fire extinguishers next to the overhead garage door," he shouted into the phone. "But don't get too close. Let the fire department handle it. Are the people safe?"

"Yes."

"Then keep your distance unless it's small enough to use the foam on."

He only hoped whoever had pulled into the station with a car on fire hadn't left it too close to the propane tanks. Hell, he thought, letting the potential scenario become a waking nightmare. That would definitely screw up his schedule.

ROSE HANREHAN TOOK one hand from the steering wheel of her red Mustang, sighed, and patted her sleeping son's shoulder. Getting Jesse to sleep in a moving car required the Almighty's personal intervention. She knew he shouldn't be in the front seat with her, but after eight draining hours for the third day in a row—Boston to Minnesota—of listening to him hum and sing, cry and chatter, and spout mileage statistics from the backseat, she'd strapped him into the passenger side belt and let him fiddle with the radio until he'd finally sagged into slumber. It only figured that they were not more than an hour from her new life.

Rose Hanrehan, Head Librarian. It sounded foreign and slightly unbelievable even though she'd practiced the title on and off since she'd accepted the job three weeks before. Yet, it rolled far more pleasantly from her tongue than Rose *Shakleford*, could-be wife of Judge Daniel Shakleford, also the daughter of Senator J. Sawyer Hanrehan and forever member of Massachusetts's Top Ten list of public curiosities.

Poor Daniel. Sweet, successful man though he was, he also played the latest role in her parents' parade of suitable prospects—potential husbands who would bring legitimacy at last to their unwed, single-mother daughter Rose. A shame they'd endured now for ten years.

Nearly eleven.

She stroked her fingers through Jesse's soft spikes of wheat-blond hair. Eleven years of joy and anguish she wouldn't change for the world. But she would, she'd told her family in her final act of exasperation, change her circumstances. If she was such an embarrassment, she would leave.

They hadn't believed her. Not until the last moment,

when she'd hired a moving company, emptied out her apartment, packed minimal clothing and supplies into her Mustang, and wished them well. Them and Judge Daniel, who would retain his mover-and-shaker status perfectly well without her.

All to take over a brand-new library in a town whose population was smaller than her father's country-club membership. It was the most exciting thing she'd ever done, and the scariest, aside from giving birth to Jesse.

Not that Jesse had been excited to move. He didn't like change.

Interstate 90 swooped across the north side of La-crosse, Wisconsin, and led to the wide expanse of the Mississippi River. A small thrill of excitement at the iconic waterway strengthened her last reserves of resolve even while it reminded her how long it had been since a bathroom stop. She needed one to the point of jiggling her left leg on and off, but she was darned if she'd stop and wake Jesse now. She could make it another fifty minutes.

She left the river and climbed through the valley on Minnesota's side, a thick canopy of hardwood trees arching from the limestone hills around her. Finally the freeway broke into the flat, and the ribbon of concrete stretched ahead of her as it had for most of the long trip. When she saw the first sign for her exit, she nearly had to wipe away tears.

Kenyon. Faribault. Kennison Falls.

Kennison Falls. The miniscule grouping of streets on Google Maps was suddenly real. She'd seen pictures of the new building she was to manage and street views of some of the other businesses. It looked like a normal small town, but she had no frame of reference for normal. She'd never lived in anything but the suburbs of Boston. She left the freeway and headed cross-country.

By the time she was five miles from town, her left leg had a permanent vibration, and the gas gauge hovered at empty. Her pulse pounded with nervousness at the inability to judge how far her fumes would take her. She would have stopped, but she'd passed no service stations on the small county road that led to her new home.

A small brown-and-white sign told her a state park was coming up in two miles, and as she continued she despaired of making it past the wilderness, convinced the park entrance was on a moving conveyor belt carrying it forward and keeping it just out of her reach.

"Come *on*," she moaned out loud. "This has to be the longest two miles in the country."

At last the entrance appeared on her left marked by a beautiful, carved wooden sign bearing a spreading tree beside a gushing waterfall. *Glen Butte State Park.*

Several hundred feet later she passed the sign she'd prayed to see. *Kennison Falls, Pop. 849.*

Her car gave its first hesitating hiccup. Nervousness rose to panic. She couldn't run out of gas now. Not now. Her bladder wouldn't hold for any kind of walk to town. And Jesse was not much of a trouper when he was tired. She eased off the gas and prayed her fumes still had the slightest bit of oomph. Her miracle appeared in the form of a square sign on a ten-foot pole that read *Mitchell's Gas 'n' Garage.*

Gas.

She reached the small building, and her relief turned to shock. Circling red lights atop a fire truck, the blue and red strobes of a police cruiser, and a milling group of people blocked one entrance to the station. It looked like the scene of a crime or accident. Rose crept past the driveway and was only partially relieved to find a second entry. She wasn't sure she wanted to drive into the middle of an accident or emergency, but the car stuttered again, and she cranked the wheel, out of options.

She coasted to the pumps and released a grateful sigh. A breathy "thank you" for blessing the last miles floated toward heaven. Then she squinted ahead to the cluster of people and lights. From this angle she could see a car—a black SUV of some kind—with rivulets of foam dripping from the open hood. Firefighters rolled up hoses and peered into the vehicle. A man, a woman, and two teenagers stood to the side wearing deer-in-the-headlight stares. One man stood out from them all—tall and muscular with broad everything: hips, shoulders, and legs. Well-proportioned and solid, he held himself like an athlete, arms folded across his chest as he spoke casually with a police officer.

And then, as if a single signal had alerted them all, every face turned toward her. The muscular man stunned her again with his Tom Selleck mustache and high, rounded cheekbones. A handsome mountain. Then the mouth beneath the thick, black mustache opened into an O and stuck.

Her car. The 2003 cherry-red Mustang she'd loved

since receiving it for college graduation ten years before was impractical at her age now, and maybe a little vain, but it, of course, not she, drew the stare.

And then she was out of time. Her body informed her in no uncertain terms it was done holding back her bladder. She glanced at Jesse, still sound asleep, and made a rash decision. They were far enough from the action that she would leave him in a locked car for two minutes. She couldn't take him to the ladies' room anyway.

"Hi, can I help you?" Muscleman Selleck started her way.

"Restroom?"

"Sure thing. Through the office."

His Minnesota accent—subtle, not Fargo-strong but tinged with the broadness that was such a part of him— made her want to smile. *He* made her want to smile. As if she'd found a big, friendly bear's den.

"Thank you."

"Need gas, too?"

"I do. I'll grab that when I get back. Four-hour driving stretch, you know."

"Fair enough. Really nice car there."

She nodded and trotted past him. "Thank you. I like it."

She knew she'd only been gone minutes by the time she left the restroom and returned to the car. But minutes were often all Jesse needed. Her heart skipped beats when she opened her door to find his seat empty.

"Jes-see," she groaned.

At first she didn't see him, but the inevitable came. "Hey, kid, I said you can't go up there."

She rushed toward the knot of people in time to see the big, friendly bear manhandling her son off the running boards of the fire engine.

"I have to see," Jesse screeched in his arms.

Rose had mere moments before these strangers were treated to a full-blown Jesse Hanrehan meltdown.

"Listen here," the big man said. "You're old enough to know better. You can't be climbing on the truck."

"Please." Rose reached him and grabbed for Jesse's flailing arms. "Put him down. Right now."

"He belongs to you?"

"This is my son. Please put him down or otherwise—"

"Otherwise he'll run right back to the truck? Lady, this is the second time we've taken him off it."

"I know. But put him down, and I'll handle this. He's overly sensitive to touch and anger."

The man released Jesse and pushed him toward Rose with a careless nudge on the shoulder. Jesse let out a cry that sounded as if he were being eviscerated. Rose glared at the man but had no time to confront him further.

"Jesse, sweetheart, take a deep breath." She held her son's face gently between her palms. "Breathe, you're okay. The firemen didn't know you were coming. We didn't make a plan with them; don't get angry."

He struggled. He'd come so far in the past three years and learned that he needed to focus and breathe, but he'd nearly passed the point of being able to help himself.

"Come on, Jesse. Nobody's angry. Now they know you just wanted to see the truck."

His eyes cleared slowly, like someone wiping fog from a mirror.

"It's a 1998 Pierce Quantum with a 1,500-gallons-per-minute pump, Mom. It's amazing. It carries 750 gallons of water, 30 gallons of Class A foam and 30 gallons of Class B foam. I want to see the gauges up close so I can draw them. I won't hurt it. But they grabbed me."

"Shhh, darling, relax. Let's see what we can do after the firefighters are completely done with their work, all right?"

The tension left his wiry ten-year-old body, and a somber thoughtfulness eased onto his face. "All right. But I'd really like to see the gauges."

"Yes. I know."

She stood. The man stared at her as if she'd just attempted to make peace with a space alien. His mustache twitched in a motion she read as scorn, and her fatigue, her adrenaline, and her hunger tumbled and fused into anger—however unreasonable it might have been.

"Do you make a habit of grabbing children willy-nilly when they're scared to death? How do you know what's going through their minds? How do you know how they're going to react? My son is traumatized by things like—"

"Lady." His voice, not deep but as big as he was, stopped her rant cold. "When I see a kid climbing three feet off the ground for the second time after being asked to stay away, and he ignores me completely? Damn right I grab him. I don't need some fool kid falling and cracking his skull on my driveway. And I don't need his mother thinking her precious baby can do no wrong. Your son got himself in trouble, that's the bottom line."

Her blood boiled at the phrase "fool kid."

"Sweetheart, will you go back to the car and get the credit card out of my wallet? You can unscrew the gas cap. I'll be right there."

"He stays away from the pumps. No one under age sixteen pumps gas."

"Go ahead." She urged Jesse off and spun on the man again. "Did you hear me say a word about pumping gas? If you want him out of the fire department's hair, then stay out of mine. I will go supervise him in two minutes, as soon as you understand something."

"Enlighten me." He folded his arms across his chest again.

"My son has Asperger's syndrome." Explaining infuriated her, but she needed him to understand her actions. "Do you know what that is? It's on the autism spectrum—a mild form. He doesn't understand social cues properly. I'm not excusing his behavior one bit, and I'm not blind to what he did wrong, but it needs to be dealt with in a particular way. Being touched unexpectedly is a strong trigger to very unpleasant meltdowns."

For a moment he considered her wordlessly, and she relaxed, hoping he'd gotten the point. She rarely explained Jesse away, but if it saved him from even one round of being judged as stupid, which he was not, she'd embarrass herself however she needed to.

"Well, ma'am, I'm sorry, but if he's that much of a social risk I'd suggest you keep him safe and not leave him alone."

It was her turn to gape. Slowly she shook away the stunned burn of his pronouncement. "Of all the arrogant, prejudicial, horrible things to say."

"It wasn't meant to be any of those things. But the world is in enough trouble without adults indulging every problem a kid has. But your son is safely away from that truck and is no longer my problem, so is there anything you need besides gas? I'm happy to help."

"Is there another gas station in town?"

He chuckled, the mustache lifting attractively toward the amusement in his eyes. If she hadn't detested him for being such an arrogant ass of a man, she'd have thought it cute. "There's a chain station about ten miles down the road."

Her heart sank. Ten feet would have been too far. She squared her shoulders and rescued a few last dregs of pride.

"Well, aren't you in luck? You get my money and my ire today. Fortunately gas is all I need, and, as I said before, I believe I can handle it fine myself."

"Glad to hear you've got control of the car. Anyone who drives one like this wouldn't deserve it if she couldn't take care of it."

"Do you stand in front of a mirror practicing your arrogance?"

He grinned, oblivious and infuriating. "Guess I must." He nodded. "I'd appreciate it if you'd supervise that boy of yours. Let me know if you need anything else."

Chapter Two

WAVES OF IRRITATION, like blasts of heat, rolled off the woman as she turned to the pumps. Rooted to his spot, Dewey watched the scene, studying her and her mystifying child. His own irritation took a reluctant backseat to curiosity and captivation. What kind of kid couldn't follow a simple directive from people in uniform? What nine- or ten-year-old kid knew the year, make, and model of a fire truck more than sixteen years old, not to mention its specs right down to the capacities of its foam firefighting equipment?

Asperger's syndrome. He knew the phrase but little about it. He certainly believed there were real syndromes out there, since he'd seen plenty of strange behavior in his life. But this reeked of a pissed-off mother simply warning him away from her weird kid. He knew very well that in this day and age you weren't supposed to touch a child but, damn it, the kid could have gotten badly hurt. And she sure as hell hadn't been around.

Then there was her car. Over ten years old and spotless as new. The red GT did *not* fit the woman. Or the situation. You didn't expect to see a mom and her son driving cross-country in a fireball-red sports car. She had some sort of mild, uppity accent and used words like "ire." In a way, she wasn't any more normal than her kid.

He tried to turn away. She wasn't from town. Thank goodness he wouldn't have to think about her once the gas was pumped. But something compelled him to watch her finish—something that told him the world would go back to being a lot less interesting once she'd left it.

The boy studied her assiduously as she hung the pump nozzle, and before Dewey could think too much about how odd *that* behavior was, the woman did the most amazing thing. She opened her door, took out what appeared to be a chamois, and bent over the gas-tank door to wipe and buff an area where gas must have dripped.

". . . she doesn't deserve it if she doesn't know how to take care of it." That's what he'd said to her.

Dang. She sure knew how to keep it . . . red.

His observations were cut off by a sudden wail. The boy lunged like a spaniel after a squirrel. The woman grabbed him, squatted, and took his hands in hers, pressing his palms together like he was praying. Her mouth moved quickly, and she leaned in close, her forehead nearly but not quite touching her son's.

It should not have been a remotely sexy picture, but it was nearly as attractive as the sight of her polishing the Mustang. The over-reactive mama wolverine morphed into someone intense and sincere with desperation around the edges, and something he didn't understand at all tugged at him, deep in his gut.

The boy finally nodded and quit fussing. The woman dropped her hands and leaned forward to kiss him on the cheek. After straightening, she glanced over her shoulder, and her son's wistful gaze followed. Dewey remembered his plea to look at the gauges on the truck. Should he give in and let the kid have his wish?

Then everything soft about the mother hardened when she met Dewey's eyes. Her delicately angled features tightened like sharp weapons, and the wisps of hair escaping from a long, thick brown ponytail seemed to freeze in place, as if they didn't dare move for fear of pissing her off further. She stood, her shapely legs—their calves bare and browned beneath the hems of knee-length cargo shorts—spread like a superhero's in front of her son. She didn't say a word, so neither did Dewey. He didn't need to take her on again. Let the kid look up the gauges online.

With a parting shot from her angry eyes, she ushered the boy into the passenger seat, darted to her side, and climbed in. The engine came to life and purred like a jungle cat. She, or somebody, clearly cared for the car. However angry she was, she didn't take it out on the Mustang but pulled smoothly away from the pump. Dewey smiled. It was her car, all right. Had it not been, she'd have peeled out to punctuate her feelings for him.

Impressive woman. A little crazy. But impressive.

He finished sorting out the fallout from the SUV fire, sent the fire chief, Duke Severson, and his crew off with the fire rig, got the vehicle owners set up with a rental car for the afternoon, and made sure Joey could work half an hour late so the deliveries would still get done despite the minor crisis.

With his schedule back under control, he headed out the rear door of the garage bay and across the wide, empty field separating his business from the family co-op that had stood since his great-grandfather's time, including through a devastating tornado three years before. The storm had demolished most of the Gas 'n' Garage and the two storage sheds once occupying the field, but Glen Butte Cooperative and Mill had barely lost a shingle.

Dewey pushed into the small office, the air thick, as it always was, with the dust of milled wheat and the sweet-sour pungency of oats, corn, and molasses. One of his brothers or a nephew would be hidden somewhere in the back with the day's order sheets. Glen would be out by now delivering cattle feed. On Tuesdays and Thursdays Dewey helped out by handling the horse feed and bedding deliveries. It kept him in good graces with the family and kept them mostly out of his hair.

"Yo!" he called.

"Duaney?"

He growled at his smart-ass youngest brother, Roger. "Aw, shut up," he hollered. "Give me what you've got that isn't grief."

Roger appeared, his face delighted at the rise he'd gotten. "Hey, bro'. What's the burr under your saddle today?"

"You. But what else is new? Any more orders come in besides what I saw this morning?"

"Don't think so. Unless you want to add a run out to Harold Olson's with that calf starter."

"Why not? I'm workin' late tonight anyhow. Gotta get Sam Baker's little Jetta going by morning."

"Does your list ever get any shorter?"

"Oh, it will. The day I die." Dewey took the clipboard Roger handed him.

"Coulda, woulda, shoulda, Duaney. We live a pretty cushy life up here running the co-op. You didn't have to go and expand."

"But I did. To get away from you. Besides, my schedule has its perks. Got to see a super-sweet older Mustang today. And a beautiful girl. Tell me, you ever see that up here? Huh? Huh? No. You see feed reps and ancient dudes in overalls. I've got the life, man. No regrets."

"A Mustang, eh?" Roger raised his brows. He, the youngest boy at thirty, and their younger-yet sister Elle were the only ones of Dewey's three brothers and two sisters who truly shared Dewey's love of cars. "Good shape?"

"Perfect on the outside. The engine sounded sweet."

"Nice. And the girl?"

"Hmm. Crazy pretty, like a Hollywood star. But a little crazy in the head, too. Had a kid with her, her son. He wandered smack dab into the middle of a bunch of firefighters and started climbing on the truck. And she comes out defending him with some autism excuse. Could have been true; he was an odd kid. I probably handled it badly because I guarantee I'm damn straight not her flavor of the day."

Roger's forehead wrinkled in concentration and then

smoothed back out with an aha! thought. "The woman. She say her name?"

"Never once. Didn't ask."

"There's a new librarian coming into town. Supposed to be here today or tomorrow, according to Gladdie Hanson. She's got a fancy degree from out East and a kid. I think her name is Rose something. Could it have been her?"

Dewey's throat went a little dry at the thought. "Nah," he said through the dust caught in his larynx. "She was too angry. Too much in love with her car and her kid to be a straitlaced librarian."

"Who says a librarian has to be straitlaced?"

True enough, he thought. Still, the image didn't fit. Except . . . that slight accent? The smart words?

"No." He repeated the sentiment more firmly and shook his head. "She didn't have anything with her, no *stuff*. No boxes or furniture. I'm sure she was just passin' through."

"Yeah, could be," Roger agreed. "We get all kinds, that's for sure."

Two hours later, Dewey headed the co-op's pickup back to the station through downtown Kennison Falls. The maple trees planted along Main Street's boulevards had taken full hold, and although they were still tiny compared to the mature trees that had shaded the town before the storm, things were looking whole again. Fewer and fewer empty spots left by destroyed buildings still existed. The newest addition to the rebuilding was the library. He passed it and slowed.

The structure had taken two and a half years and a dozen fund-raisers to replace, but it had been worth the wait, he supposed. It definitely added class to the little downtown. The building occupied a full corner on a small rise about four feet higher than Main Street. The old library had been a simple two-story brick-fronted building, unattractive on the outside but friendly enough inside, thanks to the town librarian Margaret White—a lady who'd been in the position as long as Dewey could remember.

Margaret, however, was not coming back for the re-opening. At age eighty-three, she had neither the health nor the heart to start over. So a new librarian had been hired. Dewey hadn't paid a lot of attention to the announcements as they'd come out. He liked the library. He used it. He assumed the person hired to replace Margaret would be similarly warm but stern and run the small-town library in a similarly efficient way.

The idea of a tiny little "Pretty Woman," with her strange child, running a studious place like the Kennison Falls library made him laugh out loud.

The new building looked like a stereotypical library done in miniature, with pillars and a classical façade, oversized windows on the front and a sideways set of steps to the main door, all made out of brick and native limestone. The only irony was a lack of lions. The old, plain library had boasted lions—beautiful stone figures carved by one of the town's original settlers. They'd been totally out of place against the homely building—a strange small-town quirk. Now that the town had a fancy library, however, it had no lions. To buy nice enough ones or have them made had been prohibitively expensive. For some reason, Dewey found that highly amusing. But people always told him he had a warped sense of humor.

Two blocks farther on, he passed the Loon Feather Café, the heart of town. He slowed to check traffic at the corner. And nearly slammed on his brakes in the middle of the intersection.

On the side street to his right stood a—*the*—cherry-red 2003 Mustang GT.

His pulse fast-tracked into a crazy beat, which surprised the hell out of him. He liked to think he honestly appreciated a beautiful car—arguably with more obsessiveness than the average person—but he was no longer a kid with motor oil in his veins. He'd seen cooler vintage beauties and hotter street rods than this one. What was the draw in a decade-old Mustang?

Maybe he felt sorry for it. Living as it did with a crazy person.

He laughed thinking about her, and passed through the intersection. It was the second time, he realized with a little bafflement, she'd brought him to laughter. Aside from his family, people didn't consider him someone easily amused. Focused, calm, and helpful. That was the persona he worked hard to portray.

He swallowed back the chuckles, unable to erase the memory of the woman's fiercely protective anger, and of the blazing eyes in a Disney-princess face. He knew kids, he knew parents. Nope, this princess had all the classic signs of an overprotective, obnoxious mother. Thank heavens she was not his problem any longer.

But she did have a hell of a nice car.

He shook his head to dispel the thoughts and continued on to face the mayor's Jetta.

JESSE'S HEELS BUMPED rhythmically against the legs of his chair as he meticulously stacked the plastic cups of coffee creamer before him into a tidy, upright triangle. He set them with the precision of a bricklayer, and Rose rubbed a dime-sized spot of pain between her brows, thankful for the peace this distraction provided. Her son's obsession with fire engines was nothing new, but after their close encounter at the service station two hours before, he'd had a particularly zealous afternoon of fact-spouting and "Mom-did-you-know . . . ?" monologues.

Then had come the fiasco with the apartment, and the message from the chairman of her brand-new library board. She pressed harder on the ache in her forehead. The problems blossoming before she'd even started her job weren't helping. Or maybe her head simply hurt from her first dealings with small-town mentality—specifically, the service-station owner and his heavy-handedness.

"Hi! I'm Rio. What can I get you two tonight?"

Rose popped her head up and automatically plastered on a smile. A redheaded young woman with unusual, beautiful, olive-toned skin stood beside the table like an angel of light. Hers was the cheeriest face Rose had seen since arriving.

"Oh, hi," she replied. "You know, I think I'm going for the hottest, juiciest burger on the menu. And extra fries. It's been an extra-fries sort of day."

"I'm sorry," the waitress said. "Then extra it is. On the house."

No you don't have . . ."

"Yes, I do! You're Rose, right?"

"I . . . am." She frowned in confusion. "But how . . ."

"Sorry," the woman named Rio said. "I was right where you are about a year ago—new in town—and I couldn't figure out how everyone knew who I was either. But, it's no mystery once you spend any time around here—everyone knows everyone. I heard from my co-worker who's good friends with someone on the library board that our new librarian had arrived with her son, so I guessed. We're thrilled you're here."

"My! Well . . . thanks. Thank you." Still disconcerted, Rose nonetheless latched on to the warmth in the other woman's voice. She appreciated the friendliness more than she could say.

"I also heard there were maintenance problems and you haven't been able to get into your new apartment yet. I'm sorry about that, too. What a pain after a long drive."

Rose ignored her own continuing surprise and allowed herself an unladylike snort. "It's true. A broken water pipe, I guess. It'll be four days until we can move in. I think we'll be at the little motel about six or seven miles out of town."

"Do you need a place to stay? My husband and I have extra rooms. If you didn't mind a longer drive, you'd be welcome." She looked at Jesse and grinned. "We have horses. Do you like animals?"

Jesse nodded, still laser-locked on his creamer structure.

Rio's offer nearly shocked Rose out of her chair. Who invited a complete stranger to her home?

"That's awfully nice of you. Is this the 'Minnesota nice' I've always heard about?"

"Nah, it's small-town nosiness. I grew up in the city, and I still find it crazy but fun to trust people and be hospitable."

"I'm from Boston. I *know* cafés aren't places where you get offers like this. Or if you do, it's more a cause for alarm."

"No lie. Right?"

"Well, thanks, but I think we'll stay closer to town. I have a million errands to run anyway, and the moving truck is due in two days."

"Great! It'll only be a few days, and you'll be on your feet. Meanwhile, let's get you fed. How 'bout you, kiddo, what can I get for you?"

"Mac and cheese." Jesse's eyes never wavered from his task.

"Jesse, you need to take a minute and look at the person who's speaking to you," Rose admonished.

"Whatcha building?" Rio asked him.

"An isosceles triangle."

Rose steepled her fingertips against her mouth to hold in a spurt of laughter, not at her son but at the dumbfounded response from Rio. To her credit, she recovered more quickly than most.

"Wow. I'm very impressed. Won't this turn into an equilateral triangle, though?"

"No, because the cups are taller than they are wide," he replied matter-of-factly.

"Yup," Rio said. "Amazing. All right, Mr. Sheldon Cooper, since it's mac-and-cheese day, is there anything you want to go with it?"

For the first time since sitting at the table, Jesse looked up with wide, astonished eyes. "You watch *Big Bang Theory*?" he asked.

"I do. I have a crush on Leonard."

He made a face. "That's gross."

"I'm glad you think so. What would you like to drink?"

"Milk."

"Would you like a milkshake tonight?" Rose asked. He'd had just as stressful a day as she had.

"Can I?"

"Sure."

"Vanilla, please," Jesse said.

"Ah, a man who likes it straight," Rio replied. "No chocolate, huh?"

"Chocolate goes in other things. Cake and hot cocoa."

She smiled at Rose. "I like this one. He must be a lot of fun."

That was one way to put it. Rose managed a quiet laugh. "He's amazing, all right."

Jesse watched Rio head back to the kitchen and craned his neck slightly to keep an eye on her until she disappeared.

"She's nice," he said.

"Because she likes *The Big Bang Theory*?"

"Because she knows what an equilateral triangle is."

"Hey, I know what one is, too," she teased.

"Well, duh."

The mood lightened all at once. Silently Rose blessed the first person she'd met in Kennison Falls who'd made this new life seem a shade less intimidating. Even Jesse had clearly relaxed from his hyper-exciting afternoon and went back to building his triangle with a little less seriousness in his young eyes.

The food's arrival required Jesse to take apart his creation, which he did with rare acceptance. The trade-off for his good humor was that he regaled Rose with the list of ingredients in the nondairy creamer, the whole of which he'd memorized while stacking. He then extrapolated on one, sodium caseinate, until she knew more about the substance—used, he told her, to make the fake cream thick and white and taste like real dairy stuff—than she ever cared to know.

Where *did* the child find this stuff? She knew, of course, that he was a master of search engines, but while most kids were driving parents crazy discovering inappropriate Internet sites, Jesse was following links about the most esoteric subjects on Earth. Even a librarian couldn't find what he could—she knew that for a fact.

"Hey, bud," she said. "What if you work on supper for a while and give the dipotassium phosphate and friends a breather?"

"Sorry."

"Don't be sorry. You just need to eat. How's the mac and cheese?"

"Good."

He got through two more bites. "Hey, Mom?"

She held up a forefinger. "Eat."

He nodded and dug in one more time.

"Rose Hanrehan?"

She popped her head up again and met the gaze of an older—late-sixties perhaps—woman with graying curls and a cushy, grandmotherly figure.

"Hello?"

"I'm very sorry to interrupt your dinner, but I wanted to find you before you headed for the motel. I'm Gladdie Hanson."

Of course. The voice resonated as suddenly familiar. Rose had spoken to her, the secretary of the library board, several times on the phone during the job interview process.

"Gladdie, I'm so pleased to meet you. We were going to get together tomorrow, right? I didn't miss anything?"

Rose started to stand, but Gladdie waved her back into her seat. "No, no, you didn't miss anything at all, dear. We're still scheduled for tomorrow. But I have a proposal that I wanted to share right away once I heard you weren't able to get into the apartment. I have a place for you and . . . this must be Jesse. Hello, young man."

Jesse smiled but didn't reply, which meant he hadn't made an immediate assessment, positive or negative, of Gladdie Hanson

"Yes, this is my son, Jesse. It sometimes takes him a while to warm up."

"I sympathize, Mr. Jesse. New places are intimidating. Well, to business. I know someone who owns a rental property—a wonderful older home a few blocks from the library. It was vacated two weeks ago and hasn't been rented yet. I thought maybe you two would like to look at it. It might be more comfortable than a sterile apartment—even if the apartments are new."

Rose's hopes gave a small leap of actual excitement. A house would be much nicer for Jesse than a cramped apartment.

"I might." She nodded her approval. "It depends on a lot of factors, of course, but how nice of you to think of us. I don't mean for people to go to this much trouble."

"Rose, dear, we feel very lucky to have enticed you to come. It was terrible to hear you didn't even have a place to land when you arrived. I don't want you turning around and heading back before you get started."

Rose laughed. "Please don't worry about that. I told you how excited I am for this change. Who do I need to talk to?"

"He agreed to meet me here and bring the key. I expect—"

The rest of Gladdie's words faded into a buzz of disillusionment when a figure loomed behind her, tall, foreboding, and this time *un*pleasantly familiar. Jesse sat bolt upright, his eyes wide. Rose's mood sank, and her heart followed, beating erratically the entire way.

"You," she said.

Chapter Three

GLADDIE CHUCKLED, HER gray-black brows lifting toward her hairline. "Why, Duane! You didn't tell me you'd already *met* our new librarian."

"Did you bring the fire truck?" Jesse still gaped, but nobody paid him any attention.

"You."

The gas-station owner—Duane? Who named a child Duane?—added a mocking little scowl to his echo.

"You own the house that's for rent?"

"I do not. My sister and her husband do. But they're out of town, and I've got the keys until they return."

"As long as you wouldn't be my landlord." Rose let the barest of smiles play across her lips, not sure where the teasing came from. He stared as if humor escaped him.

"Is the engine back at the fire station?" Jesse pressed his issue again, determined not to be left out.

"Safe and sound." Duane's gaze slipped to Jesse as he answered the question, but he didn't smile until he turned back to Rose. The one he offered was tinged with mocking humor. "Happily, I can promise I would definitely not be your landlord, Madam Librarian."

His gaze locked with hers, and for a long moment they searched as if gauging each other's true disposition. An upward tic at the corner of his mouth and a nearly imperceptible twitch of his mustache sent Rose's stomach into a jig that shocked her. If she'd read those miniscule signs correctly he wasn't really annoyed; still, that didn't make him worthy of one butterfly, much less a belly full of them.

"Do you know the fire chief?" Jesse asked. "Could I meet him?"

Duane stared as if Jesse had asked for bugs on his sandwich. "Got a little obsession with fire engines, do you?"

Immediately Rose's hackles rose and chased all fluttering wings from her stomach. "And if he does?"

He swung his gaze back to her and backed off with both hands lifted. "I've got no problem with it. It's unusual, that's all."

"You run a repair shop. I'll wager you can list a lot of different motors and cars, too. He happens to like fire trucks."

"Are there other trucks at the station?" Jesse asked.

"Several others."

"What kinds?"

"I don't know, kid. Sorry."

"He's got a name. Most people do."

"Lady." It was the second time he'd used the word derisively, and she bristled yet again. The man was irritation on two legs. "I am not out to hurt your boy, so would you mind pulling in the claws? What's your name, son?"

She knew Jesse wouldn't answer. He often refused to talk to people who irritated him, and Rose guessed that after being hauled down from the fire engine earlier her son wouldn't warm up for a long time.

"Jesse Loren Hanrehan," he said. Rose's mouth dropped open. "I was named after my grandfathers. Don't call me Jessica."

Another smile ghosted across the garage owner's lips. "Okay, I can make that deal. And, to answer your question, I know the fire chief, but he doesn't let anyone play with his trucks that I'm aware of. And I don't know them like you do, so I have no idea what kind they are."

"Maybe if I meet him, he'd tell me."

"Sure, kid, he probably would. Have to do that sometime."

"His name. Is Jesse," Rose clipped, sotto voce.

Full-blown annoyance bubbled up in the man's eyes, and his smile disappeared.

"Sure, *Jesse Loren Hanrehan*—" He stared at Rose. "He probably would."

Gladdie tapped him firmly on the upper arm and clucked in admonishment. "Now, you, stop it. Rose, don't you pay any attention to our Dewey here. He's got a cranky old bachelor mechanic's soul sometimes. He gets that from *his* grandfather." She smiled at Jesse.

Dewey? Duane-Dewey?

"I can do my own PR, old woman," he said, but the words were fond. "I think we need to let Ms. Hanrehan finish dinner. I can leave the key with you, and you can show her around the house."

"Nonsense. I can't answer any of the questions she might have. We'll go have some coffee, and Rose, you don't hurry. I'm serious. We'll be in the corner over there whenever you're done."

"I'm sending you to Sam Baker to explain why his car isn't done," the man groused.

"The mayor has plenty of transportation at his disposal. He won't give you any grief, you know that. Come get us when you're finished, Rose."

"Thank you," she said, although Duane-Dewey Mitchell looked far from pleased. "I don't want to put anyone out. We can easily stay at the motel."

"And you might choose to do that anyway," Gladdie said. "But have a look first. There are some furnishings, too, if I'm not mistaken."

"Minimal," Dewey agreed.

"All right." Rose acquiesced to the pressure. "We're almost done, aren't we, Jesse?"

He nodded and shoveled a spoonful of macaroni into his mouth, his attention no longer on the two people beside them.

Fifteen minutes later, Rose paid and she and Jesse approached the table where Gladdie chattered easily to a silently nodding Dewey. All traces of tension and anger had disappeared from his face, and with his hands wrapped around a heavy ceramic mug of coffee, he looked like the friendly bear she'd originally encountered. His dark-coffee eyes actually sparkled when he looked up.

"How was the mac 'n' cheese? Kid?" He winked at Rose, and her face heated traitorously.

"Good."

Gladdie pushed her mug into the center of the table. "Ready to go, Dewey?"

"Sure thing."

"Jesse, did you see the birds when you came in?" Gladdie asked.

"Yes."

"Did you talk to the little white one, Cotton?"

Seconds later Jesse had followed Gladdie from the main restaurant to the foyer, and without knowing how it had happened Rose stood alone with the man whose amenable exterior hid his heart of arrogance. She had no idea what to say that wouldn't set him off.

"She could sell an elevator to a giraffe," he said first, inclining his head toward Gladdie's disappearing backside.

"She bosses you around pretty well. Me, too, for that matter."

"She bosses everyone around. With kindness, thankfully, the old busybody."

"You seem fond of her."

"Believe it or not, she was my nanny when I was a kid."

"So you grew up here?"

"One of the poor slobs who never escaped." He smiled.

"I understand wanting to escape."

"No, it's not that. It's just small."

"So . . ." She considered exactly what to say next. "I'm thinking we haven't gotten off to the best start, Mr. . . . ? What is your name, really?"

"Dewey Mitchell."

He held out his hand and engulfed hers. But what she expected to be a doughy, impersonal grip shocked her with its warm strength—tight and sinewy, hard. Talented. His fingers squeezed hers in greeting, a wayward trill slipped into her stomach, and he released her.

"Rose Hanrehan."

"Mother of Jesse Loren Hanrehan."

"That's L-o-r-e-n, for information's sake. I realize it sounds like two girls' names."

"Noted."

He looked as if he wanted to say more, but put his lips together and twisted them thoughtfully instead. The black mustache, thick and perfectly groomed, was too sexy for her comfort. She wasn't normally a fan of facial hair, but this man wore his incredibly well.

She swallowed. "I suppose we should catch up."

"Probably."

"Thank you, by the way. I get the feeling this is pulling you from something important."

"There's always something to do," he said. "It's fine. I just like giving Gladdie a hard time."

It would be nice to have that kind of easy relationship with someone, she thought. Once upon a time she'd come close with her father . . .

In the Loon Feather's foyer, Jesse had his nose pressed to the wires of a five-foot-tall cage. Two cockatiels, one gray, one white, scrabbled on perches, cocking their heads at him and squeak-squawking. Jesse laughed.

"You rock, dude," he said.

She remembered the sign she'd noticed when entering the café: "Cotton's current phrase: *You rock, dude*."

"You're supposed to say it to her, and she'll learn to say it back," Jesse said.

"Really?" Rose looked to Dewey for confirmation.

"True," he said. "Kind of our town mascots. Cotton here says about six different phrases. Every time she learns something, Effie, the owner here, picks a new one for customers to teach her."

"How fun!"

He shrugged.

"The other one, Lester, won't talk," Gladdie said. "But he whistles tunes. He used to have only two songs, but now he has three."

As if on cue, the little gray bird puffed his chest and broke into the theme from *Happy Days*.

"That's amazing!" Rose couldn't help but be enchanted.

When Lester finished, the white bird, Cotton, chirped. Jesse mimicked the sound. "You rock, dude," he said then.

"'ock doo-doo," chirped the bird.

Jesse stared for two seconds then clutched his tummy and threw his head back in a giggle that rolled from his toes. "Doo-doo? Doo-doo!" The giggles grew to snorts.

Rose's worries dissipated, lifted from her shoulders and carried off by Jesse's bubbles of effervescent laughter. She put her arms around her son, grateful for this moment when he didn't squirm away from a mother's needy hug.

"You're completely silly," she said. "Stop being so silly."

"Doo-doo!"

She stood. "Time to go, goofball. I'm sure we'll see the birds again."

He waved at the cage and followed her willingly from the restaurant, chuckling all the way to the car. Dewey had parked across the street from her, and his bright eyes made it clear, as they had earlier at his station, that he completely approved of the Mustang. His appreciation was palpable, and she found the hairs on the back of her neck lifting in pleasure, as if he had caressed *her* with those espresso eyes.

"You drove her all the way from Boston?" he asked.

"I did. Turns out to be a great car for a woman on a long drive. It draws way more attention than I do."

His gaze swung easily to her and fixed her with a confident look. "Oh, I doubt that."

The words heated the blood in her cheeks, but she honestly didn't know if he'd paid her a compliment or simply commented on her difficult personality.

"You're wrong," she said, making herself smile. "Miss Scarlet here is better than a Rottweiler."

"You named her Miss Scarlet?" His eyes took on a "please-say-it-ain't-so" narrowness, and she waggled her brows.

"My own version of *Clue*. Miss Scarlet in the dark with a rich billionaire. I was shallow right after college."

He fisted his hand loosely in front of his mouth and pretended to cough, but not before she saw his prominent, sexy Adam's apple bob with swallowed laughter. "Touché," he said, his voice slightly higher than usual, his eyes bright. "Does that mean you've had the car since it was new?"

"Yes. I got it for college graduation."

"Nice present." He ran his gaze from trunk to hood and nodded, then straightened. "Okay. Gladdie will meet us at the house. You can follow me, then."

His accent floated lazily off the final "then," just short of charming to her Bostonian ears. He was an enigma of a man, with his broad build, his strong hands, his soft, long vowels, and his brusque self-assurance about everything. He wore sex appeal like an uncomfortable suit— something he'd owned his whole life but didn't use often enough to get used to. It was too bad. The suit was beautifully made. Given a little care, he could have made it look like a tuxedo.

The neighborhood he led her to was not what she'd imagined. She'd grown up with her parents and sister in the wealthy Back Bay area of Boston and had rented a pretty brick townhouse in Charlestown. Here, she'd pictured a slightly shabby, little-town, shoulder-to-shoulder, but the street was as quaint as anything she'd seen back home, and utterly peaceful.

The tidy houses ran the gamut from small, unassuming bungalows to triple-storied Victorian beauties in candy colors with gingerbread details. The one belonging to Dewey's sister fell somewhere in the middle and it enchanted her. The two-story, lemony-yellow house boasted round white pillars that held up the porch roof. The porch itself stretched across the entire front of the house. On top of the porch roof, another railing, black wrought iron like an old-fashioned widow's walk, balanced the façade.

"This is beautiful," she said when Dewey and Gladdie met her on the cobblestone walkway. "It looks huge."

"Four bedrooms, two fireplaces, updated kitchen. Unfinished basement, but the upper floor has a nice space for a family room." Dewey rattled off the information impassively—as if someone had made him memorize the stats.

"I would love to look at it," she said uncertainly. "But I'm not sure I can afford anything this large. And I don't think I need this much space."

Her Boston townhouse had been built vertically—four floors with two bedrooms on the top floor and functional kitchen, dining-room, and living-room spaces. She'd been picturing something even more modest for her life in Minnesota.

"I think you'll be surprised," Gladdie said. "From what I understand, Emma and Mark, Dewey's sister and brother-in-law, are very reasonable landlords."

Dewey shrugged. "I don't know exactly what the apartments you were planning to move into rent for, but they're pretty new so this might be comparable. I'll show you the lease info, and you'll know better than I do."

Jesse studied the intricate design of the stone pattern on the walkway. After that, he followed it with his eyes to the dark wood front door and craned his neck to the top floor.

"What do you think? Want to check it out?" Rose asked.

"Is there a bedroom upstairs?"

"I don't know. Let's go see."

"My old bedroom was upstairs. I'd like an upstairs bedroom."

"It might work out all right, then," Dewey said, and he caught Gladdie's eyes above Jesse's head. Something shiny and secretive passed between them. "All of the bedrooms are upstairs."

Someone had done an incredible amount of work on the older home. Earth-tone colors—beiges, rusts, and touches of subtle aqua—created a welcoming Southwestern peacefulness. Thick Berber carpet in a beautiful shade of mocha covered the floors except for the living room, dining room, and kitchen. Each of those had burnished golden oak wood flooring. Rose didn't see how the place could rent for less than the GNP of a small country.

"It's absolutely gorgeous," she said. "Did your sister do the decorating?"

"I'm sure. I helped with some renovations early on after they bought it, but I have the color sense of a clown, so she'd never have consulted me on the decorating."

Rose laughed. "I'm sure it's not that bad."

"It is. If it doesn't go in a garage, I'm lost."

She prowled the house, finding a multitude of special touches: a pair of built-in bookcases beside the living-room fireplace, a walk-in pantry, a long row of coat hooks and cubbyholes for shoes in a mudroom off the back door. It was impossible not to fall in love with the place, but she continued to fear the price despite Dewey's prediction.

Jesse hiked along with the adults, unusually quiet and studious. He opened doors and drawers and checked out cubbyholes like an official assessor. He didn't even push to see the bedrooms. Something about the atmosphere calmed him, and Rose added disappointing him to her list of concerns.

"Let's check out the upstairs," Gladdie said at last, and again the conspiratorial look passed between her and Dewey. "I think this might sell the place."

"What sort of trap am I walking into here?" Rose hid her frown with a smile for Gladdie.

"It may be a trap, you're right, dear. I couldn't help myself."

And said trap sprang the moment they entered a small room decorated in blue and red at the back of the house. A single bed with a blue-and-red-striped comforter rested against one wall. A small, simple desk stood on the opposite side of the room. But what sent Jesse into a state of near-speechless ecstasy was the set of four framed pictures—each of a vintage fire truck. He walked to the pictures as if he was in the presence of a burning bush. Rose stared at Gladdie.

"How on Earth is this possible?"

"Isn't it the strangest thing? I never would have thought about this house for you, but then Dewey told me the story of Jesse and the fire truck. I don't know why it brought these pictures to mind, but everything fell into place, and I knew you had to at least see it."

"You have no idea the impact this has. Jesse will not simply think this is cool. To his mind, he now belongs here. He likes signs that mean things."

Gladdie frowned, in comprehension. "Oh, dear, I hope this wasn't a terrible thing for me to do."

"No. No. Of course not. It was very thoughtful. And I love the house. But there will be a meltdown to deal with if I can't afford it."

"Don't kids have to learn at some point that they don't make the rules?"

Dewey Mitchell had been so pleasant, almost human, that she'd begun to forget . . . She pinched the bridge of her nose.

"Mr. Mitchell." She hesitated, thinking hard. Finally she grabbed the sleeve of his blue polo shirt and dragged him through the bedroom door into the hallway. "I would greatly appreciate it if you'd keep your opinions about my parenting skills to yourself. You don't know what you're talking about. You don't know what goes on in my son's head."

"So you keep saying. I have yet to see him react the way you tell me he will."

"Is that so. Because you've spent so much time with him?" Her voice lowered to an ominous growl. "He lives in an ordered world, because that helps him process his surroundings."

"Seriously? When will he learn how to process chaos?"

"Excuse me, but this conversation is over. I thank you for showing us this house—someone has done a beautiful job with it. But I think we'd be better off waiting for our apartment. I do not need to be beholden to you or your family."

"Hold on, hold on." He took her arm lightly to stop her as she turned back to give Jesse the news. Startled by the touch and the fizz that filled her blood beneath his fingers, she yanked herself free of his hold. "I told you I have nothing to do with this house or renting it," he said. "I'm doing my sister a favor. Don't be stubborn because you're mad at me."

Her blood stopped fizzing and started boiling. *Stubborn?* The jerk. He not only needed to stay out of her business, he needed to apologize for stepping over the bounds of propriety.

"What *is* the rent here?" She forced herself to make the query short and unemotional, steeled herself for the answer—almost hoping it would be as exorbitant as she expected, just to prove him wrong and have to move into the apartment.

"The full amount is fourteen hundred a month, but there are some things that affect that number. Do you have a pet?"

"No."

"Would you be willing to pay your own electricity and gas?"

"Probably."

"Your own yard work?"

"Yard work?"

"Emma, my sister, has a guy come and mow and keep up the landscaping. He's a hundred bucks a month."

"I can mow a lawn."

Not that she'd really ever had to, but she wouldn't tell him that fact. All animation had left his face. He recited stipulations and facts like an impersonal butler.

"We're down to a thousand-fifty a month. I can show you the last utility bills from when the house was occupied. You can decide if you think you can do better than the two hundred Emma would add for utilities. Internet and phone plans would be your responsibility."

Rose's heart raced with hopeful excitement. The apartment was nine-fifty a month plus utilities, plus a month's deposit. The library wasn't paying her a huge salary, but she might be able to swing an extra hundred dollars.

"Is there a deposit?"

"Three hundred. Since you don't have any animals."

"There won't be any animals," she assured him.

"That's about the size of things, then," he said, and shrugged. "You can read a copy of the lease. If you're interested, you can sign and stay here tonight."

That didn't sound possible to her.

"What's the catch?"

"Excuse me?"

"Business transactions don't happen this fast. Is the house on a sinkhole? Do you owe a mafia boss and need the money immediately?"

Once again he blinked in disbelief—as if she'd sprouted a horn out of her forehead.

"Where are you from?" he asked. "Someplace where people do things for each other only if they're in trouble? A mafia boss? Honestly?"

"I'm sorry." She wasn't really, but he seemed genuinely put out.

"This is a small town. We might have a mafia boss around here—but if we do, we all know him and he's hiding it well. I've run a business here for sixteen years and never been extorted once."

"I'm *sorry*." She closed her eyes and sighed. "We're clearly even on insults. I'm not used to small-town haste."

"We call it trust. Things actually move pretty slowly around here. If you don't trust me enough to take my word for things, there's no skin off my nose. I don't care if you stay here or not. Tonight or any night."

Rose wanted to have her own little meltdown. She'd dealt with businessmen and politicians, and library boards controlling half-million-dollar budgets, yet this small-town gas-station owner had her constantly fighting anger and deep guilt. She hadn't done a blasted thing to the man, and he'd been the insensitive know-it-all of the year. Was this what small-town life was going to be like?

She drew in a long, hard breath and held it several seconds. It eased from her lungs as Gladdie met up with them and smiled.

"What are your thoughts, Rose, dear? Jesse's already told me he loves the house."

"I'm sure he does."

She shifted her gaze back to Dewey. He still stood at

her elbow, a vast wall of faded jeans and navy blue polo shirt, his hot eyes cooled to chilly indifference.

"This is a cool, cool house." Jesse trotted from the room, his eyes bright enough to make up for Dewey's insouciance. "We can stay here, can't we?"

"Sweetie, in all truth I don't know yet. I need to look at some papers to see if we can afford it. Mr. Mitchell was about to get them for me."

Nearly imperceptible surprise flitted across Dewey's face. Then his eyes narrowed again, and his voice gave away none of the reaction. "I sure was."

"Mom?" Jesse said, his faded-denim eyes sincere as a puppy's. "I'll pay you my allowance if it will help."

Tears beaded in Rose's eyes. Before anyone could see them, she knelt in front of her son. If only others could see the amazing child, who offered crazily selfless things like this all the time, beneath the eccentricity. Someone like Dewey Mitchell needed a hard whack from the sensitivity genie.

Chapter Four

"I don't want to go to school."

Jesse fussed while Rose straightened the collar of his lightweight jacket. Three weeks of acclimating themselves to small-town life had been eye-opening and busy. Meeting teachers and reassuring herself that they understood Jesse's personality and needs had been the biggest task. Grocery shopping and finding necessities for the house had taken visits to three neighboring towns. Getting ready for her first official week at the library had taken more time. But once her furniture had arrived from Boston, she'd proceeded to decorate and fall so in love with the rental house that she easily thought of it as hers—and then she felt at home.

"I know you don't want to go, sweetheart. But you're ready, and it's a first day for a lot of things."

"Your first day at work."

"Right. And guess what? *I'm* nervous."

"You're never nervous."

He said it with professorial certainty, and his confidence spilled over, calming her jitters about the upcoming first day in her library building. She accepted her son's reassurance gratefully, even though their roles should have been reversed.

"Sure I get nervous. Everyone does. I'm not sure how today is going to go, you see. Not everyone likes all my new ideas for the library."

He shrugged. "You know they're crazy, Mom. Crazier than I am."

She hugged him too tightly. "You're funny, but you're definitely not crazy. You better know that."

He struggled his way free. "Mom. Don't be serious. Even if I'm not crazy, I still don't want to go."

"But you liked your teacher when we met her at the Open House. She knows where you like to sit, and she knows your best subjects. You'll be fine. It's fourth grade—you're moving into the big leagues now."

"Yeah, where the mean kids just get huger."

Her heart ached for him. People sometimes marveled at Jesse's maturity of vocabulary, but he was, in truth, a little boy who didn't understand the social niceties the world expected. That little missing piece in his mind had caused him so many wounds that leaving his old school in Boston was one of the few things neither of them had found difficult. Now Rose was excited for this new start. Jesse didn't yet share her belief that life would be better in a nicer, gentler small town.

"I'll walk you to the bus stop."

"It's only at the end of the block. You don't have to."

"Yeah, I kind of do. It's embedded in a mother's genes."

He didn't protest or make a snarky remark, which told her his indifferent face was a cover. She hugged him one last time and handed him his backpack, glad she could still read her son despite how much he protested.

The Minnesota summer of mid-August had given way to pre-fall. Labor Day the day before had been only fifty degrees and misty, and today's first day of school evoked thoughts less of apples for the teacher than of apple pies. And fireplaces.

The bus arrived minutes after they reached the corner. Two other children, both girls at least a couple years older than Jesse, got on at the same stop. They didn't talk much, but they smiled and said hi and asked if he was new. It was a good start.

She refrained from kissing him good-bye. A tug on his collar and a wish for a great day were all he got, and when he took an empty seat by a window and waved in a tiny nobody's-going-to-see-this circle, Rose wasn't sure whether the lump in her throat was for him or a result of knowing she now had to go face her own potential bullies.

A nice, gentle town that loves and misses its library.

So she'd been promised by the committee that had hired her. The original library, lost three years before in a tornado, had been a favorite gathering place, they'd told her. Everyone loved to read and loved the librarian. Rose would have a clientele aching to embrace her.

Only that wasn't exactly what had happened. After the first library board meeting two weeks before, she already had a few detractors—those who disagreed over wall colors, play equipment, and the contents of the library's collection. She had no problem whatsoever fighting for any library issues—even in a small town where she knew fewer than two dozen people. Still, she hated getting off on a controversial foot.

Inside her new library building, everything still smelled like new—wood, paint, varnish, paper. It would take a while to develop the rich, redolent scent of a well-loved sanctuary. Patrons needed to come through and scuff up the shiny new floors, flip through hundreds of books to fill the air with paper molecules and shared words. There needed to be posters and colors and tex-tured pillows and hangings—displays to soak up the echo of pristine space. A library, in her view, needed to be neat and peaceful but full, cluttered with imagination. For a few moments while she stood alone in the foyer looking left to the children's section, right to the adult room, and up the short, wide flight of stairs to the small but excit-ing research area, Rose reveled in the blank canvas she'd inherited.

The daunting task of helping turn this wonderful place into a top-notch library made her dizzy with a com-bination of excitement and mild panic. She could do this, if the little town would embrace her vision and look to the future. Unfortunately, her first challenge had already raised its head in the form of two hundred dollars' worth of bright-colored paint.

Every wall in the building had been generically painted a buttery ecru. As the board said, it was calming and went with the shiny new oak library tables and book bins and the soft blue carpeting. But the children's room needed splashes of color—a painted dragon on the wall, or Alice's white rabbit with a pocket watch, or a clichéd rainbow—along with bright throw pillows and comfy places to sit. But there were three people on the board of eight who all but recoiled at the thought of sullying the new walls, even if it only meant putting up temporary wall-cling murals.

"The color scheme was researched and planned," Pat Dunn, one of the three traditionalists of the group, had told her. "Plus, we'd like the inside to be as familiar as possible to the people of the town who lost their old beloved library. This is similar to what we had, except we upgraded the carpet."

Rose had praised their efforts and agreed the colors were soothing and neutral, but she'd also pointed out that she'd received a master's degree in library science with a specialty in children's services. She didn't push the board, she simply urged them to hear her out at a future meeting when she'd bring some examples of what she envisioned. Her only hope was that several of the members were young and excited. With luck, she'd win them all over eventually.

But, minor roadblocks aside, this was a week for excitement not anticipating problems. The library's doors officially unlocked to the public at 10:00 a.m. the following Monday. On Sunday, a big-bash grand opening would take place. That, more than wrangling with the board, had Rose's stomach Irish step-dancing. There were still a hundred things to do, and she had one hour to herself before Kate Fries, her only full-time employee, showed up for work. She wanted her newest project all ready for Kate to help with upon arrival.

The hour blew by like a fast-moving storm. When she sat in the children's book room with two giant posters spread around her on the floor, Rose didn't know Kate had entered until she spoke behind her.

"Wow, those are powerful."

Rose looked up and grinned. She liked Kate, mom to a daughter and son a little younger than Jesse. Both of her kids were in school all day for the first time, and she had the drive and eagerness of a trained athlete with nowhere to channel her energy. She'd make a perfect work companion.

"Do you like them?"

"Oh, I do. People will be shocked to see such classics on that list."

Banned Books Week was less than a month away, and Rose considered promoting it her first official task as the new town librarian. She'd spent days of her own time creating large images of famous characters and book covers from both children's and adult literature that had once been or were currently banned or challenged. She had the makings of two four-foot-long posters—one for each book room—highlighting books thought subversive or inappropriate.

"I've done smaller versions of these before," she said. "The list never fails to impress people. It's fun to watch their jaws drop when they see *Winnie-the-Pooh* and *Diary of Anne Frank* there."

"*Harriet the Spy*?" Kate pointed. "*The Lorax*? Are you kidding?"

"I'm not. And it's still happening. I expect we'll get a few comments on some of the new books coming out."

"Bring them on," Kate laughed. "Who doesn't think *To Kill a Mockingbird* is a must-read classic?"

"Oh, you'd be surprised. Did Margaret White celebrate Banned Books Week?" She invoked the name of the beloved former librarian. There wasn't a person in town that didn't seem to revere her.

"No. Not that I remember. Maggie didn't really do controversial. I love her, but I think, maybe, she was already alive when *Huckleberry Finn* first came out. That might have been her only taste of controversy."

Both of them giggled. "We shouldn't be mean," Rose said. "I've had a couple of talks with her, and she hasn't told me a thing about what to do. She just says to make it a great little library. So, I'll do my best, even if I shake things up a little along the way."

"It'll be good." Kate nodded decisively.

They worked on the posters and then hung new curtains that had already been purchased. Again they were conservative—muted blue and cream stripes—perfect for the upstairs windows and the meeting room behind the front stairs. They sufficed in the adult book room. But, again, Rose hesitated over hanging them in the kids' room. She wanted bold and fun, not staid and elegant.

"You do agree it's a good idea to lobby for some color in here, don't you?" she asked.

"You know I do. So do Lee, Abby, and Gladdie." She mentioned the members of the board who'd agreed two hundred dollars wasn't too much of the budget to invest in some further decorating. "And Donna is fine with it. We have to convince Wilma, Brian, and Pat of our vision, that's all. Give it time."

So many names. All this politicking already. Rose sighed. She was tired of being a patient visionary. She'd decided back in Boston that a vision was to follow not contemplate, and that was why she was here—to follow, at last, a life vision she'd created for herself rather than one her parents and former boyfriend designed for her. And the people of Kennison Falls had chosen her to bring part of that vision to them. She was too excited to "give it time."

At ten o'clock, Rose had to leave Kate working on new book displays and run work-related errands. She looked forward to the first day she'd get to spend an entire eight hours in her new space, checking out the existing books, making new book wish lists, corresponding with the other libraries in her system. But finalizing plans for the open house was higher on the immediate priority list.

She picked up her purse. "I'm heading to the restaurant to finalize the bakery order for Sunday, then I have a meeting with the high school principal, and after that I'm running up to Faribault to grab some supplies for the office here, and I can fill up with gas and get my car washed."

"Don't bother, it's raining."

"It is?" Rose glanced out the windows, shocked to see rivulets decorating the panes like little braided rivers. "When did that start?"

Kate laughed. "You're a librarian all right. Didn't notice the weather."

"Hey now, no mocking the boss."

"Fine. But since the car wash is unnecessary, just go fill up at Dewey's."

She hadn't seen Dewey Mitchell since he'd shown her the house. His sister Emma, a dazzling, chic woman with a no-nonsense heart of gold, had returned from her trip and handled the rental details with zero fuss. Rose had gotten the house for only two hundred more dollars a month than she'd have paid for the apartment—and it was worth every penny. She adored the place.

Not that she didn't think about Dewey and his black Sellecky mustache every time she passed his place.

"I promised myself to boycott the Gas 'n' Garage for six months."

Kate's slender, animated face nearly went blank in surprise. "Boycott Dewey's place? Whatever for?"

Rose shrugged. "Stupid personal reasons. He insulted Jesse and pissed me off."

"Dewey? You are talking about Duane Mitchell?"

"Yes. Mr. Duane I-Know-How-It-All-Should-Go-So-Don't-Argue-with-Me Mitchell. He's the one."

"Mr. Coaches-Two-Football-Teams-and-Busts-His-Buns-for-Everyone-in-Town, you mean?"

She stared at Kate and furrowed her brow. "I know people like him, but . . ."

"Like him? He's kind of Mr. Kennison Falls. High school hero and all. He was headed for a pro football career until he had to come back and run his father's business. People think very highly of him. Although I agree, he doesn't take much guff from anyone."

"I suppose I should start over with him," Rose said. "This is a small town and I can't avoid him forever. Can you tell I'm a stubborn mom?"

"I can love you for that, sister," Kate said. "But yeah, give Dewey another chance. He's a handy guy to know."

"I'll start with simply promising not to badmouth him anymore, how's that? See you in a couple of hours."

"I'll be here."

Rose pulled up the hood on her lightweight jacket and clutched it closed against the cold rain as she made a dash for her car. Once safe inside, she flicked water droplets from her shoulders and fluffed her hair, checking her rearview mirror to assess any damage to what little makeup she wore. She could dash on a little more blush and some lip gloss at the Loon Feather before heading to the high school. She wanted to look put together for the principal but not stuffy to any teens she might get to meet and talk to about helping with some reading program ideas. This would do.

But, first things first. Once in the middle of town, she considered herself lucky to find a spot within a dozen car-lengths of the restaurant. She'd already learned that in ugly weather like this, the cozy Loon Feather was more popular than cat videos on the Internet. Dragging up her hood again, she pushed open the Mustang's long door, slammed it behind her, and trotted toward the Loon's corner-facing glass doors. Hunkered into her jacket, she hopped up the two-step stoop with her eyes on the cement—and slammed into a solid wall of muscle.

"Whoa, whoa. I'm sorry!" he said, steadying her with his huge, strong hands. "I—"

He stopped short when he met her eyes and recognition burst through his apology.

"My gosh, it's you!" she said before he could speak. Embarrassment flooded her the instant the words left her lips. To have him conjured out of the storm when she'd just been talking about him gave her a fresh splash of chills to go with the ones from the rain. "I mean, no, it's my fault. I wasn't watching where I was going. I'm sorry."

Dewey tugged open the door and guided her inside. "There. Better out of the rain." His eyes took an assessment from the dripping ends of her hair, down her body, to the spattered hems of her khaki slacks. The heat from his scrutiny set little fires smoldering through her torso and all along her limbs. "You aren't hurt? We collided pretty good there."

She'd never stood this close to him. His mustache was dense as velvet—touchable, sexy. He smelled like fresh wood chips and spice, mixed with ozone freshness from the electric air that had followed them in from the storm.

"I'm fine, really. I—" She almost bit back the next words but couldn't quite keep them to herself as she followed his lead and did her own measurement of him toe to crown with her eyes. "I can't imagine I did any damage to you. Or I, ah, hope I didn't."

He smiled the same time she did, and the action transformed his eyes with flecks of cheerful gold. "I think it's safe to say the only way you'd be able to damage me is with that pretty little car of yours."

"Ah, you like my car?"

"I like all cars. But I've been coveting yours since you drove into the station way back. Which, they taught us in Sunday school when I was a kid, is a sin. I'm sorry about that."

His easy humor took her aback, although she didn't know why. Except that he'd seemed so ... uncompromising in all their other encounters. And, because she'd pricked up her ears at every snippet of chatter about him, she'd concluded that although his reputation was sterling and his admiration society huge, she hadn't met anyone who claimed to be his best friend or even know who that might be. The man was like a living statue to his own reputation.

Until this moment—when the slightly irreverent humor and the gilt-edged warmth in his eyes thawed the statue into a genial, good-looking, real man she didn't feel the need to smack upside the head.

"No need to be sorry. It's kind of an ego trip to know I've made someone jealous."

He cocked a dark eyebrow. "Can't possibly be the first time."

She shrugged and bit her lip to camouflage a smile. "I guess not. It's a pretty nice car."

"Trust me, Ms. Hanrehan. You've got more to offer than a pretty car. I hear you've got plenty of big ideas for the new library and the smarts to see them through. Lots of people are mighty impressed."

The words left her speechless. For a long moment she honestly didn't know whether he was handing her some disingenuous line designed to impress her, giving her a jab of sarcasm, or actually complimenting her. When she didn't respond, he bent forward and peered at her.

"You still in there?" He laughed.

"I . . . yes, I . . . Thank you. It's just that I've already had a couple of small battles today, so I wasn't sure how serious you were. Sorry. And call me Rose."

"I'm late for my morning break today," he said. "Got time to join me?"

"Uh—" She got only as far as that unintelligent sound before surprise struck her dumb for a second time. Hadn't she told Kate she wanted to avoid this man at all costs?

"Maybe we could use the time to start over."

He needed to stop talking and quit dumbfounding her. She wanted to—tried to—tell him she was only there to gather information and had to leave for her meeting. Instead, she nodded. "That would be nice. But I only have half an hour, and I have some questions to ask Rio about baking for the library opening."

"Fair enough."

They passed the cockatiels' cage in the foyer, and Dewey tapped the top of it absently. "You rock, dude," he said.

Lester wolf whistled and launched into the theme from *The Andy Griffith Show*. "Rock, rock doo," chirped Cotton.

"Do you have a song yet?" Dewey asked.

Nearly every regular customer was assigned one of Lester's three tunes, Rose had learned. She still wasn't sure people weren't making that up.

"I think it's *Happy Days*."

"The newest song for the newest resident." Dewey nodded appreciatively. "Smart bird."

"Is he really that smart?"

"Oh, he definitely is. Have someone tell you about the tornado sometime."

"I heard there was a bad one."

"Three years ago. Lester and Cotton here alerted rescuers to a couple of kids trapped in the rubble of the old restaurant. These birdies are town heroes."

She looked at the birds with new interest. It was a nice story, if just a story. The kind of tale she'd always imagined filled the bars and cafés of a small town. Another tiny shaft of warmth cut through the wet fall chill.

"Hey, Dewey! Hi, Rose." Rose had come to know the Loon's high-energy waitress-cook-baker Rio Pitts-Matherson in the past three weeks and loved her perpetual cheeriness. Her red hair, caught up in a high ponytail, swung like a welcoming beacon in the dreary weather. "Come on in. Two tables or one?"

"One," Dewey said.

"And when you have a free minute, I'd love to go over final arrangements for Sunday afternoon." Rose scanned the full restaurant. "Unless this time is too busy?"

"No, not at all. Sit and dry off a little, and I'll come join you in a second. I'm not working alone today. That okay, Dewey? We won't be interrupting your quiet hour?" She winked at him.

"No. I invited Rose to join me."

Another enigma blossoming, Rose thought. People asked if they were bothering him?

Dewey took his coffee strong and black, and grinned when Rose turned her mug of the lightest roast caramel-colored with two containers of cream.

"Milk coffee," he teased.

"Sludge." She grinned back, wrinkling her nose at his aromatic Sumatran brew.

"Two cups a day." He gave an unequivocal nod. "Then I move on to Diet Coke. From one bad habit to another."

"If that's your worst . . ." She shrugged. "Caffeine for me is a whenever-I-think-of-it habit."

"You're focused without even requiring coffee."

"I'm not always very focused with or without it. I make my deadlines and meet them. The rest of the time I think about everything I need to do and just try to make plans."

He stroked his mustache once with one forefinger and thumb, then pursed his lips thoughtfully. "I don't see that."

"Not to be confrontational, but how could you possibly see anything about me? We've met, what, three times?"

"But I heard the questions you asked about the house. I could tell you're organized and plan ahead."

"I didn't say I wasn't smart. But smart people can be distractible. Aren't you ever lazy sometimes?"

"I don't get a lot of time to be lazy. On the other hand, I don't much like to sit around and think. 'Cept for my hour every morning. This is planning time."

"And here I am interrupting. Now I see what Rio meant—"

He held up his hand. "You aren't interrupting. Believe me, this is more uplifting than the news."

She lifted her coffee mug in salute. "Cheers to that."

Silence enveloped them as they sipped. The last of the chill gave way beneath the warmth of the drinks. Rose marveled at the ease in the space between her and Dewey Mitchell. It was like having coffee in the shade of a protective oak with a man so comfortable in his own skin he could talk or not and enjoy it either way. She couldn't remember the last time the outside world had rolled past her without leaving some stressful mark on her mind.

"You coming to the library opening?" she asked.

"I go to most town events. Looks good on the résumé."

"That's why you go to functions? It's good promo?"

He shrugged with a touch of self-deprecation. "No. And yes. It's part of life around here. People expect to see you, and you expect to see others. It's like a continuous family reunion. Nothing really new, but comfortable all the same."

"You're pretty philosophical. Or jaded."

"You grow up in a place and it seeps in—makes you a little stodgy even if you like it."

"You're too young to be stodgy." She offered him a smile, trying to guess what his age might be.

"Thank you, but I promise I'm not young anymore."

"My age, I'd guess."

"I know better than to ask a woman her age over coffee."

"Thirty-three. I don't have time to be coy."

"Heck, if you think I'm thirty-three, I won't be coy either." Amusement propped his brows into attractive arches. "Thirty-eight. Nine next month."

"Okay, I agree. You've earned the right to be stodgy."

He sat back in the booth seat and harrumphed without bothering to hide the upward twitch in the right half of his mustache.

"How long have you owned the Gas 'n' Garage?"

He didn't get a chance to answer. From the depths of her purse came her phone's muffled ringtone. "Sorry," she said. "It could be Kate at the library. I left her with quite a list of tasks."

He waved for her to get it. She didn't recognize the number.

"Hello? This is Rose Hanrehan."

"Mrs. Hanrehan? This is Linda Verum, principal at Glen Butte Elementary."

Chapter Five

ROSE'S HEART LEAPT instantly into double time, and her stomach churned against the coffee she'd just added to it. "Mrs. Verum? Is anything the matter?"

"Everything and everyone is okay." The principal's words calmed her, and yet there was unmistakably a "but . . ." coming. "I'm afraid Jesse had a small altercation in physical education class."

Rose's head bowed under the weight of the news. It hadn't been three hours since the bus had picked up her son. "What happened?"

"We had an issue with Jesse not obeying the gym teacher's class rules. Another child called him a name, and there was a scuffle. He fell, got a bloody nose, and he's asking for you."

"Scuffle!" Jesse got into plenty of shouting matches, but there'd never been a *scuffle*. "I can be there in ten minutes."

"That would be appreciated. Although he's fine for now. No need to panic or rush."

"Thank you for calling." Her insides coiled into all-too-familiar battle readiness. "Tell him I'll be there soon. And I would very much appreciate talking to the gym teacher, too."

"I will tell them both, Ms. Hanrehan."

Rose hung up and stared around the booth in a haze of anxiety, her brain racing with how to plan the immediate future. Call the high school principal, call Kate . . .

"Is everything all right?"

Dewey's voice short-circuited the whirling in her brain, and she caught her breath, surprised—again—to see concern newly etched into the lines beside his eyes.

"My son got into a scrape at school."

She regretted telling him the instant the words were out. Clearly her mind wasn't planning all that well.

"My, my. Young Jesse Loren Hanrehan?" His broad smile wiped out all the goodwill they'd built the previous ten minutes.

"If you think this is remotely humorous—" She tried desperately to soften the steel in her voice.

"Hey, now, I didn't say that."

"That idiotic grin said it plenty loudly enough."

"C'mon, look. You have a son. I have three brothers. I remember what it was like to be a boy at school. My mom came to haul us home by the scruffs of our necks for fighting more than a few times."

"Excuse me." Indignation burned a hole in her atom of remaining self-control. The man was a complete ass when it came to kids. "My son does *not* get into fights. And I have no intention of hauling him anywhere." She gathered her purse and scooted sideways on the booth seat. "For your information, he's been punched in the nose hard enough to make it bleed, and he's terrified."

"Terrified? That's what they said?"

"This really isn't any of your business, Mr. Mitchell."

"Rose."

The calm-but-stern tone wrapped itself around her name and forced her to stop. When she allowed herself to meet his gaze, teasing had been replaced by calm self-assurance. She wanted to see arrogance there, too, but she found something that looked more like understanding.

"Dewey?" She glared, unwilling to forgive his earlier insensitivity, and perched, ready for flight, on the edge of the booth seat.

He leaned forward, forearms on the table. "Do you always go off to him in such an agitated state?"

"What on Earth is that supposed to mean? Do I go off worried sick? Of course. You've never been a mother; I wouldn't expect you to understand."

She swore he blanched slightly, but he swallowed and leaned a little farther across the tabletop. "Wait for two minutes. You don't do a kid who's upset any favors by running into the room panicked. Take a deep breath and tell me what happened. I won't say anything, but you can sort it out and calm down."

He dared tell her to calm down? Where did the man find—

"Rose."

He kept saying her name with that compelling force, yet his deep baritone softly reached something within her pounding heart that eased her low-level alarm.

"What do you want? Why do you care?"

"I don't." He wiggled his brows. "I simply don't want to have to fix your sweet little car when you crunch it up because you're upset and distracted."

Her mouth opened of its own volition to berate him again, but she stopped. Her brain engaged. He wasn't serious.

The tension left her shoulders, and she relaxed back into the seat. "You're a pain, you know that?"

"I do. You aren't the first to say so. But tell me. What happened to Jesse Loren Hanrehan?"

"I don't know exactly. Somebody called him a name. It turned into a fight, and Jesse got a bloody nose." She sighed and leaned on her elbows, pressing the heels of her hands against her closed eyes. "I talked specifically to the gym teacher before school started. I explained that Jesse is not good at physical activities. He's not all that coordinated a kid. Children with Asperger's often have delayed large-motor skills. The woman promised she'd keep a special eye on him."

Tears of frustration dampened her lashes, but she kept them from falling, knowing she was tired—and disappointed that the first day had been ruined. "I want . . . no . . . need my son to like this school."

"It's a rare kid who truly loves school."

"He could, though. He simply doesn't understand

why kids don't always care about what he likes. You already know his odd fixations."

"Fire trucks."

"One of several subjects."

"How is he at school usually?"

"He's not a genius, but he understands concepts once they're explained. He's great at history and spelling, things that can be memorized. But he's terrible at anything physical or spontaneous. Gym, art, recess."

"He's bad at *recess*?"

"It's not structured enough."

"Okay. That takes a unique kid."

Jesse had been described as everything from unique to special to disruptive, to mentally retarded. She hated every epithet, and all at once she was tired of explaining. Dewey didn't get it any more than anyone did. Than anyone could. Asperger's, or autism spectrum disorder, or ASD, was barely understood by people who studied it. They kept changing what it was called—Asperger's was simply easiest to say. She straightened again and slid fully off the bench.

"Thanks for the time-out," she said. "You were right. I'm calmer now. But I need to go. I need to have a word with one elementary gym teacher."

"I know her. Known her since grade school, in fact."

She glanced at him, confused. "I . . . guess that doesn't surprise me. I hear you know everybody. So, thanks for the coffee. I'll be sure and greet her."

"Joyce Middleburg is a good teacher. I'm sure she'd do whatever she can to help a student in trouble."

"She already hasn't."

"I could come with you and talk to her."

"In whose wildest imagination does that make sense?" She scoffed at the audacity.

"Things can be fixed if you have the right tools and information. Why not arm yourself with a good tool? I've been a plenty big one on enough occasions; I might be helpful."

She sputtered in spite of herself. It was ludicrous to think of him accompanying her, but how could she not warm to a man who could call himself a tool? Especially since he was a mechanic to boot.

"How could a perfect stranger help my cause?"

"Is this my interview for the job? I'm glad you think I'm perfect at something."

"It's not an interview. Forget it, I need to go." He raised his brows but said nothing. She took two steps and stopped, curiosity getting the better of her. "Why *did* you offer to go with me? Does your grade school friend require some kind of special handling?"

It was his turn to laugh. "No. It crossed my mind that having someone local with you would make you seem less of an outsider in a small town. And a second set of ears when it comes to problems might be helpful. But I spouted off without thinking. No problems."

"What would you say to her?"

"Hell. Nothing if you didn't need me to."

"I wouldn't." She couldn't figure out why she stood here debating with a stranger she really hadn't liked since they'd met. And yet, he had a point . . . "You just want to ride in the Mustang."

"No, I figured I'd follow you."

"Oh."

"Go," he said, his voice now warm with humor. "Sorry I slowed you down."

"You'd really keep your mouth shut?"

Genuine laughter accompanied a head shake. He scooted from the booth and took her elbow with one hand while pulling out his wallet with another. "C'mon. I can't even trust you to get out of here, much less take care of school problems."

She spun on him, ready again to let him have it.

"I'm joking. Relax a notch, Rose. The boy is going to be fine."

He was probably right, but meanwhile, Jesse was alone with strangers and scared. "You're right about one thing—this is taking far too long."

"I'll be right behind you."

"Oh, good grief, why waste the gas? Ride with me." She sighed, not remotely understanding why she should be willing to drive him but unwilling to take the time to analyze it.

She let him pay for the coffee, made her apologies to Rio for bugging out of their meeting, and led the way out into the rain.

DEWEY KEPT A surreptitious eye on the new town librarian all the way to the elementary school. That her Mustang was a five-speed impressed the hell out of him. She drove carefully in the rain but clearly knew her car's performance inside out, shifting like a pro—with smooth confidence. Her hand on the gearshift coordinated perfectly with her foot on the clutch, and the transitions purred flawlessly.

Her hands fascinated him. He would have expected a Boston-born, Ivy League girl, which she was, to have those model-like kind of hands seen in magazines, with elegant fingers made for sparkling jewelry and nails long enough to pick locks. Instead, Rose Hanrehan's hands were small and symmetrical, with short but pretty fingers and neatly trimmed nails that shone with some very pale pinkish color.

He liked the no-nonsense competence, and yet there was more to her than that—something vulnerable and totally feminine beneath the adept driving and tough-mom face. They pulled into a parking space at the elementary school, and the Mustang's engine idled smoothly before Rose turned the key and silence followed. She opened the door before she'd even gathered her purse, and tugged her hood over her thick, damp curls. Their eyes didn't meet, she didn't give him any instructions, and she barely waited for him to join her in the rain.

When they stood inside the front foyer, he finally touched one shoulder and she looked up. The genuine worry in her eyes cut short his planned ribbing. He'd hoped to relax her, but the woman refused to be rational when it came to this child. He didn't understand it, but even his male pea brain knew he had no right to truly mess with her mothering technique. In fact, for the first time he realized his rash insistence on accompanying her was out of bounds, not to mention very probably fruitless. What he expected to come of his presence was a complete mystery.

His brother would tell him to stop trying to fix stuff, but the truth was he did like and respect Joyce Middleburg. He tried telling himself this was all to save the gym teacher a tongue-lashing.

He settled for giving Rose's shoulder a reassuring squeeze and followed her into the brick-and-tile hallway in front of the office. Glen Butte Elementary served three small towns in the southeast corner of the county, a smaller demographic than the middle and high schools, which drew from all four counties that came together ten miles south of Kennison Falls.

Despite its small size, the Quad County district boasted a good reputation—solid, basic education with enthusiastic teachers and an array of AP courses, along with a high graduation rate. Very few people knew how willing Dewey would have been to teach in such a district. Very few people knew he'd once been qualified to do so.

"Hi there! You must be Mrs. Hanrehan." Deb Bowen, the secretary every parent wanted to be on good terms with because you never knew when you'd need her, greeted them as soon as they opened the office door. "Why, Dewey. Hello!"

"Deb," he acknowledged.

"I'm Rose Hanrehan." She interrupted without apology. "Is Jesse all right?"

"He's fine. He's back in the nurse's office. I think he's

more angry than upset. I can take you to him and then call the teacher."

In fact, she lifted a phone receiver first and punched a short series of numbers. "Mrs. Middleburg? Mrs. Hanrehan is here. Okay, thanks." She hung up and smiled. "She'll be right up. Come on back."

Once again Rose gave him no direction, as if she'd forgotten his presence. He knew he should hang back, wait for Joyce, but pure and simple interest drew him to shadow Rose into the small room where Jesse Hanrehan sat on the nurse's cot, holding a compress of some kind against his nose and swinging his feet. He looked anything but distressed. He didn't even look angry. Dewey finally hung back outside the door.

"Honey. Jesse!" Rose scurried into the room and dropped to her knees in front of the boy. "Are you all right? What happened?"

For an instant Jesse assessed his mother, as if deciding how to act. Dewey wondered if she could see the calculation in his eyes.

"I got pushed down and my face hit the gym floor." The report was fairly unemotional and journalistic.

"Let me see. Is that a cold pack?"

"Yeah."

She pulled his hand away and leaned closer, peering at his nose. "It looks kind of sore."

"They said I don't need to have it checked. It bled for a long time."

"I see you got some blood on your sweatshirt."

"Yeah."

"I think maybe we should take you to the doctor and make sure you didn't break anything."

"No. I didn't."

"You can't know that."

"The nurse said I didn't."

"I know, sweetheart. But really only a doctor can tell you that."

"Well, I could get out of school anyway."

"Jesse. You've been looking forward to school. What happened in gym class? What's Mrs. Middleburg going to tell me?"

"That I called Kenny Simon an asshole."

Dewey took two steps backward and looked at the floor, his lips pressed together to keep in choked laughter. He most definitely hadn't expected that reply. Certainly his mother couldn't have either. He waited for Rose's disciplinary reaction.

"Oh, Jesse," she said instead, her voice sorrowful but holding no reproach. "That's not appropriate. What did he say to make you so angry?"

Angry? Dewey thought, fighting down his slight swell of admiration for the too-honest kid. How angry did a *ten*-year-old have to get to use such language?

"He called me Jesse the Body."

"I—" Rose, nonplussed, looked in Dewey's direction for the first time.

"Ah. Like in Jesse 'the Body' Ventura," he said, leaning against the doorjamb.

"The wrestler?" she asked.

"And our former governor.

"He's not some kind of wimp?" Jesse asked.

"The guy's a little crazy these days, but he was also a Navy SEAL."

"But he was making fun of me. I could tell."

"You know about people making fun," Rose said. "How should you have handled it?"

"I shouldn't have called him an asshole."

"You shouldn't even say the word now."

"It's not as bad as *fu*—"

"Jesse!" For the first time she raised her voice. "Do not *dare*."

He shrugged, his feet swinging again. Dewey looked to the ceiling, swallowing laughter yet again at this kid who made no logical sense.

"Ms. Hanrehan?"

Dewey turned to the familiar voice, and Joyce Middleburg started slightly. She was short and still slender, athletic like a tennis or soccer player.

"Dewey?"

"Hey, Joyce. I came in with Rose."

"Ah, I see." The puzzled look didn't leave her face, but she let her questions go, passed Dewey, and held out her hand to Rose. "Nice to see you again, Ms. Hanrehan. How about we go to the conference room and chat?"

"That would be fine."

"How you doin', Jesse? Nose feeling better?"

"Kind of."

"I think we'll have it checked," Rose said.

"I'm sure it's just bruised," Joyce said. "They don't do

much for noses—kind of like ribs. Actually, Jesse could probably go back to his classroom if he wants."

"I think I'll take him to the clinic," Rose countered. "We'll start the year fresh tomorrow."

"Whatever you think. Then maybe we could have him wait here with a book while we have our talk?"

Dewey didn't think keeping Jesse from class was a good plan. Why coddle the kid? He wasn't in trouble. But that opinion definitely wasn't Dewey's to voice, and Jesse agreed happily to read and chose a book from the stash beside the cot.

Joyce ushered them into the conference room. Unadorned and slightly larger than a normal office, it boasted ten chairs around an oval, laminated-wood conference table. The three adults sat at one end, Joyce at the head, Dewey and Rose across from each other.

"So, you two are connected in some way?" Joyce asked when they were seated. "Not to be rude. I'm just making sure we can speak freely."

"Rose is relatively new to town, and I thought it would be helpful for her to have another set of ears. She's concerned."

Rose's quick, sharp glance told him he'd given enough of an explanation. He sat back.

"I know you have questions." Joyce took up the conversation. "I want you to understand that this was no more than a case of first-day settling in. I don't take any injury in my class lightly, but neither boy is in serious trouble."

"I have to say I'm a little disappointed," Rose began.

"We talked about Jesse's special needs in your class especially, and within minutes of the first day I get a call that he's been in a fight—however minor. This is a first for him, and for me. If the other child hit him, I'd like to know what's being done to assure that it won't happen again."

"Believe me, we will be certain it doesn't happen again. And Jesse wasn't struck, he got pushed and fell. But I'd like to make the point that this began because Jesse refused to participate in required activities. He drew a fair amount of attention to himself. This doesn't excuse the behavior of the other boy, but my main job is to get Jesse to become part of the class. That will go a long way toward stopping the negative interactions."

"The bullying, you mean?"

"I have to respectfully disagree that Jesse was bullied."

"You don't consider name-calling bullying?" Her face tightened into righteous anger.

"I can only tell you what I heard, of course. Jesse can tell you his perspective. From what little interaction I've had with him, he seems strong with details."

"Sometimes that's true," she murmured.

"Jesse sat himself cross-legged in a corner and wouldn't move. Several of the children made attempts to coax him into joining. Kenny Simon asked him if he thought he was too cool for school, like he was Jesse 'the Body' or something. Jesse jumped up and shouted that he was not Jesse 'the Body.' His words were 'I am Jesse Hanrehan, you . . .' And, well, I'm afraid it wasn't a very appropriate name."

"He told me what it was," Rose said stiffly. "And that will be dealt with."

"I'm sure it will be. But you can see the fault was mutual. Kenny will be disciplined for causing the fall. His parents have been notified, and they're good folks. They won't brush it off."

"What was the activity, ah, Jesse, didn't want to be part of?" Dewey couldn't help but ask.

"We're doing a unit on the Presidential Youth Fitness Program," said Joyce. "I've got the kids practicing some of the skills. We want to do everything in our power to help them do well."

"Mrs. Middleburg. Jesse will never do well on that skills test. I thought you understood that."

"I do understand. But I can't simply allow him to sit out of class. Any more than he can sit out of math or spelling."

Dewey understood the point, but Rose was clearly frustrated, her narrowed eyes giving away how close she was to anger.

"You wouldn't hold a physically challenged child to the same standard as abled children. You wouldn't hold a mentally challenged student or, say, a student with autism, to the same standard as others. Can't you come up with a creative way for Jesse to participate?"

"The problem is, Ms. Hanrehan, Jesse is neither physically nor mentally challenged. He does not have autism. Asperger's is not severe enough that I can hold him to a lesser standard."

"But he can't reach the higher standard. You'll fail him because he can't do sit-ups?"

"No, of course not. That isn't the purpose of the fitness

assessments anymore anyway. But I would fail him for not trying."

Rose struggled for composure. "What, exactly, caused him to go sit by himself? Was there something that precipitated it?"

"I don't recall anything specific. I gave my usual explanation about the physical fitness assessments, and I told them we'd have lots of time to practice so they could all get really good grades."

"Well, that explains a lot." Her voice could have been a study in defeat. "If Jesse thought for half a second his grade in gym depended on his performance, that's what shut him down. He won't try if he knows he'll fail. Period."

"I'm sorry. That's not my intention. Most kids love knowing they won't be surprised about what's on a test."

"Is that truly what this fitness program is?"

"Things have changed. It's not a test anymore, really. The kids are competing with themselves, and there are many levels at which to assess them. It's meant to be less competitive and more incentive to move."

"So, then, why isn't this a pass/fail kind of unit?" Dewey asked, genuinely curious.

"The unit is, but gym class itself is not, any more than social studies is a pass/fail class." Joyce developed a crease between her brows and seemed puzzled by the question. "I'm not saying kids have to achieve perfection to get good grades, but I'm charged with improving the fitness and lives of all the students. Some will get high marks, others lower marks. But some of my best students might struggle in math or reading. Gym class is their place to shine."

Rose's fingers drummed like charging horse hooves on the tabletop, and she took long moments, clearly choosing her next words.

"I fundamentally disagree, Mrs. Middleburg. The purpose of a phis ed class in elementary school should be to instill a love of movement and healthy habits that will last a lifetime. There will be plenty of time in high school for the athletically gifted to find their sports and raise their grade point averages. I guarantee I will not be able to get my son to participate if he thinks he's going to be penalized anyway."

"You know, I don't completely disagree with you. But the curriculum and standards are set by the state and our school board. That's where your fight needs to be. All I can do is promise to try and help Jesse fit in. It helps to know what his triggers are, and I'll do my best to assure him he won't be *penalized*, as you put it, for his abilities."

"Has there ever been such a thing as a special hour of phys ed for kids who don't *like* gym class?" Dewey asked. "There have to be others who balk at the skills tests and group games."

"Sure there are. But a special class? Dewey, you know as well as I do they can barely afford the programs we have. And, truth to tell, a third of the kids in every class would opt for a special 'fun' class. Not to mention, segregating the kids by ability would be hell on self-esteem."

"It sounds to me like you haven't ever known what it's like to be the one segregated kid in a class of good athletes." Rose didn't accuse, but her voice was weary, as if she'd explained this too many times in the past.

"I've seen it plenty of times in my fourteen years of teaching." Joyce smiled, maybe a little condescendingly, although the slight wasn't blatant. "And I hope you'll trust that I only want what's best for Jesse. Believe me, kids in his situation generally end up doing fine. There is one more thing, of course. I know you're not interested in IEPs at this time, but that might address some of the issues here, should you reconsider."

"You're right. I won't put him through that process," Rose replied, her opinion clearly immutable. "He can do fine given a little bit of flexibility on his teachers' parts.

"An Individual Education Plan?" Dewey asked, trying to remember the exact term.

"Individualized, yes," Joyce said. "And it is an involved process to set one up, but it can be helpful."

"And talk about setting Jesse apart further." More retorts were practically visible on Rose's lips. Dewey put a hand on her arm to stop her, braving the singeing sparks she shot at him from her eyes. He understood her frustration and he understood Joyce's. He didn't know enough to comment on Rose's feelings about an IEP for her son, but clearly now wasn't the time to continue the discussion.

"How about if Rose has a talk with Jesse, and if she has any more questions, she can come and ask them?"

"I'd welcome that absolutely," Joyce said.

They all stood, and if the parting wasn't easy, it was cordial. But Rose glared at the floor once Joyce left the room, and took three stalking steps toward the door herself before Dewey caught her.

"You really need to take a few deep breaths again before you go back to your boy. Remember, you have to be the calm one."

"Excuse me?" She whirled on him. "You! You were supposed to keep quiet unless I asked for something. What gave you the right to end this conversation?"

"I had no rights. I saw you were going to blow a gasket if you said anything more."

"Of all the arrogant, egotistical—"

"Nothing new there. You've told me that before."

"And you don't learn very quickly. This is my son. And I know him and what he needs."

"And I know what teachers need. Bullying at this point won't help."

"Bullying? I'm looking for help for my child."

"Then go about it one step at a time. Do not make a reputation for yourself the first day in a new district."

"I think it's time for you to stop telling me, someone you do not know the slightest bit, what to do. I've been a mother for ten and a half years and have managed fine. I don't need a busybody mechanic to step in and pretend he's got a magic wand. What makes you arrogant enough to think you're such an expert on teachers?"

"Because"—he made his face as impassive as he could—"I used to be one."

Chapter Six

IF DEWEY MITCHELL had said he'd been a truck driver on Mars, it wouldn't have seemed any more out of character to Rose than what he'd just revealed.

"You? A teacher?"

"In the interest of full disclosure, it was a very long time ago, and other than student teaching, my one classroom job lasted only seven of nine months. But yes. Sixth grade."

"You?" She knew she sounded repetitive and idiotic, but the stretch was so darn huge.

There wasn't exactly a flash of anger in his eyes, but he looked a little like someone had put mustard on his ice cream. "I kinda wish you'd stop saying that word as if it were the equivalent to *dog crap* or *cancer tumor*."

"I'm sorry. That isn't what I meant. But you have to admit—"

"That it's pretty freaking surprising a guy who gets his

hands dirty in a garage every day had enough smarts to finish college?"

"No, of course not. I—"

But that's exactly what she had meant. It was tough to deny it. He was big, strong, and handsome. But college educated and experienced? She'd jumped straight to a stereotyped conclusion.

"Look," he said. "You're completely right about one thing—this is none of my business. To be honest, I have no idea what I'm doing here. You're probably right that it was your Mustang. It's a nice ride."

Guilt was a disproportionate emotion to the situation. Rose had no reason to feel guilty for protecting Jesse's interest or standing up to a stranger meddling inappropriately in her life. A smart woman would be right and wise to harbor suspicions. The problem was, she sensed an underlying sincerity in everything Dewey had said. His advice to take problems one step at a time was spot on, even though doing so had never been her strong suit. He'd also asked good questions of the gym teacher. There was nothing untoward about anything in which he'd shown interest and his apology, this time, seemed sincere.

Her irritation slowly eroded, and she forced herself to ask the obvious question.

"Why didn't you stay in teaching?"

"Things changed here at home. I decided this life suited me better." The explanation rang with practiced dismissiveness. "Few people remember anymore that I finished my teaching degree, which is fine by me. Makes my life easier. Once in a while, though, a kid comes along, like yours, and I do a double take. Jesse's an interesting boy. Hate to see him get picked on."

Without as much as a raised voice or criticism, he'd managed to chastise her. She'd unfairly labeled him no more than a Kennison Falls good ol' boy because of her own wounded pride and protectiveness.

"I'm sorry," she said. "This is all strange for me. Everyone in town seems to get involved in everyone else's business. I'm sure it's natural and helpful to you, but it felt invasive to me. I didn't mean to insult you."

He studied her thoughtfully. A quiet smile played beneath the mustache.

"I don't insult easily. But I get pissed off as quickly as the next guy. Look, why don't you let Jesse get settled back in class, and we head back to town and call a truce? I'll stay away from school from now on."

"Truce," she agreed. "But, as I told you, I'm going to bring him to urgent care and have his nose checked. He can start fresh tomorrow."

"Don't you think he'd be better off facing . . ." He caught her eyes and held his hands up immediately. "Sorry. Bad habit. Good to check the nose."

She knew exactly what he really thought. Despite his contrite words and the truce they'd promised, he considered her an overprotective mother. Well, so be it. It was unfair, though. He'd never had a kid, she'd bet, who'd wound up in school with a bloody nose. That kind of scenario did something inexplicable to a mother's insides. Let him judge.

During the ride back to town, Jesse didn't act like a

picked-on child, or even one who needed to see an urgent-care doc. He chattered like a chipmunk about everything but the incident, peppering Dewey with questions about fire apparatus, fuel that went into them, the pictures in his room, the local fire department, and the fire at Dewey's station three weeks earlier. Clearly, to Rose's slight embarrassment, Jesse had connected Dewey to the fire engine he still hadn't had a chance to examine. The inevitable question came as they reached Dewey's car, parked outside the Loon Feather.

"You said we could meet the fire chief sometime. When?"

Dewey turned to Rose as if looking for help. He'd done a fair job of fielding the other questions, mostly by turning them back on Jesse and letting him jabber—a trick, Rose had to admit, few learned how to perform with her son.

"Did I say that?" he asked.

"Sadly, if he says so, you probably did. Not that *I* remember or will hold you to it."

She wouldn't. There was never any way to predict what words or problems would stick in Jesse's mind and fester there until they were addressed or solved. This issue wasn't Dewey's fault. To her shock, however, Dewey shifted in his seat and looked directly at Jesse.

"I'll talk to Chief Severson and then to your mom. Maybe she can get you over there at a special time."

Rose started to smile in thanks.

"But you said *you'd* introduce me."

At that, both she and Dewey sat dumbstruck. Finally,

she covered her lips with her fingers, but the smile she tried to hide threatened to morph into laughter. She'd been certain Jesse would hate this man forever after he'd dragged him kicking and screaming from the coveted fire engine. Instead, her son seemed determined to befriend him. Or exact revenge. But even Jesse's brain didn't usually run toward the vindictive.

"Are you sure?" Dewey asked finally.

"I'm sure."

"I'll have to get back to you on that, then, kid."

"Okay."

"I'll talk to him." Rose half-whispered the promise as Dewey reached for the door handle.

"All right." He climbed out of the car and then bent to peer back inside. "Here's the deal. You spend the rest of the week in school and promise me you'll ignore anyone who calls you a name. I'll let you know if I happen to run into the fire chief."

"Cool."

Dewey glanced back at Rose. "Thank you," she mouthed.

"Sorry again about forcing myself along today. Hope his nose is all right."

She started to brush off the apology but got no chance. He offered a quick, tight smile and closed the door. In three seconds her face heated to scalding and her emotions slid from stung to embarrassed. She wanted more than she should for Dewey to stop judging her and suggesting what she should do next in life, and yet the idea of having him take her son to the fire station filled her with the most ridiculous of hopes—that maybe Jesse could have a strong male role model, at least for a moment in time.

And an equally ludicrous thought—that she could look up to him, too, for that same moment—struck her, stuck to her heart, and pretty much scared her silly.

Four hours later, with Dewey relegated to a persistent but manageable memory and Jesse whining about the suggestion of tuna casserole for supper, Rose capitulated and agreed to one more meal at the Loon Feather. Jesse actually bore a piece of tape across his nose from the clinic, more to appease him than for any medical purpose. Still, it gave him a pathetic, punched-kid look that garnered sympathy.

After she'd rescheduled her meeting with the high school principal, she and Kate had finished the two oversized banned-books posters and set up impressive displays. In addition, Jesse had helped choose a dozen favorite fall-themed kids' books to display around the room. She'd come up with several activities ideas for the Open House as well as for the rest of the month.

The Loon Feather's owner, Effie Jorgenson, an ample woman with a friendly smile and the slightest limp— from a recent hip replacement, Rose had learned from eager gossipers—led them toward a table near the back of the restaurant, and the peaceful, eclectic décor of the café soothed Rose's stretched and weary nerves. She didn't notice Jesse wasn't behind her until Effie set menus on the table.

Rose spotted him beside a table where a boy approximately his age sat with his head bowed, eyes covered by thick, unruly black bangs. Rose blew out, fluffing her own bangs with the breath. "Thanks, Effie. Guess I need to retrieve my distractible son."

The older woman laughed. "That's Josh Cassidy and his mom. They're a sweet pair and won't be bothered at all. I'll be back when you're settled."

Rose set her purse and coat on the chair and headed back for Jesse. When she reached the table, the other mom looked up, a welcoming twinkle in eyes that shone a friendly golden brown. The project both boys concentrated on so hard turned out to be a drawing. The little artist worked without regard to Jesse's staring.

"I'm sorry," Rose said. "He doesn't always wait for an invitation before he stops and intrudes. I'm Rose Hanrehan. This is Jesse. And it's time for us to go sit now, kiddo."

The woman waved the apology away. She had to be one of the loveliest women Rose had ever met, with shoulder-length blonde waves and flawless cheekbones that refused to divulge her age. She could have been anywhere from twenty-one to thirty-five.

"I'm Elizabeth Cassidy," she said, her voice as sweet as her face. "This is my son, Josh, and trust me, he's perfectly happy to have an audience. Actually, Jesse did introduce himself and has been quite complimentary. It's very nice to meet you both."

Something about the woman's name niggled at the back of Rose's mind. She could have been the kind of beautiful that gave off arrogant vibes, but she exuded only approachability.

"Nice to meet you, Elizabeth. Josh, you look like quite the artist."

"Look what he's drawing," Jesse said. "It's totally awesome."

"It's just Smaug," Josh replied.

Elizabeth grimaced slightly. "He saw *The Hobbit* over Labor Day with my parents. I wasn't crazy about him watching it—too much magic and evil, in my opinion. But it is a far better dragon than I could ever draw."

At that, Josh put down his pencil and held up his sketch pad. The dragon was, indeed, smashing for a . . .

"How old are you, Josh?" Rose asked.

"Nine and a half."

She looked at Elizabeth with surprise. "That's an amazing talent."

It wasn't that the drawing looked prodigious, but the level of detail was advanced, with individual dragon scales, a clear gleam in the huge eye, and sharp talons on the claws.

"He draws a lot," Elizabeth admitted. "He had to spend the day at school without his sketch pad, and he's catching up now. Did you start school today, too, Jesse?"

"No. I'm starting tomorrow. I tried today, but I got in trouble in gym class, and I had to leave early."

"Is that why you have the tape on your nose?"

"Kenny Simon pushed me down, and it almost got broken."

"Oh, no. I'm so sorry."

Rose winced at Jesse's unapologetic honesty. She should never be surprised by it, but she often was. She thought about explaining it further, but Elizabeth simply smiled, and Rose left off the details.

"It was a tough first day," she agreed.

"They called me Jesse 'the Body,' and I didn't like it. I called him—"

Rose swooped in and physically spun Jesse from the table, covering his mouth briefly with her palm. "Something he didn't like either, right?"

"Right."

"You could be Jesse James instead," Josh said matter-of-factly. "He was a train robber and a bank robber and really tough. Nobody would mess with Jesse James."

"Can I be Jesse James?" Jesse looked up at Rose.

"He was tough, but he was not a good guy, honey. We could probably find lots of Jesses who were nicer."

"I don't want to be nicer."

"How about if you look up Jesse James and read about him, and then decide if you want to take over his name?"

"Good idea." Jesse leaned back onto the table. "Can you teach me to draw a dragon?"

Josh shrugged. "Yeah, maybe."

"Can you draw fire engines?" Jesse tried again and got another shrug.

"I don't know. I never tried."

Elizabeth laughed. "Maybe you could come and play after school sometime, Jesse. I work from home, and Josh gets pretty bored with me if I'm too busy."

Rose's chest flared with hope even as her stomach sank with dread. These kinds of friendships rarely went well. Other kids quickly got bored with Jesse's single-mindedness. If today had gone well at school, maybe she'd feel more optimistic.

"What do you do?" she asked.

"Oh, I write." Elizabeth waggled her head with a self-deprecating smile. "Kids' books, nothing major."

The memory broke free, and Rose's jaw went slack. "Elizabeth Cassidy? Of course! You write the PenPals series for middle-graders."

She nodded. "That's me. It's an honor that you know about the books. Most adults have no idea."

"I'm the new librarian. I know you very well—or know your books. At the library where I worked in Boston, we couldn't keep them on the shelf—kids love them!"

"That's really nice of you to say so."

"Have you lived here all along?"

"No, no. I've been in Kennison Falls not quite two years. I am originally from Minnesota, though. I traveled everywhere with my folks while growing up, then finally settled near Minneapolis for high school. Josh and I moved down here when he was ready to start first grade. How about you? You're from Boston, you said?"

"I am. We've been here a little over three weeks."

"I'm so happy to meet you."

"Please tell me we can get together and talk," Rose said. "I would love to pick your brain for ideas about the library. Maybe you could do a program for us?"

"I'd love to. And I was serious about the boys getting together."

Rose dug into her purse and pulled out one of her new business cards, along with a pen, and scribbled her home number on the back. "Call me anytime at home or at the library when it's convenient for your schedule. We'll set something up."

"I will definitely call. Here . . ." Elizabeth found her own card and handed it Rose. "Don't hesitate to call me either. I'm really looking forward to the library opening. The temporary one was so tiny."

"I hope we can offer some really fun things for everyone who loves to read. It's a great opportunity for me." She took Jesse's hand. "C'mon, honey, we need to go order some supper and let Josh and his mom eat theirs, too. Would you guys like to get together and play?"

Josh shrugged for the third time. Jesse nodded. Rose latched onto it as a good sign.

They sat at their table, and Jesse immediately reached for the basket holding the creamers.

"That was cool, huh?" Rose asked.

"Yeah. He's a good artist."

"He is. Do you think you could be friends?"

"It's too soon to tell."

She snorted softly and had to concede his wisdom. Life with her son always consisted of precocious understanding juxtaposed with social challenges. She often wondered if she'd ever get a handle on him.

Fifteen minutes later, Rose watched him dig into the mac and cheese that was looking like it would be his standard fare at the Loon, glad his sore nose didn't seem to be affecting his appetite. She bit into her own Reuben sandwich, enjoying the savory mix of sauerkraut and Thousand Island on rich pumpernickel. It finished melting her stress away.

Meeting Elizabeth Cassidy had made up for the day's trauma and busyness, and the calm, now that Jesse ate like a ravenous pup, brought along with it the hope that the worst was behind her. Every once in a while her son smiled over a mouthful of creamy cheese macaroni, and her heart swelled. The tape across his nose didn't bother her anymore. The day was almost done. They'd go home, watch a half hour of television, and maybe read aloud or play a game before his bedtime. Then a nice, long soak in the big, old-fashioned tub in the master bathroom for her . . .

"Hey there, kid. Whoa, Nelly-belle, did you actually bust up that nose?"

Her heartbeat started skittering before she even looked up into Dewey's eyes, and it slammed to a near halt when she saw the tall woman beside him. There was no reason for the hot acid splash of jealousy in her chest, but this woman looked like she'd been custom made for him. She had the height and self-confidence to match his, with slender femininity to make him look virile and protective. Her thick brown ponytail fell past her shoulder blades. She smiled, the perfect counterpart to his usual serious expression.

"It's not broken." Jesse looked up. Rose marveled again at how he appeared to light up around Dewey. "I can take the bandage off before bed. But I might get a shiner."

"A shiner, huh? You okay with that? You aren't gonna be embarrassed or anything?"

"I doubt it."

"Good."

He turned his eyes to Rose, and her Reuben turned to a lump in her stomach. She set what remained of the sandwich on her plate.

"Hi," he said.

"Hi back."

"I'm sorry to interrupt. I was going to stop by the house, but then I saw your car. You do know there's nowhere to hide if you insist on driving it around here."

The comical arch in his brows made her grin despite her breathing and swallowing problems. "Is there a reason that should concern me?"

"I'm standing here when I promised I'd stay away. That maybe answers your question."

"I never said you had to stay away."

His eyes darkened and softened at the same time. "Well, I won't keep you long. I wanted Jesse to know that Chief Severson would like to show him around the station on Saturday if it works with his mother's schedule. The only catch is me. If I have to be there, it needs to be after noon. If not, you can go anytime in the morning."

"You have to be there!" Jesse, his face like an eager beagle's, stared at the man who was on the way to becoming his biggest hero.

"Then it's up to your mom."

Dewey's face remained as pleasantly impassive as ever. But he'd kept his promise to a young boy, and that allowed him temporary hero status in Rose's book, too.

"Of course it's all right," she said. "Thank you. I really didn't expect you to go running off right away and making arrangements."

"Oddly enough, Duke—Chief Severson—stopped by my station this afternoon for something unrelated. Like the meeting was meant to be."

"Dewey." The brown-haired woman tapped his shoulder. "I'm going to get a table."

"I'll be right there."

She leaned around him and held out her hand. "I'm Eleanor Mitchell," she said. "But call me Elle. Dewey's told me a lot about the new librarian. Nice to meet you."

Confused, Rose took the firm handshake and smiled back. Same last name? Gentle little butterflies of envy turned into javelin-throwing ninjas of resentment. Was he married? After he'd accompanied her unasked to a conference and was now offering to take her son on a visit to the fire station?

Elle greeted Jesse and then headed for the other side of the café. Dewey stayed, holding her eyes unashamedly with his. Rose stared back.

What would that mustache feel like on my upper lip?

Oh good Lord. What in the world was wrong with her brain? Her rogue thoughts were so inappropriate she almost apologized out loud.

"Rose?"

She swallowed and focused on his voice. "Yes?"

"I asked if one o'clock would work."

"Yes. Yes, that's perfect." She took a deep breath. "Eleanor seems nice. She's pretty."

He frowned slightly, his eyes studying her like a doctor looking for a clue to a diagnosis. She saw the moment he figured it out. The broadest smile he'd offered yet turned on his sex appeal like a lighthouse beacon, and her face heated for at least the millionth time since she'd met him.

"My sister? I guess she is. And she's probably the nicest one in the family."

Her only hope was that the floor would open up and swallow her. Rose fought to keep from covering her face with her hands and making her embarrassment even more obvious.

"Sister."

"Yup."

There was nothing else to say. He knew what she'd thought. She could only pray he'd never know what thinking it had done to her. Man, she was an idiot.

"I'll see you Saturday at the fire station."

"See you then."

"And, you, Mr. Not-the-Body Jesse. You're going to give gym class your best shot, right?"

"I can't hit my nose again."

"Fair enough, don't. Stay away from Kenny Whozits and give stuff a try. It's part of the deal."

"Fine."

He winked a little too triumphantly at Rose. "A bribe can work wonders."

She laughed, holding back sarcasm. Her heart slowly approached a normal rhythm, and her cheeks cooled. "Sure, Dewey. Easy as a chick in a red Mustang. Why ever didn't I think of that?"

Chapter Seven

THE TWENTY-FIVE KIDS of the Quad County Middle
School Gold Gryphons team lined up for their last drill of
the day, and Dewey trained his eye on young Jason Peterson, impressed as always by the kid's work ethic. He'd been
named captain of the Gold team after sitting precariously
on the fence during tryouts when it came to actual skill.
Dewey had lobbied for him to make the higher-performing
Red team, since this was his last year in middle school, but
Adrian as head coach had made the final call. Jason had
accepted the decision with grace, and now helped shepherd
the younger players through the drill like a pro.

"All right, guys," Dewey hollered when the last pair
of short legs had navigated the pole grid they had to hop
through. "Tomorrow, passing and field-position drills.
We'll skip your beloved conditioning for one day. But
before you go now, I need one fast lap and one screw-off
lap around the track—build up that air."

The kids set off around the four-forty track, Jason in the lead. After once around, they all fell completely out of sync, allowed to run sideways, backward, zigzag, or however they wanted as long as they didn't walk. They took off like drunken puppets, cheering and weaving and laughing themselves silly. It was a good way to end practice every day. They didn't even know they were working.

"Hey, Coach." Jason finished first, and pulled up in front of Dewey breathing heavily but not panting.

"Good practice today. Thanks for your help with the younger guys."

"No problem. I was wondering if I could have another one of those rivet things you fixed my pads with a while back. I think the one on the other side is loose now."

"Sure. Need me to look at it?"

"I think I can fix it. Maybe."

"Good man." Dewey dug out a nylon rivet and handed it over. "Ready for our first game next week?"

"Yeah. My dad might take off work and come. That would be cool."

Jason's parents were hardworking people who owned a small farm and also held part-time jobs up in the bigger, nearby city of Faribault. He had several younger siblings, but Dewey didn't know much more about the family. They had to be good people to have raised a polite boy like Jason.

"That's great. I'll say hi to him if he comes."

"He used to play when he was in school."

"That right?"

"He says I've come a long way." Jason's chest puffed a

little with pride. Dewey knew how he felt—the same way he'd felt when his own father had praised him.

"You've worked hard the past two years. You are improving."

"I hated football when I was in grade school."

That surprised Dewey. Jason had so much natural enthusiasm for the game, it was hard to believe he hadn't been born wanting to play. "Really? Why? What changed your mind?"

"I was afraid of it. I was always kind of a fat little kid, and I couldn't run fast. I didn't like getting hit, and I couldn't jump very high to catch. I hated when my family played football at Thanksgiving and Christmas. But I have this cousin who would play with me alone, and he made up super-easy rules and didn't care if I screwed up. It was fun with him.

"Finally, I got old enough and figured out he was letting me win, and I decided I wanted to learn how to really play. Then I liked it."

"That's amazing. Good for you, Jason."

He shrugged. "I'll never be, like, a varsity player or anything, but I'm a captain. That's cool."

Dewey marveled. Few fourteen-year-olds were this self-aware. The parents deserved a medal.

"You never know. You could make varsity. You've got the right attitude."

"Hey, thanks, Coach. Thanks for the rivet."

The boy trotted off, and Dewey pinched his lower lip between his thumb and forefinger. He'd have been thrilled to have a kid like Jason Peterson. One blessed with family who stuck by him and gave him opportunities to find his own stride. The kid would be a good player by the time he reached his junior and senior years. All because one person had figured out how to meet him at his level.

He was certain his family would have been like that with any children Dewey might have had.

Not that it mattered in the least—they'd never need the chance to prove it.

He shook his head and checked his watch. Once he and Adrian picked up equipment and cleared the last of the kids off the field, he'd have ninety minutes to get some lunch and check in at the Gas 'n' Garage before meeting Rose Hanrehan and her son at the fire station. He wasn't looking forward to spending the time with the kid. He had no idea how to handle Jesse's obsessive questions. On the other hand, he'd brave as many questions as the boy wanted to ask if it meant the chance to hang out with his mother. Beautiful, smart, intense, and caring, Rose had him wrapped up in knots he didn't understand in the least.

He didn't understand because, in addition to being all those good things, she was also single-minded, touchy as a treed tabby, and mercurial as a Minnesota weather forecast. She overindulged the boy and reacted to everything as if it were a threat. It was all as irritating as hell. Yet she had mettle and good instincts. And when she laughed, it was at smart things and made her look like a kid at a carnival. Something genuine and caring shone through the quirks. She'd woven her way into his thoughts and never left.

If only Jesse Loren Hanrehan had an extended family to meet him where he was at. Dewey stopped packing up his tool kit and stared again after Jason. What if there *were* a group of kids like Jesse? Just as Rose had suggested to Joyce? All the boy needed was one person to make physical activity fun.

Thoughts that weren't quite coherent or related started to whirl. What was to stop him, or anyone, from doing something outside the school's auspices?

But do what? He didn't have any extra time in his schedule.

Jason disappeared behind the bleachers, heading for the parking lot and his ride. Dewey shook his head.

Adrian came in from the field toting a bag of footballs. "Talking to spirits?"

Dewey sniffed. "Right. Thinking about kids who manage to make it."

"The Peterson boy?"

"Works damn hard."

"He does. I was thinking maybe he'd like to move up the last couple of games this fall. He could play JV in a year."

"I think he'd like that."

"He's a decent teacher for the other kids, too," Adrian said. "A good role model. Hope he stays that way. Be nice if we taught these kids more than football skills. I think he's in the right place for now."

Dewey grunted his agreement. Jason was a good role model. How would he be with a kid who hated football?

He stopped by the station. Elle and Joey took care of the Saturday business while he was at practice. During football season Dewey cut his hours, the only time of year he did other than Christmas and Easter. This year, with his sister freshly graduated from college and begging to work for him—something he didn't understand in the least—he was able to keep the garage open for basic services like tire repair and oil changes. Elle had loved hanging around the cars as a kid. Dewey had assumed she'd outgrow the fascination as she discovered school and boys and whatever her true calling turned out to be. Nothing seemed to have called her yet.

He found her tinkering beneath the hood of a '69 Camaro that had been on his someday-I'll-restore-this-sucker-to-its-original-glory list for ten years and stepped up behind her.

"What the heck are you lookin' for under there?" He got the slightest evil-brother satisfaction when she jumped.

"Jiminy Christmas, warn a person, would you?"

"Sorry."

"You're not. And as if it's not obvious, I'm trying to get this puppy to run."

"You?"

"Yeah." She made a "duh" face at him. "Is that really so far out of the realm of your imagination?"

"I had no idea you thought you could perform such a miracle."

Elle folded her arms across her chest. "You know, I've been home most of the summer. It took me almost two months to talk you into letting me hang out down here. And you haven't once asked me what I did to work my way through college the last two years. You either still think I'm the annoying baby sister who you looked at as a dumb tomboy, or you really are a chauvinist."

What was it with women lately telling him across-the-board what an ass he was? He folded his arms right back at her.

"You're just a little pipsqueak girl," he said. "What business do you have hanging around a dirty old garage?"

"Your garage dirty? Hah, Mr. OCD. If I switched the order of two crescent wrenches, you'd see it from outside. Freak."

"You didn't answer my question." He held back a smile.

"I like cars."

"So? Lots of girls like cars, but they don't grub around in garages."

"You'd better not be serious."

"Eleanor." He leaned one hip against the old car. "What did you do to earn your way through college?"

"I worked at a garage, Duane." She offered a smug smile.

"You did?"

"You never asked Mom what I was up to?"

To his shame, he had to admit he never had. He'd asked after her, of course, but the details had never come up. "I knew you were fine. What else did I need to know?"

"That a guy named Todd Winthrop taught me everything he knew about engines."

"You're serious."

"I am, you bonehead. I've been trying to tell you all summer I know what I'm doing."

"I'll be danged."

He stared at his baby sister, thirteen years his junior and still as sweet-faced as she'd always been. Now, however, there was a determination in her eyes that had been no more than stubbornness at age twelve.

"Let me fix up this engine, Dewey. If I prove I can do it, let's talk about me working here and handling more repair work for you."

"Okay, okay, hang on." His moment of nostalgic fuzzy feelings passed, and he straightened in a rush. "You're putting a big old cart before the horse here, Elle. I've never hired another mechanic, and if I did it'd be someone with a hell of a lot more experience than you have. Go ahead and play with the Camaro if you want. And I'm happy to have your help. But don't make plans for the future yet."

She shook her head, leaned forward, and kissed him on the cheek.

"You sound more and more like what I remember of Daddy every day, you old fart. Thanks. I'll get her running."

She had grown up, dang her. No temper tantrums, no finagling. She'd been only nine when their father had passed away. He guessed he and his brothers had done all right raising her. He grabbed her around the neck, planted his own kiss on top of her head, and then rubbed his knuckles into her hair while she screeched at the noogie.

"Butthead," she laughed.

"I'm going to grab lunch and then head to the fire station. Be back maybe two-thirty or so. Have it done by then."

"Double butthead."

He laughed this time and sauntered to his car.

Saturdays at the Loon Feather could be either crazy busy or slow as a ghost town, depending on the weather. Today was sunny and wrapped in the kind of soul-deep, satisfying warmth that only a Minnesota September could produce. A couple of people sat at tables in the café. Others were out enjoying the last days of yard work or picnicking.

"Hey, Dewey. We don't see you often on a weekend." Effie patted him on the arm and led him to his normal weekday table. "Everything all right?"

"Sure, Effie. It's football season. Things slow down at the garage because I'm cranky and tell people to stay away."

"Cranky." She giggled like a much younger woman. "That'll be the day. What can I get you to start with, dear?

"Simple's all I need. A burger and a Coke."

"Easy enough. Rio and I baked our first pumpkin pies yesterday, and I'll give you a day-old piece on the house if you want to try it."

"You think I could say no to that?"

She shook her head, winked, and walked away.

Things like day-old pie for free were definitely the perks of living in a small town. As was having business owners who knew you as well as your own mother did. Of course, there were all too many times when that was also the biggest problem with a small town. He'd learned to deal with it by presenting only the face he wanted his fellow Fallsians to see. The skill was sharply honed.

Once Effie brought his Coke, he nursed it slowly, letting his mind roll over the crazy day that wasn't half-done. His sister was cracked—wanting to spend her days grubbing in grease and engine oil? He stared at his hands and rubbed off the one spot of grime he found. Even he hated oil-stained fingers and, however unmanly it might be, spent a fortune on hand cleaners that he used religiously after every job. He did too many other things besides fix cars to allow himself to look like a grease monkey. And although he like his job fine, he wanted more for his brilliant, sociable sister.

Then again, she'd been the one of all their siblings who'd loved mud pies better than apple pies, and finger painting, and running around in the rain. Hell. Girly girls or tomboys. Who could figure females out at the best of times?

Which brought him to Librarian Rose. Sitting here by himself, he found the zing of attraction at the thought of her stronger than ever. He'd met many beautiful women in his life, but other than his ex-wife they hadn't affected him. After his divorce he'd dated a few. He'd gotten physically close to a few. But emotionally, everything remained superficial even at the most intimate times.

He'd barely touched Rose Hanrehan, yet she was like itching powder in his undershirt. He couldn't get her, or her hair, or the curves she covered in practical pleated slacks and tidy sweaters worn over other sweaters, out of his mind.

What would it be like to divest her of the grown-up clothes and put her in nothing but a pair of Daisy Dukes—

Whoa. Holy hell, where had *that* come from? He was about to go meet the woman and her son, for crying out loud, and he hadn't had such a blatantly immature thought in as long as he could remember.

And yet the picture of her as a sexual—sexy—woman wouldn't leave.

A soft touch on his shoulder jolted him back to the present and he jumped, his guilty conscience heating his face from deep within. To his surprise, Abby Stadtler-Covey stood beside him, gentle amusement in her eyes.

"It's not often I say hi and don't get a response," she said, her voice as bell-like as he'd known it for twelve years. "Everything okay?"

He was definitely off his game today. Everyone had to ask him if he was all right, and that suddenly annoyed him.

"Fine. It's football season and there's lots to think about."

"Of course. How could I forget? You guys won your first game, if I heard right."

The high school team had won the night before, and he nodded. "Yeah. Good game. Lots to fix, though."

"Spoken like a true coach."

Abby. The one near-exception to the truth that he'd never gotten close to a woman since his ex-wife. Several years before, he'd thought he could marry Abby in a heartbeat if she'd only returned his interest. She'd always been made of gentle grace and a lot of class. And then she'd met the rock singer, Gray Covey, and it had been, and still was, hard not to admit he was perfect for her. Although he hadn't been particularly gracious at the time.

He smiled at her, and noticed a wan quality to her cheeks that he'd never seen before. He peered more closely and took in an anemic smile and a slight purple tinge on the skin below her eyes. He'd long ago gotten over any romantic feelings for her, and since she'd married Gray they'd all become good friends. Now his concern didn't stem from anything deeper than friendship, but it hit strong and hard.

"I think I should be asking if you're okay," he said. "You look a little . . . peaked."

He cringed at the old-fashioned word his mother had used whenever someone was sick. Abby sighed and set her hand on his shoulder again. For an instant he was sure she'd say "fine" and reassure him, but instead a distant smile flitted across her lips and disappeared.

"Sit down," he said, and to his shock she did.

"Oh, Dewey, can you keep a secret? Wait, that's stupid, you're the best secret keeper in town. The only one who knows everything and says nothing."

"What's going on?" A flash of caring shot through him, and he dreaded what she might say. Something was wrong with her? With Gray? With one of her kids, Kim or Dawson?

"I . . ." Her eyes brimmed with unshed tears, and Dewey's heart punched in his chest. She covered his hands with hers. "I'm fine. I'm fine. I'm . . . pregnant."

A wave of relief so powerful it hurt swept through him first, and he grinned.

"That's great, Abby. Unless it isn't?"

"Oh, it is. I think. But it's the scariest thing that's ever happened to me."

"It shouldn't be. You're the world's greatest mother. But why are you telling me?"

"I have no idea. Except I think I needed to try out the words. I saw you here, and suddenly I wanted to tell someone safe."

"Nobody knows?"

"Well, Gray does, of course. He's beside himself with excitement. But nobody else. You've been such a good friend. I'm sorry if this is too personal."

"No, Abby, I just . . . you know I'm not good at emotion. I have no idea why this is scary, but if it is, I'm sorry."

She laughed. "It's scary because I'm thirty-eight and you know how much I hate the media attention around Gray. He handles it perfectly and protects us like crazy but, well . . ."

"I get it." Hadn't he just been thinking about what a positive thing it was to have a town that knew you inside and out? "But the baby itself—that's okay? You want this?"

"Oh, I do." She made a face like sour lemons. "Or I will when I stop feeling like crap."

"Aw, I'm sorry. What do pregnant women drink? Tea? Milk?"

"Tea. You'll let me impose?" She propped her chin in her hands and looked a little better.

"Impose. That's a laugh. Anything to let you know it's going to be fine."

"You're a special guy."

He laughed, but the compliment sliced through him like a knife blade instead of uplifting him. Everyone's special guy. If they had a dead car or lawn mower. And as Abby's relaxed joy started to shine through, replacing her earlier tears, the knowledge of how lucky she was not to have hooked up with him slammed Dewey right behind the knife stab. She was sick but so happy—and he never could have given her this moment. He could never give it to any woman.

And that was something not a single person in this small town but his own mother knew.

Chapter Eight

"Do you have any USARs?" Jesse asked the question while engrossed in a printout listing the locations of fire stations in every town and city within a fifty-mile radius of Kennison Falls.

Rose smiled gratefully at what had to be the fiftieth time Chief Severson gave a patient smile for one of Jesse's rapid-fire questions. He leaned against the gleaming door of Engine #2 with his arms folded.

"Urban Search and Rescue, huh? You know what 'urban' means, right? A big city?" Jesse nodded. "Since we aren't too urban here, we don't have a full USAR apparatus. But we have our light-rescue truck and Engine #2 here that carries more extraction equipment."

"Jaws of Life?" Jesse asked, wide-eyed.

"That's right."

"Can I see the rescue truck?"

Rose glanced at her watch, and a wave of guilt lapped

at her thoughts. "Jesse, honey, you've kept Chief Severson for an hour now. I'm guessing he has other jobs he needs to get done."

She looked from Duke Severson's smiling, lined face to Dewey, who stood silently in a corner. He'd ensconced himself there half an hour before, once Jesse had decided he wasn't afraid to talk to the chief on his own. It was probably a good thing; Dewey had been grouchy since the moment he'd shown his face.

"Let's look at the rescue equipment."

Chief Severson led Jesse away and Rose sighed, lost as to what to do while she waited. Two tentative steps took her to Dewey. Neither of them followed the older man and his little shadow.

"He's more than earning his hero stripes today," she said.

"The kid sure can come up with questions. Have you ever talked to him about going into journalism?"

She nodded and smiled. "I know he can be exhausting. Thank you, too, for taking this time. You get stripes, too."

"Don't want any stripes," he grunted. "Consider it my good deed for the month. Making up for earlier transgressions."

"I'm sorry about how ungrateful I've been. I know you've been trying to help. I'm nervous about the Open House tomorrow, and anxiety makes me short tempered."

"It takes a while to get your sea legs in a place like this."

"I guess so. I thought I was ready for small-town life, but it's . . . interesting."

"You ever lived in a small town?"

She shook her head. "Boston suburbs. And the branch of the Boston Public Library I worked at had thirty employees. Here I have an entire board questioning my every move."

"Is there that much to question?"

"Are you still planning to come tomorrow?"

"Yeah."

"Then you'll see what it is some of the board members don't like. I'm promoting Banned Books Week coming up at the end of the month, and it's a hot topic."

"They still ban books?"

"They try. People challenge books all the time."

"I'd have thought we were beyond that these days."

"Well, come and see," she teased.

They went in search of Jesse and Chief Severson. When they found the pair, Jesse was trussed up in a complicated harness, beaming. He turned, an exaggerated grin on his face. "Look! I'm in a rescue harness. Plus, we found a broken carabiner. Chief says I can have it. And *Jaws of Life* is a brand name, and they're huge and awesome."

"That's really cool, sweetheart." Rose bent to examine the hook-shaped oval of metal in Jesse's hands.

"Don't let him use that for anything like climbing or weight bearing," the chief said. "It isn't safe."

"Thank you so much," Rose said. "You're more of a collector anyhow, aren't you, Jess?"

He nodded and held the new prize out to Dewey. "See?"

"Neat, kid." Dewey gave a good impression of caring, but Rose got the feeling he'd rather be anywhere else.

"I think we still have some of our chocolate fire engines in the kitchen. Come on and check out the rest of the station."

The large, modern kitchen boasted stainless-steel appliances and a long narrow island down the center of the room with plenty of storage cupboards and a hanging rack over the stove holding every size of cooking pot. A large glass bowl on the end of the counter held a mound of foil-wrapped candies that, on closer inspection, proved to be chocolate fire engines, just as promised.

Two other men sat around a family-sized table at the far end of the space. They waved and called hellos.

"Jack 'Church' Hubbard and Pete 'Buzz' Franklin." Chief Severson introduced them. "They're putting together a training schedule. We're the three full-time members of the squad; the rest, about fifteen men, are all volunteers. Help yourselves to the chocolates." Chief Severson pointed at the bowl. "We order lots to bring around to schools and give out at times like this."

"I can't thank you enough for this," Rose said, keeping an eye on Jesse, who already had four of the chocolates in hand.

"My pleasure. Always glad to show a fellow aficionado around the firehouse." He ruffled Jesse's hair. To Rose's amazement, her son didn't flinch. "What else do you like to do, Jesse?" the chief asked.

"Draw things. Play with dogs."

"What?"

Rose couldn't help blurting out her surprise. Jesse had mentioned dogs once in his life, when his grandmother had taken him past a mall pet-shop window and a litter of five Jack Russell pups had caught his attention. Rose had put a fast kibosh on the idea of bringing one home and made it clear there was no room or time for a dog in their lives or small apartment.

Because there hadn't been.

Jesse hadn't ever brought up having a dog again. And where he'd gotten the idea now remained a mystery until the chief laughed and pointed to the table.

"You saw Loki playing, didn't you? Church! Bring the dog over here. Someone wants to meet him."

The firefighter nicknamed Church, a tall and extremely good-looking guy who could only be described as ripped beneath his tight blue KFFD T-shirt, jumped up and slapped his thigh. A pretty dog with husky-like markings but the wavy coat and softer features of a retriever joined him immediately.

"Hey!" Church said. "Nice to meet you guys. This is Loki. He's pretty new with us, actually. Only been here about six months."

As if his only purpose that day was to shock his mother silly, Jesse dropped to his knees and embraced the dog, who lapped eagerly at his face. He giggled and craned his neck side to side, trying to avoid a tongue in the mouth.

"Loki! Stop, boy, stop. You're funny. Loki!"

The adults looked on wordlessly, smiles growing as Jesse's laughter increased.

"Boy needs a dog." Dewey's breath in her ear sent a shower of sparks down Rose's neck and across her shoulders.

"Well, it's a good thing your sister doesn't allow pets," she replied, rubbing her arms to ward off the sudden breakout of goose bumps on her skin.

"She allows them. She just charges extra."

"Same thing."

"You don't like dogs?"

"I didn't say that. We weren't pet owners growing up. My mother was too OCD for animals in the house, and my father was a state senator who had no time. Besides, my sister was allergic."

"Defensive much?" His voice carried the lightness of teasing. She glared over her shoulder and saw the mustache twitch.

"Rude much?" She shot back and got back a chuckle, the reply still in her ear.

The firefighter named Church called out. "Jesse! Catch!"

Rose turned her attention as a tennis ball sailed across the room. Jesse held out his hands awkwardly but flinched before it touched his fingers. The ball smacked the floor, bounced hard, and careened off the wall. Jesse chased it down and without much aim, tossed it too hard to the dog. It bounced yet again but this time caromed off the candy bowl on the counter and crashed it to the floor, where it shattered and scattered red-foiled candy like a paint spill. Loki twisted and bounded after the ball. Jesse stared at the mess, his lip starting to tremble.

"I . . . I . . ."

"Hey, hey, Jesse, it's no problem," Church said. "I didn't give you any warning, and I threw the ball too hard. You grabbed it and did what I did."

Church collared Loki, who came sniffing back after a piece of the chocolate. The chief snatched a broom from a tall cupboard beside the door and started gathering glass shards into a pile.

"Jesse, here you go." The second firefighter, Buzz, walked around the counter and placed a treat bone directly into Jesse's hand. "Come on over here, and I'll show you how to make Loki beg. "

Jesse shook the firefighter's hand, but still looked on the verge of tears.

"Hey, sweetie." Rose stepped forward. "It's okay—"

She knew he was hypersensitive to such gaffes, especially in front of adults. This was the exact reason he'd had trouble in gym class the first day.

"Leave him." The whisper entered her ear again, along with goose bumps as Dewey caught her around the shoulders. "Let him get through this."

Why was the man so damn infuriating? Did he honestly think he was some superhero stud when it came to kids? She spun and lost all train of thought when her torso wound up pressed to his, and he smiled down the same way he had four days ago in the rain.

He smelled like outdoors and a hint of something mind-confusingly masculine. Her heart hammered against his chest. "What happened to not butting in?" she whispered furiously.

"I'm not. I know you think he needs to be comforted because he dropped the throw. Let Buzz and Church take care of it."

"You know them, too, naturally."

"Didn't you say I know everybody?"

Again with the rare grin. The man was a chameleon—dour one second, cheerful the next. Her knees threatened to give way like the smashed glass bowl.

"I'm quite sure you probably do." She wanted her words to reflect disgust. Instead they came out softly, and she had a hard time swallowing. This was stupid. She hadn't run away from Boston and one man in order to fall into the arms of another. Certainly not one who didn't understand her or her son in the least.

He saved her from making a complete fool of herself by spinning her around again so they stood back to front. He dropped his arms, the heady male scent of him faded, and her brain cleared. Slightly.

"Talk to me after this is over. I have an idea about this exact thing for Jesse."

Now what?

She nodded again and refocused, breathing a sigh of relief to see Jesse nod at Buzz and follow him. Once at the table, he held the dog's treat straight out from his shoul-der. Loki lifted onto his haunches and folded his front legs in, begging perfectly. Jesse fed him the treat and everyone clapped.

"See, he can do fine," Dewey said.

She wanted to resent the assessment. In fact, resentment was such a familiar feeling to associate with Dewey

Mitchell that she shocked herself when her head bobbed in agreement.

"I always expect a meltdown. Trust me, they truly aren't pretty."

"Then don't expect them."

She sighed. There wasn't any point in arguing with him further. Nod and smile. Accept him as a natural-born busybody and move on, she told herself. She knew nothing about him anyway, other than that he'd taught sixth grade and not even been able to finish the year. She didn't have to listen to his advice.

"Other than your erstwhile class of sixth-graders, do you have kids?"

He stepped back as suddenly as if she'd scalded him. "No."

The strange severity in his reply made her look at him again. His smile had vanished, and he now looked as if one wouldn't stay on his face if someone painted it there. She hadn't truly meant the remark as a jab, but the dark brown of his eyes boiled nearly black. Out of pure astonishment she held the hot gaze.

"Sorry. I only thought maybe you had."

"Well, I don't."

"All right, then."

Her face stung. They'd been squabbling since day one. What had been worse this time to cause such an angry withdrawal?

They didn't speak another word until the visit ended. Jesse left the station with a KFFD mug in addition to his carabiner, and a handful of fire-safety brochures. Loki had received one last huge hug. Rose apologized again for the candy bowl, and they all left through the truck-bay doors with Captain Severson, Church, and Loki waving good-bye.

Rose stopped by the Mustang. Jesse studied his carabiner, and Dewey halted, too, awkward for the first time since she'd met him.

"What do you say to Mr. Mitchell?" she asked.

Jesse looked up, his little-boy eyebrows puckered in thought as if he was deciding. With no warning, he threw his arms around Dewey's waist. Dewey jerked like a rabbit in a snare.

"Thank you, Mr. Mitchell. This was the best day of my life. Except for the bowl breaking."

"Man, uh, Jesse. I hope that's not really true. This is just a fire station." The discomfort in his eyes confounded Rose. The man was normally nothing short of a rock.

"Yeah, but a fire station with a 2001 Spartan E-1 75-foot aerial apparatus, and a 2006 E-1 Typhoon pumper, and a 2010 Ford F-550 Ferrara light-rescue truck, and—"

"Hey, hey, sweetheart." Rose placed a hand on one shoulder. "How about you write them all down for us when you get home? I'll never remember."

"And they had Loki," he added, switching gears without a blink.

"Loki is definitely a cool dog," Dewey replied.

Finally Jesse released his hug, and Rose swore Dewey rocked backward as if riding out a shock wave. She met his eyes a little hesitantly.

"Thank you again. I think you'd be surprised how special it was for him, despite the, ah, excitement."

"Well, good, then."

"What did you want me to ask you about? You said you had an idea for Jesse?"

"It was nothing." The words were too abrupt, and he didn't elaborate. "He figured stuff out like a pro. Ready to be a firefighter someday, right?"

"Nuh-uh." Jesse shook his head. "I only like the apparatus, not running around with fire hoses. That's for brave guys."

"Come on. You're plenty brave." Rose squatted and gave him a hug.

"Nope. I'm a lover, not a firefighter!" He shrugged away and grinned, pleased at his joke.

She glanced at Dewey, but he stood solemnly, his smile still under cover. She wanted to ask if he was all right, but it felt too intrusive, despite the fact that he never seemed to have any compunction about intruding in her life.

"Well, then, I guess maybe we'll see you tomorrow?" she asked.

"I'll try to come."

Try?

Although his six-feet-plus towered over her and his broad shoulders gave him a perpetual air of invincibility, she could ignore the intimidation factor when fighting on Jesse's behalf. She dug her keys from her purse and handed them to her son.

"Here, sweetheart. Go ahead and wait for me inside. You can read your brochures."

He took the keys and turned with no preamble. "Bye!"

When he was safely in the Mustang, Rose swung back to Dewey. "Would you like to tell me what I did that's got you so pissed off?

"Who said I'm pissed off?"

"Personally, I don't care, but whether he shows it or not, Jesse hears every word and feels every nuance around him. For some reason I don't understand, he likes you. If you don't show up tomorrow, that's your business, but I will have to explain why you aren't there, and I'd like to be honest with him."

"You didn't do anything." He didn't look at her but hiked up his shoulder to get a hand in his front jeans pocket, where he fished until he pulled out his own keys. The simple action was surprisingly fluid, and she wondered how up until this moment she'd missed the gracefulness in his movements.

"How am I supposed to believe that?"

"Rose, look. Not everything is about you. Not everything is about Jesse. If you want to know the truth, I don't understand why the kid would like me either— he needs a nice guy in his life. Someone to teach *him* to throw a ball and keep *you* from worrying about him all the time."

The words stunned her into speechlessness. She honestly didn't know if she was going to strike him or burst into tears. Neither happened when he finally had the guts to look her in the eyes and she looked deep into his. No disapproval shone there; in fact, he smiled at her, although it wasn't a happy smile. Sadness, deep and unreadable, fueled it, and the unexpected emotion punched Rose in the gut like a physical fist.

"I'll be there tomorrow." He turned.

"Dewey, I . . ." She what? Still didn't believe she'd done nothing? She didn't. Suddenly, however, she didn't want to be the one who'd caused such a look of ingrained worry in his eyes. "I'm sorry."

He looked briefly over his shoulder. "Honest, you have nothing to be sorry for."

She watched while he tucked himself into his black Sonata and kept watching until he drove away. Numbness enveloped her as she tried to make sense of the bizarre turn the afternoon had taken. Hard as she worked at it, she couldn't raise the righteous indignation he usually caused. Not that his words didn't prick. She'd never considered herself a selfish person. Of course *the* world didn't revolve around her or her son. But *her* world did.

A mini-pall replaced the numbness as she turned to her car, as if something had gone missing, or something irreparable had occurred. But that was complete nonsense. Nothing had happened.

Only the top of Jesse's head was visible through the door window, bent over his brochures. She tapped on the glass as she passed and waved when he looked up. When she settled behind the wheel, she felt better. Enclosed in her own world, where she belonged with her son, the events didn't seem as dire.

"Have fun today?" she asked.

"Yeah." His excitement had settled. "They won't stay mad about breaking the bowl, will they?"

"They were never angry. It was an accident."

"I don't like balls."

"I know, sweetie."

"Do I have to learn to throw a ball?"

"You can throw a ball." She glanced at him, confused.

"I mean throw it good."

"You don't have to throw it *well*," she promised. "But there are lots of times throwing a ball is fun."

"Not for me."

"Oh, Jesse, don't say that. Everything can be fun. You have to try things you don't like. Don't tell yourself you're not good at things just because other people can do them better."

"Yeah, yeah. I know."

"You do know you're a pretty special guy, right?"

"Yeah, yeah."

"I mean it."

"Mom. You say it all the time. I know."

Let him get through this. Dewey's voice in her head startled her, and she fought the urge to argue with a memory. How could a kid figure out good self-image if he didn't have it to start with?

She had no idea. The stupid thing was, she'd believed she knew how to give it to her son until Dewey Mitchell, with his handsome mustache, snarky, busybody tongue, and sad eyes, had bulldozed into their lives. She rubbed her own eyes tiredly and then pulled away from the curb.

Just as she merged with the traffic, her cell phone rang from her purse.

"Sweetheart, can you grab that?"

Jesse found the phone. "Hi, this is Jesse. Mom is driving." Rose smiled. She'd taught him well. "I can ask. Mom, can I put the phone to your ear? Kate says she has to tell you something."

"All right." He pressed the phone tight against her skin. "Kate?" she asked.

"Hey, Rose. I know it's Saturday, and the library doesn't open until Monday after the Open House tomorrow, but you'd better come now. We have a little, uh, problem."

"Little?"

"Well, no. Really, it's big."

"What is it?"

"We have our first protestors."

"Seriously?"

"Yup. A whole raft of them. And they don't want to talk to me."

"Okay. Okay. I'll be there in five minutes. How many people are there?"

"Gosh, you know what? I think I'll let you be surprised."

Chapter Nine

AS IF THE day's events so far hadn't been unusual enough, the crowd of people milling on the lawn outside the library pushed them into the realm of absurdity. Surprise didn't begin to cover Rose's emotion. As she parked the car, she did a swift count of thirty-six.

The group quieted as she approached, holding Jesse's hand. There were no signs, no ominous subsets of people looking like potential lynch mobs. Scanning hopefully for a familiar face, Rose was forced to a stop by a man she didn't know who stepped into her path. Short and squat as a fire hydrant, with a gleaming pate, bulldoggish jowls, and clever eyes, he spoke with a politician's authoritative voice.

"Mrs. Hanrehan."

"Ms. Or just Rose," she said, holding out her hand. "Mr. . . . ?"

"Reverend. Nathaniel Coburn. I'm from the Spirit of Trinity Church up toward Dundas, and I—"

"Reverend, excuse me. I'd like to take my son inside."

"We've waited for nearly an hour. We can wait an-other minute or so." He acquiesced with indulgence and theatrical understanding.

She moved through the group, acutely aware of the firmly set faces and the low-level murmuring like bees gathering. Frowning, she refrained from asking the obvious what-are-you-doing questions until she reached the front doors. The first familiar figure stood there, clearly awaiting her arrival.

"Pat?" She took in the board member's neat blue slacks and gray knit turtleneck. Pat Dunn's presence sent Rose's stomach sinking. They hadn't seen eye-to-eye from day one.

"Hello, Rose. I'm sure you're not surprised to see us here."

"On the contrary, I'm stunned. What's going on?"

"After the last meeting, you couldn't guess that if you went ahead with the emphasis on banned books for the library opening you'd upset a lot of people?"

"Are you serious? You're protesting something librar-ies across the country celebrate every single year?"

"Not here. This is a quiet, conservative little town. There's never been any need to tout controversial books."

Rose hid a sudden seething anger behind a smile so forced she feared it might crack her face. "All right, let me get my son inside so Kate can set up him up with one of the library's dangerous books, and we'll talk. Are you the group's spokesperson?"

"No. Wilma, Brian, and I are simply concerned citi-zens. Reverend Coburn is the organizer."

"Fine. I'll be back shortly and look forward to speaking with him." She refrained from looking for the other two mentioned board members and opened the door with more forced outward calm.

"Mom, why are there all those people?"

With a deep breath, she relaxed her smile. "You remember all those books I've told you about? Books people haven't liked over the years because they thought they had bad messages?"

"Banned books? Yeah."

"I think the people are angry because I want to talk about those books at the library."

"That seems ridiculous."

Laughter cleared her head and instantly buoyed her spirit. Why was she angry? She loved this kind of battle. She loved this particular battle best of all. She swooped her precocious Jesse into a hug and squeezed him like a stuffed animal.

"You're absolutely right, brilliant son of mine. It is ridiculous. So I think I need to go and tell them so. In a nice way." He smiled and squirmed out of her embrace. "Will you stay in here with Kate?"

"I'll come out and tell them it's ridiculous with you if you want."

"Thank you, sweetheart, but I'd better talk to them first. You can help later, don't worry."

She bustled into the children's room, where Kate sat behind the reference desk computer logging in some last-minute book data on her own time. Her eyes sparkled with amusement.

"Welcome to the circus. They let the loonies out today, huh?"

Rose rolled her eyes. "They're concerned citizens. Pat Dunn told me so."

"Sure, boss."

Kate was a keeper.

"Can Jesse stay with you while I go talk to them?"

"Of course. Are you sure you want to go, though? Personally, I don't want anything to do with them."

"Heck, what's the saying? This ain't my first rodeo. But I do want to call Gladdie Hanson before I face them. She has much more moral authority with these people than I do. And I *think* she'll back me up."

"Gladdie? That's an understatement. You might see her as a benign little old lady, but that's her Clark Kent disguise. I'll give her a call for you, see if she's home."

A cool breeze met Rose on the steps when she opened the main door and returned to the group of protestors. She had to admit, as every pair of expectant eyes turned her way, protestors in Kennison Falls were far more genteel than they were in Boston. She hugged her lightweight jacket close and smiled. Gladdie had promised to be there shortly. This was in the bag.

"Thank you for coming back to talk to us, Rose." Reverend Coburn had made his way to the steps and stood beside Pat Dunn. This time she also saw Wilma Nesrud and Brian Duncan, her other two troublesome board members.

"There's no reason to avoid talking to you, Reverend. Perhaps you can explain what it is you're having a problem with today?"

"Rose, now, it's come to our attention that you plan to highlight books, both old and new, that have been banned from libraries and schools around the country. The group assembled here has met several times, and we've come to make a formal request that you refrain from celebrating these books. Especially at the grand opening of this beautiful new library."

"Am I to understand that you are not here to protest a certain book?"

The reverend's eyebrows, gray but surprisingly bushy given his billiard-ball head, arched as if telling her she should know better. "On the contrary, we have a list of ten books we know are on your recommended reading list."

"I see."

"But that's secondary to the bigger issue, which is the glorification of all these books that over the years many parents, teachers, and readers themselves have found objectionable."

"Wait. You're protesting books written in the past?"

"Books that have not been on our public shelves until now."

At last he'd managed to flabbergast her. Rose stared, unwilling to speak until she processed his words. She gazed at all the faces, and for the first time saw them as potential enemies. Resolutely she pushed that image out of her mind. She had to see them as neighbors and friends, or this would never work. Nonetheless . . .

"You don't mean to tell me that you've kept books off the public library shelves and nobody has noticed?"

"We've tried to explain this to you at our meetings." Pat spoke for the first time. "If there was concern about a book, Maggie White simply didn't order it. We didn't advertise that fact. We didn't expect people to keep from buying it for their own homes. If someone really wants to read such a book, there are large libraries in Faribault and Northfield."

"This isn't a difficult question, dear." Wilma, the oldest board member at seventy-three and, as far as Rose could tell, Gladdie's exact philosophical opposite, nodded her head as if to reassure the entire crowd. "The books are available in other places; we can't stop that. But we don't want this material in the direct path of our children and teenagers. Or adults, for that matter."

It took all Rose's effort to ignore the woman and draw in as deep a breath as she could and release it slowly. She opened her mouth and closed it. Finally, at a loss, she simply held her hand toward Reverend Coburn.

"Do you have an actual list of these ten . . . dangerous books?"

He produced a sheet of paper, almost with a flourish, from a manila folder he'd been holding the entire time. She glanced at him skeptically and lowered her eyes. After several seconds, she almost laughed.

"I'm sorry, but this cannot be serious. Several of these books are now modern classics."

"I warned you this would not be a simple matter." Pat Dunn looked past Rose to Reverend Coburn.

"We take the shepherding of our young people seriously." The reverend's smile grew a tad frosty. "I'm disappointed to hear you turn our request, made in good faith, into a joke."

"I absolutely do not take any of this as a joke," Rose replied. "Taking away the freedom to read is no laughing matter." She glanced back at the numbered list. Each book title was followed by a short list of descriptors explaining what made it objectionable. "Do you really mean to tell me the Kennison Falls Public Library has never had copies of the Harry Potter series? Or *Twilight*?"

"We do not approve of witchcraft or sorcery. Or abominations of God-given love that include sex with vampires." Reverend Coburn's smile had disappeared.

"Have you *read* the *Twilight* books?" she shot back.

"I have read part of the first Harry Potter book. That was disturbing enough."

"First of all, I'm sorry for you. They're wonderful books. Full of allegory and classic good versus evil."

"And ungodly spells."

"Have you heard of teaching your children the difference between fiction and reality?"

"Young children do not have the ability to make those distinctions."

"On the contrary. Studies have shown that children are quite adept at knowing the difference. But this is not the place to have this debate." She took another calming breath. "The second thing you need to know is that I have some literature on how to challenge a book. The most important thing it will tell you is that you must have read the book in its entirety."

The reverend tightened his jowly round face. "I'm not at all sure about that. No one can be forced to read a book that would go against his beliefs."

"One of my points exactly. But if you haven't read a book, you have no frame of reference for telling someone else they can't.

Reverend Coburn contemplated her a long moment.

"All right, I will look into that if you say it's a requirement. As a gesture of good faith, can we be assured that, at least for the Open House, you will remove the banned-books theme from the calendar of events? Give us time to assimilate the books?"

"I'm afraid the answer to that is no. The Open House does not have a theme as such. Banned Books Week starts a week from Monday. There will be information available tomorrow on some of the programs, and I won't be removing that."

"You aren't going to work with us?" Pat cried.

"I'll definitely talk with you more, just as you'll talk with me."

"But your mind is made up."

"As is yours, Pat." She looked the neat, middle-aged woman straight in the eye. "The thing is, I have the Constitution on my side."

"And we have righteousness on ours."

"You have an opinion on yours." She was getting sucked into the anger, and Rose knew she had to end the conversation or risk starting an all-out blowup. So far the crowd had been silent, waiting, unable to hear most of what was going on. That would end as soon as Reverend

Coburn repeated what had been said. "Look. This list certainly invites discussion, but you—"

She stopped as a name she'd glossed over jumped out at her from the list. She stared again at the crowd led by the frustrated minister and the three board members.

"You have Elizabeth Cassidy's new book on here? Why in the world?"

"Have you read it?"

"I've read everything she's ever written, and now she's one of your own neighbors. She writes the most moral books I can think of. The PenPals series is amazing for young teenagers."

"Well, read the newest one. She includes premarital sex and even rape. It's very disturbing. Especially coming from her."

Rose thought about the lovely woman she'd met at lunch days before. It had been just short of a fan-girl moment, and she couldn't imagine Elizabeth doing or writing anything that would offend anyone. Her books were inspirational stories—witty and edgy sometimes, but always containing a strong positive message.

"It's about a young girl struggling with something that happens to her sister. And Elizabeth might be participating in some events this year. Maybe we'll get the chance—"

"Good gracious, what's going on at the library a day before the opening?"

Gladdie Hanson, her thick figure nearly dancing up the flat steps from the sidewalk, turned every head in the crowd with her powerful voice. Rose released a grateful breath, surprised at the knot of tension twisting at the base of her neck.

"Good afternoon, Nathaniel," Gladdie said to Reverend Coburn. "Praise the Lord for such a fine day, don't you think?"

"I do, Gladys."

"Patricia. Wilma. Brian. You're taking a civic interest on your busy Saturdays?"

"As you should be," Wilma replied.

"And here I am."

Gladdie reached Rose and handed her a large cardboard container with a carrying handle and a capped spout. "Hello, Rose. I'm sure you didn't expect this."

"True, I didn't. But they've brought up an important issue."

"A lot of unnecessary fuss, but you may be right. Here's some coffee from Effie. Paper cups and some accompaniments in the bag." She held up a brown paper sack. "Do you think we could use one of the beautiful new tables in the meeting room? Any talk goes better with a little caffeine."

Rose could have kissed her right there in public. In mere seconds, Gladdie had diffused the immediate tension and offered the modern-day equivalent of a peace pipe.

"Absolutely." She bent forward. "Thank you," she whispered.

"We can't end this today," Gladdie whispered back. "But we can shorten the conversation a little bit. Are you all right?"

"I'm fine. This is not new. Just surprising that it happened here."

She nodded. "No town is perfect."

They managed to get the full contingent of protestors into the community meeting room and set up the coffee. Effie had thought of everything from a plastic table cover to creamer, sugar, and stir sticks. The hot coffee seemed to soothe, and smiles returned. Rose milled through the group, meeting some of the other townspeople and trying to listen without giving her own opinion. She'd never been good at it, but something about knowing she'd be unable to hide from her words in a small town kept the lid on her irritation.

Unfortunately, coffee could only mollify the reverend temporarily. He made his way to a prominent spot in the space and called his makeshift flock to attention.

"I'm sure we all have things we'd rather be doing this afternoon. I'd like to propose we come to some sort of equitable agreement and then leave the lovely Ms. Hanrehan to her own busy schedule."

Gladdie didn't wait for Rose to respond. "Why don't you avoid beating around any burning bushes, Nathaniel, and tell us what you want?"

"I believe I did that before you arrived. I'd like to remove any mention of banned books from the Open House tomorrow and call a meeting of the board before the proposed Banned Books Week festivities."

"We can certainly call the meeting, Reverend Coburn," Rose said.

"And tomorrow?"

"Did you know that *Winnie-the-Pooh* was once a banned book?" Gladdie asked. "Tell me. Did your children ever watch the cartoon or read the book?"

"That was quite a bit different."

"It was no different at all. People thought it an abomination against God and nature to depict talking animals. Am I right, Rose?"

"One hundred percent."

"And you have two delightful children, Nathaniel. Grown and reading *Winnie-the-Pooh* to their kids, I imagine. Some people might still find that disturbing, even if you don't. Shouldn't we take another look at that book?"

"This is a ridiculous conversation."

"I'm afraid you've started it."

His face flushed a half shade darker. "You know that the subjects *we're* talking about with these books—disrespect, the occult, sinful behavior like rape—are legitimately harmful to young people. Why would you want to be a party to this?"

Rose couldn't keep quiet. "Because these books don't simply throw subjects out there in order to hijack minds. They also teach, and show children the world, and give them coping skills. Not to mention reading skills. There are books I don't let my son read yet because he can't understand the concepts, and there are television shows I don't let him watch. But it's *my* job to keep them from him until he's ready. It's not yours. It's not the library's. And that's why I will be leaving my banned-book posters up tomorrow."

The room burst into noise and protests. On the verge of throwing up her hands, Rose plunked into a chair at one of the computer carrels and surveyed the growing anger. A light scraping across the carpet caught her attention, and she smiled ruefully when Gladdie set a chair next to hers and sat.

"Good. This is going well."

"Well?"

"They're arguing among themselves about what you've said. Means there'll be no more call for a decision today, and Nathaniel will have to re-rally the troops. But there'll be a handful of people protesting again tomorrow, I'm afraid."

"I suspect so. I'll be ready."

"This is new to them, like it is to you. This group isn't used to someone who knows what's going on in the world. Your predecessor, God bless her, is as old school as they come. You made a simple but good point about parents being responsible for the kids."

"It's true. And I loved your *Winnie-the-Pooh* example. Kind of makes the whole exercise of calling books 'ungodly' look a little silly. But I know I can't brush off their concerns. I need converts, not enemies."

"And now you're showing me why we hired you."

"Thanks, Gladdie. Not that it isn't annoying."

"Being right usually is."

They shared a moment of laughter. "C'mon, we need to be nice." Rose giggled.

"We're plenty nice. They got coffee, didn't they? They're not right in this case, and they can't win because your board is with you except for the three, and I don't think Brian will be that hard to get back. Don't give up."

"Oh, do not worry. This is one fight I'm a bulldog about."

"I'll go tell Nathaniel it's time for him to retreat."

"How do you do it?"

"Do what?"

"Command such respect?"

She scrunched up her face in thought as she stood and then winked. "First, I don't pay attention to anyone who doesn't do what I want. Second? Short women are cute."

Rose's burst of fresh laughter brought several pairs of eyes zeroing in on her, and she clapped a hand over her mouth. Gladdie patted her once more on the shoulder and made her way to the snarl of people surrounding Reverend Coburn.

SUNDAY AFTERNOON, DEWEY scuffled his way up the steps to the front of the library like a petulant teen. His funk from the day before hadn't lifted, and now he was just plain mad at the world. The world never kicked him in the ass anymore; he was the one who did the kicking— if it was needed. Two years in college fighting cancer and picking up the pieces after his father's death had shown him that if you gave in and let the world have its way, you ended up whipped. You either fought and you fixed. Or you were miserable.

Abby's pregnancy was something to rejoice over;

instead, it had bowled him over as thoroughly as the tornado had three years before. Abby's happiness only dredged up the pain—a pain that wasn't supposed to lay a manly man low.

So why now, idiot?

Because of Rose Hanrehan. Because she could turn out to be different.

But he'd thought Rachel had been different, too. And she had been for six years, until the day she'd said it was too sad. Too sad never to have children.

But Rose already has a child.

A child who needed someone not yet old and half-jaded to the world. Abby always referred to Gray as her white knight. Rose deserved a white knight.

Thanks a ton, Abby.

His mind stayed on the circular wheel it had been riding like a demented hamster for the past twenty-four hours. It was the reason he had no business going anywhere near Rose. She'd already gotten a pretty decent look at his sullen adolescent act.

But he'd promised.

Familiar faces filled the library. Kennison Fallsians loved any excuse for a town party. But this rivaled the last fund-raiser they'd held to buy books—a hot-dog-selling affair that had filled the town park to capacity. Now that the books had been purchased and the library they'd worked so hard to build was finished, everyone wanted to see the handiwork up close and firsthand.

"Hey, Dewey!"

He turned to the town's favorite MD, Chase Preston, and had no choice but to lose a little of his glower. Chase and his wife, Jill, had to be the cheeriest couple in town, and nobody rocked volunteerism better than they did. Made Dewey look like a slug.

"Chase." He shook the doc's hand. "How's that bike doing? Have to put it up for the winter soon, I'll bet."

Chase rode a vintage Triumph Bonneville Dewey had helped him with a number of times, although he himself wasn't much of a motorcycle guy. Still, he knew how to appreciate a classic.

"I might eke out another month, depending on how October starts." His easy Kentucky drawl slipped over the words. "I'm learning how the weather 'round here is 'bout as predictable as a pea in a paint shaker."

Dewey grinned and winked at Jill Preston, who shook her head at another of her husband's famously outlandish sayings. "I can't trust him to speak in public some days," she laughed. "How are you, Dewey?"

"Life is never dull. How's the vet business?"

"I can say the same. Spring and fall are crazy. Plus keeping up with my riding students. Plus the special-education kids that come to our place. What are your busiest times?"

"Winter."

"All those dead batteries in the freezing cold."

"You got it."

"Well, here's to both of us enjoying the fall. Maybe we'll get some good Indian summer this year."

He smiled, said he'd see them later, and went looking for Rose. It took a long time to wend his way through the crowd. People weren't quite shoulder to shoulder, but there were pockets of congestion wherever Rose had set up an activity.

He found himself in the children's section, obvious because of the nature of the games and the bins of picture books. At one small table, kids scribbled pictures of their favorite book characters. At another, children could write down what adventure they'd go on if they were friends with Frog and Toad from what he guessed was a famous book. At yet another station, kids were asked to suggest subjects or characters for a wall mural.

He wondered how much of this was Rose's doing as he scanned the room again, still missing her. A sense of pride overcame him as he realized the town was out in force for her. Not that he had a thing to be proud about—he'd had nothing to do with her success. But a success it seemed to be.

He turned at another clap on his shoulder and came face to face with Gray Covey. It no longer shocked him to see the famous rocker in the midst of town functions. Nobody in Kennison Falls paid much attention to his celebrity any longer.

"Hey," Dewey said, and caught Abby's eyes. She looked more rested today. After a moment of uncertainty, she eased his concern.

"I told him I told you," she said.

That warmed him, and he was proud of the fact that he didn't harbor a hint of envy for his friends. His problems because of the news were all his own.

"Congratulations, man," he said, pumping Gray's hand.

"Thanks, Dewey. It's still a bit of a secret. Until we're past the first few months, anyway. We don't need a circus."

"I understand. I'm honored to be one of the few."

"It was nice to have your ear yesterday." Abby stepped forward and gave him a soft peck on the cheek. "Thanks."

"My pleasure."

He watched them drift into the crowd. And then he saw her.

Abby's action had reminded him to start being nice, but niceness evaporated as if some wicked witch from one of the books buried in this room had come to life and cast a spell. Rose stood beside an elaborate poster, pointing out the features on it to Church Hubbard, the firefighter she'd met yesterday. The man stood with one hand resting lightly between her shoulder blades. The other absently tousled Jesse's wheat-colored head.

Without warning, the light in the room went dim.

With a solid green tinge.

Chapter Ten

DEWEY TURNED IN place, ready to leave before he acted like a complete a-hole in front of everyone who knew him. This was ridiculous. Hadn't he told himself he didn't *want* any kind of entanglement with her? He hadn't been this knocked off his game by a female in a very long time, and that alone was proof he needed to pull himself together.

"Dewey!" A bullet in the form of a Jesse Loren Hanrehan hit him in the legs and halted his retreat. "You're here."

"Hey, kid."

He didn't want to be glad to see the annoying child, but he patted Jesse on the head.

"Did you come to hear Mayor Sam read?"

"What?"

"He's gonna read from Harry Potter. Mom says he can do a really good imitation of Dumbledore. But everybody is kind of mad about it. The mean lady from the library board is going to bring signs saying it's bad."

"Mean lady?" Dewey had no frame of reference for Jesse's waterfall of words.

"Most people are nice. One is mean."

Dewey's curiosity got the better of his bad mood. "Why does the mean lady think it's bad?"

Jesse shrugged elaborately. "Mom says some people don't like spells."

Dewey didn't like spells either—absolutely not the one that seemed to be working on him now. He wanted to peel the kid away from his side and beat feet out of the room.

"Come on." Jesse tugged on his hand. "Come and see Mom."

"Oh, she's busy." He looked at her, laughing now with Church.

Jesse looked, too. "No, she's talking to Church. He's kind of weird. He keeps patting me on the head."

"Wait. Like I just did?"

"No, you didn't."

Dewey's brows shot up as high as they'd go, tightening his forehead in surprise. The kid didn't like to be touched, but he hadn't noticed Dewey's? An evil glow of satisfaction spread slowly through his midsection as Jesse pulled him resolutely toward his mother.

She looked up, and he was relieved to see that she didn't react as if he were pond scum—after he'd been so out of sorts at the fire station.

"Hi!" she said.

"Hi."

"I see Mr. Jesse has found you. Thank you for coming."

He nodded. "Hey, Church."

"He was telling me why they call him that." Rose smiled, entirely too happily, up at the fireman, who was not quite as tall as Dewey but undoubtedly in much better shape.

"Don't know that story," he admitted, not caring.

"Middle name's Winston. Winston Churchill equals Church." He shrugged. "Less obnoxious than some firehouse nicknames."

"Don't talk to me about nicknames. I can't get rid of mine." Dewey offered a self-deprecating smile.

"Dewey's not your real name?" Jesse asked.

"Yeah." He nodded at the boy. "It is, don't worry. How about you? You got a nickname? One you like, I mean?"

"Jesse James."

He hadn't expected that. Rose stared at Dewey as if it was news to her, too.

"The bank robber, huh? Well, he had a fine name, but I hope you don't plan to get rich quick."

"I read about him, and he got shot in the back. That's not cool."

"Is there anything you don't know about?"

Jesse shrugged.

"Hey, I need to get back to the station. I have maintenance duty," Church said, and ruffled Jesse's hair again. This time the boy ducked from the touch and bumped into Dewey's side, scowling.

Church turned to Rose and offered a grin that reminded Dewey of a big dopey lap dog. "I'll call you, then."

"And I'll talk to you then." She returned the smile. And then, as Dewey was starting to feel like a kid who should be banished to the reading corner until he could behave, Rose turned the smile on him. "Good crowd, isn't it?"

He returned a sheepish grin. "It is. I hear the mayor is going to read."

The tiniest shadow flickered in her eyes. "Yes. From the first Harry Potter book. We'll see how that goes."

"Jesse said something about people being upset?"

"I'm expecting my contingent of protestors any moment. This time they might even bring signs."

"You have your own protestors?"

"Aren't I lucky?"

"Want to tell me about that?"

"Sure. Start with this quiz, though." She gave him a piece of paper along with a secretive little wink that sent a flight of sparks surfing through his veins. "Check off the books—all on this poster here—that you think have been banned."

He took a skeptical glance at the poster and found himself hooked. Twenty different characters and books with familiar titles stared back in an intricate collage. *Winnie-the-Pooh* sat on a stack of books including a Dr. Seuss title. Anne Frank stared out a window. Some cartoon kid in a cape and underwear was pointing at a picture of Alan Rickman as Snape from Harry Potter.

"Is this a trick test?" he asked.

Her shoulders lifted in a careless shrug. "You never know."

He looked at the list of books and then set it down without marking anything.

"They all are or were."

She nodded, impressed. "Excellent. You know your banned books."

"Not really. Who's the mostly naked guy in the underwear?"

"Captain Underpants? The creation of two fairly rude, naughty little boys in the books. Hilarious but disrespectful. Teaches children bad habits."

"I see."

Excitement bloomed in her eyes. Dewey's stomach danced, catching her enthusiasm even though he really didn't understand it. To see her so animated, so impassioned, without it having anything to do with worry about her son, only intensified his captivation with her. The enthusiasm brought her entire body to life, as if she'd only been a stiff and proper cutout of herself. This Rose was a hot, fiery, beautiful flower.

"Do you see? There are about three dozen adults who are on the warpath against characters like Captain Underpants. They want me to keep banned books off the shelves and not celebrate them."

"So you were serious yesterday? They really do want to ban books."

"They gave me a list of ten when they came by yesterday."

"And they're coming back."

"Oh, yes. They do not want the mayor to be reading an occult book to our children."

"Oh, brother."

She stared in surprise at him. "Yes! Exactly."

"What are you planning to do?"

"Have him read anyway."

As if they'd summoned him, Mayor Sam Baker emerged from a parting crowd and approached, a copy of *Harry Potter and the Sorcerer's Stone* in his hands. He grinned, but behind him a line of grim-faced people followed, with signs at the ready. Dewey recognized a minister from a church in the area, along with Pat Dunn, whose husband owned a sporting-goods store downtown, and several other people he never would have guessed to be anti-book.

"I'm here for my audition," Sam said, his round belly shaking like a Santa's with a laugh. "And it looks like I have an anti-fan club."

"It's nice of you to come, Mayor. This will make a big statement. Are you okay with that?" Rose asked.

"I'm not in favor of banning free speech or books," he said. "This isn't political, though. I'm going to let you deal with the group. Tell me where I'll be sitting."

"I can't thank you enough."

Rose showed Sam where his chair was, and Jesse poked at Dewey's forearm. "C'mon, Dewey. Let's go listen."

He watched the group of sign holders encroaching on Rose's poster. He squatted in front of Jesse.

"Will you save me a place? I think I'd like to hang out here for a minute and make sure nobody picks on your mom. Is that okay?"

Understanding sprouted in his eyes. "Are they going to do anything bad?"

"No. No, not at all. You don't need to worry about that. They're just going to complain. But it's like when Kenny Whatshisname was being mean. You kind of wished you'd had a friend with you, didn't you? I'll be your mom's friend for now."

The boy nodded enthusiastically. "Should I stay, too?"

"That's cool of you, but you really want to hear Mayor Sam be Dumbledore, right?"

"Yeah."

"I got this."

He hadn't used this cajoling, reassuring voice in fifteen years. Not since that sixth-grade class. It felt unnatural in retrospect—rusty. But it had slipped out with little effort. With slight heat in his face, he straightened to find Rose studying him with thoughtfully crinkled brows. He had no time to question her, however. Pat Dunn reached them and practically sucked all the air out of the room with her sour face.

"You know we warned you we wouldn't let this go unopposed, Rose."

"You did. And I explained that I wasn't going to change my plans."

"We're willing to fight this."

"That's clear," Rose replied. "And you have the right to protest, of course. I have some literature for you that will tell you how to make an official challenge. And some of what I give you will talk about the books on your list. I only ask that you don't disrupt the day by being loud. If you'd like to stand in a group, maybe over by the stairs, and let people know your opinions, go for it."

She seemed calm and unaffected by the disrespect these people had for her. For the first time he could remember, Dewey felt a sense of shame in his fellow Fallsians.

"I think we'll stand right here." Pat's retort nearly caused Dewey to snap right back. With effort, he held his tongue.

"Please don't fully block the poster." Rose's reasonable voice and request resonated with far more moral authority than Pat's angry tone.

Without really thinking about it, Dewey picked up a book from the examples of banned books standing and lying artfully around the poster. It was a copy of *To Kill a Mockingbird*. For a moment he was lost in disbelief. It had been years since he'd read the classic, but he remembered it having a powerful impact. How could anyone have been narrow-minded enough to ban such a story?

"Dewey Mitchell. You come from a good Christian family. What do you mean by supporting such a blatant display of disrespect for the people of this town?"

Speechless, he looked into the face of Wilma Nesrud, her round cheeks rosy with her own brand of passion, her skin deeply etched with age lines. She'd been around as long as he could remember, probably longer than Gladdie or her sister Claudia. Old Sunday school lessons were etched in Dewey's brain because of Wilma.

"Mrs. Nesrud," he said at last. "I'm not sure how I'm disrespecting anyone. This is a copy of *To Kill a Mocking-*

bird. I assume you've read it. I think every adult should read or reread it."

"That is not the book I'm talking about, young man."

"It's on the display," he said. "So is this one." He picked up *Brave New World.*

"There are books there that simply do not need to be put in front of our noses. We're working to get them relegated to the privacy of people's homes."

"Did you know that the Bible has been banned in many places and countries over the centuries? If that was banned somewhere, wouldn't you stand up for the freedom to have that out in the open?"

"Why, that's simply disrespectful and blasphemous."

"I don't understand that even a little." He held her angry gaze.

"Well, I never." She huffed at him, pursed her lips in disgust, and turned away.

From the corner of his eye, he saw a figure rise above the crowd. Rose stepped onto a wooden chair she'd pulled from a table and stood like a graceful siren.

"Ladies and gentlemen," she called. "Can I have your attention?" It took a moment, but eventually the room quieted. "I wanted to announce for any of you who haven't seen the schedule of events, that Mayor Baker is about to start reading an excerpt from *Harry Potter and the Sorcerer's Stone.* The reading circle is in the back corner of this room. And across the library in the adult room, there's coffee and tea and other refreshments. And in half an hour, Jemma Katz, a beloved Minnesota poet, will be reading from her newest collection. I'd also like to welcome a few members of our library board who'd like the chance to speak with you about Banned Books Week, coming up in about ten days. They have concerns and are interested in the idea of keeping certain books off our public library shelves."

Her words were drowned out by a swell of questioning voices that morphed into low booing. Dewey smiled at the floor.

"Wait, wait." Rose held up her hands. "The group will be standing over near the stairs in the foyer. Share your opinions with them, and listen to theirs. Thank you all for coming today! It's so nice to meet everyone. And leave your suggestions in the boxes around the library. Or come and talk to me anytime."

She stepped off her chair, then turned to the bald minister, who stared at her with uncertain eyes. She didn't give him a chance to open his mouth.

"Freedom of speech, Reverend Coburn," she said. "I believe in it. Feel free to try and make your case."

With a tug on Dewey's sleeve, she averted her face from the protestors. "Come on. Let's go listen to the mayor. Let this group sort itself out."

He set the book back on the shelf and followed her away from the center of the room. Half the crowd followed them, and the other half drifted toward the front of the library.

"You were amazing," he said.

"Look who's talking." She chewed on her bottom lip, a small smile struggling to free itself. "I can't believe you turned the Bible on them. Brilliant."

"Hey," he teased. "I come from a good Christian family. Wilma Nesrud said so. Can't let 'em think I don't care about the Good Book. Besides, they needed a little jab in their righteous indignations."

She stopped at the edge of the standing-room-only group, settling in to listen to the reading. Shocking him completely, she took his hand and squeezed it. "I mean it. Thanks, Dewey. It meant a lot that you were there to back me. You hold a great deal of sway in this town, and your words had an impact."

She dropped his hand nearly as quickly as she'd taken it, but the heat from her touch remained, radiating up his arm and spreading warmth through the base of his skull and across his back to the depths of his belly. Her eyes shone, her lips parted as if she'd just finished a sprint. It was all he could do to keep from wrapping her in an embrace that pulled her close and let him congratulate her on the victory in his own way.

"I don't know if that's true. But it was fun to see their faces. And you don't look like they bother you at all."

"It bothers me, but only because I get frustrated with people's ignorance. Believe me, I am not afraid of this fight."

"I think you relish it, actually. It's a little scary."

"It's that obvious, huh?"

"I think the board hired a warrior."

"Better keep your eye on the new librarian."

Boy, howdy, he'd definitely like to apply for that job. He laughed, but only for show. Beneath the false easiness, little flames of newly hatching desire were popping up in very intimate places and scaring the crap out of him.

The mayor's Dumbledore impression garnered wild applause and rave on-the-spot reviews, and the magic from the famous book seemed to have spread into the real world, because by the time the crowd dispersed, so had the group of protestors. Only Pat Dunn remained, and all she said to Rose in passing was that the next library board meeting needed to be as heavily promoted as the controversial books. Dewey marveled at Rose's calm politeness in the face of such antagonism.

But he said nothing. He also found it impossible to leave the gathering he'd been so reluctant to attend. Wandering through the crowd, watching people explore the library while he explored their reactions, he couldn't hold back a bit of pride that his new librarian was bringing one part of Kennison Falls into the twenty-first century. It wasn't that his hometown was completely stodgy, but a few musty corners remained. The library had been one of them, despite its revered status.

He stopped in front of the science fiction shelf in the adult book room and stared at the floor, rewinding what had just gone through his brain.

His new librarian, he'd called her. The thought was outlandish. He had nothing to do with her success, past or future. He had no connection to her other than a few ill-conceived encounters due mostly to her son.

Yet he really did feel genuine pride—in her and for her.

And it scared him again.

The building was still filled with enthusiastic patrons when the last author had read his excerpt and the official Open House hours ended. Kids milled around the picture-book bins, and Dewey came across Jesse sitting at a reading table with another boy, not poring over books but drawing intently on sketch pads. An attractive blonde woman he knew, but not well, sat nearby, her nose buried in a thick novel.

"Dewey! Look!" Jesse saw him before he could turn away. The boy held up a rudimentary drawing of a fire engine.

"Hey, nice," Dewey said. "I didn't know you were an artist."

"I want to be an artist."

The second boy lifted his head, displaying soft serious eyes and a shock of curly black hair. Dewey couldn't remember the kid's name, but the mother, he remembered, was a quiet, conservative woman who lived a few miles out of town not too far from Chase and Jill Preston. Cassidy. Liz, if he wasn't mistaken. She didn't spend a lot of time in town.

"Josh draws really great fire engines," Jesse said.

That was true. The other boy's rendition was surprisingly sophisticated.

"Amazing," he said sincerely. The woman smiled.

"My goodness, Dewey, are you still here?" Rose's voice interrupted anything Liz Cassidy was going to say. Dewey spun, his heartbeat ramping up, mutinying against the calm he wanted to project. "This is above and beyond." Her smile actually held warmth that didn't look forced.

He doubted the warmth was really for him. Her shindig had gone well. She had far better reasons to smile.

"I stayed for the pie and doughnuts."

"I get that." She nodded, and fully took in the grouping around the table. "Elizabeth!" she said. "You came. I'm so glad."

"Of course. We were late, but I had to be here."

"Did you see the section of your books? I already had kids asking to check them out. They'll be back tomorrow; I'm sure of it."

"You're too nice about that," Elizabeth said, and offered a slightly mischievous smile. "I understand I may have a problem book with some of the patrons."

Rose grimaced. "Can you believe it? I have the silliest argument on my hands. But we'll sort it all out."

Dewey had no idea what they were talking about, and he'd almost forced himself to butt in and ask when a sharp, terrifying crash shattered the peace, and shrieks emanated from the adult side of the library. Rose blanched to the color of a book page and turned to the boys.

"Don't you two move."

She took off like a sprinter, but Dewey caught her in two strides. "Hang on, don't tear in there. Slow down. Go in with your eyes open."

She listened to him, but he could hear her elevated breathing. He set his hand lightly between her shoulder blades and followed her into the room. Voices blended in a frantic chatter, and a dozen people stood in a semicircle around a huge spray of shattered glass. In the center of the shard debris sat a cantaloupe-sized, gray-speckled rock.

"Oh my lord," Rose cried, her eyes glued to the mess. "No, no! Who would do this?"

Dewey dropped his hand and replaced it with his arm, engulfing her shoulders. He looked at the huge shattered window to his right. The rock had been aimed perfectly to shatter the largest pane of glass, a section approximately ten feet high.

Rose covered her mouth with both hands and slumped hard against him. He squeezed her tighter.

"It's all right," he said. "It's going to be fine."

"It's not," she began, and tried to move forward toward the rock.

"No, don't touch it," he said. "You should let the police know and have them move things."

"There aren't going to be fingerprints on a *rock*." Her words emerged wrapped in half a moan.

"Mom?"

Dewey looked over his shoulder. Elizabeth stood with her son and Jesse, a hand on each of their shoulders.

"Get back into the other room." Rose barked the order without looking at her son.

"But the window is broken."

"Okay, guys. You saw what happened. Your mom's right, Jesse. Let's go to the other room." Elizabeth started to turn the boys, but Jesse broke free and darted toward Rose.

Without thinking, Dewey let go of Rose and scooped Jesse up mid-stride before he could hit any of the glass.

The boy kicked a little, but when he realized it was Dewey who'd grabbed him, he quieted.

"What happened? Why is the window broken? How are we going to fix it?"

"You have to hang tight, kid," Dewey said. "Everyone is real surprised, and we don't know."

Rose turned, too, her face slightly less gray, and put her arms around Jesse, enveloping Dewey in the process. For several seconds they stood, a trio bound by a convoluted knot of holds and hugs. Her hands quivered against his arms. He looked down at the crown of her head, and his muscles went slightly mushy.

She straightened at last, and Dewey set Jesse on the ground.

"Go with Mrs. Cassidy, honey," she said, without anger this time. "I'll come get you in a few minutes. Don't worry. Everything's okay. There's a lot of glass here now, that's all."

"What happened?" he asked again.

"I'll tell you as soon as we know."

It took an hour with the Kennison Falls chief of police to get everyone's story and then shepherd them out of the library. While the questioning took place, Dewey rushed to the co-op and loaded two pieces of plywood into his delivery truck along with an extension ladder. He grabbed Glen and Bart, the only two brothers already at his mother's house preparing for their bimonthly family Sunday dinner, and hauled them back to the library to set to work. By the time the building was empty of everyone but Rose, Jesse, and Police Chief Hewett, they had the window boarded.

"You really are the town hero, aren't you?" Rose asked.

"You can't leave the library open to the weather, right? No big deal."

Tears wet her eyelashes. "I can't open the library tomorrow," she said, turning to watch Jesse, who sat morosely at a carrel, swinging his feet.

"Why not?"

"Look at this mess."

"There's some glass on the rug. Chief Hewett is going to take the rock. We'll vacuum it up and go."

She spun on him. "It's *not* that easy."

He pulled her to him, not caring that his brothers, Tanner Hewett, and Jesse all looked on. "It is, though," he whispered. "You're in shock. C'mon, it'll be done in no time."

She gave one short sob against his chest, and then it turned into a tough little growl. She straightened and swiped her eyes. "You're right. You're right. I'll go get the vacuum and a broom."

Twenty minutes later the biggest shards of glass had been hand-tossed into a wastebasket and the rug had been vacuumed to within an inch of its new, blue life. Rose put the tools away and set the wastebasket in a back storage room. Chief Hewett had gone to start asking questions around town, and the three Mitchells and two Hanrehans surveyed the re-tidied room.

"A job well done." Bart high-fived Glen.

"Thank you more than I can say," Rose added. "It wasn't a very auspicious way to meet you both."

"Heck, it was fine." Glen smiled. "I'll bet you're ready to get out of here, though."

"I am. I have to stop and thank Effie and Rio for cleaning up all the food." She looked at the watch on her arm. "Oh my goodness, how did it get to be nearly five-thirty?"

"Dinnertime," Dewey said.

"You riding home with us, Duaney? I'm sure Ma didn't start without us," Bart said.

"No. I'm driving Rose's car. She's coming for dinner."

Dewey waited for, and got, her slack jaw and narrowed eyes.

"Excuse me? I don't think I am."

"You are. Jesse, too. If I leave you, you'll go eat at the Loon Feather and fret. You need to process this. Talk about it."

"I need to process it at home, on my own."

"Nope. It's pot roast and gravy and a whole lot of people for you." He looked at Jesse. "And probably something with chocolate in it for dessert. You're coming, right?"

"Okay."

"Dewey, don't do that."

"What?"

"Play him against me."

"Then you can join us and make a united front. You're outvoted, Rose, so get over it. You're coming for dinner."

"You are the bossiest, most pigheaded person I've ever met."

"Heck." He winked at her. "Wait until you're sitting in the middle of ten or twelve Mitchells. I'll look a whole lot better. Now go get your coat."

Chapter Eleven

FIFTEEN PEOPLE SAT around the gigantic pine table in the Mitchells' oversized dining room. Rose prayed there wouldn't be a test at the end of the meal, because she'd never remember everyone. They chattered over her, through her, and with her as if this were her hundredth meal with them, and she marveled at the easy atmosphere, so different from the stiff and formal meals she'd grown up eating with her own small family.

Jesse sat wordlessly between her and Dewey, focused on his food, not looking at the big boisterous family who'd given up trying to force conversation from him. Even Dewey's four nieces and nephews, ranging in age from four to thirteen, paid him little mind since he'd been so quiet.

"Nobody saw anyone toss the rock?" Elle, to Rose's left, set down her wine glass and stabbed her fork into a piece of carrot.

"They didn't," Rose replied. "We hope someone saw the person from outside."

"And you're sure it wasn't one of those banned-book haters?"

They'd been over the theory, and Rose couldn't see it. "They're adults. They aren't going to resort to childish vandalism." She shrugged. "But I don't know this town yet. You guys would know better than I if such a thing would be likely."

"Of course it wouldn't." Evelyn Mitchell, matriarch and phenomenal cook, had won Rose's heart with her open manner and the no-nonsense way she wrangled her expanded family. Rose couldn't imagine the woman having a bad thing to say about anyone, although she wasn't above reminding her grandchildren—or grown children, for that matter—of their manners. "I know all those people you've mentioned, and they're good-hearted. They might be wrong in this case, but they only want what they think is best. They wouldn't destroy something the town has worked so hard to build."

"People do stupid things when they're angry, Ma." Dewey shrugged as if he had no opinion but was simply shoving the idea out there.

"Well, I'm glad it was the library building and not your car." Elle grinned. "That thing is gorgeous, and I'm totally jealous. I think *I* would have cried if they'd gone after it."

"I admit, that would have done me in." Rose laughed. "I'm pretty pathetic about my car."

"Dewey said you seem to know how to care for it. It's in perfect condition."

"My dad taught both my sister and me how to maintain our cars. We had to prove we could change tires, change oil, and at least start to diagnose what might be wrong in an engine so we could talk intelligently to a mechanic. He didn't want anyone to take advantage of his girls."

"Cool dad."

"Hmm." Rose wiped her fingers on her napkin. "I don't know if 'cool' fits my father. Practical, stern, smart—scary smart. He loves us, but he was rarely around. He's a United States senator, and that, we always knew, takes an enormous amount of time."

"That's impressive."

"He's impressive."

"He must be proud of you for getting your own library to run. I think that's impressive." Elle grinned. "I'd be a total loss at it."

"In all honesty, he and my mother think I'm crazy. I kind of had to run away from home to be here."

"You're kidding?"

"Only a little. If I'd stayed home, my mother was expecting a wedding sooner rather than later in order to legitimize her single-mother daughter."

"Really?" Elle asked.

"My mother is not shy about matchmaking. The latest was a judge. Oh, how my father was hoping."

"So it's not someone likely to show up and haul you down the aisle?" Dewey's laconic question was laced with his typical dry humor, but the narrow crease between his brows belied a seriousness that gave Rose a secret little jolt.

"Wouldn't matter if he did. I'm not heading down any aisle with anyone."

"That right?"

"Why? Were you about to propose?" Teasing him was fun, even though conversation around the table halted and all eyes turned to her.

"I really was," he replied without a lost beat. "But I think you've made it pretty clear what your answer would be."

"Okay. Glad we cleared that up."

Conversation resumed with no more than amused glances and wry smiles. Clearly this family lived for ribbing humor, although Dewey's quiet style stood out among his highly social siblings. She looked around the table, set as elegantly as if this were a fancy dinner party, with china edged in delicate forget-me-nots and rimmed in gold. Two slender, sky blue tapers burned on either side of a small fall bouquet but the centerpiece still left plenty of room for the bounty of food—a fall-apart pot roast, the sweet carrots roasted along with the meat, fluffy mashed potatoes, and dishes of pickles, olives, and fresh horse-radish. Rose had scarfed down the melt-in-your-mouth meal like addictive candy.

Emma and Mark, with their eleven-year-old daughter, Aubrey, and thirteen-year-old son, Aiden sat across from Rose. Of all the siblings, Emma was most like Dewey, but she wore her smiles a little more lightly and chatted more readily. Elle was like a tomboy version of Barbie, tall and leggy, maybe a little more like an Amazon princess than a blonde bombshell, but gorgeous, exotic, and as talkative as Dewey was quiet.

Glen and Bart both acted like overgrown kids despite the presence of their wives, and in Glen's case two girls aged four and six. Dewey was the straight man, feeding into his brothers' silliness as if he actually liked the position. His littlest nieces, Madeline and Fiona, sat to his right and clearly adored him. He treated them with the same calm aloof humor that he did Jesse. He reminded her of a man allergic to animals who attracted them in hordes. Like he wanted to play with them but didn't dare.

"Can we watch one movie before we go home?"

Little Fiona pushed her plate slightly away from the edge of the table, the first to start fidgeting. Clamors from the young kids followed her requests. Aiden, with the bored insouciance of a new teenager, said nothing. He hadn't said much anyhow, since his cell phone had been banned from the table.

"I have two new ones," Evelyn said. "If your parents say it's okay, you guys can eat your ice cream bars in the family room."

The cheers rang as loudly as if there were a dozen kids.

"Jesse?" Evelyn asked. "Would you like to be excused, too, and watch a movie with the others?"

He shrugged and looked up at Rose. She nodded. "It's fine, sweetheart. Go ahead."

When the other four hopped away from the table, Jesse followed slowly.

"He'll be fine." Dewey touched her arm.

"Probably."

"You really do worry about him too much. And I only

mean that because it's stressful for you. You need to be able to enjoy your life, too."

She sighed, far too tired to argue that Jesse was her life—what she most enjoyed. And the truth was, Dewey had a point—worrying about her son was stressful. She kind of liked sitting here with adults who weren't questioning her life choices. She kind of liked sitting here with Dewey Mitchell.

"I enjoy my life fine." Her words emerged in a weak protest.

"Can you prove it?"

She shook her head at his persistence. Lifting her gaze, she drew her lips into a jack-o'-lantern grin, top and bottom front teeth together. "I'm schmiling, shee?"

He laughed. "It's a start. How 'bout you come take a walk with me? See what my family does for a living? Guarantee it'll take your mind off the rock, the banned books, and your kid."

"Kids are goats, Dewey," she said, and wrinkled her nose teasingly. "Just call him Jesse."

"Let me ask you something. Have you ever looked at his face when I call him 'kid'?"

"I don't know what you mean."

"He gives this little half-sized grin, like someone picked him first to be on a team."

"He doesn't."

"Yeah. He does."

"Even if that were true, why would he? Nobody likes to be generic."

"Boys do, kind of. They don't want to be different.

They want to be tough. They want to be 'hey, kid,' like every other cool guy."

"Jesse—"

"Is different. I get it. But he's still a little boy. Forget it. Come on. I'll give you a tour of the feed mill."

"Wow. Are all your dates this romantic sounding?"

"Hey. Don't knock it." He leaned toward her ear. "Lots of secret corners in a place like the mill."

"I think I'm definitely staying here." She crossed her arms and grinned at the floor.

"Aw, c'mon. Do I need to get my brothers over here to haul you up and force you to have fun?"

She glanced around the table. Dewey was speaking low enough that nobody paid them any attention. The benefits of a big, rowdy family.

"Again, I maintain, everyone has a different definition of fun."

He stood, and she peered up at him by turning her head ever so slightly. He put out his hand, large, sexily masculine, and inviting. Reluctantly, but with curiosity that couldn't be contained, she slipped her fingers into his palm. His hand closed around hers like a security bar coming down on a thrill ride, and he tugged until she rose from the chair.

"You can like all kinds, though. Of fun."

She made sure Jesse knew Mrs. Mitchell would come find her if he needed anything at all, and he waved her off, engrossed in the cartoons on the big+-screen TV. Evelyn, too, dismissed Rose's concerns. "He'll be fine. I raised six kids. Seen it all. Go on and enjoy the nice night."

She went, some of her reluctance eased by Dewey's big, accepting family.

The cool air smelled sweetly of rain-washed grass and the remains of summer flowers. Although darkness hid it in shadows now, Rose had earlier noticed Evelyn's huge garden, still full of gorgeous blooms despite September nearing completion. Since childhood, and a disastrous period where everything from her room to gifted clothing had been festooned with roses, she'd avoided her namesake flower. Tonight, however, the cool breeze carried a hint of the familiar perfume from the garden, and it tinged the air with romance.

Romance? She shook the thought away. She'd had plenty of romance—her parents' choices for beaus had seen to that over the years. Nothing but the best for the daughter of an influential senator. Wining, dining, bed-and-breakfasts, presents, and roses by the dozens had been hers without ever asking.

But, sought after as romance could be, there was more to life than being swept off one's feet. She wasn't in Kennison Falls, or walking hand in hand with Dewey Mitchell, to find romance. Everyone made youthful mistakes. Everyone suffered the consequences, and life got built around those falls and rises. Her "mistake," however, had led to Jesse, who'd become, unquestionably, the best thing in her life. The consequence was that he deserved a kinder life than she'd been able to make for him in Boston. Now she'd come halfway across the country to find it and she wasn't going to sacrifice that goal for the scent of a lovely night, or a man's protec-

tive grip enticing effervescent bubbles from her blood-
stream.

She looked at her hand clasped in Dewey's. He'd
taken it so naturally, it hadn't occurred to her to protest.
He started a windshield-wiper motion with his thumb
against the heel of her hand, and microseconds later
shock waves jolted through her. His thumb continued,
creating more and more sensation in her blood—molten
little bubbles turning into a warm, intensifying boil.

The tiniest ember of panic lodged in the pit of her
stomach. She had no idea where, physically or emotionally, Dewey was headed right now. The idea that he
wanted anything nefarious out of this nighttime stroll
was ludicrous on the face of it. Dewey Mitchell had to be
the safest man in town. On the other hand, what did she
really know about him?

"What's wrong?" His voice startled her, and she realized she'd pulled her hand free.

"I . . ." Her pulse pounded at the base of her throat.
"It's been a long time since . . ."

"Okay." The shadows blurred his smile, but it came
through in his voice. "I get it, sorry. Wasn't thinking. I
admit I got to feeling a little Neanderthal-like when that
rock went through the library window, and this is a hold-
over. But you don't need protecting here."

She stopped. Deliberately, she took his hand again
and laced their fingers together. "I only meant it's been a
long time since someone has offered to protect me. Since
I never feel like I need to be protected, I don't know what
to do with that. It scares me a little."

He squeezed her hand gently and started walking again. "How long have you been on your own? Without his . . . Jesse's, father, that is?"

She ignored his hesitation over saying Jesse's name. The odd little discomfort in his voice was almost as much a part of him as his mustache.

"Since the beginning. He chose from the start not to be a part of our lives."

"You were never married to him?"

"Hardly." She couldn't keep the derision out of her voice. "He was someone I got star struck over in college—a pharmacology student who spent hours in the library where I worked, someone who had the world at his fingertips and every girl who saw him swooning. One day, he picked me."

"You can't really blame him, can you?"

She laughed. "Don't turn silver-tongued on me. I'm kind of used to the Neanderthal."

"Huh. I don't know how I feel about that." The corner of his mouth twitched, she thought. It was hard to tell in the dark. "Still, I'm just sayin'."

"Right. Whatever, Dewey. Anyway, I dumped a boyfriend my parents adored for this guy. I was in my 'I'd-rather-be-like-my-sister' rebellion, tired of being the good girl. One thing led inevitably to another, and a month after we met I was, as my parents insisted on saying, a girl in trouble."

"Really?" They reached a narrow depression filled with water, and he stopped her. "Careful. This is a drainage ditch. It's pretty muddy. Here . . ." He lifted her as if she were not more than a wisp of dandelion fluff and stepped across the wide ditch. His arms tensed as he cradled her for one last second and then set her down on the other side.

He continued talking as if the interlude hadn't happened, but her heart beat so loudly she could barely hear him. "I would have thought in this day and age, having a baby before you're married wouldn't be all that unusual."

"Uh . . ." She struggled for composure. "No, it was definitely scandalous for the daughter of the junior senator from the Commonwealth of Massachusetts. I had caused the Great American Family Tragedy. And they haven't rid themselves of the stigma yet."

"Did they disown you? Or not support you?"

"In all honesty, they did neither. My circumstance might have been an embarrassment, but by gosh we were going to tough it out together. I was pretty much the opposite of not supported. I was over-supported; I was practically a public charitable institution. Strong, independent Rose. Bad, runaway, unnamed father. Which, I suppose, wasn't entirely untrue."

"He left?"

"He wanted me to have an abortion. When I nearly punched him over that idea, he insisted I give the child up for adoption. When I refused that as well, he finished school and vanished from our lives."

"Asshole."

"Yes," she said quietly. "But I don't think of him that way anymore. I can't. I know his name and family members' names, and if Jesse ever wants to find him someday, I'll be as honest as I can and give him all that information. I can't raise him with anger in my heart; I can only raise him with enough love and attention to make up for one parent being absent."

"That's a tall order."

"Yes, it is."

She knew he wanted to say more. She already understood fully that he fundamentally disagreed with how she treated her son. But he didn't say anything more; he kneaded her fingers gently and refused to let go. She ignored the little warning pings telling her he was another man who'd find constant fault with her decisions. Even so, something made her cling to him right back.

"My parents gave me support, but it was conditional. Sending Jesse to the best preschool and then private schools showed I was willing to do whatever it took to make up for my indiscretion. Most importantly, however, finding the proper father for him—one who would legitimize the fallen daughter and her illegitimate son— became mission number one. They claimed it wasn't true, but that was pretty hard to believe after I lost count of the blind dates and dinner-party setups. Mother would get almost Victorian and take to her bed when I broke up with someone I'd seen more than once."

"Wow."

"Yeah, kind of wow."

"So here you are. In the safety of small-town Minnesota. Is that the idea?"

"Pretty much. Having escaped from the final straw."

"Oh? Was this final straw another blind date?"

"Oddly enough, no. It's someone I've known a lot

of my life, the son of a Massachusetts Supreme Judicial Court Justice who's one of my father's best friends. Daniel is eleven years older than I am and a decent enough guy."

"Did you break Judge Daniel's heart? Leave him at the altar?"

They reached the back door of the smallest of three buildings. Dewey gave his little quirk of a smile and squeezed her hand again before letting it go. He fished in one pocket and dragged out a set of keys.

"No, never got nearly that far. I disappointed him a little. But I'm pretty sure his heart is intact. He's a plenty eligible bachelor."

He tsk-tsked as he put the key in the door's deadbolt lock and turned it. "So callous, Madam Librarian."

"I must be," she said, surfing a wave of satisfaction into the dark room with Dewey's hand on her back to guide her.

Dewey filled her with a sudden sense of being in control. Of being unexpected. Maybe a tad disobedient. All things she hadn't allowed into her character for fear of disappointing someone. She was being a little like her sister, and the idea made her smile. Daisy the Wild Child, the one who never did the expected and who was the ever-fêted prodigal daughter.

Well, Daisy could eat her heart out. Who, after all, was the one walking into the dark with a man she neither needed nor had been set up with, but who smelled delicious and sexy like hot spice and Shiraz? Who gave her shivers by holding her hand. She couldn't, in fact, remember anyone creating such a simple but powerful sensation.

Dewey walked beside her through a dark hallway, his hand still on her back, and the blackness held no more forbidding shapes or feelings. It held . . . potential.

"Let there be light." His declaration rumbled in her ear, and the room burst into a bright, unexpected view. Rose blinked in astonishment. She'd never had a need to come to the feed mill and hadn't realized there was a retail component. The store was large enough that she couldn't see to the front door, and a riot of smells bombarded her as if they'd jumped out with the light. Musty earth, sharp fertilizers, plants and paper, leather, unidentifiable odors that intrigued and made her nose twitch like a curious cat's.

"Look at all this!"

"It's just a feed store. A little pet food, a lot of gardening supplies, a few tack items."

She'd never been in a feed store. It pummeled and delighted her senses like a spicy Marrakesh bazaar.

"Horse stuff!" She fingered a purple-and-black halter hanging on the wall. Beneath it stood a rainbow of buckets—green, blue, pink even. "I'm scared to death of horses, but this is adorable."

He raised an amused brow.

One by one she picked up and studied garden trowels and gloves, small, rough-hewn bird feeders, and sleek garden gazing balls. She ran her fingers over bags of sunflower seeds and wild bird food. In another aisle she found odd containers of udder balm and calf starter and huge feeding bottles.

"I know all this stuff has to come from somewhere,"

she said, "but I've never been to the source. I'm sure you think I'm completely bonkers."

"I think you're a funny city girl," he replied. "Cute in an *Alice in Wonderland* kind of way."

"Now I know you're making this up to flirt. Using a book reference."

"I may be a dumb jock gear head, but I have a little schoolin'."

"You must have plenty if you were a teacher."

"A fallback when I couldn't play pro ball."

"If I had to guess, I'd say football."

"I played Division I at the University of Minnesota and was scouted fairly seriously. But then, in my junior year, I was diagnosed with cancer and that derailed my career—"

"Oh, Dewey, no! I'm sorry. Are you . . . ?"

"I'm fine. Been fine for fifteen years. Same kind of cancer Lance Armstrong had, but a lot less widespread."

She must have looked as stricken as the hole in her stomach made her feel. Dewey strode toward her and placed both palms on her cheeks, enveloping her chilled skin in warmth. His eyes settled on hers and commanded her to look deep. In the hot espresso pools she saw flecks of silver light, earnest and comforting.

"It's all good, Rose. There's nothing to feel sorry for or worried about. I didn't mean to shock you like that. It was rude. I forget you haven't been here long enough to learn what's old news for everyone else. But thanks for being concerned."

A mix of foolishness and embarrassment sent feverish

heat through her face beneath his hands, but she couldn't pull away. His breath, still slightly sweet from the wine at dinner, whispered against her nose, and his mustache, perfectly groomed and thick as velveteen, beckoned for her touch. No way could she test its texture with her lips the way she fantasized, but she slowly lifted a forefinger and stroked it. His Adam's apple bobbed.

"I had to find out if it's as soft as it looks. I had an awful flash of you not being here and never being able to find out." She withdrew her finger and finally pulled away. "Sorry. That was forward."

"It was . . . nice." He swallowed again, his eyes no longer as certain as they'd been. "It felt honest."

She shrugged. "Impulsive. I'm hardly ever impulsive."

He smiled suddenly and took her hand, turning for another door on the side of the store. "C'mon, then, on with the tour. Who knows what you'll find if this is all new to you?"

The atmosphere shifted back to normal, and she relaxed as her embarrassment faded. Her finger still tingled from touching him. Or, more likely, from being so bold. But he'd said a person had to have fun in her life. This was, for whatever oddball reason, fun.

The next room was a simple, unadorned wood-walled square piled high with bags and sacks in every color and texture from paper to burlap. One wall looked like an enormous sliding door.

"What's this?"

"Feed storage."

"Cow chow?" She grinned.

He laughed. "All kinds of cow chows. Here's our own branded sweet feed blend for horses."

Their own brand of feed? Then, in astonishment she read through the other labels. "Rabbits?" She looked to him, and he acknowledged with a nod and a smile. "Pigs. Sheep. Guinea pigs? Kangaroos?"

"There's a feed for everything if you need it," he said. "Monkeys, elephants, big cats. You ever get into exotic animals, I'm your man."

"Your family started this?"

"My great-grandfather, William. In about 1920 or so. Been around a long time."

"Impressive."

"A different kind of an empire than a political one," he said, "but it's important, I guess."

They made their way across another small office, this one sparse, with nothing but two calendars and two huge message boards on the walls, and finally he opened a last door into what he said was the final destination. In the dark, with only pale moonlight coming through a row of rectangles along the top of the room, the space appeared filled with giants, angular creatures with freakish growths and mad limbs. Instinctively she pressed closer to Dewey.

"Light again," he warned, and a sharp click sent illumination over the darkness.

Machinery like something out of a steampunk movie filled the room, and she gasped. "Now we are in Wonderland."

Her gaze wandered over huge chutes, a motionless

conveyor belt, machinery that looked as if it could grind dinosaur bones, and countless bins and vats. The air hung with a thick, sweet aroma like molasses and flour, concentrated until she nearly tasted it.

"This is where we unload grain. Over there is the mill; it can grind anything from oats to corn. There's the mixer. That's where we blend our branded feeds. You can tell they just made fresh sweet feed, because it still smells of molasses."

Carefully, he led her through the maze to the far side of the room, where he pointed to a small, neat metal cage on a platform. "Climb in," he said.

"Oh, excuse me?" She laughed. "I'm not that stupid."

He grinned and stroked his mustache like a melodrama villain. "I can force you, you know."

"I'll scream." Her chuckle turned to a giggle.

"Who'll hear you? I told you this place was full of secret hiding spaces."

"Great. I guess I am this stupid. My body won't be found for weeks."

She had no idea why her laughter continued to grow. Potentially this was a very unfunny subject. But just as he'd confused her with his earlier shutdown, he intrigued her with this unfamiliar Dewey. One she trusted for no reason that made any sense.

"Nya ha ha," he cackled, and made a twirling motion at the end of his mustache. "This is my personal elevator, and I'll take you to new heights if you'll trust me."

"I think in books they'd call me too stupid to live," she said, and climbed into the cage.

He followed her and closed the little door. The space was only about six feet square and maybe six feet tall. She caught sight of a small box containing two push buttons hanging beside the door. Dewey pushed one of buttons, and the wooden floor of the cage buzzed beneath her feet. Slowly, smoothly, it began to rise.

"Whoa!"

"Better than the glass elevator in *Charlie and the Chocolate Factory*."

"Stop with the literary references. You had me at 'new heights.'"

"Good. Guess I haven't lost my touch." He stopped the little elevator just before they reached the final level—a step onto the top of the vertical grain elevator. "There you go. The whole candy factory spread out for you."

Indeed, she could see the entire floor of the mill from their new perch twenty feet up the side of the wall. The sense of order was clearer from above, and Rose smiled, surveying Dewey's world.

"Is this safe?" she asked.

"A modern pulley system and brand-new floor. I can secure the cage multiple places along the route." To prove it, he flipped another switch she hadn't noticed, and two steel bars slid from the base of the elevator and locked into brackets on the side of the wall. "We can use this for heavy storage or to keep something big off the floor. It's very convenient."

"This is a really cool toy."

"Yeah, you think?" He grinned. "We loved it when we were kids. It's not that unusual even now to find one of Emma's kids up here reading."

To her next surprise, Dewey slid down the side of the cage and settled onto the floor. With one soft tug, he pulled her to sit beside him. There wasn't much more room side to side than for the two of them, her thigh snugged up to his, her hip pressed against the denim of his jeans. His size was even more evident like this, with his feet touching the far side of the cage while hers fell shy by six inches.

"What position did you play? In football?" she asked.

"Linebacker. Or I could make my way as a defensive back."

"I can see that."

"You know football?"

"I don't really love football, but it's the one totally guy thing my father did love. I used to let him tell me about it so I could spend time with him. I kind of like baseball. I always wanted my son to grow up to play first base for the Red Sox." She laughed. "He couldn't care less about sports."

She swore another shadow passed through Dewey's eyes, but it cleared quickly.

"He might yet."

"You haven't seen Jesse with a ball." She shook her head, no longer stung by the reality of her son's clumsiness. "But you. You couldn't go back to playing football after your illness?"

He pursed his lips and raised one knee, resting his large, handsome hand against it. "I lost a lot of strength while I was ill," he said. "Besides, after that, football didn't seem quite as important. I figured I could teach football, teach phys ed or something, and that would make a better use out of the life I'd been given back."

"But you didn't. Why?"

"My father passed away three-fourths of the way through my first year of teaching, and I couldn't leave the business or my mother hanging. I came home to take over, and I've never left. It's all fine. I found out I was good at fixing things. This is probably a better fit for me."

He meant it. She could see his sincerity. But for some reason she didn't believe him. She thought she could see a connection between his inner shadows and the mention of children. What was he really missing?

"You went through a lot."

"Everybody does. Look at your story."

A rush of gratitude washed over her. He really could be a nice guy. For all his intrusiveness and oftentimes banal outlook on life, this was a depth he'd never shown before.

The new insight made her turn and rest one hand above his knee, the other one still stretched flat against the floor. He started slightly at the touch but turned toward her, too. Without giving herself time to think deeply, she leaned forward and placed a soft kiss on the side of his mouth, catching the gentle bristles of his mustache against her top lip. She meant the kiss to be quick and platonic, but a ripple of sweet gooseflesh swept down her neck and into her arms.

She started to pull away, but he stopped her, shifting to take both her upper arms in his hands.

"Uh-oh," he whispered. "This place just got very unsafe."

Chapter Twelve

THE ONLY EMOTION racing through Dewey's mind when Rose first turned back into his kiss, parting her lips with pliable acceptance, was disbelief. Then the darts of pleasure shooting through his belly wiped out any need to wonder why the unbelievable had occurred, and the more he tasted of her and the longer her lips played against his, the more intense the pleasure grew.

She didn't simply let him kiss her, passively allowing him his own pleasure. Her mouth encouraged him, invited him to play. She caught a portion of his lower lip and touched the tip of her tongue to the skin. Fireworks crackled within him. He twisted, changing the pressure of their kiss, returning the lip bites, soft and enticing. Sweet as dessert.

He didn't ask for more. The exploration of this unexpected kiss excited him plenty—maybe too much, given the state of his nerve endings and the sparks that pulsed from them as if they were live wires lying exposed on the ground. Her fingers, light as breath, touched the corner of his mouth and stroked his mustache. That delicate sensation fanned his internal sparks into flames, sending his stomach jumping with a wayward thrill so intense it pulled him away from the kiss.

Her eyes, blue as cornflowers, didn't flinch from his gaze. Her fingers remained against his upper lip, and she stroked it only millimeters at a time, like she was petting a hummingbird. His heartbeat certainly had to be hummingbird rapid.

"It tickles," she whispered.

"Sorry."

"Don't apologize." She giggled, a sound that brought impish light to her eyes. The brightness calmed him—slowed his crazy heartbeat—and he placed his thumb against her upper lip to imitated her stroking. "I was the rash one. I'm sorry."

"You'd better not be sorry."

The musical little laugh escaped again. "Do you want to know the honest truth? I haven't decided to kiss someone on my own for a very, very long time. I think that's why I did it. Not that I knew I was going to do it until I did. Librarians gone wild, I guess—I don't—"

He pressed slightly harder against her lip, feeling her rush of explanations and justifications start to kill the magic. "It's okay, Rose. I liked the surprise."

"It was that." She lowered her hand from his face and set it in her lap.

"Don't start analyzing it." The mood was slipping, inexorably.

"Nothing to analyze. I followed a wild impulse, and it was . . ."

"Maybe just fun?"

"Super fun." The twinkle in her eye lasted another brief moment. "But I've been gone a long time. I should get back to Jesse."

"Jesse." His heart sank. He'd hoped to take her mind off him for more than a few minutes.

"Why do you say his name like it's distasteful?"

"I don't mean that. I honestly don't. I want you to relax about him. He'll be better off if you let yourself be a normal mom. You really, truly don't have to be his dad, too. You can't be. He knows he's got someone who'll always protect him—that's all you have to be."

"You don't understand."

"I think I do."

"That's kind of your problem, you know." Her words came out quietly as she stared at her hands, tangled awkwardly in her lap. "You think you know about everybody, and you think you can help them all." She lifted one hand slowly and cupped his cheek. "But you don't have the perfect wisdom for everyone. You don't have everyone's cure."

"I wouldn't claim to." A stirring of resentment dampened the pleasure of her touch. "That's a little harsh, when it comes right down to it."

"No. I don't mean it to be. I look back, and in an awful lot of ways you've been the best first friend in town a person could have. Jesse likes you—that's a gift to me. But you do have to let me be the kind of mother I am."

"Not my intention to change you."

But maybe it was, he thought, as he clambered to his feet and offered her a hand up. Unlocking the cage and starting it back down, he said nothing. He believed with all his heart that a less uptight, less controlling Rose would make for a happier, less weird Jesse. To the extent that her son would see good role-modeling for easygoing behavior, he did wish Rose could change.

He'd seen the tiniest sliver of that relaxed Rose moments ago—lips pink from their kiss, eyes shining with a little rebellion, movements slow with exploration. That was the librarian he could fall for.

They reached the main floor, Dewey opened the elevator door, and Rose popped out like she'd been claustrophobic. The euphoria from their kiss receded further as reality set in.

"Mitchell? Glen, Bart? You the ones in here?"

The loud, authoritative shout made both him and Rose jump. She put a hand to her mouth, stifling a cry. Seconds later, a flashlight beam danced on the surface of a grain bin and two police officers appeared around the big mixer.

"It's me," Dewey called. "Just giving a tour. Is there a problem, Chief?"

Tanner Hewett eyed the two of them uncertainly at first, then relaxed and holstered the Maglite. His partner, a new officer who couldn't be more than twelve, Dewey thought, followed suit and stood behind the chief.

"We noticed the lights on and thought it was unusual for this time on a Sunday night. What with the vandalism at the library and the fact you were there, I thought maybe someone was targeting your place, too. Everything's all right? Evening, Ms. Hanrehan."

"Hi," she replied.

"Everything's great," Dewey said. "Like I said, I was giving Rose a tour. She and her son joined us for dinner."

"All right, then," Hewett said. "Glad to hear it." He gave a half smile as he eyed them up and down. The chief wasn't known as the warm fuzzy type either. Dewey had always liked his no-nonsense approach and crisp style, so his knowing little grin now stood out a little too glaringly. The man had only been in Kennison Falls a year. Sad to think he'd already been corrupted into thinking small-town gossip was fun. "Enjoy the . . . tour."

"I'm sure we will." Dewey offered a benign smile in return. "By the way, any news on the rock thrower?"

"I'm afraid not," he said. "We'll have more luck finding folks to talk to tomorrow. Someone will know something."

"Thanks for all your help." Rose cut in before Dewey could reply.

"Just doing my job. Okay, we'll leave you two."

"We'll follow you out," Dewey said quickly. "This is the end of the line in here anyhow."

In more ways than one, he thought with a tinge of moroseness as he flicked out lights along the return route. Fully subdued Rose had made it clear what she thought of his "help," and he knew beyond a doubt that no matter what fun a stolen moment might be, she would never fully give herself to anyone but her son.

Not, he thought vehemently, that he wanted very much from any woman. Rose had simply shaken him with unexpected desire. She'd claimed this had been the first kiss she'd initiated in a long time. Well, it had been the first time he'd let down his guard. If he did anything, he did casual. Maybe it was a good thing she'd put the lid on this, whatever it was.

He said good-bye to the police and thanked them for being vigilant.

Not until they'd locked the store back up and were headed back across the field between the mill and his mother's house did she speak.

"Way to get me in trouble with the law, Mitchell." Teasing came through the words, and he relaxed.

"Yeah, I guess I did. You know, this'll be all over town by midweek."

"The police chief would spread rumors?"

"Nothing malicious. But we were found in an empty feed mill, alone, with no good explanation except that I part own the place. I'm warning you now. If you want to avoid gossip, you might want to avoid being seen with me for a while. I'd understand."

He tried to put a note of teasing in his voice, too, but had no idea if he'd succeeded. Her eyes held no laughter. She didn't take his hand.

So, fine, he thought. A freakish, one-time kiss, an awkward end to a nice night's walk. He wondered what his intentions had truly been tonight. To kiss her?

Maybe—if only to satisfy his curiosity. He hadn't satisfied anything, however. He had more questions about her than ever. A woman wanting to rebel. A very controlling family. A runaway father. He wanted more information, and yet he wanted nothing more to do with such complications. She didn't seem inclined to want more complications either, judging by her stiff, aloof walk. In fact, at the moment, the only course of action that sounded palatable was to go back to simple—his simple, boring life.

Except there had been that kiss.

THE WEEK WENT well. For all the calamity at the library on Sunday, the official opening days were fun and, as Gladdie put it, ran smooth as chocolate silk pie. Books flew from the shelves, and the first story hour on Wednesday night enticed thirteen children to sit with mouths agape as Gladdie read *Curious George* to them—the best grandmotherly reader Rose had ever heard.

The protestors mostly stayed away, although Rose surmised the shattered window had more to do with that than a change of heart. Nobody wanted to be associated with vandalism. There were no calls from school about Jesse. Her coworkers and volunteers seemed cheerful and enthusiastic.

Other than the fact that the rock-throwing vandal seemed to have gotten away scot-free, opening week was idyllic.

She should have been excited, fulfilled, buzzing with

plans. Instead, a hollowness lay under all the excitement, restlessness moved her through the days, and the only reason she could come up with for her discontent annoyed the heck out of her.

Dewey.

How had she not realized the number of times per week she'd usually seen since the day she'd arrived in town? The man had been nearly underfoot, his handsome, mustached face poking into her business, helping her out of stupid situations, forcing her to dinner . . . kissing her.

Dang him for letting her start *that*.

But this week he'd been as absent as snow in Hawaii.

She'd known something had gone wrong as soon as they'd been caught by Chief Hewett in the feed mill. Whatever crazy spell had been cast over them in that stupid wire box twenty feet off the ground had been immediately uncast.

She dithered about it a little more every day. And the entire stupid week was wrapped in irony because Dewey had been spot on in his prediction. At least twice a day someone came in and asked about him. About *them*.

"How's Dewey?"

"I heard you're seeing Dewey?"

"Good for you, a great guy like Dewey deserves a great girl."

By Friday she wanted to tear her hair out—or at least put a sign in the window: "Dewey doesn't work here; Dewey doesn't date the head librarian; the head librarian doesn't know how Dewey is."

Even Jesse mentioned having dinner at Dewey's house to "the other kids" in his class and asked after him all week. He surprised her, because Jesse didn't wax nostalgic about people. She began to resent the mystical hold Duane Dewey Mitchell had on everyone in the town.

Finally on Friday at three-thirty she left the library fully in Kate's capable hands. All week she'd been bringing Jesse back to the library after school to hang out until closing. Tonight she'd planned a date with her son to celebrate a successful first week. Letting Kate stay until closing by herself not only freed the evening but built a lot of goodwill. Kate had proven to be incredibly valuable and totally in love with her job. Rose needed her to know how trusted she was—and how much she was liked. Her two other part-time employees were fine but very limited in their schedule flexibility, and one was Wilma Nesrud, who still sided with the anti–banned-book group and had been cordial but cool during her ten hours of work that week.

No. She definitely couldn't afford to lose Kate.

She put her work thoughts on hold and headed out to retrieve Jesse from the bus stop, looking forward to their twenty-mile trip to the bigger Minneapolis suburbs north of tiny Kennison Falls. The idea of dinner at a fancy restaurant, a movie, and an excursion to get her son some new gym shoes had her anticipation running ridiculously high. Whether it was truly the thought of quality time with Jesse or also the idea of getting away from Dewey's stomping grounds, she didn't know. But getting out of town for a few hours suddenly seemed like an outing to heaven.

Her excitement dipped to concern at the stop sign just past downtown when the first unmistakable whiff of coolant filled the Mustang's interior. She knew the hot, sickly sweet smell immediately and swiveled her head, praying to find she'd pulled up beside a broken-down car. Not a single vehicle stood anywhere near her. Her heart plunged.

Slowly, she rolled through the intersection. Nothing felt different, but her eye caught the temperature gauge and she knew. It had moved toward the red and now climbed slowly but inexorably upward. Frustration burned as a choking sensation in the back of her throat. She'd had the entire car checked and serviced before leaving Boston not a month ago. This couldn't be happening.

Stubbornly she drove another two blocks and stopped at the next sign. When she saw the steam wisps curl like taunting ghosts from the sides of the hood, she pulled to the curb and set her forehead against the steering wheel.

"No. No. No."

For a moment, the crisis was all about herself: repairs she couldn't really afford. Bruised pride that the car she pampered like a second child would make her look careless. Inconvenience . . .

Jesse.

"Shit." She growled at her own vulgarity. When all else failed, she usually had her decorum to fall back on. The lessons drummed into her by a fairly devout set of parents extended to some odd places, but clearly not to car breakdowns.

She blew out a sigh and her mind churned through the frustration searching for solutions. She was a mile and a half from the bus stop. She could limp there at least, right? But she knew better. If the radiator was dry—if she'd broken a hose or, please God, no, worse—driving was bad for the engine. Those repairs she definitely couldn't afford on a car like this.

But Jesse . . . He would start to panic if she wasn't there. Schedules were imperative to his life.

Who did she know? So many new faces. So few honest-to-goodness friends yet.

Elizabeth Cassidy crossed her mind. Rose had her card. But no, Liz would be waiting for her own son to get home.

Gladdie.

Rose breathed a little easier. Gladdie had her small-town idiosyncrasies—for one, she refused to drive on the freeways, relying instead on her slightly younger sister, Claudia. She did, however, drive perfectly well around town in her old, maroon-colored Monte Carlo. If she was home, maybe she'd find Jesse and bring him to . . . her heart sank further. Dewey's. There was nowhere else to bring the car.

With a last frustrated growl that sounded childish even to her own ears, she found Gladdie's number on her phone and swallowed her pride. Problem solved. That was all that mattered.

Gladdie answered immediately, and Rose swore she sounded perfectly delighted at the prospect of fetching Jesse. She had to go out anyway for a gardening meeting in an hour. This would work out perfectly.

"You're wonderful." Rose breathed easier.

"Pish." Gladdie dismissed the compliment. "Can I help with anything else?"

"Do you have the Gas 'n' Garage's number? I never put it in my phone."

"Have you got something to write on, dear?"

Rose dug a pen from her purse and a napkin from the glove box. When she had the number, she showered thanks on her grandmotherly savior again and hung up. Then all she had to dig up was the courage to call Dewey, even though it irritated the heck out of her that such a stupidly simple task required anything like bravery.

Wimp. Coward. Chicken. Idiot.

"Hello, Gas 'n' Garage, this is Elle."

The breath she'd been holding whooshed free, and relief eddied in her chest with a surprising rivulet of disappointment.

"Hey, Elle. It's Rose Hanrehan."

"Rose! Nice to hear you, how's it goin'?"

"At the moment, not great. My car seems to have sprung a leak. Probably the radiator. I don't know if it's a hose or something more serious, but I don't really want to drive without having someone check it."

"I'm so sorry. Where are you?"

"Just past Main Street and Third."

"Well, Dewey's not here. He's off on a delivery, but I can come and check it. Do you think you need a tow?"

"I honestly don't know. If we could fill the radiator and drive temporarily, maybe not. But if you could come, I'd be so grateful. If nothing else, maybe you could bring me back to the station. Gladdie Hanson is meeting me there with Jesse."

"Of course! On my way, hang tight."

Good to her word, Elle appeared seven minutes later. The surprising thing was, she arrived in the station's tow truck with "Mitchell's Gas 'n' Garage" emblazoned on the doors. She pulled up in front of the Mustang, and hopped out, frowning in sympathy.

"Sorry. This is such a bummer. I hate car issues when they're with *my* car," Elle said.

"I know." A smile formed easily on Rose's lips as Elle strode confidently toward the Mustang, tall and trim in a pair of gray work trousers and a fitted pink T-shirt that read "Let's go racing, boys!" Workmanlike and sexy all at once.

"Love your shirt," she said.

Elle laughed. "I have a whole drawer full of car-slogan shirts I got for working with Dewey. Trying to brainwash my darling oldest brother into the current century."

"He's old-fashioned?"

"When it comes to cars. Although I don't know if he's really a chauvinist or if he's jealous of his business. Between you and me, though, I can handle your problem." She winked.

"Sister, you've got it. I can do a lot of maintenance on this car, too, because my dad made sure I could take care of it. This car is pathetically like a baby to me, but I'll only admit that out loud to you. Or anyone who tries to mistreat her. I trust another girl to be kind to her."

"Does she have a name?"

"You wouldn't think it ridiculous if she did?"

"Heck, no. Girls love naming things."

"Miss Scarlet. Cliché, but better than Sally."

"Agreed. Scarlet she is. Let me take a look."

The hoses were all in place, the clamps tightened properly. Elle frowned again and admitted that didn't bode well for the radiator. "It could be a small leak that we can patch. Want to try topping off the water and see if we can get three miles to the station? Or, we can tow her in."

"What do you recommend?"

"Probably doesn't matter. Let's pamper her and hook her up. She'll be super easy to load."

"Sounds like a plan."

All Rose knew about Elle's background was that she was the youngest Mitchell sibling, twenty-five years to Dewey's thirty-eight. That made her nine years younger than Rose, too, but she moved around the tow truck and car like a seasoned pro. She'd graduated from college with a business degree. Why she worked at her brother's garage was a mystery.

"Have you always liked cars?" Rose asked when the Mustang was winched up and ready to go.

"I have. I hung around the station all through high school. Everyone thought I should be cheerleading or playing basketball because I was freakishly tall. I liked volleyball, but I loved the cars more. Nobody had a clue I was absorbing knowledge. I was the weirdo tomboy. Dewey hired me semi-reluctantly after I got back from college last spring. He can't believe I worked at a garage the last two years away."

"Do you race?" Rose pointed at her shirt.

"Nah. I don't have the time or money to put into a sport like that. I watch a little NASCAR, though. I'm a Jeff Gordon fan. Kinda cliché, maybe."

"Well, at least I know who he is."

Elle laughed. "I'm not a fanatic. And I'm not the fix-it person Dewey is, but I get along. Come on. Hop up in the truck."

"Never ridden in a tow truck before."

"Gosh, then I'm glad I can give you *that* thrill." She rolled her eyes theatrically. "We'll take Miss Scarlet to Dewey."

"Is the problem something you could fix?"

Elle held Rose's eyes, truly surprised. "I probably could. I don't do many major repairs like that, though. Dewey's protective of his business reputation and I'm unproven."

"But if you thought you could, can't I pick the mechanic I want? Like I'd pick my hairdresser?"

"I expect so." She beamed like a child. "You'd trust your baby to a newbie?"

"I'd trust her to another woman who wouldn't want anything to happen to her."

"Dewey wouldn't let anything happen. He is the best, you know."

"I have no doubt he'd do a perfect job. But I think you would, too. And I trust you to tell me if you can't."

"That's a huge compliment. Thanks, Rose. I'll look at it when we get back."

On the way back to the garage, Elle admitted she'd never taken the tow truck out alone before. She'd been with Dewey many times and driven the one at the shop she'd worked at during school. Rose could not help but love the young woman's free spirit that exuded such honest confidence. If she'd heard an inkling of braggadocio, she'd have been suspicious, but Elle showed her skill rather than spoke it. Her passion shone from every pore.

Gladdie's car was already parked at the station when Elle guided the big truck to the long side of the two-bay garage. She set all the brakes and left the motor running so she could run the winch from behind and let down the Mustang.

"Mind if I go tell Jesse everything's okay?" Rose asked. "Then I'll come back and see what you need from me."

"Go for it. I'm good."

They each exited their side, but neither made it to her destination. Just as Rose reached the corner of the building and Elle the back of the truck, Dewey strode toward them, his expression thunderous. He passed Rose with barely a glance, for which she guessed she should be grateful. Even so, her heart did a little jig-twist in her chest at the sight of him.

"What the hell were you doing with my tow truck?" He advanced on Elle like Darth Vader on a bad day.

"Hi to you, too, bro."

"Don't 'bro' me. You don't have permission to drive that truck alone."

"After what? Ten, twenty times *not* alone? Get over it, Dewey, you know I can handle it fine."

"That's entirely beside the point, and you know it. This is an insurance issue."

Elle jumped angrily around the back end of the Mustang, nearly ramming into her brother and stopping him in his tracks. Chest to chest with him, she narrowed her eyes.

"I call bullshit."

Dewey's brows shot up, and he actually took a step back. Rose nearly laughed.

"This is because you don't think a girl can handle your precious equipment," Elle continued.

"I—" Dewey stared, openmouthed. "What did you say?"

"I meant it—including the innuendo. You're a chauvinist moron, Duane."

"You're crossing a line here, Eleanor."

"Then fire me."

"I'm sorely tempted."

"Hey, now!" Rose tapped him on the shoulder. "Easy, Dewey. Elle really helped me out. You're lucky to have her. And if you'd like a critique of her performance, I'll gladly give her an A-plus."

He spun, surprising her. "I do not want a critique. This has nothing to do with you."

Purposefully, she sidestepped him and took up a spot beside Elle. Deliberately, provocatively, she folded her arms.

"It most certainly does, since I just hired her to fix my car."

"You . . ." He squinted, his mouth opening and closing like a guppy's. He rubbed a hand down the side of his face as if desperately trying to figure out what was going on. "Excuse me?"

"Something's up with the radiator. She thinks she can fix it. I'm happy to let her try."

"Over my dead body."

Rose leaned toward him and smiled, thoroughly enjoying his discomfort. "If it comes down to murdering you, it is two against one."

Elle's laughter burst around them, and she held up one open hand. "All right, Rose!"

Rose aimed a wink directly at Dewey, then she high-fived his sister with an ostentatious and highly satisfying smack.

Chapter Thirteen

DEWEY HAD NO clue what was happening. Ten minutes before, he'd been in control of his life, or at least of his own business. Now he was facing the assault of the warrior women. One tall but slightly skinny business school grad, and one curvy, brown-haired, very beautiful, very obstinate . . . wrongheaded librarian.

Who kissed like a fantasy.

Stop it. You're not going there.

He swung his gaze toward Elle to reignite his annoyance. What was his stubborn little sister thinking? This was serious. But there both women stood, as pleased with themselves as if they'd cured cancer.

"What's really the problem here?" Elle asked. "Admit it. You don't like a girl being good at your job."

"That's ridiculous."

She was quick to call him sexist, but it wasn't true. He just . . . he didn't want her to get injured on his watch.

That was it. As if she'd read his mind, she stepped forward again.

"Is it? You've let Joey take the truck out. By himself."

Gladdie's grandson, Joey, had worked at the station for two years. At twenty, he'd proven himself a smart kid, and one of the few who could handle Dewey's slight OCD when it came to his garage rules. Joey knew the procedures. Elle made up her own.

"With permission. I trained him."

"Is that it? I don't do things your way, so I must not be competent?"

"Will you stop trying to get into my head?" He reined in his frustration with effort. "I never said you weren't competent. You just . . . I never know what you're going to do next or how you're going to do it."

"You throw vague instructions at me as if I'm a cleaning lady and then you leave. So yeah, I do things my own way."

Without thinking, he lifted his eyes and gazed past Elle to find Rose chewing her bottom lip in fascination. Her brows arched when their eyes met, and it looked like she tried to suck back a grin. Heat crawled up Dewey's face. Elle was simply spitting-kitten mad now and blowing things out of proportion.

He didn't know why he cared what Rose thought. It hardly mattered. She'd been cuddly as a steel beam after the kiss that stayed stubbornly on his mind all week, and she'd evidently taken his teasing suggestion to stay away seriously. It seemed pretty clear they couldn't be in the same room—hell, the same gas station—for more than ten minutes without irritating each other. Fascination was not enough to overcome basic incompatibility.

Out of the corner of his eye, he caught movement from the station office and turned to see Gladdie and Jesse approach, all smiles and anticipation. His will to argue drained from him like spent energy. He closed his eyes, then turned back to Elle.

"You know what? Fine. You two liberated females have at that radiator. But remember, if you break it, you bought it."

"That was condescending." Elle glared at him.

"Just telling you the rules, like you asked."

To his shock, Elle backed down immediately. Her perpetually sunny smile replaced the angry frown and she nodded, satisfied. "Fair enough. You go worry about manly things like straightening your wrenches. I'll let the car down and test the radiator. Can I use the empty left bay?"

He honestly didn't know if the emotion charging through his chest was fury or pride. Elle's confidence had always amazed him, but when she aimed it at his expertise, somehow it galled him, too.

"Sure. Why not? Whatever you need, Eleanor."

He turned away again, but not before he clearly caught the triumph that passed from Elle to Rose. Stomping past Gladdie and Jesse in a full-fledged snit, he barely heard the boy call out.

"Dewey!"

He slowed the tiniest bit. "Hey, Jesse James. I gotta run, but your mom's over there."

"Where are you going?"

Someplace away from girls. You should run, little buddy. "I have some work to do on a car."

"Can I help?"

"Don't think so, but thanks."

Jesse frowned until it looked as if his features folded in on themselves trying to understand. Guilt slowly overshadowed Dewey's anger. He'd answered as if the kid were an adult offering assistance only to be polite, when the request had been dead serious. He was out of practice dealing with kids younger than twelve.

"Look, your mom probably wants to go home while Elle finds out what's wrong with your car."

"Actually, I think I'm going to stay while she does her diagnostics." Rose hopped into the conversation from behind him, and he started, spun, and stared. "I'd like to look under the hood with her, if Gladdie can spare a few more minutes."

Her eyes glistened, as excited as Jesse's had been over the fire engine. Astonished at the genuine interest, Dewey's resolve to ignore her slipped a notch.

"I have about ten minutes," Gladdie said, and inclined her smoke-colored curls in his direction. "But Dewey here can entertain our young man until you're done."

Dewey bit back the retort that formed on his tongue at Gladdie's blithe offer. What the frickin' hell was going on with the women in this town today? His poor garage needed an infusion of testosterone, fast, and what he had was Jesse, totally oblivious to the estrogen storm raging around him. The boy stared past all the drama, head tilted so he could see into the garage. His eyes didn't move, didn't flicker. Dewey wanted to wave a hand in front of him to see if he was catatonic.

"I don't want to impose—" Rose began.

"Nonsense," said Gladdie. "Dewey, get Jesse some pop and then show him around."

"Sure. Why not?" He might as well retreat from the ambush with honor until he could regroup.

"You can come and watch us if you want," Rose said. "Elle's going to try and fix the car."

Jesse didn't move.

"Jess?" Rose touched him on the shoulder.

"Huh?" He turned his head and focused on her.

"Come and watch Elle fix the Mustang, or go with Dewey."

"Dewey," he replied without hesitation.

"All right. But you stay out of his hair."

Jesse looked up at Dewey and squinted at his hair.

He laughed in spite of his cranky mood. "It means you won't bug me. You won't, right, kid? We'll get away from the girls."

"Yeah. Away from the *girls*."

"Oh, don't you start brainwashing him." Gladdie patted Jesse's shoulder. "You'll like girls fine in a few years."

"C'mon, Jesse James. Let's go rob a train or something." Dewey guided the boy away.

"Rob a train?"

Dewey scowled. Did the kid take everything literally? "Uh. Not really."

"Okay."

Strange child. Still, he had an innocent appeal about him. It fascinated and baffled Dewey at the same time. Without further discussion, checking, or permission, Dewey led Jesse toward the office. They fell into step together and didn't say a word until Jesse glanced back over his shoulder.

"Mom's coming, too," he reported.

"What are you following us for?" Dewey called without looking. "You have work on the red car to do."

"Why are you being so weird?" she replied.

That stopped him. He considered her words for a moment and dug into his pocket. He pulled out four quarters and handed them to Jesse. "The pop machine is next to the counter in the office. Go ahead and pick what you want."

"Okay." Jesse trotted ahead.

Dewey turned slowly in a half circle. "Being weird? Why do you sound like a five-year-old?"

"Don't give me that. You know what I mean. You sure weren't this cool in the elevator last weekend. What's got you in such a sulk that you will barely talk to me? You disappeared this week."

"Me? Where have *you* been?" Defensiveness wasn't normal, but she drew it out of him like she was exorcising an evil spirit.

"Mad at you for disappearing without as much as a 'gosh, that was nice.'"

He blinked. "Hey, you could have called."

"Oh, no. You can't have it both ways. I'm the *girl*, remember? You don't like us to take the initiative."

"Will you stop? Do not let that evil, conniving sister of mine brainwash you."

"Then stop acting like an ass. To her."

Ass?

He'd been called many things in his life. Dour. Quiet. Talented. Sometimes even nice. He'd never been called an ass. The word wounded with surprising sharpness.

"Wow. Tell me what you really think."

"Look. You treat Jesse better than you do Elle. And you don't like him that much."

"Hey, now, that's not fair."

"Dewey." She snared him with knowing eyes.

"Rose," he countered, suddenly angry. Her answering giggle disarmed him. "What?"

"Have you ever noticed that? Dewey Rose?"

"Oh, for the love . . ."

She stepped to within inches of his face and placed one finger on the corner of his mouth, tugging it up gently. "Smile. I'm not mad at you anymore."

"You called me an ass and said I didn't like your kid. Maybe I'm mad at you now."

"Okay." She dropped her finger and turned with a flirty flip of her hair. "I respect that. Still—be nice to my kid. This isn't his fault."

"I never said—wait, did you call him 'kid'? His name is Jesse, you know."

"Ah ha."

He grabbed her wrist before she moved out of range and twirled her back to face him. One quick glance around told him Elle and Gladdie had both disappeared.

With swift certainty, he covered her mouth with his and dispensed immediately with the chastity that had marked their first two kisses. Hot and hard, he plunged his tongue through the surprised O of her lips and plundered her mouth with it like a marauding pirate.

Her sweetness nearly convinced him to slow down and savor, but that wasn't his intent, and he ignored the impulse. Lifting his head, he looked deeply into her shocked face and tried to give a cruel, conquering smile, but his muscles suddenly didn't want to hold him upright, much less channel Blackbeard. He cleared his throat.

"You think I'm an ass? I can be one."

"Try stubborn ass."

Her tongue swept her bottom lip slowly, as if tasting the kiss. Blackbeard's Ghost left Dewey high and dry, with only weak knees and hard desire.

"Is that a challenge?" he asked.

"No. An observation."

"I was going to ask you out tomorrow night, but I think you're too mean for me."

"That's all right. You're too arrogant for me."

Her voice teased and flirted. He tried desperately to quell the laughter bubbling toward release. For a book-learned librarian—however sweet tasting and perfectly curved—she turned something on in his brain as well as his body. With Rose, he didn't feel like good old Dewey. The trouble was, he didn't yet recognize the man standing there in his stead.

"Stop calling me arrogant. It bugs me. Are you free tomorrow night? I'll pick you up at seven. I'll even find you a babysitter if you need one. Elle likes kids."

Her face lit with unmistakable interest, and then it fell, taking his heart with it. "Oh, Dewey, I'm sorry. I truly am. I, uh, have plans tomorrow night." And then, surprisingly, her eyes dulled further. "We were supposed to have plans tonight, too. Miss Scarlet sort of put a crimp in those."

"What plans?"

"Heading up to Burnsville. Tennis-shoe shopping. Nice dinner. And a theater is having a month-long Friday night Disney Classics festival. Tonight it's *101 Dalmatians*. I think."

"Sorry. That sounds like it would have been fun. Maybe Elle can find the problem fast enough for you to make it."

With every fiber, he wanted to offer to take her. But the courage to ask her out and the courage to intrude on time with her son were two different things. He knew better than to get involved in their relationship.

"Even if she's a girl?"

"Huh?" He forced his mind off the fantasy.

"Elle could fix it fast even if she's a girl?"

"You know what?" He drew in a calming breath. "I never said I have a problem with her being a girl."

"Then what is your problem?"

"I think I'd better go check on the kid Gladdie palmed off on me. You're gonna miss your diagnosis if you don't get back there."

"Fine."

They separated with no more sparring. He decided then and there any kind of relationship with her would simply take too much effort.

But there was yet another kiss . . .

Five minutes later, Jesse followed him through the garage bay not occupied by the women and Miss Scarlet, heeling like a well-trained pup and jabbering like a person who'd just discovered speech.

"What kind of wrench is that?"

"Monkey."

"For monkeys?" Jesse chortled at his unfunny joke.

"No."

"What is it for?"

"Holding weird-shaped things tightly."

"What's this?"

"Hey, that's heavy, careful. It's a big pipe wrench."

"Can monkeys use it, too?"

Okay, that was a worthy fourth-grade joke. "Sure, why not?"

"What's that car here for?"

Dewey put the large wrench back in its spot. "Needs new brakes."

"Can you put them in?"

"Yup."

"Is it hard?"

"Not if you know how."

"I don't care if I know how."

"Don't suppose you do." He picked up a chamois cloth and folded it.

"Why are your tools so neat? My grandpa's tools are all jumbled. He has to search for them."

"I hate searching for a tool. Makes me plain mad when I can't find something, so I want my space neat."

"I'm like my grandpa. My mom would say I should be more like you."

A surprised flicker of pride sent warmth through Dewey's belly. "I highly doubt that, kid."

"What's a lawn mower doing here?"

"I fix lawn mowers sometimes."

"Can you fix . . . boats?"

"Mostly."

"Toasters?"

"Yeah."

"Washers? Furnaces? Sinks? Toilets? Barns?"

He didn't have to answer. Jesse was on some sort of roll, and only he knew where and when it would end.

"Hey, can you fix fire engines?"

"I've worked on the small tanker engine a few times. Depends on what's wrong."

"Sometime, if you fix it again, can I come and watch?"

"I don't know. It could happen."

"Can you fix anything?"

His sudden capture of Jesse's earnest eyes actually stopped the boy's incessant flow. This time, the question that usually stoked Dewey's pride gave him pause. The answer didn't come glibly. "I can fix most things. Well, I can fix a lot of things."

Like he could stop this insane parrot-on-steroids interrogation! He grabbed an always-handy football off a shelf. Jesse was as handsome a kid as Dewey had known. Wheaty hair. A guileless face with even, perfect features. A regular child movie star. But the boy needed to do something that a normal ten-year-old male did.

"Jesse James," he said. "Let's go out and play a little catch."

Jesse shook his head. "I hate football."

"That's okay. We won't play football. We'll play catch."

"I can't catch."

"Anyone can catch if he's the right distance from the ball. C'mon. If you're gonna be a bank robber, you'll have to know how to catch the sacks of money that get thrown at you."

"Jesse James robbed mostly trains. From 1866 to 1876."

"I see. So would you rather be a train robber?"

"I'd rather be no robber. Just Jesse James."

"Okay, you be Jesse James, and haul your brainy little self out the door. You don't need to stay in a garage when it's this nice."

Jesse protested all the way to the field behind the station, but he set his features into admirable determination when Dewey handed him the football, let him roll it around in his grip, then showed him how to place his fingers along the laces.

"This is too big."

"Yeah, footballs are big. But they're shaped cool enough that anyone can throw them. Give it a try. Just toss it."

A moment of warmth filled him. From the time he and his brother had been football fanatics in high school and college, he'd imagined teaching sons how to play and carry on his passion, if at no bigger a venue than football games after Thanksgiving dinner. Every member of his big family harbored the wish to extend his or her part of the Mitchell legacy. He'd had to give up that dream after his illness, but it wasn't something anyone other than his mother knew. His private wound had made him stronger at many things. He'd healed the scar with the football teams. And now, for a brief second, the fantasy flared again.

"Okay," he said. "Bring the ball back beside your ear and push it forward. Let it go just before your hand starts toward the ground."

Jesse hyper-cocked his arm and twisted his torso in an ungainly windup. When he flung the ball, it was with all the finesse of a penguin trying to pass with its flipper. The oval wobbled and dropped to the ground at Jesse's feet.

"No problem," Dewey said. "Try again. This time, don't bring your elbow out so far and don't twist your body. Use your arm."

A carbon copy of the first throw followed.

Dewey scratched his head. "Okay. One more time."

Three more attempts failed miserably.

"It takes practice," he said.

"I told you."

"Bah. Don't worry. How 'bout I toss you a few?"

"Won't be any different."

"Hey, no defeatist attitudes around here." Dewey gave him a mock scowl. "Dig in there, Jesse James, you've got this."

True enough, Jesse could catch the ball in two hands from four feet away if Dewey threw it to him with the ends pointed side to side. The instant he tossed it properly, the boy flinched and let the leather dribble from his hands like a hot potato.

Ten throws. Fifteen throws. Jesse caught the ball no more than three times. He didn't seem to have the eye-hand coordination to clap his arms like pincers at the right moment. He tried without complaint until one final drop cracked his passive face. Red crept up his cheeks like liquid sunburn, and he swung his foot violently at the ball. It sailed ten feet—the most coordinated move he'd made all afternoon. His face turned from adorable to sour in less than a second.

"I don't want to do this anymore. Stupid ugly damn football."

Dewey stared at the transformed child, unable to find words. Jesse kicked again at a grass tuft and then another, little growls erupting with each effort. Slowly, Dewey's brain engaged. Rose had told him he'd never seen a tantrum. This was what she meant? Well, he wasn't going to coddle a tantrum.

He knelt in front of him and grasped the two slender upper arms. Jesse struggled and growled. "Hey." Dewey let the word zing from his tongue. Jesse peered at him, little blue eyes narrowed. "Knock it off, you did great. Tell me you're done for the day, and I'm happy to quit too. But you don't have to get mad at the grass."

"Whatever."

Dewey almost laughed at his baby-trying-to-sound-tough defiance. "You okay now?"

"I'm stupid."

"Knock that off, too. You're one of the smartest kids I know. I told you, you did fine."

This time, Jesse merely stared as if Dewey was insane.

There wasn't any point sitting here trying to convince the boy he was a perfectly fine athlete. The tantrum seemed over, but football was done. What next?

The answer came like serendipitous lightning. Dewey jumped to his feet. "Come on. We're going to find your mother."

The look changed from skepticism to utter defeat. Dewey dropped to his knees again. "Not because I'm leaving you. I just have something to tell her."

"How bad I am because I swore?"

"No! I'm not a tattletale. I swear sometimes, too. Not that you get to at your age," he amended quickly.

"Oh."

His chest burned with regret as he patted Jesse's shoulder. What was this boy's story, really?

They rounded the corner to find Elle and Rose deep in discussion.

"What's the verdict?" he called.

Elle shook her head. "Radiator's cracked. Unfortunately, we can't get the part until Monday. We're discussing where to get her a car."

"No need for a car, she's coming with me."

Rose rolled her eyes and sighed loudly enough for him to hear. "Here we go again."

"Wait." He kept his brain in the game. "I'll try again. Please, I'd like you and Jesse to come with me."

"Where exactly are we going?"

Jesse, too, stared up at him, expectant and confused. Dewey took a deep breath and plunged. "Someone told me this old cartoon movie about dogs is playing up in Burnsville."

The surprise on her face made him hold his breath in a moment of uncertainty, and then her surprise melted into a soft smile.

Chapter Fourteen

ROSE HADN'T SEEN *101 Dalmatians* since she'd been a teenager. She'd all but forgotten the awkward-sweet human characters and how truly awful Cruella de Vil had been. Nobody forgot or didn't love the adorable, animated puppies, however, and Jesse sat through the entire movie enthralled. Since he often got bored by the three-quarter mark of a film if he didn't find a story compelling by whatever standards he kept in his unfathomable brain, seeing the ending was an unexpected pleasure.

Dewey had insisted he didn't mind that staying to the end wasn't guaranteed, but he'd sat for the whole movie as outwardly riveted as Jesse had. She couldn't imagine a big, hunky guys' guy not having something he'd much rather be doing, but as the final scene faded with Pongo, Perdita, and their ninety-nine safe-from-Cruella puppies tucked into their cozy home, Rose glanced down at her hand, clasped securely in Dewey's.

Holding hands at a movie. She couldn't remember the last time she'd done something so astoundingly simple and pleasurable with a man. The walk and kiss a week ago no longer loomed as simple in her mind. That had been confusing and complicated.

This was . . . nice.

His eyes found hers in the flickering dark, and he squeezed her fingers, not looking bored at all. Jesse didn't notice their hands. He sat mesmerized by the few end credits. At one point in his recent past, he'd looked up descriptions of movie-crew job titles, and now knew what every position from gaffer to key grip entailed.

"Did you like it?" Dewey asked in her ear. He flexed his fingers, then untangled them from hers, running his thumb along the ridges of her knuckles. She shivered.

"I've loved that movie since I was his age. I wanted a Dalmatian for a long time after that."

"I would like a Dalmatian." Jesse spoke, matter-of-factly and expressionless, as the big screen went dark.

"It's kind of a universal reaction to this movie. You must have liked it, sweetheart."

"It was silly. How could someone want a coat out of dogs?"

"That's why Cruella was really bad. Why her name sounded like 'cruel.'"

Jesse blinked as the theater lights went on. "I liked it." He gave his unequivocal assessment with a nod.

"Then I'm glad." Rose smiled at Dewey. "Thank you. You didn't need to pay for the movie. We should have paid for you, since you drove all the way."

"No need."

"Did you like it?" Jesse hopped up from his seat and started pushing his way past first Rose and then Dewey.

"Hang on there, buddy." Dewey put a hand out like a gate. "Let the folks next to me go, and then we'll head out. I liked it, yeah."

"Do you want a Dalmatian now?" Jesse asked.

"Nope."

"Why?"

"They're pretty expensive. If I was going to get a dog, I'd go find me a nice mutt from the Humane Society."

"I'd do that, too. I'd get a Dalmatian from the Humane Society."

Rose giggled, but put a hand on her son's wrist. "I don't think that's how humane societies work, honey," she began.

Dewey shook his head and put his finger to his lips. He didn't blink at Jesse's incorrect conclusion. "If anyone could find a Dalmatian in a dog pound, you could. You like dogs?"

"I love dogs," Jesse said.

"Since the fire station." Rose laughed.

"Do *you* like dogs?" Dewey asked her.

"I think they're beautiful. I don't really know much about them."

"But you're not afraid of them. Or allergic to them?"

"No," she said slowly. "Where are we going with this?"

"Just gettin' the facts." He winked.

When they made their way out of the theater, the seven-thirty sky was dark and starless, and a chilly wind had come up. Jesse hunkered into his jacket, whining about the cold. Rose shivered in her sweatshirt but kept one hand on Jesse's collar to keep him from rushing into the parking lot to get to the car.

"Go get him shoes now?" Dewey asked.

"We don't have to, Dewey. This was above and beyond. You don't need to get stuck running all our errands."

"But you said he needs them. When else will you go?"

"Elle said she'd find a car ... I could come back Sunday."

"That's sure a little crazy, since you're already here in town."

She grinned. When he relaxed, his broad, easy Minnesota accent fanned out like a comforting blanket, warming her.

"I guess I can't argue with that. I'm glad you suggested we stop and eat before the movie."

"I think Jesse James here needed energy. He got a workout playing football."

The two males, one young, one grown, exchanged a look Rose couldn't decipher. It was as if they were creating some sort of secret code there on the spot, Jesse pleading—or maybe demanding—with his little narrowed eyes, and Dewey towering over him, that friendly grizzly bear. They hadn't given a single detail about whatever they'd done during their half hour together that afternoon, and the slightest envy that she wasn't invited into the newly formed boys' club tinged her curiosity.

The shoe store at the mall was geared toward kids.

Rose headed straight for the boys' running shoes, not looking forward to the ordeal. Jesse hated trying on shoes. He had no patience for things that pinched or flopped and had driven more than one shoe salesperson in Boston to rethink life. She'd learned a few tricks over the years, but having Dewey there watching didn't make the potential adventure any more palatable.

"Come and show me which ones you like." She motioned for Jesse, but he hung back at the store entrance with Dewey.

"Go, pick out some football-catching shoes."

"That's stupid." Jesse scowled.

"Nah. The faster you can run and the higher you can jump, the better you catch. I think you have the wrong type of shoes right now."

"Then you pick them out."

"Nope. I'll tell you if I think the ones you pick are good catch-playing shoes, but you have to pick. I'm not wearin' 'em."

"I'd rather have these." Jesse took two steps toward a display of boots. On the end of a row was a pair of black cowboy boots with blue leather-filled cutouts.

"Cool boots. Bad football catchers," Dewey said.

"I don't care about catching footballs."

"You will when you learn it in gym class. You might as well get the right kind now. Help your mom out."

"Mom, I'd rather have the boots."

This was a new one. Usually he didn't want to look at anything. And with his pickiness, Rose couldn't imagine he'd like the feel of boots for more than three seconds.

"Cowboy boots can be kind of tight feeling," she said. "I don't know if you'd like them very much."

"I would."

"Honey, we came to get new tennis shoes because the old ones have holes. You don't need cowboy boots for anything."

"I need them."

"Jesse . . ."

"Jesse James," he said firmly. "He wore boots. I need boots."

At that, she looked helplessly at Dewey, who rubbed a hand over his mouth to hide a smile.

"Kid's got a point about Jesse James." He squatted in front of Jesse. "Your Mr. James was a lot older than you are. You could probably wait a few years and then buy boots."

"If I want everyone to know I'm Jesse James, I need them now."

"If you have cowboy boots, you have to have a place to use them. You got a horse you ain't telling me about?"

"No. I wish I had a horse."

"I think Miss Emma would charge way, way too much for a horse to live at our place," Rose said. "Dewey's right. You need a horse to justify cowboy boots. And Mrs. Middleburg won't let you wear them in gym. How about we find the tennis shoes we came to get?"

"I would *like* the boots." He planted his feet firmly in place and crossed his arms.

The set face and defiant pose were familiar—harbingers of all-out anger. Rose sighed, knowing she should simply take her son from the store and come back another time. But it would take days, if not weeks, for him to forget the boots. She could let him try them on and hope discomfort would prove he wouldn't like them. On the other hand, if for some strange reason he did like them, there'd be ugliness to spare when she told him he couldn't have them.

These were the times she despaired of finding a proper parenting balance. Teach her son he couldn't always have his way? Or give in to avoid a scene?

"Look," she said at last. "Here's the deal. If you find a pair of tennis shoes you really like, and I mean you have to properly try them on and make sure they fit, then I'll let you try the boots on and see if you like them. If you do, you can ask for them for your birthday."

The parenting gods took pity. Her suggestion got a nod of approval from Dewey and eager agreement from Jesse. When her persnickety son actually chose the second pair of shoes he tried, Rose allowed herself to believe the night would be a success.

When the saleswoman brought in the box holding the boots, however, she realized too late she'd been played. Jesse was going to like the boots even if they crushed his toes into flat little flippers.

The boots were, sadly, adorable. Jesse paraded in front of a mirror like a model for cuteness and announced he should have his birthday present early.

"I knew it," Rose sighed, slumped in a chair beside Dewey. "I should never have let him put them on."

"At the risk of getting myself in hot water like I usually do, what would be the problem with buying them?" Dewey asked. "Couldn't he wear them to school like regular shoes?"

"I suppose, but honestly? I don't see the fascination lasting. These are far out of his normal interest range, and they aren't that cheap."

"True." He sat silently a moment, fingers thoughtfully covering his mouth. "I have an idea," he said finally. "But it'll only work if you agree to two things."

"Oh?"

"You let me pay for half of the boots, and you agree to come out with me tomorrow afternoon."

"I don't see how those two things follow in the least."

"Trust me."

"Oh, sure." She laughed. "Because we have such a good track record, right?"

"Nah. Because I'm your best hope right now."

She shrugged. "I work until noon tomorrow. I have plans . . ." She hesitated, reluctant to reveal them. "I have plans at seven. We can go out, but I'm buying the boots myself. If that works into your amazing secret scheme, go for it, Mr. Fix-It. Get me out of my dilemma."

He grinned. "All right. I've got this. Follow my lead. Hey, Jesse J. Come 'ere."

Rose swore the child actually swaggered. "Can I get them?" he asked.

"Your mom said you can get them now for your early birthday present. But. Did you know that cowboys have to earn their boots? If you get these, you have to do something worthy of being a cowboy."

"What?" The first edging of suspicion laced his question.

"You have to come with your mom and me to a horse place I know about. Tomorrow. You have to catch your own horse, saddle it up, and ride it. You'll get lots of help, don't worry, but you have to do this. No wussing out. No scaredy-pants little city slicker changing his mind. You ride the horse, you get to keep the boots."

"Honest?" He looked to Rose for confirmation, his eyes shining as if he'd won the ten-year-olds' lottery. She, however, was dumbfounded.

"Honest," Dewey said.

"Riding?" she squeaked.

"Remember Dr. Preston and his wife? They have a farm outside town and Jill teaches special-needs kids. That has nothing to do with Jesse, it means she has some great gentle horses, and I know she could find one for him to ride."

"I could ride like Jesse James?"

"You can. If you're willing."

"I am! Mom! Mom, this is the coolest. This is the ultimate coolest."

If his little uncoordinated self didn't fall off and die, she thought, shivering and burying her face in her hands. She'd been afraid of horses since age twelve, when one had run off with her and dumped her at a friend's birthday party.

"This is terrifying," she admitted.

"Awww . . ." A throaty, sexy chuckle filled her ears. The sound, along with his touch, the pressure of his fingers rubbing little circles between her shoulder blades, kept her from sinking into the hope that the idea was simply part of a ridiculous bad dream.

ROSE HAD TO admit, more of her city-bred stereotypes had colored her expectations of the sort of place a small-town doctor and his wife would live. In truth, the big, comfortable home she'd pictured didn't exist. Chase and Jill Preston shared an old farmhouse with the elderly farmer who owned it along with the land his family had farmed for two generations. Dewey had told her how they'd befriended the old farmer and saved his land from being turned into a gravel pit by an unethical builder. The stuff of classic David-and-Goliath stories.

The farmyard was neat, the two-story house painted a crisp white, the barn across the yard a traditional red. Beside and behind the house were two riding arenas, one small and fenced with simple chicken wire and boards, the other larger with traditional rail fencing. Rose stood beside the gate of the smaller one, Dewey beside her, holding her breath while Jill worked with Jesse and a large, dark brown horse in the center of the arena.

"Relax," Dewey told her for the twentieth time. "Jill's an expert at this."

"I know. I know. It's . . . I still can't believe you thought of this."

"When you think of riding horses around here, you think of two people—Jill Preston and David Pitts-Matherson."

"Rio-from-the-Loon-Feather's husband?"

"Our local Englishman," he said.

"I met him once. Didn't know he was a horse person."

"Big-time. David's father rode in the Olympics for England and tried to get Jill to ride with him a while back, but the bottom line is, Jill turned down a chance to be in the Olympics for this—working with kids. Especially kids with issues. She's got a talent for bringing out the best in them. People like her a lot."

"She is nice. Jesse might be a perfect candidate for her, then." She tried to joke, but somehow it didn't feel all that funny at the moment.

"I didn't mean . . ."

"No, no, I know you didn't."

Jesse had somberly taken in everything Jill had said from the moment they'd met. Rose couldn't say he looked excited or even happy, but he was engaged, and that was something.

"Dewey!"

Rose looked up when Jill called from the arena.

"Yo," he answered.

"Could you come join us? Jesse has an idea he'd like to try."

Dewey flashed Rose a bemused smile before slipping through the gate. He approached the trio and lifted one hand to pat the horse. Sun was its name, they'd been told. Jill spoke earnestly, far enough away that Rose couldn't hear the words, but a moment later Dewey's deep guffaw flew clearly across the space.

"Really?" he asked.

"You game?" Jill asked.

"I haven't been on a horse in five years," he said.

"No matter. You'll do fine." Then, to Rose's surprise, Jill beckoned to her. "Rose, c'mon in. You can be here for this. Got a camera?"

Rose fished her phone out of her sweatshirt pocket and nodded, suddenly smiling.

"Mom, Mom, Dewey's gonna take me riding."

Jesse practically skipped out of his new blue and black boots. Dewey made bug-eyes at her.

"Can't wait to see this." Rose grinned. "Dewey hoist on his own petard."

"Don't be smug. Your turn will come."

"I'm perfectly fine right here."

"'kay, Dewey, up you go." Jill held the horse's reins while Dewey twisted the stirrup, lifted the toe of his work boot into it, and swung up more-or-less gracefully. "Sweet!" Jill said. "Now—Jesse James. Dewey's a big guy, so there's no room for you in front. You'll go behind him. You can wrap your arms around him and hang tight. Sun's got a really smooth walk and trot; you'll like it back there."

She cupped her hands and had Jesse step into them. Without effort, she lifted his weight and had him throw his leg over Sun's rump. Jesse glommed on to Dewey so fast they looked like two magnets. He pressed his cheek tightly against Dewey's back.

"O-Okay," he said, his voice muffled by Dewey's light-weight jacket.

"All set?" Jill asked.

"Ready, Jess?" Dewey asked. "The James Gang rides again?"

Jesse squeezed his eyes until the lids were no more than wrinkled slashes in his face. He nodded against Dewey's back.

"Woo-hoo!" Jill called when Dewey pressed his heels against Sun's sides and the horse ambled off.

They made half a dozen circuits of the arena, and Rose snapped ten times that many pictures, laughing when Jesse laughed, marveling at the sight of a big man on a medium-sized horse with a little wart of a kid behind him. Dewey sat comfortably and looked like a pro to her. Jill made a handful of suggestions but otherwise let them wander at will. When the horse broke into a slow jogging trot, Jesse screeched with delight and bounced a little like a rag doll. Rose found herself holding her breath until Dewey brought Sun back to the middle of the arena.

"Mom, Mom! I did it. I earned my boots. Dewey says so."

"That you did," Dewey agreed.

"You ride now, Mom. Your turn."

She inadvertently took a step backward. "Oh, I don't think so, sweetie. This is your day."

Jill winked at her. "Dewey can take you around for a ride, too."

The thought mortified and intrigued her. "I . . ."

Jill reached up for Jesse, who willingly slid into her arms and onto solid ground. He jumped like a little spring. "It was fun! You can do it, Mom. You can."

Before she could protest any more, Rose found herself stepping onto a mounting block Jill dragged from beside the arena fence. Dewey grinned down at her, his mustache shining almost auburn in the bright, cool sunlight. He removed his foot from the stirrup, Rose placed hers into it, and Jill gave her a push, launching her twenty feet into the air—or so it felt. A second later, she sat astride Sun's broad rump behind the saddle. Instinctively she grabbed Dewey around the waist as her son had done.

"Howdy, little lady." He laughed.

"Don't 'little lady' me. If I fall off, I'll turn *you* into a little lady."

His laugh deepened. "Afraid much?"

"Hey, I cracked my head open falling off one of these things when I was twelve. Sorry if I'm a wimp."

She hadn't admitted the story until now, but she had to explain the quivering in her torso somehow.

"Really?" He placed a hand over hers, where it fisted in his shirt against his belly. "I'm sorry, I didn't know. I wouldn't have made fun of you."

"It's fine."

This time when he laughed, he shook against her body. It didn't help the quivers any, but it did make them form from something other than fear. She noticed immediately how heightened every sensation was from her spot on Sun's back. She could feel when Dewey squeezed his legs together, because the tension spiraled through his entire body. When Sun stepped out, his haunches lifted beneath her, throwing her balance left and right. As Dewey swayed with the rhythm of the horse's walk, her body motion evened out, relaxed even, and she pressed closer to him, his body her only safety equipment.

"Better?" he asked.

"Where the heck did you learn to ride?"

"I don't ride all that well, but Emma and Elle both had horses at one point. We all used to go out on trail rides once in a while. I can do this much, but nothing fancy."

"This is good enough."

"Relax, I won't let you fall."

He meant it literally, but the words sank into her mind, soothing her past the fear of falling off a horse. For an instant, she knew what it was like to let worry go. Jesse was right there and safe; he was happy; she could close her eyes and think about herself and the strong, spice-and-horse-smelling man without anybody caring or knowing he was with a senator's daughter. She didn't have to move her own legs or make a decision about where she was going. This had to be what living on clouds in heaven was like.

"What do you think?" His voice rolled beneath her cheek like soothing surf. "Could you do a longer ride like this?"

"I'm pretty sure I could," she murmured.

"You sound a lot more relaxed."

"Once I found out you're a real cowboy."

"Yah, okay, let's go with that."

The next five minutes passed like the breath in a first kiss. Too quickly. Completely unexpected. He let Sun trot, and Rose giggled, slipping side to side until she found the rhythm with Dewey's strong back as a guide. She reveled in his width, his height, his solid male strength. He made her want to sit with him forever and let him guide her. He made her want to climb on a horse by herself and run through the fields with him beside her—to prove she could do it without being scared of her twelve-year-old self.

Far too soon, he pulled back up beside Jill and Jesse.

"Awesome, Mom!"

"Awesome, Rose." Dewey turned his head and whispered it over his shoulder. She quivered again.

"Thanks."

Jesse rode twice more, once with Dewey and finally by himself. He more than earned his boots, Rose thought, marveling at the man who hadn't even seemed to like her son at first. For the first time, she got an inkling of why everyone in town revered this guy, yet for all the time they'd spent together, she didn't know him at all, really. Every other minute, he was crashing through the last picture she'd created of him.

When Jesse dismounted for the final time, it was he who asked if they could come back again.

"Would you like to go on a real trail ride next time?" Jill asked. "I've got a cool little place you could ride to that has a miniature waterfall and picnic spot."

"Can we?" Jesse looked at Dewey.

"Up to your mom, Mr. James."

"Sure. We can do that sometime."

"Great!" Jill grinned. "This is a pretty time of year to go. The leaves are starting to turn. Give me a call, and we'll set something up."

They left Jill's place, and Rose didn't have to worry about any kind of conversation because Jesse immediately unleashed his usual stream of chatter, rehashing everything Jill had taught him during the forty-five minutes they'd spent with her. Quietly, without asking, without making a big deal, Dewey took her hand as he had at the movie.

She loved his hand, more each time she held it. This time, however, instead of sending pure shards of pleasure up her arm, his touch filled her with guilt.

They had absolutely no claim on each other. He'd held her hand a few times. He'd ignored her for a week. She'd ignored him. They weren't dating. They were barely friends, who'd kissed twice. She had no reason to fear the question when it came—the question she'd prayed he wouldn't ask. But he pulled up in front of her pretty rented house and smiled when she extracted her hand from his.

Every marvelous moment of their short horseback ride flooded back. The crazy warmth and the deep sense of safety. When Dewey cocked his head, she knew he was going to make her tell the truth.

"What's on your calendar tonight? You goin' on a hot date?" His eyes twinkled, teasing.

She wanted badly to sink through the seat of his car.

"Mom's going for drinks with one of the fire guys."

The silence in the car roared. Rose needed the fire guy to come put out the flames in her cheeks.

"That right?" Dewey searched her eyes, the twinkle in his gone.

"Church Hubbard asked me way back at the library Open House if I'd meet him sometime. This was the first available night for both of us."

"Well. I'd best let you go, then."

His tone went cool and dismissive in the heartbeat it took him to process the words. Suddenly, it pissed her off. Royally. She *didn't* have any attachment to Dewey, nor he to her. He'd been a great guy. He didn't need to go macho and wounded over something this stupid.

"Yes. We'd best," she mimicked. "Thanks for an amazing afternoon."

"If Jesse had fun, then it was successful."

If Jesse had fun? Thanks a lot.

"I think he did."

"See you later, then."

Dismissed, like that. About the time she'd decided he wasn't a typical jerk of a caveman.

She stood outside the car. Dewey didn't attempt to join them or see her to the door. He barely said good-bye to Jesse before he drove off.

For the love of Pete.

She hadn't actually been looking forward to the date, if drinks with Jack "Church" Hubbard at a Western-themed bar in the next small town to the east counted as a date. But now, she told herself, she couldn't wait. Firefighters were supposed to be sexy and sensitive. Maybe this guy wouldn't be as hard to deal with as a certain Jekyll-and-Hyde, macho, possessive mechanic.

Chapter Fifteen

"WHAT'S THIS PILE of rags sitting here?" Dewey bellowed over Robert Plant belting out "Whole Lotta Love" on Elle's beloved classic-rock station. "Who left these wrenches out?"

Nobody answered, if they'd even heard him. Elle's butt, sticking out from beneath the hood of Rose's Mustang, swayed in time to Led Zeppelin. Joey was nowhere to be seen. *Frickin' heck.* Dewey stomped to the radio and turned it down.

"Hey!" Elle's muffled voice protested from inside her car cave.

Dewey ignored her. "Joey!"

"I'm here, I'm here." The boy trotted in from out front. "Pumping gas. Didn't you see Gray and Abby pull in?"

He hadn't. That he'd missed them only ticked him off further.

"What's with this rag pile?" Dewey growled at him. "It's been sitting here all afternoon."

Joey didn't flinch at the bark. Dewey knew he was an exacting boss, and he never tried to hide it. He'd told every kid who'd ever applied to work for him that the only thing he required was things be done his way without question. Unfair, perhaps, but that was the way it was. Joey Hanson had lasted in Dewey's employ for two years, compared with most other kids' three to six months. Dewey relied on Joey. He half-loved the kid. So he barked at will.

"Yup, it has," Joey replied. "I have Ethan Potter's car left to shine up so he can come pick it up this afternoon. Then I'll clean up all the rags and wash 'em for you. How's that sound?"

He was also the only kid who dared tease Dewey when he was cranky. He'd earned the nickname "Braveheart" from Bart and Glen because of it.

"Did you take out the metric wrenches?"

"Nope."

"Aw, leave the poor guy alone, Crabbypants." Elle surfaced and wiped her hands on a rag tucked into her waistband. "I took 'em out for that Mazda this morning, and I'll put 'em away. What's got you pissed off today?"

"I'm not."

Elle and Joey exchanged a look they didn't try to hide.

"Then for sure nobody wants to see you when you are." Elle shook her head as she headed toward him. "You were high as a treetop yesterday. Cheerful as can be. What happened in less than twenty-four hours?"

"Nothing happened."

"Fine. Then pick up your own dang rags and wrenches if you can't wait for us." Elle planted a kiss on his cheek as she brushed past.

He sneered at her, but the angry wind left his sails. She was right, as usual. He hated that his baby sister had more wisdom about much of the world than he did. Her endless optimism and practicality reminded him of his early years, when he'd known how to handle everything, too, but now, he was losing wisdom by the day.

He had no right to let Rose or anything about her life affect his mood, much less determine how he treated his employees. So she'd gone out with another guy. Why wouldn't she? She was gorgeous and fun and smart. It was a wonder she didn't have single men lined up awaiting a turn.

Hell, maybe she did.

Nonetheless, that was no concern of his. He liked her. He'd admit it. But three shared kisses didn't make him and Rose a couple. One ten-minute horseback ride or holding hands during a movie didn't constitute an exclusive dating relationship. And yet, Jesse's announcement the night before had sent a Rocky Balboa punch to his stomach. And it still stung.

All because he'd lost his head, he told himself sharply. He'd let himself forget what the future didn't hold. For the first time in years, he'd dropped his focus from all the things that had saved him over time: his job, his reputation, his control, his football kids. He'd let his focus go soft and fuzzy over a pretty face, a someone new, and forgotten he couldn't hide his past forever and that an ex-jock turned grease monkey could never compete with firefighters or rock stars.

Rose had made him forget that he never thought about such things anymore. Not since Rachel had shown him he was better off sticking to what he was good at—fixing other people's things.

"Elle," he called, following her into the office. "I'm sorry."

"I know." She smiled. "Joey knows, too. Anything you want to talk about?"

"Nope. I was pissed off because Rose went out with Church last night."

"Church Hubbard?" She looked mildly shocked, which pleased him.

"Yeah."

"He doesn't seem like her type at all. He's a nice guy, but he's kind of pretty."

"And your point is . . . ?"

"She's more into guys like you." Elle pulled her lips back into a toothy fake grin and punched him.

"I definitely raised you wrong."

"You definitely raised me right. But you're still an idiot. If you're jealous of Church, then go get Rose yourself."

"I'm not going to be stupid and tell you I don't like Rose," he said. "But I don't do serious relationships. She's better off with someone like Hubbard."

"And I'm not going to waste my time and argue with you. You make your own happiness. If you want to be a cranky, lonely dumbass, I love you anyway. Just quit yelling at Joey because of rags and stuff."

"I hardly ever yell at Joey. It's good for him once in a while."

"Boss of the year, that's you. I'm going to get something to drink, and then I'm finishing Rose's car. After that, because I'm not dumb either, I'm going to ask you to check my work."

For the first time, he smiled. "I have a mind to let you sink or swim on your own."

She smiled back, and flipped him the finger.

THERE WEREN'T HORDES of people at the park, but a half-dozen kids made a big enough crowd that Jesse didn't want to go off on his own to play on the swings and climbing equipment in the playground. He'd always done better with adults than other children, and he'd always known he wasn't as athletic or coordinated as the other kids. So he wouldn't expose himself to ridicule, no matter how Rose promised him nobody would tease him for swinging. She knew better than to push him. She had to save her battles for things that really mattered. Like she'd tried to do with the cowboy boots.

That certainly hadn't gone as planned. Yet she had to admit, giving in had turned out to be the happiest decision of the weekend. A warm shiver shimmered in her stomach at the memory of Dewey working out a deal that didn't look like Jesse simply begged for the boots and got his way. He was such an enigma. One minute, he didn't seem to have the time of day for Jesse. The next, he was a brilliant mentor.

And he was moody. Sometimes it felt like he walked through life without any genuine joy. But that couldn't be true. He had a big, rowdy family that adored him, an entire town that was ready to offer him up for sainthood, and a smile beneath his crazy mustache that could light up a heart without any apparent effort. And yet, the light in his eyes could dull just as effortlessly, as if happiness refused to stick to him.

Completely unlike her firefighter from the night before. Man alive, if a guy ever wanted to know how to do everything exactly right on a first date, Rose would send him to Jack Hubbard. He'd been as polite as a Marine, fascinated with every word she spoke about Jesse, sympathetic about the troubles with the library board, and had even asked if he was stepping on toes when it came to Dewey, because he'd *heard* . . .

Not only that, Jack—she'd asked to call him by his given name instead of his firehouse nickname—was *GQ*, *Men's Health*, and romance-novel cover material all rolled into one. The kind of man that turned heads because he truly was rare and beautiful. She couldn't deny it had been fun to watch the admiration. The thing was, even though Rose couldn't say Jack had been vain, she'd noticed all evening his answering grins, his subtle smiles, his awareness of the awareness.

Dewey might not have garnered as many stares and flirtatious winks, but he wouldn't have noticed anyway. Not if someone had walked up and asked him to buy her a drink. And he was solid as a brick wall, but his strength seemed natural, nothing he had to work at. Jack had been solid, too, beneath his KFFD polo shirt. But his were gym-created abs and pecs—impressive and maintained. Not that she couldn't appreciate a great set of muscles. They were just so . . . perfect.

He'd asked if he could see her again. She hadn't said no. She hadn't had a bad time. But she had asked him to call in a week, once her schedule was more set. That had been a delaying tactic, of course. What she didn't admit was that it was more to see if Dewey climbed down off his macho high horse and acted civil. She'd rather have a verbal sparring match with him than sing karaoke with Jack. On the other hand, she didn't want to burn any bridges.

"Mom? My toe hurts."

Jesse's complaint brought her spinning back to reality. She glanced at the boots he'd insisted he could wear on the four-block walk to the park. They were far from broken in, so she'd known he wouldn't last in them. Full of maternal smugness, she stopped a few steps later at one of the benches scattered through the four-acre town park, this one beneath the granite statue of J. W. Kennison, explorer, raccoon-hat wearer, and discoverer of the actual Kennison Falls, located in the neighboring state park.

"I thought these might not be ready for a long hike," she said, taking Jesse's booted foot in her lap and tugging at the heel until the boot slipped off. She peeled off his white cotton sock and found the bright red baby blister.

"Ow," she said. "That's a beaut."

"I don't want my boots to hurt."

"They won't always, you have to stretch the leather by wearing them a while. Lucky for you, though, I'm the smartest mom in the world."

"You can't prove that." He grinned.

"I can. Watch." She slipped off the backpack she was carrying and unzipped it. With a flourish, she produced his old tennis shoes and a small pouch containing antibiotic cream and plenty of bandages. "Instant blister relief."

"Wow."

They laughed while she administered the first aid. The breeze had warmed, and the leaves were crisping and yellowing almost as they watched. The day had redeemed itself with the lovely fall weather. As she was finishing up with Jesse's foot, she caught sight of the poster.

"Honey, here, put your tennis shoes on for me."

"I can wear the boots. You put bandages on the red spot."

"No, you can't wear the boots. You can wear them tomorrow."

"But—"

She handed him the tennis shoes and picked up the boots from the bench. "No."

His face tightened, but she ignored him—which she never did easily. This time, however, she stood and actually left him to pout on his own. On a small community bulletin board across the path from the statue, a brightly highlighted flyer, quite glossy and professional, drew her like a poisoned spell.

"Public Announcement—Everyone Urged to Read," the sign said. "Protect Our Children. Boycott 'Banned Books Week' at the Kennison Falls Public Library, September 24–29. Attend the next KF Town Council Meeting, Tuesday, September 25. Voices for Quality Literature has a spot on the agenda when we will be urging our council members to save our library from inappropriate and dangerous material."

"Voices for Quality Literature?" she read out loud. "Save our library from inappropriate and *dangerous* material . . . ?"

What was wrong with these people? She couldn't imagine what was that frightening about reading a book with a curse word in it. Or one that contained a message, even if you didn't agree with it. It wasn't like she was promoting liars—these books were simply . . .

"Gah!" She actually made that sound out loud, too.

The whole concept of this protest infuriated her to the point she feared going back to Jesse and letting him see her anger. For a moment she turned helplessly in a circle, looking for support or poison-dart guns . . . or calm. She reached for the flyer to pull it down, but stopped herself. She couldn't keep the group from posting its opinions if she was fighting against censure.

Finally her anger settled, and she took a deep breath. Fury wasn't going to get her anywhere. She'd attend the meeting, all right, and she'd promote the heck out of the library and any programs she and the board chose to present. She had a big week, culminating in Gray Covey coming to read at story time Saturday morning. The town, she'd learned, had embraced their world-famous singer with protective arms, but that didn't mean he wouldn't draw a huge crowd. People were not immune to his popularity. He'd be reading *The Lorax*, once upon a time a banned book. Now, there'd be something to get the good citizens of Kennison Falls riled up.

She tamped down her rising irritation again.

"Rose?"

She spun to find Liz Cassidy smiling at her, and Josh trotting down the path to where Jesse still sat on the bench, still sans tennis shoes.

"Hi, Liz!"

"I'm so glad to see you. What's all this about?" She pointed at the offending sign.

"Oh, gosh. Don't get me going. A handful of narrow-minded people are trying to get me to remove the banned books from the library. Evidently, the last librarian swept Banned Books Week completely under the carpet."

"I don't get it."

"Thank you!" Rose forced her own smile. "I understand individuals not wanting to read a certain book, or avoid exposing their children until a certain age. But you can't ban books because they aren't to your liking."

"I admit, I'm pretty picky about books myself. I think there are lots of inappropriate things out there. But I agree they can't be banned. Besides, I'm apparently one of them now. It's kind of an honor."

"Well, maybe you'll come to the council meeting with me and hold my hand, then," Rose joked.

"Oh, I'd love to be there."

"Fantastic! I know we don't know each other well yet, but I get the impression you're pretty strong in your religious beliefs. If you're willing to stand on the side of freedom of expression, you could be a pretty powerful ally."

"I've got a little bit of a conservative side," she agreed. "I made enough mistakes in my teenage years to sympathize with those who are struggling to learn what's right and what's wrong. But I'm an artist of sorts, and I'll stand by other artists. For sure."

"Not to change the subject, but look." Rose pointed at the bench where the two boys sat head to head. "I was just fighting with my son about changing his shoes. Long story, but I think Josh got Jesse to put on his tennis shoes. I may owe you money for that. Or at least coffee."

Liz laughed. "Hey, I'd be thrilled to have Jesse befriend Josh. Between you and me, he's been hanging out with a boy a year older than he is, and some of the things he's starting to say are concerning me. Things about hating school, and certain teachers being 'dumb,' and other kids being stupid. It's minor, but Jesse seems like a nice boy."

"He is nice," Rose said. "But Josh will find out, he's also not a normal kind of friend. I should tell you, he's been diagnosed with Asperger's, and he frequently misses a few social cues. Maybe explain to Josh that if Jesse ever hurts his feelings, it's not intentional."

"Very interesting," Liz said. "I'd like to learn more about that. Someday, it might make a good book subject. I love trying to portray things real kids deal with in a sympathetic way. And of course I'll talk to Josh. For now, we'll see how they do."

"I have a very forward question," Rose said. "How would you and Josh like to come over for pizza tonight? I'm stuck at home without a car, and now that the council meeting has me riled up, a distraction would be awfully nice."

"You know what? That would be fun. Thank you! I have brownies at home that I made this morning. Can I bring those?"

"Only if you want them gone. I should warn you about my chocolate addiction."

"Soul mate! What time?"

The pizza distraction turned out to be a godsend. Rose found Elizabeth an engaging friend, and reveled in the stories of her travels across the country and the world with her parents, who'd been itinerant doctors. She'd lived in twelve major U.S. cities, including Boston, and had spent her junior year of high school in Liverpool, England.

"If I tell you a secret, will you keep it?" She laughed over their second helping of brownies.

"Of course. I'd never tell on a new friend who brings me some of the best brownies I've ever tasted."

"Well, then!" Elizabeth grinned. "My secret is that I moved here because one of the first people I met in town was David Pitts-Matherson. I fell in love with England all those years ago. I've never been back, but when I heard David's accent, I couldn't move on. How's that for sad?"

It was the cheeriest story Rose had heard in a long time.

"David doesn't know this?"

"Heavens, no. Not really. He knows I lived in England

once. That's good enough. I crush on his accent from afar."

Rose lifted her glass of sparkling cider, since Liz didn't drink, it turned out. "Here's to good, secret crushes."

"Would it be too nosey to ask if you have one?" Liz clinked glasses and grinned.

"Ha. Don't pretend you aren't asking me about Dewey Mitchell."

"Moi?" Liz put her hand to her chest.

"*Every*body asks about Dewey, but here's the thing. It's not a crush. And it's certainly not a secret."

"Dewey's one of the—"

"Nicest guys you know. Yeah, yeah. You know what? He can be. No, he is. Dewey is quite amazing. But he . . ." But he what? She couldn't start telling tales on Dewey. That was the cardinal sin of friendship—no matter how much she would have loved a confidant. "He's so busy he makes me tired."

"He definitely is a one-man town-builder. It seems like he gets called on for everything and takes on every-thing willingly."

With or without permission, Rose thought, but smiled to herself. He drove her a little crazy, but he did come up with some creative ideas. Ideas that left deep, tingling impressions. She shook her head. Tingles didn't make up for the fact that they could barely go an hour together without an argument.

"Josh's dad, Charlie, was a good guy, too. Steady, de-pendable, dedicated."

Rose knew he'd been a Minneapolis police officer,

killed in the line of duty almost ten years ago. "I'm sorry again. It's hard to lose the love of your life."

Liz smiled, but it was very far away. "He was close," she said. "Another confession. I loved him, but I married for security as much as for true love—maybe more so."

"So was there another true love?"

"True? No. Great? Yes. Once. A boy."

"Wait!" Rose couldn't stop a silly grin as understanding dawned. "England! Your great love sounded like David Pitts-Matherson, didn't he?"

"He didn't sound anything like him—he had a very different accent." Liz laughed as Rose poked her in the arm.

"You go, girl with the great memories. Those will never let you down."

"Good memories, for sure."

The doorbell startled both of them, and they laughed a little harder. "Hope those aren't ghosts we've invoked," Rose said.

"I don't believe in ghosts, we'll be fine."

The boys were on the couch in the family room, safely watching cartoons. Rose stood as the visitor followed up the ring with a knock.

"Who on Earth? Nobody comes around at eight o'clock on a Sunday."

She opened the door no more than a couple of inches and gaped. Speak of the devil.

"Hi," Dewey said.

Her heart gave a little kick, and she opened the door fully. "Hey! This is a surprise."

"I'm sorry to bother you." He looked surreptitiously past her.

"Liz Cassidy and her son are here, that's all."

He had the grace to color slightly. "I just . . . Hell," he said. "I think you need to come with me. There's something you should see."

"Dewey, I can't leave my guests . . ."

"I know. I wouldn't have come, but it's about the library."

Panic rose in her throat. "Did something else happen? Is the building all right?"

"It's not that."

"Hi, Dewey, I heard your voice." Liz joined them and sent Rose a knowing wink. "There's pizza left if you want any."

"Thanks," he said. "But there's something going on at the library. I think maybe Rose should come."

"All right, that's twice you've hinted at trouble without telling me anything. What's up?"

"Your protestors are back. With a vengeance."

"What? On a Sunday night?"

"Who are they protesting?" Liz asked.

"I think they're setting up for tomorrow."

"Come in for a minute." Rose tugged on the sleeve of his jacket, a sexy denim one with a shearling collar and lining. She closed the door behind him. "What could I, we, do if I went there now?"

"Honestly? Simply know what's coming before tomorrow morning. The truth is, when I drove by and saw all the people, the only thing I thought was that I needed to tell you. I was going to call, but I remembered you don't have a car."

"It was good of you, I just . . ." She looked toward the great room, she looked at her watch, she tried to ignore the pounding of her heart and the sick anger rising behind the need to be a responsible mother.

"You should go," Liz said. "I'll stay here with the boys."

"It's already nearly eight. I'm sure you want to get Josh ready for bed, too. There's school tomorrow."

"Well, does Jesse have an extra pair of pajamas? If we could borrow them, I'll get both boys ready here. If you're late, I'll tuck them in somewhere together and haul Josh home whenever you get back. It'll be fine."

The idea was so practical, the suggestion made with so little fanfare, Rose didn't know how to signal her gratitude for Liz's swift and genuine friendship. She could think of ten reasons Jesse wouldn't like this idea—he didn't like sharing a bed, he might not want to give a pair of his pajamas to anyone else, he had a very specific bedtime routine . . .

"Are you sure?" She ignored the negative warnings.

"Very sure. Dewey's right. You should at least see what you're in for come morning."

Rose's heart sank further. Maybe she didn't want to know. "All right. But it really shouldn't take long. Should it?"

"It doesn't have to," Dewey agreed.

She knew she had to go. With a heavy sigh for the curtailed night and for being thrust back into combat mode, she went reluctantly to explain to Jesse that she was leaving.

They drove in silence for several blocks, the atmosphere in Dewey's car awkward but not painful. The air crackled more with electricity than discomfort, and Rose was sharply aware of his hand, which she'd held willingly, now resting on the shift lever. She wanted to touch him. Their last interaction had been so cool, she couldn't understand why every moment around him was so hot.

"Did you have a good time with Church?" His question, although quiet, startled her as much as if he'd shouted it.

"I get it, that's what this is about. Is there really something going on at the library?"

"Okay, I'm an idiot, but I'm not cruel. Making up a story like that would be downright mean."

"It would be."

"I was making polite chitchat. Isn't that what girls like?"

She smiled, staring at the dashboard. "First of all, thanks for·calling me a girl. Second, no. Chitchat from another girl. No chitchat from a guy. Meaningful conversation— now there's a fantasy."

"Fine."

"The date was nice. He's a sweet guy. Kinda pretty."

She didn't understand the look of pure shock he gave her. "Is that bad?" he asked.

" 'Course not. Everyone likes pretty things. They're fun to wear out to parties."

"Oh, for crying out loud," he said. "I'm not talking in metaphors with you. That's stupid."

"Hey, at least you know what a metaphor is."

"I know lots of stuff. Just tell me whether or not you like the guy."

"Why, are you jealous?"

"I kissed you, and I liked it. Sure, I'm jealous. But it's not like we're going out. If you're dating the man, I want to know."

All the worry, the fear, the anger over the library dissipated as warmth burst through her veins. He was jealous? And he admitted it?

"I didn't tell him I wouldn't go out again," she said. "But I didn't tell him I would either."

"Well, that made my position clear as mud."

"What do you want your position to be, Dewey?"

He didn't have time to answer. They pulled past the Loon Feather, and a full block from the library Rose could see activity on the small hillside. Two, maybe three small lanterns sat along the edge of the sidewalk, illuminating ghostly figures. Dewey pulled closer, and Rose could see what the figures were doing. A hard gasp escaped her throat.

"Oh, no, Dewey. This is insane!"

He finally reached over and took her hand. Along the sidewalk and halfway up the hill were signs—not a few, but hundreds. Her small group of protestors had turned the library into a graveyard, and every single sign looked like a tombstone.

Chapter Sixteen

DEWEY COULD SEE Rose struggling like a caged lioness in her seat. He could feel it through her skin and in the rigidity of her fingers. Anger wafted off her, and he wasn't sure he should stop the car. Maybe it was best if he let her have this look and then took her home to process it.

"Let me out." She took the decision away from him with a tight, heated demand.

"It won't do you any good to antagonize them now."

"It didn't do *them* any good to antagonize *me*."

"Rose, listen. Why don't we see if Sam Baker is up? Or one of the council members. Or Chief Hewett. Maybe the group is in violation of some kind of law. This is library property, and they shouldn't be trespassing."

Her steeled eyes showed she thought about his suggestion—for a microsecond. "Look, there's Pat Dunn, and there's Brian Duncan. They're about to find out what happens when you piss off the librarian. Stop the car and let me out."

"I'm not going to do that until I see you're rational. You're too smart to jump out half-cocked—"

"Dewey . . ." She sounded like approaching thunder.

He dropped her hand and maneuvered into a spot along the curb. Unease gurgled in his stomach. She launched herself out of the car before he'd shut off the engine.

"Hey, I'm coming with you."

"Fine."

She marched directly past the half-dozen people planting signs with the intensity of master gardeners and found Pat directing traffic like a construction boss.

"Would you like to explain exactly what's going on here?" Rose demanded.

"Good evening, Rose. I think it's obvious we're organizing a protest."

"You're organizing a mob scene—this is extremely inappropriate."

"Excuse me?" Dewey thought Pat sounded openly hostile now. "You are hardly one to lecture about what's inappropriate. We've asked you as politely as we can to honor the traditions of our town. You've come blowing in here and have thumbed your nose at everything we hold to be important. You're the one not being appropriate."

"Do we live in the same country?" Rose countered. "How can you be serious? The United States was founded on the principle of free speech. You cannot simply ban a book because you don't like it. Besides, there are procedures. I showed you what they are."

"Of course we can. If the town votes to keep something off the shelves, then off the shelves it will stay. This is a campaign to show people who've been perfectly happy with the way things have been run for a hundred years that newcomers can't come in and run roughshod over our town."

"Roughshod?" Rose's face flushed beneath an outward expression of calm. "Just because nobody has ever brought this town into the twenty-first century doesn't mean I'm running roughshod because I'm trying to do it now. I'd like you to remove these signs and act like the thinking adult I believe you are. What kind of example are you setting for our children? For our adults who love to read? That one small group of people gets to choose what's appropriate?"

"That's precisely what they need to learn. That one small group of people can effect change against wrong-headed decisions."

Dewey placed a hand on Rose's upper arm, gently, half-afraid she was going to punch the woman.

"Pat," he said, "this is a lot of signage for a small library. I think it might be a little overkill."

"And you've fallen in with the devil, I see."

"Now, wait a minute." He pulled Rose beside him. "That's getting a little personal. You might want to be careful."

"You know I mean the ideas," she said. "It's nothing personal—this is all about decency."

"Well, this number of signs is indecent," Rose said. "I plan to contact the police and mayor first thing and have you removed."

"You can certainly try, but we did our homework. We are on public property more than a hundred feet from the building. We are fully within our rights."

Dewey felt an angry retort rising within Rose before she spoke a single word. It was time to get her off the battlefield.

"I'm not sure what happened in your life to make you such a frightened, closed-minded person," Rose said. "But I'm sorry for you. Fight this all you want, but I think you'll find you've gone about this the wrong way. All these signs are only going to draw attention *to* my cause."

"Come on," Dewey whispered in her ear. "Time to go. You can't accomplish anything here tonight."

For an instant, she stubbornly held her ground. Finally, the tension left her body although her face remained scrunched and angry. She opened her mouth, but Dewey spun her toward him and placed a finger on her lips.

"You ended with the last word. Come on."

She slipped from his grip and marched back to his car. He sighed and looked back at Pat along with all the protestors who'd stopped to listen to the exchange. "This is ridiculous, people. It's a stupid thing to protest. You aren't going to fix anything with these tactics."

He followed Rose to the street, where she stood shaking beside the car door. Sorry for her pain, he wrapped his arm around her. "Don't worry," he said. "It'll be all right."

"Darn right," she said through gritted teeth. "Two can play at this game."

Liz fairly danced in delight when Dewey and Rose reported back to the house. The boys were newly clad in pajamas and sketching away in one of Josh's notebooks. Dewey could hear them arguing about whether Jesse should change something in his drawing.

"I tell you what," Liz said. "This town could use a good controversy. It's a great place, I'm glad I moved here. But it's caught in a bit of a time warp."

"They seem to think I'm the devil come to corrupt them."

"Oh, don't let them say that! You're an angel. And tomorrow you'll be an avenging angel. Would you mind if I came by and watched the action?"

"I would be thrilled and honored if you came. How would you like to help me make my own set of posters?"

"Really? What are they going to say?"

"I want people to come by and see what all the shouting's about. A 'come and see if YOU think these books should be banned' kind of thing. I don't know—you're a writer, you could think up a good slogan for us."

"Okay, I will."

Liz winked at Dewey, and he smiled. All at once he felt like a musketeer—on the side of right, but outnumbered. It got his blood pumping almost as hard as Rose's flushed and determined face did. Maybe Liz was right. Kennison Falls could use a little shake-up. *He* could use a little shake-up.

Liz and Josh left soon afterward, once the boys made peace over Jesse's fire engine.

"I can't believe she's actually going to help," Rose said when they'd pulled away. "I feel like we honestly bonded.

I haven't had a friend like that in more years than I can remember."

"That's sad."

"It's not. I don't mean I didn't have friends, because I did—through Jesse's school and at the YMCA where I belonged. But they weren't do-anything-for-you friends. Elizabeth Cassidy? I've loved her books for years, and now she steps in and I feel like I've known her forever. It blows me away. Your sister is kind of like that, too."

He wanted to be included in that list—as unmasculine as that sounded—and he had to stop himself from begging for an invitation into her new circle of friends.

"Elle can talk to a lamppost and get its life story," he said. "She'd invite Jack the Ripper to coffee and have a good time."

"She called me before you got here tonight, by the way. Says she'll pick me up in the morning and have my car back to me before lunch. How'd she manage that?"

"I told you—she can sweet-talk a vampire out of his fangs. She wheedled a radiator out of the distributor in Minneapolis and drove to get it herself."

"She's good at this, Dewey."

"Yeah." He agreed reluctantly, still not sure why he bucked so hard against his little sister choosing such a grungy, unfeminine lifestyle.

"Be nice to her."

"Hey, I love Elle. I want her to be smart and have it all."

"How she does smart is her choice."

"Yeah. Well, look, I should go."

"Would you . . . wait? I'm going to put Jesse to bed; it'll take about ten minutes. Liz is a teetotaler, so I drank cider with her, but I would love to open the bottle of wine I have in the refrigerator."

The invitation honestly took him by surprise. His heartbeat picked up speed and flipped around his chest like it belonged to a teenager asked to the dance.

"All right. If you want," he said.

"I do want."

"Come on. Say good night to Jess, and then maybe you'd be willing to open the wine?"

By the time Rose got back, Dewey had finished sneaking around the house he actually knew well from his weeks helping remodel it. He'd checked out the surface changes she'd made, and there was no denying she'd turned it into a comfortable home in the past short month. She liked blue and sage green and touches of sunset colors like purple, yellow, and deep, rosy reds. She'd hung several floral pictures and one beautiful landscape. The kitchen now boasted a Tuscan wine and grape theme in the floor rug and towels and a couple of fabric thingies covering the table and counters. It was quite different from his dark, rustic log house four miles out of town. He'd built it almost ten years before and had changed nothing since his mother and sister helped him decorate it in '90s slate blue, off-white, and the peachy color they called salmon. He kept it neat enough, but all the decorating was Early American Guy Technology or with things he'd picked up at thrift stores because they fit some weird space. It definitely didn't have any fabric thingies or themed throw rugs.

"Hi," she said, finding him in the first-floor family room checking out her forty-two-inch plasma TV.

"Hey," he replied and picked up her glass of wine from the coaster he'd found on an end table.

"Thanks for staying. I . . . I didn't want to wander around here alone rehashing the scene from tonight. I wasn't very polite or smart, even though you warned me."

"You were perfect. Although I thought you might hit Pat at one point."

"I felt the urge." She smiled. "But that would have been really stupid."

"Yup. It would have been."

"I wanted to say thank you, too, for coming in the first place. Not everyone would take that big an interest."

"Look, it still bothers me that they haven't found the rock thrower. On my way home, I kind of swung by the library to see if someone happened to be skulking around. I hit the mother lode tonight. I didn't think about anything except telling you."

"It's funny. I don't own that building, but it feels every bit like my home. I'm sure that's the wrong way to look at it. I need to let this stuff roll off my shoulders a little better."

He guided her to the big sofa she had in front of the television and sat with her.

"No, it's not the wrong way. Your love for the library shines all around you. It's your most attractive quality."

She laughed, and like always, the music of it turned his brain to a purée of words and feelings he didn't know how to sort out. "Wow, there's a line sure to sweep a girl off her feet."

"That's me. A regular Cyrano de Bergerac."

"Again with a literary reference? Mr. Mitchell, are you trying to seduce me?" She giggled—actually giggled—after her three sips of wine.

"If I thought I had a chance in hell of it being successful, I'd say yes."

He swallowed, trying to sound lighthearted, hoping she couldn't feel the heaviness in the air or the heat suddenly radiating from every pore of his skin because her mere proximity turned his insides into superheated emotion.

He must not have succeeded, because her giggling stopped. Her lips paused at the rim of her wine glass, plump, beckoning, wet from the sweet Riesling that had just passed over them.

She didn't meet his eyes. Instead, she focused lower, on his mouth, and neither of them moved or spoke. The air grew heavier still, affecting his breathing, weighing on his entire body and creating a pull so deep he couldn't control the desire it produced. Slowly, she lowered the glass and licked her bottom lip unconsciously.

"You never know until you try," she whispered.

He groaned in surrender and took her glass. Without analyzing anything, he drank from it, set it down on the coffee table, and pulled her to him, swallowing just before their lips met and fused, and he closed his eyes to sink into the soft, wine-infused kiss.

THE NIGHT'S EVENTS, the worry, the physical room around them disappeared when Rose surrendered to

Dewey's hot, unexpected kiss. He opened his mouth and invited her into the intimate warmth. The wine he'd sipped from her glass glazed every surface and melted against her tongue before going straight to her head.

He pushed back with his own tongue, bringing the sweet alcohol taste to her. She tangoed with him there, then moved back into his mouth, where he suckled a moment before moving to her lips and gently worrying first the bottom and then the top with his teeth. The soft hairs of his mustache tickled the skin beneath her nose, sending tender shoots of desire twining through her body.

He grasped the sides of her head, and she copied him. He groaned, and she groaned in response as the kiss intensified. A tiny mewling sound filled her ears, and she recognized it as hers. She allowed it to swell into a moan of capitulation and clambered onto his lap, straddling his thighs, pressing her breasts to his hard chest.

"Oh, yeah," he whispered into the kiss, sending a fresh army of goose bumps down her back. He dragged on her hips until she meshed with him in timeless perfection.

A thrill, hard and sweet, shot through her, and their tongues moved together in play and discovery. He was masterful in the way he kissed, raising their desire in increments so steady she didn't know how close she was to the next level of passion until she gasped and pulled away in shock.

His large, warm hand slipped beneath the back hem of her sweater and splayed across her back, kneading and soothing and sweeping cautiously around her ribs until he found her breast through the soft fabric of her bra. Her eyes drifted closed, and she arched into the touch.

"What are we doing?" she asked.

"I think that's fairly obvious." He twisted his head to the side and kissed her throat. Again the mustache tantalized like feathers drawn across her skin.

"Don't be obtuse." She whimpered at the chills raining over her.

"I'm not. I work out plenty and eat healthy."

"Dork."

He captured her mouth again, and kneaded through the satin over her breast to raise the sensitive nipple. Her chills turned into a storm, pelting her with sensations she couldn't fight.

She combed through his thick, sable hair and pressed into his scalp, learning its topography, journeying across his entire head, loving the shivers she could physically feel in him. Without planning she rocked forward, and her hips took on a slow, slow rhythm they found all by themselves. He pushed her bra up and over her flesh and touched her bare skin, allowing a deep, rumbling laugh when she groaned and arched harder.

"Nice," he whispered.

"Dewey?"

"I know. This is unexpected."

"Pretty." She closed her eyes when his fingers played against her like a pianist. "Very."

"This is what happens when a fix-it guy gets jealous."

"Maybe I should go out with Church again—"

He growled and flipped her off his lap and onto her back so quickly she laughed with the surprise. Dipping his head at the same time he shoved up her sweater, he found a spot beneath her exposed breast and nuzzled it ruthlessly.

"I can't tell you what to do," he said.

"Oh, I think you're making your wishes pretty clear."

His mouth closed over her sensitized nipple. She sank into the euphoria and pulled his head closer. But when the shivers pierced too deeply, and the liquid within her turned into a heated river, she pushed him away from his amazing work and made him look at her.

"I think I like you," he said.

"Under the circumstances," she panted, "I'm awfully glad to hear it." She wriggled to push him farther away, and he allowed it, pulling her up to sit. She curled into his embrace, burying her head against his chest, clamping her arm tightly across his stomach. "But I have to slow down. Things . . . are happening awfully fast, suddenly."

"But you're all right? With this?" he asked.

"I . . . am." The answer surprised and pleased her. "But how is it possible? This is probably the longest we've gone without irking each other."

He didn't answer her question; he smiled. "I think one of the things I like most about you is the way you use words nobody else uses."

She ran her hand over his abs, smoothing up over his chest and around to his back. She tested the taut muscles through the cotton of his plaid button-down shirt, learned the breadth of his body, and reveled in the immovable quality of *him*.

"I may know some words," she said at last. "But I don't know one for this. For us. I might like this. I might want it. But I don't know what it means. I've never wanted a relationship."

"You've never been married? Never been serious?"

"I've been serious, always because my parents wanted it. But married? No."

"I was married for six years."

"Really? What happened? I'm sorry; I didn't mean that to sound judgmental."

He was quiet such a long time she pulled back to study him. His face was a pallet of emotions—slight uncertainty, which she'd never seen in him before, a shadow of hurt, and desire that mirrored her own.

"I couldn't give her children."

Blunt and matter-of-fact, the words shocked but only told a small part of what had to be a larger story. After he spoke, however, the unfamiliar emotions eased away from his features.

"I . . . I'm sorry," she said.

There was nothing else *to* say. She didn't know what it meant that he couldn't *give* her children, and the explanation left more questions than it answered, but she hesitated to ask them. The ease of their teasing and the comfort in the way they bantered fled while she waited for him to explain. But he didn't. He shrugged. "We were young at the time, but I thought Rachel was the love of my life. 'Life stinks sometimes.' That's the reason she gave when she asked for the divorce."

"Oh, Dewey, that's harsh."

"It was. On the other hand, it was a long time ago now."

"How long?"

"Ten years."

"Well, you're definitely a free man, then." The joke felt vaguely inappropriate, but she wasn't sure what to do with the awkwardness that had sprouted.

"I am. And I'm not looking for sympathy, and I'm not asking you for anything serious. I'm happy because you didn't kick me out when I got to second base."

The awkwardness vanished. He seemed to be very good at easing difficult situations when he wanted to.

"Are you okay if that's all the further you get tonight?" She wiggled her brows, hoping to mask her own disappointment at stopping.

"If you make the decision it'll be easier to convince you that I would have stopped myself in another heartbeat."

"Would you have?"

"Fortunately, we don't have to find out. Let's just say this was the wise place to strand the players."

She relaxed against him, her arms loosening so her hands could roam freely again. The complete lack of expectation, the need to do nothing except explore their desire, left her drunk with luxury. He didn't want anything—he'd said so. She believed he meant it. Her parents would have loved the polite and heroic Church with his eager attitude. They'd roll their eyes at the laconic Dewey, content with second base. She laughed softly.

"What?" he asked.

"I know you're a football guy, but this is why I kind of like baseball. It's slower, more thoughtful."

"Nothing wrong with baseball." He kissed the top of her head and drew small, exact circles with his thumb on the palm he upturned in his lap. "The great American pastime, right? But maybe someday we'll practice a few end-zone runs, too. I'm not a bad coach."

He proved it to her with another kiss, long, sweet, deep and, very quickly, dangerous.

"Now," he said, lifting his head and stopping it himself this time. "What are you going to do tomorrow morning about the horde of insane people? Do you need moral support? Or an early breakfast to give you strength?"

Chapter Seventeen

JESSE WHINED FROM the moment he got up the next morning. Rose had no idea what his problem was, but she was too sleep deprived to question him. She all but shoved him, reluctant and sullen, onto the school bus, with barely half a bowl of oatmeal and a crustless piece of toast smeared with too much Nutella for his breakfast. She hadn't even fought about the cowboy boots. He wore them, his toe still bandaged against a pretty decent blister, and promised grumpily to change into tennis shoes for gym without complaint.

Elle pulled up right on time, but Rose had waffled over her wardrobe so long that she was the late one. For the briefest moment she flirted with staying home and letting the protestors have the run of the library grounds. But that wouldn't be fair to Kate.

And she'd bragged about not running from this fight.

Unfortunately, her fighting spirit was still curled up in a little ball, sleeping in. What she really wanted was for Dewey to come back. Maybe he'd shoot for third base . . .

A laugh nearly escaped as she sat beside Elle on the way to the library. It definitely wouldn't do to let Dewey's sister hear such inappropriate thoughts about her brother. Then again, maybe Elle was what she seemed: bright, eager, intuitive—she probably wouldn't think twice. Rose shook her head to clear it. She had no intention of spilling news of her tryst with Dewey to anyone.

Elle whistled as she pulled up in front of the library. "Wow, Dewey wasn't kidding."

The sight was creepier in the daylight than it had been at night. On two sides of the corner hill, signs plastered the lawn. This group had certainly gotten organized—there had to be a hundred and fifty hand-drawn and printed placards.

"Save Our Children's Minds." "Support Morality." "Keep Kennison Falls a Family Town." And twenty or so books had their own signs, including Elizabeth Cassidy's *I Thought It Was Love,* the young adult book supposedly too full of talk about rape and feelings about sex to be considered appropriate.

"This is out of hand," Rose muttered.

"Amen to that," Elle replied.

"Well, you can let me out here. I'm pretty much planning to ignore them while I figure out my moves. The smartest one is probably to do nothing until the town council meeting."

Elle smiled sympathetically. "If there's anything I can do, let me know."

"Stick up for the library if anyone says anything to you."

"Consider it done. I'll have your car here by lunchtime. Going back to finish it right now."

"That sounds great, Elle. Thank you."

"Do you want me to walk up there with you?"

"No. Thanks, but they aren't dangerous, just aggravating. I'll see you later."

She made no eye contact with any of the protestors even though they started a chant as she walked toward the door. "No Banned Books Week. No Banned Books Week."

She made it to the door before she was confronted by Reverend Coburn who, this time, offered no cordial greeting.

"I hope we have your attention this morning, Ms. Rose."

"You've had my attention every day, Reverend Nathan." She met his eyes, unflinching.

He hesitated, then allowed a thin smile, as if he realized the battle was joined. "I do hope you've reconsidered your position. I think you can see that we're willing to make life a little unpleasant."

"First of all, I don't need to *reconsider* my position because I've considered it thoroughly from the beginning." She adjusted her purse and the bag containing her own library books. "Second, the library is warm, bright, and cheerful, and that's where I'll be all day—along with the patrons who come to enjoy their right to read. You all might be uncomfortable out here, but I intend to be the opposite."

She left the reverend's slack jaw behind and unlocked the front door. Once inside, she locked it again and pulled out her phone. On the way to her small office, she texted Kate to come in the back door when she arrived. All that was left to do besides set up for the day and take a first look through her e-mail was worry that the protestors might scare off patrons.

"G'morning, Rose!"

She looked up half an hour later into Kate's perpetually happy face. "Hey!" Rose said. "How'd you sneak in without me hearing? I didn't think I'd be able to concentrate at all."

"Good. Glad you got some work done. It's time to open the doors. I think there are actually people out there who aren't part of the knuckle-draggers carrying signs."

Rose grinned. "I thought we'd agreed to be kind and professional."

"Nuts to that. Let's . . . I dunno. Toss peanuts to them like they're monkeys in the zoo. They're starting to give me a permanent headache."

"I know. If it's like mine, it's pounding. Okay, unlock the door. But today, no protestors allowed inside. I'll play bad cop."

"No fair."

"Okay, you play bad cop."

She pumped her fist. "Yes! I'll go open the door."

With Kate's good humor, Rose had the audacity to think the day was looking up. No sooner had the first ten curious patrons come through the door buzzing with opinions about the rally outside, however, than Rose's cell phone rang. Her stomach dropped when she saw the number.

"Rose Hanrehan," she said.

"Good morning, Ms. Hanrehan. This is Linda Verum."

God, give me strength.

She should have known better than to put Jesse on that bus in a mood.

"Good morning, Mrs. Verum. What's happened?"

"I have Jesse here with me. I'm hoping you might have a few minutes to come and help calm him and take care of a small disciplinary matter. It seems Jesse slammed one of his classmate's fingers in a book and called another one an inappropriate name, but we can't get him to tell us what happened in his own words. He's a little distraught."

"Of course." She sighed, her heart aching. "Oh. Wait. I don't have a vehicle today. It may be a little while before I get there. Half an hour, perhaps. I'm sorry."

"We'll keep him occupied. Thank you, Ms. Hanrehan."

Hangover-caliber throbbing started behind her eyes and thrummed in her temples.

"Anything wrong?" Kate asked.

"It's Jesse again. I'm so sorry. I have to go talk to the principal. It shouldn't be more than an hour. Probably less. I'm hoping they'll send him back to class after we discuss whatever it is he's done."

"Poor Jesse. Adjusting is tough."

"I don't know what it is. He was out of sorts this morning. Maybe he's coming down with something. I can only hope there's some excuse. Is there any chance I can borrow your car?" She made the request somewhat sheepishly.

"Rose, I'm sorry. I had Ken drop me off today."

Of course she had.

"It's no problem. I'll call Elle and see if she's got an idea when my car will be done."

She punched Elle's number.

"Dewey Mitchell."

The surprise of hearing his voice took away her voice at first. Then warmth burst through her chest, easing the worry lodged there. "Hey! I was sure I called your sister."

"Hi there, Ump."

"Huh?"

"The one who stopped me at second base."

"Very funny." She smiled into the phone. "And as nice as it is to hear your voice this morning—believe me—I was hoping to talk to Elle."

"She's off with the tow truck. I'm not thrilled that she left her phone on my desk."

"You *let* her take the truck?"

"Okay, okay, I was a jerk. Give a guy a break. I let her go this time."

"You did. And we should celebrate. Unfortunately, I need a car. I need to go deal with some kind of Jesse crisis at school again. I was hoping maybe she'd know when the Mustang would be done."

"It's finished. We were going to return it when she gets back. I'll be right there."

"Dewey, you don't have to come—"

"If I don't, how do you expect to get to your son?"

"All right. I'm sorry to pull you away from work."

"Joey's here—we'll be fine. See you in five."

She didn't want him to keep taking her to school. She didn't want him to keep seeing Jesse at his worst. If he was ever to change his mind fully about her son . . .

"Rose!"

She looked into Liz's breathless features. Her new friend leaned over Rose's desk and set an eight-and-a-half-by-eleven-inch flyer in front of her. The mini-poster was stunning.

"What's this? Already?"

"I couldn't sleep last night."

"Lot of that going around."

"Wait. Dewey didn't stay overnight?" She actually looked scandalized.

Rose chuckled. This must be the conservative side Liz always talked about rearing its head. "No, not even close. Second base."

"Oh." She shook her head. "It's none of my business, sorry. The thing is, I started working on these and couldn't stop. I took the liberty of stopping at the copy place and made fifty copies. If you like them, I'll make more. Or we can tweak them. But I wanted to start countering the other signs as quickly as I could."

"You've already put some up?"

"I have. Wherever I could, I put them next to one of the other side's signs. But I put them other places, too. Hope you don't mind."

"Mind? I'm flabbergasted. You're amazing. *These* are amazing!"

Across the top in big block letters was the phrase "Come and Join the Banned." The poster had a few book covers, including Liz's own. Drawings of kids decorated most of the page. They were reading, using the books as musical instruments, holding them while princess tiaras and cowboy hats floated ethereally over their heads. In a standout square at the bottom, Rose read "Want to see what all the fuss is about? Come check out the fun of Banned Books Week at the new Kennison Falls Public Library. Come and find your good 'bad' book!"

Rose jumped from her chair, rushed around the desk, and threw her arms around Liz's shoulders. "You are wonderful. Did you draw the kids on here?"

Liz shrugged. "I'm not good, but I can sketch easy fun things like these."

"What's this? Group hug?" Dewey walked in on the embrace.

"You wish." Rose grinned. "Thank you so much for coming."

"Not a problem." He dangled a set of keys in front of Rose. "Miss Scarlet has been repaired." But when Rose grabbed for them with a sigh of relief, he pulled them away. "I'll drive you to school. I'm still testing the workmanship."

"Dewey," she warned. "This is *not* your—"

He held up his hands. "I can be taught. I'll wait in the car. If you have to bring Jesse home, which I pray you don't—or won't, I don't want you mama bearing him while you're driving."

"Mama bearing?"

"Being a mama bear. You know."

"Coddling him, you mean." She tried to look annoyed. It was impossible while looking at the mouth that had thrilled her the night before.

"You? Never."

She marveled that she didn't want to smack him for meddling. My, how things changed after one night at second base.

"Come on, Mr. Buttinsky. Let's go."

The lighthearted banter disappeared in the car. Dewey drove as promised, and he took her hand once they were underway, kneading her fingers softly together, comforting her but unsuccessful in halting her growing agitation.

"What's up with Jesse Loren Hanrehan today?" he asked.

Her sigh sounded pathetically nervous even to her. "I wish I knew. Something about slamming someone's fingers in a book and using bad language again. I don't know *what's* going on. He had troubles on and off in his old school, but he was never the source of the problems. Not directly."

"One bad thing about small towns and small schools is that the kids are a little, what do kids call it? Cliquey. When you're new, it's hard to blend in, because most of the kids have known each other since preschool. Jess has to hang tough, and eventually he'll make friends."

"But you know him, he's not tough."

"Rose. He's way tougher than you think he is."

She didn't respond. Truly, she wasn't annoyed with him, but Dewey didn't understand. Jesse's brain didn't work exactly like other kids' brains. She'd spent ten years figuring out when to sit him down and tell him what he'd done was inappropriate, and when to sympathize and let him know that he was fine the way he was. He wasn't a tough little boy. He was a tenderhearted, easily bruised little boy who might never understand the social cues most people took for granted.

When Dewey pulled the Mustang into the small elementary school parking lot, he put it in park, lifted Rose's hand again, and brought it to his lips. The gesture warmed as much as thrilled her—a chivalrous act from the guy who didn't always get social requirements himself.

"Go fix it, Mama Bear."

"You mean you really are staying here?" She'd fully expected him to renege on his promise to wait.

"I said I would."

She leaned over at that and kissed him on the side of the mouth. "Thank you."

He shook his head. "Don't act so surprised."

She smiled and opened the passenger door. "Be back with or without child as soon as I can."

"Leave him there if they're not making you take him home."

"There are some CDs in the console if you want something other than the radio." She sweetly ignored his directive. "See you in a few."

His mustache twitched.

This time, Jesse was not as sanguine as he'd been her first visit to school. He sat on a bench in the main office unmoving, his face a study in sad and mad. When he saw her, his little body slumped a little.

"Hey, kiddo, what's going on?"

"Kevin told everyone I was retarded and Seth took my book and I grabbed it back and his fingers got in the pages when I closed it, but he told Mr. Joseph I did it on purpose and I said Seth was a lying cheat and Mr. Joseph sent me here and Mrs. Verum said I had to sit and wait for you because I wouldn't tell what Seth did."

The breathless explanation barely made sense as Jesse let the story gush. He'd clearly been holding it all in. Rose knew the tactic. Jesse didn't bother with explanations if he thought nobody was going to listen or believe him. Somewhere along the line, he'd taken to heart the idea that he would only get into deeper trouble if he argued. In many ways, it was a lesson more people should learn. Other times, however, like this one, his silence only bought him the trouble.

"I'm sorry, honey. You could have told Mrs. Verum what happened."

"She doesn't believe me. I told her she wouldn't believe me anyway, and she said if I couldn't get along she would have to call my mom and I said good, you can call her."

He was like a little faucet that had been unclogged, and the words spewed out in front of pressure that had been building for hours. Usually only time relieved his agitation.

"Ms. Hanrehan?"

She turned to the principal's passive-featured face. She'd only met Linda Verum twice, and those times she'd been in cheerful meet-and-greet mode. This time, with black hair pulled back into a severe chignon, and her eyes giving away nothing except the look of an administrator used to dealing with defensive parents, she was slightly more intimidating.

"Thank you for calling me," Rose said.

"Come on into my office." She offered a half smile then, not cold but devoid of true warmth.

They settled into the small space crowded with files and adorned with plenty of family pictures.

"Normally," she began, "we wouldn't have called you in for a minor scuffle in a classroom. But Jesse seemed to need you here, and I thought it best we let you know."

"Sometimes he has difficulty making his feelings known."

It took a solid ten minutes to get the full story from her son. When it turned out that the teasing had begun once again because he'd sat mute and refused to participate in a class discussion, Rose sighed with frustration. Not because she was upset he'd clammed up—the teacher supposedly understood that little quirk, too—but because she didn't know how to help Jesse or the administration understand that this was a matter of educating everyone. Of helping the kids who teased him understand that Jesse would eventually even out his behavior, and of helping Jesse understand that he needed to stay calm when other kids teased.

"Jesse," she said. "You know that if you don't like what the teacher is saying, you can't blurt it out. You need to talk to him by yourself."

"But he was wrong."

"It sounds like he wasn't wrong. He didn't give as much detail about where the Declaration of Independence was signed as you wanted him to give." Jesse was accomplished at anything that required memorization. He knew too many esoteric tidbits about too many things. No other fourth-graders cared.

"Well, he should give the details. He told me I could use what was right in my own work, but I didn't need to share it all with the class."

So he'd shut down completely and refused to answer questions. During a break, the "retarded" name had come out.

"And Jesse, you can't take revenge by hurting others," Mrs. Verum said, a bit sternly.

"I didn't mean to. He took my book."

"And you snapped his fingers in it."

"He didn't move his fingers when the book shut."

"Jesse," she admonished.

"Look," Rose said. "I don't like parents who think their children never do wrong. But I would like you to consider that one thing Jesse doesn't do is lie. He's very black and white about most things. He should apologize for catching the other boy's fingers, but if he says he didn't intentionally snap the book, then that's how he perceives it. Sometimes he needs to be shown how things are perceived by others."

The principal looked at Jesse slightly less critically. "Do you think you can apologize to Seth?"

Jesse shook his head.

"Honey, even if you didn't do something on purpose, if someone gets hurt it's good to say you're sorry he got hurt."

"But he doesn't have to say I'm sorry for calling me retarded?"

He had a point.

"Yes, he will," Mrs. Verum said.

"There you go." Rose gave him a hug, which he shrugged off. "You can go back to class, and everything will be good."

"I don't want to go back."

The kiss of death. Rose's heart dropped. "Sure you do."

"No. Tomorrow."

She lived in deathly fear that Jesse would melt down in front of his teacher or, worse, the class, and then his reputation would be solidified. If she forced him to go back, that was a definite possibility.

"I think you'll find that everyone has forgotten what happened," Mrs. Verum said. "And your class is about to head for gym."

Rose nearly groaned out loud. If she'd wanted a way to assure Jesse's noncooperation, she'd found it.

"No gym," he said and folded his little arms like a miniature politician.

"You don't like gym?"

"We're learning football. I hate football."

For the first time, Rose thought of Dewey sitting in the car waiting for her to come out without Jesse in tow. He'd never understand a kid who was skipping school because he didn't want to play football.

"You still have to try," she said. "You can't skip gym class."

"I'll go tomorrow."

It would be much easier on him and on her to take him now. But then she remembered the forest of signs on the lawn at the library, and knew she'd only have to protect Jesse from whatever confrontations might arise because of protests. Burying her head in her hands and crying would have been a comfort. Burying it in the sand and ignoring all this would have been heavenly. She sighed—yet again—and very nearly gave in. She knew exactly how Jesse felt. If he went back, he was afraid he'd get teased more. If she went back with Jesse in tow, she was afraid Dewey would lose all respect for her.

It made her a little angry that she even cared what Dewey thought. She'd already decided he didn't understand. And she'd never bowed to pressure over how she dealt with Jesse. But the sad fact was, now it did matter.

So who won, mother or son?

"You need to go back to class," she said, before she could change her mind.

"I don't want to."

"I know. People are still angry at me at work, too," she said. "And I don't want to go back there either. But we're smart enough to know we have to, right? How about if I come all the way to school and pick you up after you're done? You don't have to ride the bus today."

He stared and started bumping his feet against the legs of the chair in which he sat.

"Jesse?"

"Okay."

"And you'll apologize to Seth?"

"If he apologizes to me."

"I will make sure he does, and so will Kevin," the principal promised.

Jesse shrugged.

"Come here," Rose stood. When Jesse trudged the two steps into her arms, she squeezed, and this time he allowed it. "You can do this."

"You can do it, too."

By some miracle, he'd let his anger go. She felt fairly confident he wouldn't fall apart this moment. She wouldn't place a bet on two hours from now.

Chapter Eighteen

DEWEY ARRIVED AT the middle school practice field early, expecting to have time to set up a couple of drills before the kids arrived. His mood soared, sunny as the early autumn day. He'd found himself whistling, for crying out loud, after Rose had dropped him back at the station once she'd finished her meeting at the school. She hadn't said much about the problem, only that Jesse had calmed down and gone back to class. And she'd kissed him, Dewey Mitchell, good-bye of her own volition, right in front of the garage where anybody could have seen. The pleasure from her boldness still lingered six hours later.

The lone figure seated on one of the sideline benches with his hunched back to the parking lot, took Dewey by surprise. By the time he was halfway from his car to the field, he recognized Jason Peterson, but the boy didn't look right. His missing humble-but-optimistic attitude was as obvious as a broken limb.

"Hey, Coach," he said as Dewey drew up beside him. "I got here early."

"You did. Wanna help me set up some poles?"

"Sure, okay."

Jason stood and made an obvious effort to smile. Dewey usually left the emotional mentoring to Adrian, but he couldn't see letting the boy lumber this morosely through the next half hour.

"Everything okay, Jason?"

"Yeah." He hesitated. "No."

"Want to spill the trouble?"

"Yeah. I was kinda hoping you'd be the first coach here."

Dewey took the compliment in stride without giving away the pleasure he received from the words. "What's up?"

"I . . . you know how . . . they're trying to find the person who threw, you know, the rock at the library?"

Dewey honestly didn't think he could handle a confession from this kid.

"I do."

"I think, I mean I might, know who it was."

"You do?" Again, Dewey hid his inner reaction. Chief Hewett had run out of leads along with ideas for finding them. Whoever the vandal was had so far succeeded in getting away with the Kennison Falls crime of the year. "Can you tell me?"

"I don't want to tell on him. I want him to come forward by himself. But he's kind of mad and stubborn."

"I suppose. He probably doesn't want to get in trouble."

"No. But you're pretty good at knowing what to say to

guys to get them to do what they're supposed to. I thought maybe you could tell me what to do."

At that, Dewey couldn't keep the surprise out of his voice or, he assumed, off his face. He rubbed the corner of his mouth with one thumb. "Jason, that's real nice of you, but it's pretty hard to convince someone to turn himself in for a crime. I'm not sure what to tell you. Don't you think it would be better for you to tell someone and let the authorities deal with this?"

Jason stood silently for so long Dewey almost asked him again, but something made him wait. Finally, Jason looked up and Dewey was horrified to see tears in the boy's eyes.

"He's my cousin."

Oh jeez, what the hell do I do with this?

"I'm sorry," he offered at last. "This is tough for you. Are you close to him?" Dewey placed a hand on his shoulder.

"Not really. Not anymore. He's like my second cousin or something, and he's like a year younger than me. I used to play with him, but now I only see him at school and family stuff. He hangs out with different guys."

"What makes you think he threw the rock?"

"We had my grandpa's birthday last weekend, and this cousin was there. I heard him bragging how his mom hated the new library and he did, too. He said she thinks there are bad books in there, and she doesn't like the lady who runs the library now."

Dewey's heart rate accelerated at the oblique reference to Rose. He found it hard to keep from grilling the boy for every piece of information he could get out of him. But this wasn't Jason's fault, of course. "Is his mom one of those people protesting at the library?"

"I don't know. I don't think so. I think she just agrees with it. His family is kinda weird, actually."

Dewey's heartache eased, and he allowed a short laugh. "We all have weird family members."

"Anyway, he said he was doing stuff to make trouble at the stupid library. He said he'd damaged it already, and all it took was a couple of rocks. I mean, he must have thrown the one that broke the big window."

"He told you this?"

"No. He had one of his friends with him. They didn't know I heard."

The whole thing was surreal. "Do I know this cousin of yours?"

"He doesn't play football or anything."

"Are you sure it's a good idea to talk to him yourself?"

"He doesn't hate me or anything. I talk to him sometimes, I just don't hang out with him. I'd say something if I knew what to say."

Dewey blew the breath he held out in a loud whoosh. "C'mon, sit down." He sat on the bench with Jason beside him and leaned forward, elbows on his widespread thighs. "This is a tough one. I really don't think it would be telling on him if, first of all, you aren't really sure he did it and, second, if you aren't breaking a promise not to tell."

"I know, but I think he has some, like, learning problems. He's always in special classes. I don't want him to get in trouble."

Jason was too nice for his own good.

"Sometimes it's better to get them in a little trouble before they get into worse trouble because nobody cared to help them."

Jason pondered that and leaned forward, too, mimicking Dewey's posture. "I guess."

"You can think about it. How about that?"

"Will I be in trouble for not telling right away?"

"No." Dewey chuckled. "Haven't you told anyone? Your folks?"

"No way. My dad is cool, but he gets kind of mad when people are stupid. He'd go rushing over, and then it would make everything weird."

"Yeah. My dad was kind of like that, too. Well, listen. I think you should tell your dad or your mom and have them take you to the police. All you have to do is say what you heard. Let them take care of the rest. They don't have to let on who told them."

"They don't?"

"No. They can say they followed leads."

"It would be better if I told him, and he didn't think I was a snitch."

"Well, you can think about that, too."

They sat quietly again for several long seconds. Jason jiggled one knee nervously, as if the question he wasn't sure he should ask was shaking itself loose.

"What?" Dewey asked.

"Would you talk to him?"

"Me?"

"If I got him here?"

"You think you could?"

"I don't know. Maybe."

"Aw, Jason. I want to find the person who threw that rock. And I'd like him to be punished. But if what you say is true, I'd also like him to get help. I'm not sure me talking to him would make any difference."

"I don't know either." His crestfallen features flickered between sadness and anger. "I wish I hadn't heard him."

"Don't blame you. But you think about how good it will make people feel to know who did the damage."

"Yeah. Coach?"

"Huh?"

"Are you going to tell I told you?"

"No. That's your job."

"Thanks."

"And you know if for some reason you got your cousin here, I would talk to him. But that's not your first option. Okay?"

"Okay."

"Let's get that drill grid set up. You have a good practice today, and you'll get rid of some of that worry." He slapped Jason on the back. "Buck up. We'll fix this. Like your shoulder pads, right?"

He got a genuine smile at that.

It was all Dewey could do not to tell Rose that night about his talk with Jason. She invited him for dinner and, thankfully for once, Jesse rattled on about his day at school and how the boy who'd gotten him into trouble had finally said he was sorry, but he really wasn't. And how they were learning football in gym, but Dewey knew how crappy he played football; that was why he hated it.

Dewey's interest picked up at that. What little boy hated football and every other sport that had to do with balls? He wondered what on Earth he could do to turn the boy into less of a pale, geeky kid. Yet, he shouldn't be wondering such a thing at all.

Rose would be infuriated.

He watched her over the dinner table, rapt at her son's lengthy report of his day. Something special shone from her eyes at his words. As much as Dewey was growing to care about her, and the boy, he knew nothing that he could give her would ever come close to competing with the relationship she had with Jesse.

"What would make you like gym class?" he asked.

"If they had Wii bowling or horses."

Dewey exchanged a glance of amusement with Rose. Her eyebrows lifted into her caramel-colored bangs with such attractive surprise he wanted to go kiss them back into place. Instead, he focused on Jesse.

"You really did like the riding, huh?"

"My boots don't hurt much anymore. I can ride by myself now."

"You think so?"

Jesse nodded matter-of-factly.

"Maybe one more time with some help." Rose looked to him for backup.

"I can call Jill and see if she can help you again."

"She said we can all go on a trail ride. Mom, too."

"Whoa there, partner." Rose's eyes held genuine fear.

"You can! You don't have to be afraid. Jill has nice horses." Jesse nearly jumped from his chair.

"You and Dewey can go," Rose said.

"You'd really give up a chance to learn to ride again?" he asked.

"You bet I would."

"We'll talk about it."

"We *are* talking about it. You and Jesse can go with Jill." Her eyes twinkled, but she wasn't joking.

For several seconds, they locked gazes, and hers softened from one of defiant teasing to one filled with intriguing shadows. His stomach flopped lazily. She might not look at him with the intensity of a mama bear, but the smoke she did turn on him wasn't bad.

"I'll call Jill and see about this weekend. Is Sunday better for you?"

"It doesn't matter, remember? I don't have to be there."

"Riiight." He winked at Jesse. "We can pretend horseback riding is gym class, and this time it's your mom who doesn't like it."

His grin at her glare came easily and felt devilish. Teasing her when they weren't really angry was some of the best fun he'd had in a very long time. He found it more and more difficult to be annoyed at anything she did. She had vulnerable spots—enough to make him feel strong when he helped her—but she definitely wasn't weak. He marveled that simply being around her made his own weak spots feel whole and almost healed.

"This is why I told my mother I never needed men in my life." She grinned back at him and ruffled Jesse's hair. "Stay young, buddy. You're not *quite* this obnoxious yet."

"Didja hear that, Jesse James? We're obnoxious. Maybe you *are* an outlaw!"

"Awesome."

Rose let Jesse sit in front of the television while Dewey helped her with the dishes. They worked comfortably together, and he let her keep her thoughts to herself as they worked. She'd briefly mentioned the protests from the day but hadn't given any details. He knew they upset her. And he knew the council meeting was still scheduled for the next night. The thing he wished he knew was how to help her. It seemed like such a waste of time to be fighting over books in a library.

He was about to hang up her dishrag and guide her to the living room when her cell phone rang. He grabbed it off the nearby bookcase and caught the name as he handed it over.

"It's Gladdie's number," he said.

She frowned and answered. From the start, he knew something was wrong.

"Oh hi, Claudia." Rose paused to listen. "Oh, no! I'm so sorry. Is she all right?"

He had only her half of the conversation, but it didn't get any better sounding. "Where is she? What do they say? Of course I understand. Give her our love."

She hung up and stared.

"Well?" Dewey asked.

"They plunked Gladdie in the hospital this afternoon. She has pneumonia."

"Good gosh. I've never known the woman to be sick a day in her life. How serious is it?"

"Sounds like she's pretty miserable, but they think she'll be fine. She won't be home for several days, though." Her lower lip protruded in a thoughtful pout. "You know, I wondered why I hadn't heard from her recently. Even on the library's first day. I feel awful that I didn't check on her."

"Hey, you can't take care of everybody."

Rose sank heavily into a kitchen chair, her face a gloomy mask.

"She'll be fine, Rose. She's tough."

"It's not that. I'm a horrible person."

He laughed out loud. "Okay, now you're delirious."

"I'm not." She covered her face. "I'm angry because Gladdie was my security blanket for the meeting tomorrow. She has all those people in the palm of her hand, and now she's not going to be there."

"Oh, you're right. You're awful."

She looked up nervously and groaned. "See?"

"I'm kidding. You're worried about the meeting. That doesn't mean you don't care about Gladdie."

She slid her arms straight out in front of her across the tabletop and flopped her head down between them. "Ugh. I hate this. I should let the council meet and do what they want."

"Good idea."

"What?"

He laughed again, swept her arms off the table, and pulled her up to stand in his embrace. "You would no more skip that meeting than let someone hurt your son. Buck up, woman. You'll convince that council to take away the protest signs."

"When did you suddenly get to be such a believer in librarians?"

"Not in librarians, one librarian. I've been watching you. You act all nice, but you're a little terrier. You like a good fight."

She muffled her laugh in his chest. The vibration and the moist warmth from her breath wicked through his shirt and into his skin, making him shiver. "I guess I do a little," she said.

"Relax." He kissed the top of her head. "You've got this, with or without Gladdie."

She lifted her head, and her eyes filled with a touch of disbelief. She placed a palm on each of his cheeks and drew his head toward hers. Soft as her whisper, she sought a kiss. He hummed in surprise and met her lips with relish. Despite its eagerness, however, the kiss remained soft, almost careful. Exploratory. Light. Fun. It almost created more sparks and shivers than their hotter, heavier kisses the night before.

Or maybe he just wanted her that much more tonight.

But there was Jesse to consider, and Rose pulled away first, her hands lingering on his face, her fingers brushing softly at his mustache.

"I'll bet you're a stunning man underneath this."

"You don't like the 'stache? The truth comes out?"

"I do like it. But if you're this handsome with it, what must the naked face look like?"

"You know, most women don't find me all that attractive. Face is a little uneven, forehead kind of wide. That's what I usually get. What Rachel used to say."

"Poor, blind Rachel."

He grinned at that. "I grew the mustache after she left, to become someone different. It worked. The face looks a little better."

"It looks better than better. Someday, you can show me a picture of you without it, though, so I can prove to you what a dolt your ex-wife was."

He normally felt it was a little uncharitable to bad-mouth Rachel. She hadn't been evil. Just sad. But when Rose said the words, a little piece of leftover hurt and anger broke loose and drifted away. He lifted her an inch off the floor and twirled her once.

"My own personal 'Mean Girl.'" He set her down.

"Not mean. I just don't lie. Or pull punches. And I say you deserved better."

The last words sent a cloud of aching fear through him. He shuddered and forced it away, but all the doubt he felt anytime he got a little close to a woman welled up and tried to crowd out his bravado. He'd told her the truth. But she hadn't questioned him at all about children or his divorce. He was sure she didn't really understand.

He let her go and shook all the gloomy thoughts away. Of course she understood. She was smart. She was a fighter, but she was kind, and she wouldn't play with these new, exploratory feelings callously. After this last kiss, he couldn't be completely stupid to take a chance.

"Come on. We promised Jesse we'd play his game."

And then there was Jesse. He knew the boy liked him, but it was only because he needed a role model, someone strong to counteract Rose's quickness to baby him. And she did often baby him. It was easy to play the strong tough guy once in a while, but Dewey was sure he and Jesse would drive each other crazy, given too much time together. Dewey tutored his football kids in the thing he loved. He gave marching orders, and the kids marched. He hollered directions at the high-schoolers, and they fell into line. He fixed their shoulder pads and taught them to block and think on their feet. He taught them to hit safely.

Jesse could understand none of that. Dewey would make him a terrible father figure. Jesse needed someone more nurturing as a full-time dad.

Hell, he thought as Rose flipped off the TV and placed the game box on the coffee table, who was he kidding? Great kissing and mutual attraction wouldn't impress her for a lifetime. She wouldn't be happy with anyone who couldn't be the perfect person for Jesse, too.

He watched the boy unpack the game pieces and then listened as he chattered in his breathless sentences about the rules. Rose laughed, and Dewey put up a few good chuckles, but somehow, in the space of three minutes, his optimism had fled the room.

THE SIGNS STILL peppered the library lawn the next morning, but Rose, Kate, and Liz had spent all afternoon the day before plastering Liz's counter-signs all over town, too, and they'd clearly generated interest. Several people had commented and cheered her on when she'd stopped for coffee at the Loon Feather. She doubted the town was coming to blows over the silly library fight, but at least she was heartened that a few people noticed.

Kate's cheerful greeting lifted Rose's spirits further. Jesse had been less sullen this morning. Dewey had played games until Jesse's bedtime, and although he hadn't stayed later, he'd made his good night, um, memorable. She flushed at the memory. With him on her side, she believed she could take on the council. Not that she'd asked Dewey if he'd be there. She wasn't ready to push yet—the whole *thing* with him felt both sudden and as if it had been ordained from their first argument.

The better day disintegrated before eleven-thirty with another call from Linda Verum. Jesse was back at it in gym class, this time refusing to participate in football because he was going to have a special extra gym class on Sunday when he went riding.

She didn't know whether to cry or curse on the way to talk to her son in the principal's office for the third time. On the one hand, Dewey had made her son excited about physical activity for the first time she could remember. On the other, Dewey had equated it to gym and, unwittingly, given the child an annoying loophole out of real class.

And the school. Were these teachers completely incapable of handling unique situations without resorting to formally written teaching plans? IEPs—she'd been through the process of creating one for Jesse in Boston. It had been awful. Somehow Quad City had to find the key to her son without one—they were the educators.

Her meeting with the principal was short and to the point. Today, Jesse had called Mrs. Middleburg an inappropriate name. About all Rose could tell herself for comfort was that it had not been swearing or vulgar. Still, "you're being stupid" was unquestionably inappropriate.

This time, Linda Verum asked her to take Jesse home and have a long discussion about appropriate behavior and, of course, this time Jesse was reluctant to leave because there was going to be a movie about animals in science. Good punishment, the principal scolded.

"Are you mad?" Jesse asked on the way back to the library.

She sighed. "Yeah. I'm pretty mad. I'd like to figure out why you're so unhappy at school here. You were never the one who started trouble back in Boston. Why won't you at least try here?"

"I do try." He put on a pathetic pout. "But this school makes us do too much gym. And Mrs. Middleburg is really strict, and she makes us run if we don't do stuff right. I hate to run."

"Well, then, we have to talk about that. You cannot call adults who aren't trying to hurt you names. Ever. Like they can't call you names. Do you understand that?"

He nodded solemnly.

"I hope so, Jesse. We can't keep doing this."

"I'm sorry. I shouldn't have said Mrs. Middleburg was stupid."

"Thank you. Now, I'm afraid you're stuck with me all day. And I'm putting you to work."

"Doing what?"

"I don't know yet. Something awful."

He laughed. "I know that means you really won't."

"Don't try me."

She tousled his hair. She could not stay furious at him.

To her shock, Dewey was waiting for them at the library. He greeted them both like a stern parent. "Huh," he said to Jesse. "Are you sick?"

"No."

"Then they must have canceled school."

"No."

"Are you playing hooky?"

"They made me leave because I was rude."

"Is that really true?" He looked at Rose.

She shrugged. "It is. This time, I tried to talk her into keeping him. She wants me to make certain he understands proper behavior."

"Jesse James. Do we have to change your nickname? Is this one making you act like an outlaw?"

"Yeah."

"Don't bug him," Rose said. "Jesse. You can go through the picture books and make sure they're in the right bins. Do at least the A's and the B's."

"Somebody needs to bug him, Rose," Dewey said when Jesse was gone.

"Believe me, I know. And I have been, and I will. I don't know what's wrong, Dewey, but don't lecture me about my son."

"Hey." He caught her arm and pulled her around a corner to the back of the stairs where no one could see them. "I won't lecture you. It's not my place. I'm sorry he's having a tough time."

"He told Mrs. Middleburg that he didn't have to play football because he's going to gym class on Sunday and he's doing a unit on horses."

"Shit." Dewey covered his mouth. "Sorry. That's my fault, isn't it?"

"Not because you intended any consequences. It's really Jesse's warped and slightly devious little mind." She closed her eyes and took a calming breath. "Why are you here?"

"I came to wish you luck tonight. I probably won't get a chance to see you and say it later."

"Oh?" Her heart fell in disappointment. "You're not coming tonight?"

"I'm sorry." He truly looked it, which gave him a point at least. "Tuesday nights right now mean middle school football games."

"Oh. I get that." And she did. But she still felt like crying for no reason other than the day was starting to stink to high heaven.

"You'll do great."

"I will."

"What are you doing with Jesse?"

"He'll come along. Everyone I know who could watch him is going to be there."

He raised his thick, gorgeous eyebrows. "I'm not."

"Okay, well, one person will be at a football game." She made a face.

"Why not send Jesse with me?"

"Um, maybe because he hates football?"

"Precisely. Maybe . . ." He stole a kiss on her nose. "There'll be a miracle."

Chapter Nineteen

WITH TEN MINUTES left in the game, Dewey checked on Jesse who, after his initial spate of questions when he'd arrived, had sat watching, surprisingly quietly, on the end of the home team's bench. His face gave away no emotion, not disinterest, boredom, or understanding. At one point, he'd asked if Dewey had a cell phone. At first Dewey had refused to hand it over, but finally, when Jesse himself had brought up phone calls and promised not to make any, he'd let him have it. Several times now, Dewey had found him engrossed in the Internet.

Sadly, it didn't look as though there'd be a miracle with Jesse and the sport of football, but at least the kid was quiet.

"How's it going, Jesse James?" he asked. "Doing okay? The game's almost over. Ten minutes is all."

"I'm fine. There are eight minutes and forty-six seconds left." He pointed at the clock on the scoreboard of the big high school field where the middle school Gryphons loved to play. "Plus, the other team has a timeout left. And the Gryphons have two."

Dewey stared, speechless for a moment, impressed to his core. "That's right."

"I looked up the rules."

That's what he'd been doing? Dewey squatted in front of him. "I'm impressed."

A little half smile tilted Jesse's mouth, even though he didn't raise his eyes from the phone screen. A ref's whistle sounded, and Dewey spun on the balls of his feet to face the field.

"Third down," Jesse murmured. "The Gryphons have to get six yards for a first down, or they have to punt. Did you know the creature griffin is usually spelled g-r-i-f-f-i-n? If you cross a griffin and a horse, you get a hippogriff like Buckbeak in Harry Potter."

Clearly, he'd been self-entertaining and quiet too long. Dewey shook his head.

"You're an amazing kid, Jesse James. I'm glad you're not a train robber—you'd be the smartest one out there, and that's a scary thought."

"I'd be a scary thief. Mom says so, too."

"I'll bet she does."

He patted the boy's knee and stood. And came almost face to face with Rose. She'd made her way onto the sideline and stood a few feet behind the bench. Immediately, Dewey saw the dazed light in her eyes when she smiled at him. So pretty, so incongruous in her conservative blue skirt, black tight-like stockings, and a soft, thick sweater in bright orange and blue swirls. With her caramel curls disheveled around her face from the breeze, she looked like a delicious dessert.

"Gotta finish," he said, pointing to the field. "Come sit by Jesse?"

She nodded and made her way around the end of the bench. Few players sat there anyway—they all stood at the sideline cheering crazily for the first down.

Seven minutes later, despite gaining the needed six yards, the Gryphons lost by three points. It took until after the consoling and the game wrap-up for Dewey to find his way back to Rose. She looked like a carbon copy of her son—staring at her phone with nothing but blankness on her face.

"Hey, you," he said.

She looked up, a quick smile giving her features a little of their animation back. "Oh, hi. I'm sorry the team lost."

"Thanks. They win about half, so maybe next time. They did well, regardless. But that's nothing. Tell me how things went at the council meeting. I expected it to go late—it's only nine o'clock."

"Yeah." Her rueful laugh told part of the story. "I'm not sure what to tell you happened. They put us nearly last on the agenda, and the entire book discussion lasted fifteen minutes. There were maybe fifty or sixty people there, but only Reverend Coburn and I spoke. Someone called for my resignation. Barring that, they'd like me fired. That got a couple of points on the applause-o-meter."

"You're not serious."

"I'm not worried, but the suggestion was serious. The

person, I don't even know her name, confronted me after the meeting."

"The town is going crazy."

"You know what? Asking for my resignation wasn't crazy, but what the council decided they have to do is. They divvied up the book list, and they want to read the books." Her eyes had dulled again, fatigue turning them into muddy pools of weariness. "Can you believe that? They didn't ban the books, but they didn't stand up for freedom to read either. Unbelievable."

Her voice should have risen in anger. Her cheeks should have flamed with indignation. Instead, everything came out in a monotone. After two sentences Dewey could tell she wasn't acting normally.

"It is unbelievable. But there's nothing you can do about it right this moment. Come on. We're going home—going to your place. Your day needs to end."

"Yeah. But I doubt I'll sleep much tonight."

"I don't know. You look like you could sleep right here."

"I'm acting catatonic to keep me from yelling." At that, she smiled again.

"Well, gotta love that plan. Okay, then, up you go."

"Haha. 'Ohh-kay.' That sounded like Fargo-speak."

"If it makes you laugh, I'm not gonna argue with you."

"It happens when you're tired. You must be, too."

"Been a long Tuesday."

EVEN JESSE SEEMED nearly dead on his feet by the time Rose unlocked her door and let the two men into the house. It felt weirdly natural for the three of them to file through the door and for her to set Dewey to making coffee while she got Jesse up the stairs and ready for bed. After Jesse padded downstairs in his bare feet and pajamas, thanked Dewey, got a drink of water, and went back upstairs, Rose returned to get her own cup of coffee, ready for the boost of energy it would give. She hated feeling so . . . battle weary.

Instead, Dewey greeted her with a cup of one of her herbal teas.

"It said 'Sleepytime' on the box," he said.

"That would be, like, the opposite of caffeine."

"Exactly. Drink it."

"I have things to do."

"Oh, c'mon. What?"

"More posters. A written response to . . ."

He placed a finger against her lips. "That can all be done tomorrow. Drink the tea. I don't bother with tea for just anyone, you see."

They sat, and he said nothing except to ask her what the council had actually said.

"They weren't ungracious. They said they understood both sides. Traditions and 'the way things have always been done' need to be taken seriously. They said they want the town to move forward, but they were also willing to see if any of the books made the council want to take a stand for the proud family traditions of Kennison Falls." Her heart pumped fresh, angry adrenaline into her system, and she could feel the heat in her face.

Dewey turned beside her on the couch and made her

face her back to him. "It's time to let it go. I have a feeling the council will do the right thing."

"Really?"

"Yeah. Sam's a pretty good guy, pretty progressive."

"I hate the religious arguments. I believe in God. He's really important to me. But I don't believe for one minute he's that judgmental or narrow-minded. You're an upstanding guy. Your family says prayers before supper and seems to operate on good old-fashioned principles. Do you think God cares if people read Harry Potter? Or teenage girls think vampires are attractive?"

"I do not. And I also don't think He minds if they find singers attractive or fantasize about movie stars, but people disagree with me on that, too. You can't dictate someone's deep-held beliefs."

"Sure I can. Watch me."

He laughed behind her, placed his hands on her shoulders, and kneaded deep into the muscles, setting off a shower of electric sparks. Her eyes closed in glorious ecstasy. "Stop thinking," he whispered.

She did—about everything in the world except his hands. His fingers traveled around her body, kneading in knot-busting circles, casting enchantments down her spine and up into her scalp. Wave after wave of goose bumps flowed across every inch of skin. He pressed his knuckles along her spine, spread his palms wide to fan beneath her shoulder blades, and stroked his thumbs up the cords of her neck.

Nobody had ever touched her this thoroughly and with such undemanding skill. She thought she might burst into a thousand pieces of joy if he continued, or a thousand tears if he ever quit.

"This is honest-to-gosh heaven," she said.

"No. This is first base on steroids." He dropped his hands, and she really did feel tears of release and disappointment in her eyes. "What would you try to do around here if I left now?"

"Bawl like a baby."

"Can't have that."

He stood, bent over her, and scooped her into his arms as easily as Superman had lifted Lois Lane before their first flight together. She felt as amazed and dazzled as Lois must have when seeing the ground from the sky for the first time. She buried her eyes in his shoulder as he carried her up the stairs.

"Kick off your shoes," he commanded when he set her on the carpet in her bedroom, and she toed off her comfy, wedge-heeled ankle boots. "Now, anything else tight or restrictive. You can put PJs on if you want."

"PJs? Now there's an unsexy seduction line."

"Seduction would do neither of us any good right now."

"Speak for yourself."

"Fine. Here's what I have for seduction tonight." He turned her back to him once more, slid his hands beneath the back of her sweater, and glided up her back to the clasp of her bra. With a quick flick, he undid the hooks. "Pull your arms out of the sleeves."

She obeyed, grinning into space. Gliding his fingers to the tops of her shoulders, he drew the bra straps down her arms and away from her breasts, and dropped the bra from beneath her sweater to the floor. Oh so briefly he cupped a breast in each hand and drew his thumbs across the nipples, sending a shock directly to the juncture of her thighs. She gasped and rocked against him.

"See? That is not relaxing." He kissed her neck and withdrew his hands.

"You're the only one who seems to think I should be relaxed."

"Then I'm the only smart one in the room. Time for the rest of the clothes, but keep your mind out of the gutter."

"Boy. You are as romantic as a traffic cop tonight."

"Good. Exactly what I was going for."

She wriggled her tights and panties off from beneath her skirt and dropped them on top of the bra. Every cell in her body felt suddenly awake and hot.

"PJs or no?" She shook her head. He lifted her again and laid her gently on the bed. "I'm serious. No hanky-panky. How likely is it that Jesse's gonna come wandering in here?"

"Almost zero percent. One of his eccentricities is that he won't leave his bed once he's in it."

"Score one for the kid."

He pulled down her quilt and opened up the sheets. Once she was settled to his satisfaction, he crawled in beside her, took up a spoon position but with half an arm's length between them, and began the back rub anew. Head, shoulders, back, and to the swell of her bottom, he worked methodically and masterfully. One by one, tingles of plea-sure worked like relaxation drugs on each muscle. One by one, each released its tension until she was fighting sleep.

"Dewey?"

"Yeah?"

"This is boring."

His resonant, from-the-belly chuckle rolled like a distant comforting thunderstorm into her ear. "I've heard I'm really good at boring."

"Well, I believe it."

The last thing she felt was the tickle of his mustache on her cheek.

She cracked one eye open to find she could see nothing in pitch darkness. Confusion fogged her brain until she registered a warm wall behind her and a weight across her middle. A person? A man?

Dewey? Still here at . . . she lifted her head half an inch off the pillow. Two-thirty?

Happiness engulfed her, and she sank back into the pillow. Deep, rhythmic breathing behind her lulled like a metronome. He didn't snore. He didn't move, even when she curled backward into the curve of his body. All she wanted was to stay awake and marvel at the man in her bed, but his breath, his scent now permeating the very air she breathed, and his arm solidly around her dragged her back into sound, motionless sleep.

Her permanently set alarm went off at six-thirty.

Dawn light brightened the room, and the body in her bed shifted, sending her shooting to sitting with a shocked cry, startled all over again to see Dewey beside her. His eyes flew open and, for one satisfying moment, he looked as disoriented as she was. Then he smiled.

"Heck, I didn't expect this when I started last night. I'm going to be the envy of all the boys at school."

"And my reputation is shot."

"Then my work here is done." He stretched with a long attractive motion. "Is this your normal time to get up?"

"It is. Forty-five minutes before Jesse. I try to do my yoga and get a head start on him."

"This is why you're the mom." He threw back his half of the covers and sat, setting his huge hand on her thigh and stroking it through the sheet and blanket. His unbuttoned plaid shirt was wrinkled, the navy T-shirt beneath it slightly twisted. His touch gave her as much pleasure this morning as it had the night before. "This is nice, but I'm leaving now. I need to go home and change so I can get to work, too. I usually open at seven."

"Not even time for coffee?

"Nope. You go about your normal routine. How does the world feel this morning?"

"After eight hours of sleep during which I never moved? Like Christmas."

"That's my girl. Hold that thought. I'll talk to you later—after your super-spectacular day."

My girl. The words meant nothing—it was a generic endearment—but they opened a floodgate of questions in her mind. She'd never wanted to be anyone's girl, but she also noticed how full the house felt, how safe with Dewey in it. What would her parents really think about a big ex-football jock with a laborer's job? What would Jesse think if he happened to find them together, however innocently? This time it had worked out. Did she want there to be a next time?

Duh.

No, really, she argued with herself. Next time, if she allowed it, innocence would be easy to toss out the door.

Still, duh.

He kissed her good-bye quickly—a chaste, almost husband-like kiss.

She pried that thought away and tossed it as far from her mind as she could. She was not going near the marriage scenario.

He waved cheerily, heading down the sidewalk to his car. He waved one more time driving away. And only then did her heart start pounding and everything go haywire in her brain. Why couldn't she have something like this every day? She dug in her drawer for yoga pants and a T-shirt to replace her rumpled skirt and sweater. She definitely needed to balance her chi. Or she needed to stop sleeping with strong men and leaving out the sex.

HE COULDN'T SEE Rose on Wednesday. A quarterly meeting with the feed-mill tax accountants took up three precious hours after work, forcing him to decide ten o'clock was too late to call on her. Only the fact that a day off to cool his crazy, burning libido was an excellent and probably necessary idea kept him from pining like a teenager. He still found it hard to believe he'd spent the night unintentionally with her. And done a big fat nothing.

He'd forced nonchalance that morning and acted as if the entire sleepover had been planned all along. In reality, he'd awoken in the middle of the night and gone around to turn off lights and lock the doors. Then, self-ishly, he'd climbed right back into bed with her. Had she come awake, too, he knew unequivocally he'd never have left her and her naked-beneath-her-skirt beautiful body alone. Instead, he'd fallen into an unconscious sleep, probably the most peaceful he'd had in longer than he could remember.

The tension, the frustrated longing, the desire hadn't started until she'd bolted upright in the bed, her skirt hiked up to the top of her creamy thigh, her hair tangled sexily around her face. When her surprise had turned into warm acceptance of his presence, it had been all he could do not to grab her.

By Thursday afternoon, after a full, grubby morning working side by side with Elle on two big repairs, he finally decided he had his senses back. He was *not* a randy teen, and he didn't want to make any mistakes with Rose. Right now she was warm and willing to have him around. Too much pushing, and she might show thorns—a prickly side he already knew.

He wasn't prepared, then, for her panicked side. His phone rang deep in his pocket just after lunchtime, and he grunted in frustration, scrubbing his greasy hands quickly and inefficiently on a rag before digging the phone free. He didn't even look at the number, afraid he'd miss the call.

"Dewey Mitchell."

"Dewey, it's Rose. I hate like heck to bother you." He couldn't miss the mini-sob in her voice, and his heart rose and skipped beats in his throat.

"Hey, you're not. What's wrong?"

At that, she burst into tears, something he'd never thought he'd hear. "I'm sorry," she said again. "I don't know what to do. It's Jesse. He's melting down, I swear. He's boycotting gym class this week. I got a call from school for the fourth day this week. And I have . . ." She choked. "I have a . . ."

"Babe, stop. What do you need me to do?" His repairman's heart kicked into high gear.

"Mrs. Middleburg, Joyce, is insisting on talking to me, and I can't get away for at least an hour. I know that makes me an aw-awful m-mother."

"That's ridiculous, Rose. I can go get him if you want me to."

"Pick him up. That's all I need. Oh, and tell Joyce Middleburg I'll make an appointment to talk to her tomorrow. I'm sorry."

"Will you stop apologizing? Let me take five minutes to clean up, and I'll go get him. You want me to bring him to the library?"

"I guess. I have a conference call I can't miss. Kate will watch him. I need to negotiate a raise for her." Her voice shook a little less, and her sobs stopped.

"All right."

"Dewey, I . . . Don't . . ." She hesitated, and her voice dropped to barely audible. "Thank you."

"See you in a little bit."

He scrubbed away the grease, changed to a clean T-shirt, and told Elle he probably wouldn't be back until after football practice.

"Rose is okay?" she asked from under the hood of a fifteen-year-old pickup truck chronically in the shop.

"She's fine—Jesse's going through a tough time at school. She can't get there to pick him up. Maybe it's a good thing. He seems to respond to a little firmer hand. Kid is smart. He knows how to get coddling from his mom."

"Aw, she's a great mom."

"She is. But boys need to have boundaries, not guidelines."

"Don't take on too much with him, Duaney. He's not ours to fix."

He actually smiled at her use of the word "ours." She was right. Still, this wouldn't be a bad chance to have a man-to-man with young Jesse Hanrehan.

"Whatever you say, sis." He headed for the door and then turned back. "Hey, Elle's Bells? Did I ever tell you it's nice having you here?"

She popped her head up from the truck and stared. "Say again?"

"You heard me, dork."

"No," she said, "you never have. But thanks, butthead."

"Dewey!" Jesse jumped off the chair in the school office and threw his arms around Dewey's hips.

"Uh, easy, champ." It was hard to be stern after a greeting like that, and Dewey's cheeks warmed with a little embarrassment and a lot of puffed-chest pride. He patted Jesse's back awkwardly and dislodged his hold. "What's going on here?"

"Where's Mom?" He ignored the question and looked around as if expecting to find Rose hiding behind Dewey.

"She couldn't come, buddy. She had a big meeting. You know, she can't always come running whenever you don't like something here at school. It's not fair to make her do that."

"I just—"

"Dewey?" Joyce Middleburg strode from around a corner, her surprise obvious.

"Hi there, Joyce. Rose couldn't get away this time. She'd like to call you later this afternoon and set up a meeting."

"That's fine. You're here to take charge of this young man?"

"She said she'd call with permission."

"All right. Dewey, between the two of us, I think Mrs. Hanrehan has a pretty serious problem on her hands. You're not the boy's guardian or parent, so I can't discuss him with you, but I hope you'll impress on his mother that this is very important."

"You know I will, but I don't think she needs to be told. Rose is pretty upset. Jess? Hey, remember those books you were reading? How 'bout you go sit in that room and read a while? I'll come get you in a minute or so."

Jesse shrugged and shuffled off, his blue and black cowboy boots scuffling along smoothly.

"There's probably no need to send him away. There's not much I can say to you."

"But I have a couple of questions. The answers might help pinpoint things for his mom to talk about."

"Okay. Without divulging any teacher/student/parent information, I'll answer what I can."

"What is it he seems to dislike?"

"Anything that has to do with learning a skill or practicing it with the other kids. He's fine with individual things like calisthenics. I can't even get him to play catch."

The images of Jesse struggling so hard with the football rose clearly in Dewey's mind.

"Have you ever watched him try?" he asked.

"He's not gifted physically, I get it."

"Have you thought about things he might be able to do that would make this easier for him? Ask him about the rules and the stats for the game? Ask him about the history? Let him work on his skills against a wall by himself or with someone else who could use the practice?"

Joyce laughed humorlessly. "I can tell you haven't taught for a very long time, my old friend. You have the idealism of inexperience. If we can't get Ms. Hanrehan to think about an IEP for Jesse, I don't have time to treat him differently in a regular class."

"It's not time, just a little extra creativity on the spot. This isn't criticism, Joyce. It's hard to help the kid when we can't tell him there'll be something he can succeed at."

"Maybe he'll be better at the next unit. Maybe he'll never love my class. Regardless, he has to try. He's not the first kid to hate phis ed."

And that's okay with you?

"Okay," he said out loud. "I'll pass this on to Rose. Can the boy go back to class?"

"If you can convince him. He's insisting he can't. This is why I believe there's a more serious issue than gym class."

Frustrated, Dewey watched her leave, her blonde ponytail swinging, her toned arms bared beneath a sleeveless shirt despite the season. He'd always liked her, but her attitude disappointed, even angered him. She'd become the clichéd tough phis ed teacher—the one all the kids feared unless they were natural athletes. "He's not gifted physically," she'd said. "He's not the first kid to hate phys ed."

Damn it, he thought. Every kid should love gym class. Especially at this age.

He wandered into the room, where he found Jesse sitting quietly, no book in his hand. He looked up.

"Are you mad at me?"

"Hmm." Dewey squatted down. "That's hard to answer. I'm peeved you won't tough it out in gym. But I kind of get it."

"Peeved." He grinned. "My grandma used to say that. It's a funny word."

"I suppose it is. But making your mom sad because she feels bad that you keep getting in trouble—that's not funny."

He didn't say anything, but he bowed his head slightly.

"You going back to class?"

He shook his head.

"Wanna tell me why not?"

"They all tease me as soon as I get back from the principal's office. They don't if I come back in the morning."

"There's a real easy fix for that, y'know." Jesse eyed him dubiously. "Don't come to the principal's office."

"But they send me here."

"Yeah. Because you're not obeying the rules in class. If you quit messing around there, you stop coming here. Simple stuff, Jesse James."

"You don't get it either." He folded his arms and kicked with his familiar frustration at the legs of his chair. "Nobody gets it. They want me to be like everyone else."

"Kid, I do get it. Believe me. You aren't good at things like football, and it's no fun to drop balls and get teased. Plus, the teacher said you get graded on all this, and so, if you're going to get a bad grade anyway, why get teased, too? Am I sort of right?"

He nodded a little morosely. "Why can't I just go ride horses and tell the teacher I did the skills? That's what I want to do."

"That would be cool. But the teacher doesn't get to decide what you have to do to pass gym. The school does. For now, you have to try to do what you're supposed to. And you should go back to class."

At that, he shook his head adamantly.

Well, Rose was expecting him. He sighed. The idea came to him like a smack to the head.

"Well, okay. But here's the thing. You can't get off school and go have a great time at the library while other kids are working hard. I think if you're not going to be at school, you have to be in your room without your computer. Or you have to work hard at something else."

"What else?"

"You have to come to football practice with me for a week."

Chapter Twenty

"WHAAT?" JESSE DREW out the word like Dewey had told him he'd found a flying horse.

"Yeah. You can watch how the older kids learn to play. You can carry equipment around if I need it. You can keep some of the player stats." He added that on the spur of the moment. The boy seemed to have enjoyed learning about football. If he truly couldn't or wouldn't play, maybe he could delve into the rules.

"Like a team manager?"

Dewey laughed. "More like a team grunt."

He wrinkled his nose. "I don't want to be the grunt."

"Okay. Come up with any name you want. Servant. Slave. The job's the same."

"Can we go there now?"

"Not for two hours. We have to run this past your mom, anyway."

"I wish she could have come now. I like it when you both come."

He hadn't expected that. "You do?"

"Yeah."

Jesse didn't elaborate, and Dewey didn't force the issue. But the boy's strange admission left an uneasy question in the pit of Dewey's stomach. Now that he thought about it, this wasn't the first time Jesse had asked to see them together. And yet they were, at the moment, the two most important adults in Jesse's life. It shouldn't be that unusual if he wanted them with him at the same time.

Still, he wondered. The kid was odd but not stupid.

Conspiracy?

Dewey snorted inwardly at the thought. His imagination was getting the better of him.

Rose gave her approval to the plan Jesse labeled Football Slave Class. He accompanied Dewey early that afternoon to the practice field and ogled the stack of PVC poles used for making drill grids, the two dozen orange traffic cones, the huge bag of footballs, and the thick playbook Dewey carried with him.

"Who makes up all these pages of plays?" he asked, thumbing through the three-ring binder and all the plastic-sheathed papers of what had to look like indecipherable scribbles.

"I do. And Coach Miller."

"You have to be pretty smart for that, I guess."

"Sure." Dewey winked at him. "Smart. I like that. Come on. Let's haul some of these poles out to the field."

They laid out a series of lanes, and Jesse huffed and puffed valiantly, clearly not a kid who got a lot of physical exercise. Still, he didn't complain and fetched one pole after the other like a little pack horse. They were about to start on another grid when Jesse stopped.

"Someone's coming."

Two figures approached from the far end of the field. Dewey recognized Jason immediately, but he'd never seen the second boy. When they arrived, both stood silently, shifting in uneasiness. With sudden insight, Dewey knew exactly who the new kid was.

"Jason," he said.

"Hey, Coach. Can we, uh, talk to you?" Jason glanced uncertainly at Jesse.

"Yeah, of course." Dewey thought quickly. Jesse was like a little radio transmitter with no filters. He would hear and report as the whim struck. "This is my friend Jesse Hanrehan. He's helping out for a while. Hey, Jesse, could you maybe pull four more poles out to the field? And then, here . . ." Dewey dug out his cell phone. "Do a little research on . . ." He ran through ideas in his head. "On M-Drills. If you find anything, see if you can figure out how to set up those orange cones for it."

A dubious shadow crossed his face, but Jesse took the phone. "Okay."

It was a simple drill, easy enough to find online, but figuring it out would keep him occupied while Dewey sorted out what Jason wanted. Once Jesse ambled off for the pile of poles, he turned to the two teens.

"What's up?"

"This is my cousin," Jason said, as if that answered everything.

The cousin did not meet Dewey's eyes. A shock of mousy hair hung down his forehead and across one eye. His mouth, slack and pouty, gave him a young Johnny Depp carelessness. His jeans bore one shattered knee, but his jacket, a navy blue Columbia, was new and not cheap.

"Do you have a name, Cousin?"

"Taylor," he said with a lack of attitude that surprised Dewey. "Dunn."

Dunn. Dunn . . . *Pat Dunn?* The library board member who'd rallied the protestors?

"Do I know you?"

"Everybody knows my mom."

"Is your mom Pat?" He kept his voice even, with effort.

The boy nodded, his lip twitching into an angry curl for the first time.

Dewey had to take a breath. This was, of course, the cousin Jason had talked about, but if he was Pat Dunn's son . . . His mind reeled.

"His dad and my dad are first cousins," Jason explained.

"All right. What can I do for you?"

"Taylor wants to tell you something."

Dewey absolutely did not want to hear it. He didn't want to deal with a problem this big. Still, he waited.

After a very long, uncomfortable time, the boy finally spoke, almost too quietly to hear. "I did it." Dewey kept his eyes on him, still silent and waiting. Taylor finally realized he was going to have to spill it all. "I broke the library window. I'm going to be in big trouble."

"I can't lie," Dewey said. "You're right about that. Why are you telling me?"

"Jason said it was better to tell you than to have him tell my mom."

Jason looked a little like someone had strapped him into an electric chair. Yeah, maybe this hadn't been such a good idea, right, Jason? Dewey thought.

"How could that possibly be true?" he asked his star Gold Gryphon defensive end-slash-offensive guard.

"Because he said you can fix stuff. Even stuff like this." Taylor answered for Jason, suddenly hopeful. Probably because Dewey had been foolish enough to engage in this conversation at all.

"Boys," he said. "I can't *fix* vandalism. You really do have to go to your parents or to the authorities and tell them what you told me."

"But I can't. My mom will . . ." Taylor stopped, his lip no longer sneering, but almost trembling. Clearly, this kid wasn't anywhere near as tough as he wanted to look.

"Will punish you? Don't you think maybe you should do a little time for the crime?"

Taylor nodded mutely, but he didn't look like he wanted to agree.

"You can tell him," Jason coaxed.

Taylor's young shoulders drooped like an old man's. "You," he half-whispered.

"He told me yesterday that his dad gets so mad he

scares him if he does anything wrong. He always says he's going to hit Taylor with a belt."

Dewey's heart fell in sick fear. "*Has* he hit you, Taylor? Has he hurt you in any way?"

He'd have no choice but to tell authorities if Taylor was being abused.

"No! No. He swears a lot and says he's going to. But I've never told anyone that." Taylor pleaded with his eyes. "He'd be real mad if he knew. And if my mom found out about the window, she'd have to tell him, and . . ." He folded his arms around himself, unconsciously curling inward.

The boy was soft-soaping this; he feared his father. This was beyond Dewey's experience and nowhere near his comfort level or expertise, but the thought of a potentially abused child standing in front of him made his blood boil. He glanced behind him. Jesse had dragged the poles out to the field, and now he sat on the bench, head bent over the phone.

Dewey sighed and tried to keep his anger hidden.

"Can you at least tell me what possessed you to throw that rock?"

"I was mad at my mom. She's making this big deal out of the library books, and everyone is starting to hate her. I wanted her to stop making the signs and stop being at the library with them. I don't like reading anyway. Why should she care? I won't read the stupid bad books. I thought maybe if she could see that people were that mad at the protests they would wreck the library, she would stop. Only, it didn't work. She thinks people who agree with her broke the window. She'll be almost as mad as Dad when she finds out."

Dewey held back a groan. The story grew more convoluted the longer he stood here.

"Taylor, man, I'm not sure what to tell you. What did you think I could do?"

The boy brightened slightly. "You're friends with the lady who runs the library. Maybe you could, like, ask her if I could work to pay off the window, and she wouldn't tell my parents."

Criminy, the kid had actually thought about this.

"I can't keep a secret like that, man. Neither should you."

"So you're going to tell."

Taylor had so obviously expected this reaction that his voice didn't change, but defeat deadened his eyes.

"No. But you are. And I can make this much of a deal. I won't say a word until you're ready to talk yourself. Now, that doesn't mean you can wait until your next birthday." He offered a brief smile. "And if you want to talk to me about how to do this and what might happen, I'll be there."

"Really?"

"And there's one more catch. Are you in any school sports?"

Taylor shook his head.

"Anything after school?"

Another shake.

"Then you're coming to football practice with Jason every day. I'm gonna get to know you. Find out if you're going to be good to your word." He cringed slightly at the magnitude of what he was saying. "Of course, your parents have to say this is okay, but I'll have Coach Miller give you a permission slip for them to sign. You can tell them the team needs a student assistant, and your cousin talked you into coming out for it."

"Okay!" It was the most enthusiasm Taylor had displayed.

Dewey thought a minute more, and an incongruous question popped into his head. "Tell me why you don't like reading."

Taylor shifted on his feet and stared at the ground. "I can't do it. I mean, I can't read things very good. Everything is all scrambled and confusing."

Dewey had only taught for seven months, but he'd had a dyslexic student in his first and only class. Teaching was years in his past, but he knew the symptoms. This boy had more problems than a math book.

"Well," said a voice that couldn't possibly be coming from his own throat. "That's something else we can talk about."

He looked up when he caught sight of Adrian heading their way. How in the world was he going to explain this fiasco and the need for a parental permission form? Then, before Adrian reached them, Jesse trotted up and tugged on his jacket sleeve. He pointed to the field, where he'd set cones in a mostly accurate representation of the drill Dewey had given him to study.

And so they stood, side by side: two kids, each only one step from being a special-needs student. What the hell was he going to do with a ten-year-old hooky player and a thirteen-year-old master vandal? He was a part time coach.

And what the hell was wrong with Jason's father?

ROSE GENTLY STROKED the neck of a squat, sturdy, brown and black horse—bay being the proper color term, according to Jill—named Tampa. She'd been promised this little gelding would not only never buck her off, but would rather walk a hundred miles than gallop a hundred feet. After surviving the week from Hades, all Rose could think was that the promise had better be true. She was only here because she had no choice. Mothers couldn't renege on promises.

Between Jesse's horrid week at school, Pat Dunn and the good Reverend Nathaniel's open-warfare campaigning, calls for her resignation, Gladdie Hanson's illness rendering her unavailable to run interference, sweet Church Hubbard acting a little too wounded over being turned down for a second date, and a phone call from her mother opining that the brokenhearted Judge Shakleford, her ex-fiancé-who'd-never-really-been-a-fiancé-at-all, was begging to know if there was any chance she hated the new job and would come back to him, Rose felt like the only plague she'd been spared were flying monkeys from the land of Oz.

Now, here she was about to mount a horse—something she'd sworn she'd never do.

But Dewey had made the deal. If Jesse stayed in school the entire day on Friday, they could go horseback riding again. Rose had fulfilled her parental duty and gone to a fairly unsatisfying meeting with Joyce Middleburg, but Jesse had made it through gym class without incident and stayed in school.

Be careful what you wish for.

"Come on, Mom."

Jesse already sat astride the cutest little horse Rose had ever seen. This one was something called a Fjord pony—a buff-colored animal with a black-tipped mane that stuck straight up from its neck like the bristles on Marvin the Martian's helmet. And its name was Thor. How sweet was that?

She'd have been content to take pictures of Jesse in his boots and little riding helmet sitting all by himself on the horse and call it good, but no such luck.

"Yeah, come on, Mom," Dewey called from the back of a tall, gray horse named Rafe.

Rafe was big enough that he actually took up Dewey's height and solidness. Rose had to laugh. Dewey wasn't nearly as adorable in his helmet as Jesse was in his. In fact, she'd looked at herself and Dewey together in a car window after they'd put on the required helmets and thought they looked like alien nut cases. But she couldn't argue with safety.

"You'll be fine, Rose. I guarantee it." Jill, beside her, gave her a confident grin. "Step on the mounting block. Tampa's an old pro at this, she won't move until you tell her to."

Seconds later she was in the saddle. It was big, cushioned, and surprisingly comfortable. She grasped the saddle horn and forced her shoulders away from her ears.

"Are you sure we should be doing this alone?" she asked. "Don't most riding places make you go with a guide?"

"Every one of these horses knows this trail blindfolded," Jill said. "And Dewey knows it because he helped us clear it. Rafe's main job around here is to lead kids around on Thor. And Tampa here, she's cured a lot of people of their horse fears. Just let her follow. Take your time and have fun. If you're not back in two days, I'll send out the search and rescue."

"Will you send a fire engine?" Jesse's eyes lit.

"You want me to?" Jill asked.

"No!" Rose laughed. "No rescues. We're coming back on our own."

"Yes, we are," Dewey replied. "Come on, cowpokes, let's hit the trail."

It wasn't so bad. Fifteen minutes out of the old farmyard, Rose found herself trusting Tampa's steady, cheerful walk. She didn't rush, nor did she lag. She kept her nose beside Thor's saddle and bobbed her head in a soothing rhythm. Jesse chattered on and off and held reins that were attached to sides of the bridle rather than the bit to keep him from pulling on Thor's mouth. Dewey led the way, holding Thor's lead rope in one hand. He rode like an honest-to-gosh cowboy, and noticing the sexy, almost suggestive way his legs draped around his horse's sides had as much to do with Rose's diminishing nervousness as anything.

"Y'all doin' okay?" He turned in his saddle to check.

"Fine until I heard that fake Texas accent."

"Ouch. Here I thought it was so authentic."

"Do you want me to lie to you? What kind of lesson does that teach?"

He let roll a genuine belly laugh. "Sounds to me like you're doing fine, Madam Librarian."

"Okay, I admit it, this is kind of fun. You having fun, Jess?"

"Cool."

High praise.

They rode quietly a few more minutes until Dewey nearly shocked the helmet off her by starting to sing. His voice, a deep, slightly scratchy baritone, nonetheless stayed in tune.

"Rollin', rollin', rollin' . . ."

He sang until he got the dogies movin' through rivers and streams that were swollen, and by the time he got to the chorus, Jesse was laughing. "Git 'em up, move 'em out, Rawhide," Dewey bellowed.

His absolute abandon, something she'd never seen or expected to see, given his almost pathologically even-keeled personality, wormed its way into her heart, helped along by Jesse's giggles. For the first time, she saw a man who might break the mold. Someone who could love her son for the strange and wonderful little person he was.

Forty minutes into their ride, they left an open grassy field and entered a stand of woods, bright golden and scarlet leaves whispering softly, getting ready to fall. The path was gorgeous, the air sweet with the scents of leaves and pine and earth.

"I have to pee."

Jesse's blunt announcement shattered the magic woodland spell. Dewey sputtered.

"Jesse!" Rose half-covered her mouth. "That's not polite."

"But I do."

"Well, you have to wait until we get back."

"Why?" Dewey stared at her. "We're in the woods."

"So?"

"Please don't tell me the kid has never watered a tree in the woods."

"Urinate outdoors?"

"You and your ultra-proper words," he teased. "For cryin' out loud. Stop the horses. The boy's education is sorely lacking."

"Don't you dare!"

"Rose. Clearly, grandpas who are senators don't go camping and teach their grandsons how to do this. It's one of the few perks of being a guy, so stop, dismount, and get over the fact that your son has the equipment to pee in the woods."

She wanted to be appalled, but he was right. She'd never had brothers. Her father was about as far from outdoorsy as one could get.

"Fine." She moved up beside Rafe, pulled back on Tampa's reins, and the mare halted. "But I guarantee you, this is not his style. He's not a woodsy, grubby kid. He'll want to wash his hands."

"Stop fussing. Leave the guy stuff to the guys."

He grinned, swung his leg over the back of the saddle to dismount, helped Jesse off, and aimed him toward the woods. He turned back to Rose and kissed her quickly. On the lips. Making her stupidly weak and acquiescent. "We're going to whiz in the woods. Girls can do it on that side." He pointed. "Use a leaf."

"Eeew!"

He kissed her again.

She waited only a few minutes before Jesse came charging out of the woods, laughing like a little howler monkey.

"Mom, Mom, I watered a seedling by spelling my name."

"Oh dear . . ." Rose covered her mouth to hold back a choking laugh. "Words cannot express my pride in you."

"I didn't look, but I think Dewey wrote the whole alph—"

Dewey swept in from behind and clamped a hand over his mouth. "Private boys' club information there, champ. Trust me, she doesn't want to know."

Jesse struggled and broke free, still laughing. He clomped back to Thor. Dewey leaned in and kissed Rose again. And once more. "He rubbed his hands off on a basswood leaf. I'll make sure he washes when we get back. Okay?"

"You are without a doubt a whizzing genius."

He grinned, looking delighted and insufferably proud. "I keep telling you. He's a boy. You have to treat him like a boy."

She forgave him the cute little bout of arrogance. In all honesty, she was happy, relieved even, to have him role-modeling for Jesse. He still had no idea what Jesse could be like when he lost his emotional rationality, but there was no doubt Jesse listened to Dewey like he did very few others.

"What's your favorite song?" Dewey asked when they were on their way back.

"'Yellow Submarine.'"

A pair of stunned black-brown eyes met Rose's over Jesse's head, and she laughed.

"That is completely *not* what I expected him to say."

"One of the few bonding experiences with his grand-father. My dad taught him that song, and it was a five-year-long earworm. Thanks ever so much for this."

Jesse was already belting out the mini-saga of the ma-a-an who sailed to sea, who'd told him of his life on the yellow submarine. "We all live . . ." he wailed, loudly and almost in tune. Dewey joined in and, finally, unable to resist, Rose lifted her voice as well. All the ugliness from the week vanished, and they were all still singing when Dewey led them back into the farmyard.

Jesse carried on by himself, piping out the words to Jill's amusement as she helped them untack the horses and give each a quick brushing. He was still humming when they put the horses back in the pasture.

"Don't you think it's time to park the yellow sub back at the dock?" Dewey asked.

"Hahaha, earworm," Rose replied.

Jesse kept humming with impish defiance until Jill halted the singing with an enticement.

"I have something to show you before you go. In the barn."

"What?" Jesse swapped curiosity for the Beatles.

A minute later, Jill opened a wide, wooden stall door, and Jesse squealed at the sight of—Rose counted quickly— nine wriggling, curly haired, multicolored puppies.

"Someone dropped a stray dog off at the clinic six weeks ago," she said. "She was ready to have all these pups, but nobody wanted to adopt a dog in that condition. These little guys are five weeks old and looking for homes."

"I want a puppy!" Jesse pushed into the stall, flopped to his knees, and let them swarm him.

"They're adorable," Rose said. "But no puppies."

"Real boys need puppies," Dewey whispered.

"Do you have a puppy? Maybe you want a puppy." She leveled a warning glare.

"Ha. Maybe I do."

"You do not. You're saying that to be difficult. And this is not a rite of passage like peeing in the woods. Don't you *dare* suggest a dog."

"Mom! Can we have one?" Jesse turned to her, two pups in his arms.

"No."

"But I could train it like Loki."

"Loki?"

"At the fire station," Dewey whispered.

Of course.

"What kind are they?" he asked.

"Mutt crossed with mutt," Jill replied. "Mama looks like a Lab, spaniel, shepherd, husky, something. She's out with Chase and our dog, Angel, fixing fences. Giving her a break from the babies. They're big enough to do without her for an hour."

"Never know, maybe I'll take one for my birthday—it's next week." Dewey shrugged.

"It is?" Rose asked.

He leaned in and whispered yet again, "More on that later." To Jill, he added, "I'm mostly joking. But if you have trouble finding places for them, let me know. I haven't had a dog since Jeff died. Kinda miss him around the station."

"I really, really want one, Mom."

"I'm telling you right now. There will be no puppies. There is no time at all for a puppy." She couldn't figure out why nobody was looking at her. Nobody was saying a word. "No puppies," she said again, feeling like the Grinch.

Chapter Twenty-One

JESSE'S FIRST REAL meltdown since their move from Boston finally happened. Rose didn't begrudge her son the wonderful day, but it grew ever clearer, once Dewey had left them for the night, that overstimulation and sheer exhaustion were going to take their toll no matter how hard she tried to stave off the inevitable.

The catalyst was the dog—the puppy Jesse had picked out despite everybody's, even Dewey's, admonition that he couldn't have one—a brown-and-tan fuzzball he'd taken it upon himself to name Hotshot after his current interest in wildfire fighting.

"Why can't Dewey stay?" Jesse's voice already held a half whimper as he climbed reluctantly into the bathtub.

"He can't stay here, sweetheart. He has his own house."

"He stays late sometimes."

"We all have work and school tomorrow. And you have to help with the football team all week, remember?"

He plunked down into the water. "Dewey wants a dog. What's wrong with a dog?"

"What's wrong is they start out as puppies that piddle all over the house unless you're here all the time to train them. We aren't here all the time."

"I would take care of it."

"Jesse. You have to take care of school first. You're still having problems staying in class for a whole week. Puppies are harder than school."

"They are not!" He slapped the water with his palms, the spray missing her because she stood at the doorway, but drenching a towel on the floor.

"Hey, now," she warned.

"They're cooler than school. Way cooler. And if I had a puppy, I would stay in school."

"First you stay in school. Besides, Emma doesn't really want dogs in this house."

"Why does everybody *hate* dogs?" His voice reached for a screech, and he slapped the water again.

"Jesse, it's time to take some deep breaths."

"No!"

For a few minutes she waited, holding her own breath. Sometimes his rages came and went like lightning. Other times . . .

He stared unblinking while she watched, and the lines between his little brows deepened while his features soured.

"I want a dog."

"This is not up for discussion any longer. Come on, you need to calm down. Finish your bath, and we'll read. There are lots of good *books* about dogs."

"That's just stupid!"

"Wash up."

"I'll be dirty if I want to."

"Fine. Come on out, then."

"I'm staying here."

"Okay."

She left the bathroom, hoping against hope he'd calm down once he couldn't see her. But he wasn't a baby, he only acted like one when his world went out of whack, and he knew she could and would hear everything he said. Or yelled.

"Don't leave me here alone!" he demanded, and then waited. "Mom! Mo-om!" She still refused to answer. "Come back here!"

He continued issuing orders, slapping the bathwater after each. She let him continue for a full five minutes, and then she slowly entered the room again. "Yes, Jesse. What do you need?"

"I want a puppy."

"No puppies."

"Then I want Dewey to come over."

"No Dewey. You'll see him tomorrow."

Not that she wouldn't have given a lot to disappear into Dewey's wide embrace. The magic of their long, adventurous day was quickly dissipating into misty memory, and she longed for its return. He'd never seen Jesse in tantrum mode, however, and introducing him to one of them wasn't something she relished. She wasn't ready to lose their connection quite yet. It was tenuously new as it was.

"Can I call him?"

"He's home sleeping already."

If he were lucky and smart, she thought, forgiving herself the fib because she couldn't definitively say he wasn't, however unlikely at eight o'clock.

"That's bullshit."

"All right. Out of the tub."

Only out of long practice did she keep the command calm. He didn't always curse, but sometimes, if agitated enough, his brain flipped the forbidden words out as if it were having little tic seizures.

She held out a huge towel and tugged gently but firmly on his arm. Enough of the day's dust and horse stink had sluiced off that she didn't care he hadn't soaped, and he resisted, but only a little. He was quickly approaching the age when it wouldn't be appropriate for her to be in the bathroom with him. She didn't want to think about how she'd convince him out of a bad place as he got older.

"You head straight for that bedroom."

He dropped the towel and ran, dripping wet, out the door, slamming it in her face and tearing down the hall. His bedroom door slammed. She marched after him. He'd scrambled under the covers and now sobbed piteously. She gathered pajamas from his drawer and sat, forcing his comforter from in front of his face.

"All right. Look at me."

"Everybody has a dog. Everybody has a horse. Everybody has a pet." The words broke and shattered around him, and his blubbering was almost comical, except that in his mind this moment was end-of-the-world serious.

"You might think so, but you still can't swear and slam doors. Now, if this is something important to you, what should you have done?"

As slowly as water seeping into earth, Jesse's tears ebbed and his sobbing stopped. The irrational little boy receded, and the real Jesse awakened, as if from a spell. "I shouldn't have used the word *bull*—"

"That's right." She cut him off. "And what should you do when you want something?"

"Talk about it and wait if I can't have it now."

The conversation was hers now. It had been a relatively short-lived burst, but the emotions, however used to them she was, left her exhausted. By the time she'd fully calmed him, read to him, and tucked him in, she had no energy left except to go to bed early and try not to fear that tomorrow the flying monkeys would finally arrive.

Dewey hadn't lied; it really was his birthday on Thursday of that week, which he proved by waving his driver's license under her nose and suffering her merciless teasing about the somber most-wanted picture. He exacted retribution by making her agree to a date—one, he said with slightly lascivious relish, that didn't include children.

The thought thrilled her. Another grown-up night out? This time with someone she already knew she liked? But at the same time, the idea terrified her. Each moment spent in Dewey's company was like another drop of heroin into her veins. She didn't know how much more she should take, because any moment she might go over the abyss into a place from which she couldn't escape.

She had no excuse to put him off, however, when out of the blue Liz Cassidy called to see if Jesse could spend the night on Friday. When Jesse said he wanted to, it was clearly Fate who'd set the plan in motion. Jesse rarely if ever stayed anywhere that wasn't home. The plan had the added benefit of being a carrot on a stick. The promise of his first sleepover was powerful incentive to behave at school.

She hated bribing him. She worried about the fact that Dewey seemed to be worth compromising her parenting morals for. But despite Rose's slight guilt, the bribe worked. Monday, exhausted from his meltdown, he spent a quiet day at school. Tuesday and Wednesday he sailed through, evidenced by the lack of phone calls from Principal Verum. Thursday, Rose planned supper for Dewey's actual birthday, since he wasn't celebrating with his mother and family until the weekend, and Jesse arrived from school pumped for the micro-party and the present he'd helped pick out. He was too excited to remember either the gold star on his spelling test or the sealed note from Joyce Middleburg. Rose only found them going through his backpack looking for homework.

"What's this?" she asked.

He shrugged. "I kinda sat in the corner during gym today."

A large crack developed in her up-to-then-perfect week. "Oh, Jesse, what happened?"

"Nothing. I can't throw the football. I only like knowing about the guys who do. But Mrs. Middleburg said I couldn't look stuff up for gym class."

Rose didn't ask further. Resignation warred with worry as she tore open the envelope.

Dear Ms. Hanrehan: Jesse had a minor incident in gym today. He staged a little boycott against our passing practices for the football unit and seemed to think he should be allowed to study quarterback statistics instead of participate. I did not discipline him when he wanted to sit by himself. He has spent the week trying hard in class, and I appreciate that. But I wanted you to know and thought perhaps you could talk to him, as you've obviously been doing, to explain that he can't use the Internet in lieu of being active. Thank you for all your support as we work with Jesse this year. Yours, Joyce Middleburg.

Almost exactly what Jesse had told her.

She had no idea how to handle this anymore. And she didn't know what the appropriate response was. How did you discipline a kid who didn't care about punishment?

Suddenly, she didn't care. Maybe she'd lose her job at the library after all, and they'd leave this town before they'd even begun to settle, and the next place would be fairy-tale perfect. As tired as she was of all the hassles in Kennison Falls, the idea wasn't unpalatable.

Except for Dewey.

He'd be hard to leave.

She sat Jesse in a kitchen chair and took one next to him. "Look," she said. "You are good at memorizing things, that's why you like the statistics on the Internet. But gym is about moving around. If you aren't good at football, it's okay. But you have to try. That's all. It's a rule both at school and here and anywhere else. Just try. Now, it's time to wrap Dewey's present."

It probably wasn't the lecture Mrs. Middleburg had wanted her to give, but that was too bad. Mrs. Middleburg wasn't exactly looking like a whiz at problem-solving herself.

Two hours later, after their dinner of lasagna, roasted garlic Brussels sprouts, and Italian bread, Dewey accepted his present, wrapped in colorful Sunday comics pages, and shook it. "This is a pretty big box for little old me. Will I break anything?"

Jesse laughed. "It's not breakable. It's smashable. I thought of it."

"What?" Dewey's deep hearty laugh, something Rose heard more often lately, filled the living room. "You got me a smashable present? Wow, must be cheap and flimsy, then."

"Not cheap."

"And *not* expensive," Rose added swiftly. Although it really hadn't been all that cheap. And Jesse had indeed thought of it and picked it out.

"So it's not a giant Rolex watch?"

"Not on my salary."

He wrinkled his nose at her, which made her want to hug him like a teddy bear.

Well, no, not at all like a teddy bear.

She nodded at the package to cover her sudden flush. "Open the darn thing and quit asking questions."

"Yes, ma'am."

He tore off the paper and squinted at the picture on the brown cardboard box. "Is this accurate?" he asked.

"Open it."

He did and lifted out a hat—a classic black Stetson with a softly curved brim and a low, unostentatious crown. It was banded with a narrow belt of fine blue beading. Dewey whistled. "Wow. I mean, really. This is something."

"It matches my boots." Jesse stuck one foot straight out.

"It does that." He caught Rose's eyes over Jesse's head. "Thank you," he mouthed.

"If it doesn't fit, I can take you to the shop and they have the same style in other sizes. Your sister gave me an old ball cap you wear sometimes at the garage. We kind of went by that."

"This is . . ." He seemed genuinely lost for words.

"Now when we go riding you can wear your hat and I'll wear my boots."

"Together you're one whole cowboy," Rose teased. She'd never once brought up the fact that they had to wear helmets when they rode. She'd deal with that later.

"Pretty darn cool." Dewey held his palm up for a high five from Jesse. "Thank you both. This is kinda . . . well, I've never had anything like it."

"Try it on." She couldn't help urging him, silly as the gift had seemed when Jesse had first insisted they look for a cowboy hat.

He rocked it gently onto his head, and it slipped into place over his brow like it had been custom made. Her heart jumped a little. He looked, well, dang fine. "Nice," she told him, a little breathlessly.

He acknowledged the catch in her voice with one dark lifted brow. Her heart stumbled again.

"Didn't I hear that you have a birthday fairly soon, too?" He turned to Jesse.

"October twenty-fifth."

"Maybe we'll get you a hat as well. Then we'll be one and a half cowboys."

"The boots were supposed to be for my birthday."

Her literal and honest son. Rose smiled.

"Oh. Well, I'll get you something little, then."

"I want a puppy."

"Oh, good gosh." Rose stood. "No more puppy talk. Time for dessert. You have birthday cupcakes from the Bread Basket," she said. "I totally wimped out on making you a cake. There wasn't time after work. But next year, I promise it'll be homemade."

"Oh? You're promising me next year, too?"

"Unless I get fired. In which case, I may not live here, so you'd be on your own."

"Get fired." He mocked her. "Wouldn't worry."

"Then I'm sure in a year I'll at least still know where you work."

Two cupcakes each, a rousing game of Wii bowling, and a hair tousle before sending Jesse off to bed later, Dewey stood at the door with Rose, his new hat cocked sexily back on his head à la Bret Maverick. She played with his bangs, straightening them beneath the brim.

"Tomorrow night," he whispered, "can't come soon enough."

"I don't know. You seem a little dangerous now in that black hat. Kind of villainous. Maybe I should stay away."

"Oh, no, you don't. And you'd best not leave town before I get a chance to tie you to the railroad tracks."

"But isn't there always a guy in a *white* hat that comes along then and gets the girl back?"

"Hey, you picked the black, sweetheart."

"I didn't. Jesse did. There was no talking him out of it."

"You wish it was white, then?"

She rested the four fingers of each hand on his cheeks and stroked his mustache with her thumbs. She'd grown so used to it she rarely really looked at the thick, well-groomed hair above his lip anymore. She liked it. It was as much a part of him as his nose. But she still wondered what he'd look like without it.

"No. You're such a goody guy in real life—I guess I like this little bit of black-hat action."

"Goody guy?" His nose wrinkled at her again, this time in disgust. "Might as well just call me a girl."

"Trust me, buddy, you ain't no girl."

They kissed, and it filled her with bubbling longing from her lips to her heated core.

"See you tomorrow at six-thirty," he said against her mouth.

Rose worked the entire day on pins and needles, fully expecting a call from school. But it never came. Then she waited for Liz to call with some reason Jesse couldn't stay with Josh—flu, whooping cough, deadly toe jam—but at five-thirty on the nose, Liz and Josh drove up, chatted for ten minutes, gathered Jesse's things, and took him off.

At last, Rose dressed—in an honest-to-goodness party dress, deep cadet blue covered with delicate pink rosebuds—and she waited to wake up and find her entire life had been nothing more than a long, intricate dream.

No evil befell the night. Instead, Dewey showed up as promised in black jeans, a black button-down shirt, a leather jacket with a dark plush fur collar—and his hat.

"Sweet Pollyanna Pureheart," he growled, pushing the hat brim up with one finger. "I'm here to take you to your doom."

She sputtered and laid a hand over her heart, then batted her lashes furiously. "Please don't hurt me, sir. I'm a poor single woman with a fatherless boy in need of a hero."

"Well, I ain't no hero. Can't you see the black hat? But I know where there's a good last meal."

"That's surely something, at least."

He laughed then. "You're a quick one, Madam Librarian."

"I'm good with impromptu stupid."

"It was that."

And with that perfect intro to the evening, Dewey ended up being the one to ruin it. Or at least make a valiant attempt at destruction. She ushered him in and went to grab her coat. When she returned, he was looking at the note from Joyce Middleburg that Rose had left open on the kitchen counter.

"When did this happen?" he asked, his voice sympathetic. "I'm sorry I snooped. But only a little sorry."

She curled her lip and blew out a breath. "It happened yesterday. Today was fine."

"It's not awful." He raised his brows hopefully.

"Yeah, I'm not sure what's going on, but sounds like Jesse's at least trying. And your friend the gym teacher recognized the effort a little. Maybe it's a start."

"Okay, this leads into a thought I had. Just an idea."

"Oh?"

"I'd like to get Jesse a dog. And . . ." He held up his hand at her gasp, rushing on before she could get off the tongue-lashing of disbelief ready to fly. "Keep it at my house until it's housebroken and less of a brand-new pup. Jesse can do a lot of the work, and it'll be like the boots. He'll have to earn the right to keep the dog."

Rose didn't hesitate for a breath of a second. "That's the stupidest, most ignorant idea I've ever heard, Dewey. What have you been smoking? Have you not heard all the reasons I've given, very clearly I might add, that we cannot have a dog?"

"All reasons I can help mitigate. Jesse responds to positive reinforcement. Boys and dogs grow naturally together."

"I don't see you having a dog."

"I did. Until about eight months ago. Jeff. He was an Australian shepherd/golden retriever mix. He was fifteen. I miss him."

"I'm sorry," she said, halted for a moment by his sincerity. But her resolve hardened again quickly. "So why don't *you* get the puppy?"

"I thought of doing that, too."

"And you nixed it why?"

"I didn't nix it. Jill has nine puppies. Enough to part with two."

"You have got to be kidding me."

The tension escalated as the topic morphed into parenting. When he told her—again—that all Jesse needed was to be treated like a normal boy, it was a match to tinder.

"You have absolutely no idea what you're talking about," she railed, her voice rising. "In all these weeks you still haven't seen one of his breakdowns. Would you like to know when the last one was? Sunday night. After our *normal* day. Look, you get to plan all these fantastic outings, walk around like the adored superhero, and then leave the tired, overly sensitive, volatile kid to me."

"Every kid has tantrums."

She had the serious urge to strangle him. "Stop! Stop acting like you get it. You don't get it. Why do you think I watch him like a hawk? Why do think his bedtime routine is set and this is his first sleepover ever? Over the past nearly eleven years, I've learned the difference between normal little-boy anger and Jesse Hanrehan eruptions, and I've learned the signs that tell me one is imminent. You blithely tell me to leave him in school after an incident, but you wouldn't have to pick up the pieces with authorities if he truly flipped out in front of them."

She stopped and hung her head, her insides still roiling. It shocked the immediate anger out of her, however, when Dewey placed his fingers beneath her chin and raised it.

"I'm sorry."

Her heart melted against its will, as it always did lately when his deep-set, dark, and hooded eyes took away her breath and ability to stay rational. She steeled herself.

"And the whole school thing is new to me. He's never acted this way before, and I don't know what comes next with any given incident. I'm not there to control it if his mood escalates. I'm trying as many different things as I can."

"But I've seen how he is at school, too. To me, it's normal. Kids who feel picked on go into protection mode. You can't control his whole life unless you keep him here in a bubble. And he's way too normal for that."

He smiled, tenderly, and squeezed her chin in his palm, running his thumb along the corner of her mouth. Her annoyance melted in the wake of his touch.

"I hope you never have to see one of his swearing, screaming tantrums."

"Oh, I hope I do. I want to get to know all of Jesse." His mouth lowered, and her eyes fluttered shut. "Like I want to know all of you."

The spell weaving over and through her was insidious, dangerous, pulling her under before she was ready. What they been talking about was important. It was easy for Dewey to make grand promises at a moment like this, but she had no desire for another man who only wanted her and didn't understand her son.

But, oh, she had desire for this one.

"We should get to dinner," she whispered.

"Dinner be hanged. I'll change the reservation."

More resolve bled from her, replaced by the incense of his aftershave, the sweet mint of his breath, and total weakness in her joints and mind. Her blood raced and sang through her veins. And then he kissed her. Lip to lip, mustache to tender skin, he roamed her mouth, tickling, thrilling, raising her once angry insides to the boiling point again for a much different reason.

With effort, she pushed him away.

"Too fast," she murmured.

"Or not fast enough," he teased.

"I'm still mad at you."

"No, you're not."

No. She really wasn't. She let him lead her into the kitchen, only steps away from where they stood in the front hallway, and he sank onto the closest chair, pulling her to straddle his lap.

"No dogs," she whispered, laughing and gasping as he hitched her skirt up and slid his hands along the outside of each thigh.

"This is not the time to be talking about dogs."

"It's the perfect time. You're horny and vulnerable. You'll do as I say."

"No." His fingers reached her hips, and he pulled hard on them, settling her firmly against the confined ridge of an unmistakable erection. Desire flashed like heat lightning between her legs and up into her stomach, leaving her trembling. "You'll do exactly what *I* say and stop talking now."

She sank onto him, little eruptions of pleasure building where they meshed, and she didn't say a word.

Chapter Twenty-Two

ROSE ROCKED SLOWLY against him while he held her close. His answering rolls—so subtle she should barely have noticed them—struck like flint on stone. Sparks ignited and caught until she wanted him and his solid body beneath her in a way she hadn't wanted anything in a very long time. Each gentle arch and motion of their bodies built on the previous until, before she knew it, she was gasping for control.

"Easy." His voice soothed in her ear, low-pitched and breathy in its own right.

"This is crazy."

"Maybe."

He wrapped his arms around her thighs and stood, his hands clasped beneath her bottom.

"I didn't really want you to move," she said.

"Believe me, I needed to move."

They reached the sofa in the living room, and he lowered them onto the cushions, settling her once more on his lap but pushing her torso away until he could reach the row of buttons down the front of her dress. They were mostly decorative, but he loosed the bodice to below her bustline and spread the fabric to expose the low-cut bra she'd chosen for . . .

Her thoughts stuttered.

For this, she realized. For his eyes.

Leaning forward, he kissed the hollow of her throat and darted his tongue against her skin, sending shivers dancing down her neck, across her shoulders, and into her stomach. She giggled as, slowly, he worked his way lower, kissing, pushing her farther away from him, supporting her spine until he reached the valley between her breasts. Swiveling his head, he nibbled the soft side of one and then the other and tried to push the flowered dress fabric out of his way.

"How do you get this blasted thing off?"

She giggled anew. "A newfangled invention called a zipper." She pushed forward and nuzzled her lips beneath his ear, loving his groan, and arching against his chest so he could find the zipper pull at her back.

"This was designed by a puritanical father, right? Double fasteners?"

"Can't make it too easy."

The zip rasped, and Dewey growled in triumph. Moments later, he pulled the dress down her shoulders. "That's what I'm talking about," he said.

After unclasping her bra, he pulled it off, too, and dropped it to the sofa. Then he simply looked at her while the heat rose in her face and liquid sluiced to her core at the pure erotic reverence in his study. Finally, when she thought his worship alone might bring her to the brink, he circled her rib cage with his hands, twisting them until his thumbs stroked softly against her peaked nipples.

"Wow!" Her breath caught on the word and gushed out, leaving her airless and with nothing more than the desire to pitch forward into an endless embrace.

"No," he whispered, holding her upright and leaning in for a kiss. "Let me play."

"Fine. But not alone, you don't."

He still wore the jacket and the hat over his black T-shirt. She pushed the jacket backward over his shoulders and struggled to work it free. The gyrations and resulting lap dance nearly did her in. His jacket landed on the floor behind her.

"Shirt," she demanded. The aching excitement left her winded.

She didn't wait for him but dug for the hem of the shirt and yanked upward, hurried and impatient. Once the T-shirt had joined the jacket, it was her turn to stare. At the broad, smooth expanse of his chest. If she'd expected to find dark whorls of hair to match his mustache, she'd been wrong. His sleek skin, warm and taut across his pecs, begged to be stroked; his flat, masculine nipples stood erect and hard to tickle the palms of her hands as she explored.

He managed to flip their positions while they played and lay her on her back. He hovered above her until she scooted her hands and fingers lower onto his belly and delved as far as her fingers could reach beneath the front of his waistband.

"Whoa-ho," he laughed. "You don't get to go there until I get the same. Isn't that how you've set up the rules?"

She grunted.

He grasped both her wrists in one hand and lifted her arms over her head, holding them like a velvet vise. "I'm not finished up here; you have to wait."

Tongue, lips, and teeth tantalized her as he took the tip of one breast in his mouth, dropped it for the other and tasted back and forth until wave after wave of pleasure turned her into nothing but shivering desire. She wriggled to get free, to touch him back, but he held her firmly in place. Her eyes slid closed and her back arched, begging for more touch.

At last he freed her, and her hands flew to his back, grasping at his skin, raking it with her fingertips, eliciting moans and arches from his long, heavy body. He pulled from her slowly, kissed down her stomach, and made his way to the top of her thigh, still clad in mocha-colored tights. Deftly, he smoothed up her hips, found the waistband of the hose, and hooked it with his fingers. They peeled off almost effortlessly.

"Now I'm ready for this part," he said.

"You need to be very careful with this part," she replied.

"Are you worried?"

"Very." She smiled drunkenly, a buzz of anticipation filtering through her limbs as he removed the stockings and her panties at one time.

"Don't be."

She jumped in delight when his lips met the skin above her knee and began a journey up her thigh toward the hot spot between her legs. She moaned as tickles turned to need. One large, solid hand smoothed her stomach, caressed her hip, her other leg and, finally, brought his fingers to rest against the hot folds protecting her desire.

"My turn to say wow," he whispered against her skin. "So beautiful. So ready."

He ran a thumb along the cleft. She sucked in her breath. He groaned.

"I want to touch you, too," she said.

"Believe me, I want you to."

He pulled away, dismaying her until he stood, bent, and cradled her in his arms as he had the night he'd carried her to bed. This time, however, he dropped kisses onto her cheeks as he walked, trailing them to her shoulders, bending almost enough to reach her breasts. They got to the stairs, and she wriggled to lift herself closer to his lips. She'd always wanted this kind of decadent night. A night not cloaked in guilt and fumbling that resulted in a family's shame. A night of clothing trailing through the house because her man couldn't wait for the privacy of a bedroom.

"Stop," she said after he'd mounted the first stair. "Let me down."

"No."

"Yes."

She squirmed free to his laughter and landed on the step above him. Her dress slipped all the way to the carpet, and she kicked it aside, leaving her only remaining article of clothing a blue half slip, then squatted before him and worked the button of his waistband through its hole. Slowly, purposely teasing him, she drew down his zipper, then worked the black denim off his hips and down his thighs. With a groan, he stepped out of the pants, leaving her gaping at what remained.

Hard male excitement waiting behind the darkest pair of briefs she'd ever seen. Something about the surprise of their total opaqueness turned up her desire yet another notch.

"A good guy almost all in black." Her heart thrummed so hard it labored her breathing. Again.

"My thoughts at the moment aren't those of a good guy."

"That's all right."

He lifted her again and let her wrap her legs around his hips to settle against his long, hard body. She thrilled with each lift as he climbed three more stairs, and she pushed closer to him, almost throwing him off balance.

"Hey!" His rumbling chuckle filled her senses, and he grabbed the banister. "You're going to dump us backward, crazy woman."

"I am crazy. I said it before. I just normally have a small person here to counter it."

He leaned forward and set her on the landing step, pushing her backward onto the carpet.

"I can't wait for this anymore."

She thrilled to his impatience. Before she could react to *him*, he'd found the tender skin of her inner thigh and lipped his way to the juncture where he gave her no warning. Hot, wet, tenderly he kissed her in the most intimate kiss a person could give, and lightning seared through every cell in her body.

His touch and tongue strokes, soft and powerful, took only a minute before lightning turned to pressure and then to explosions that sent her cries echoing around the two of them, binding her to him as surely as his arms had done.

He rested his lips against her thigh once more, and she cried out again against the exquisite supersensitivity.

"Dewey . . . !"

"Shhh."

He lifted her from the stairs and strode to her bedroom. Seconds later, they lay entwined skin to skin and kiss to kiss, moving with each other as if their bodies had known how to do it for years.

"Dang," he rasped when he was ready, and she more so. "My pants are at the bottom of the stairs."

"So what?" She pulled on him, trying to bring him closer.

"I need what's in the pocket."

He left her, disappeared, and she collapsed into her mattress, shivering and bereft until he returned, the foil packet already open.

"You're so prepared. You can't be the bad guy."

He smiled, a little distantly, and was back with her in another two seconds. "If I am, then right now I'm *your* bad guy. You ready for me, Sweet Polly Pureheart?"

"I'm not sure I'll ever be ready. Surprise me."

He did, rocking into her body as if he'd been custom created to rescue her. For as big a man as he was, she fit with him as if she'd found a missing half of herself. Her second climax came with his first, and burst in heat and colors that didn't belong to any rainbow spectrum she'd ever seen on Earth.

She lay on her side facing away from him, with his arm wrapped under her neck, supporting her better than a pillow. close behind her she could still feel him pressed against her back and bottom, he cradled her head and leaned over her, kissing her cheek, making her smile. She could barely tell where she ended and he began.

"I think we missed dinner," she said, dopily.

"Is that all you think about? Food?"

"No. I'm thinking about how very good you are at so many things."

"It's been a long time for this."

"For me, as well. I should be . . . embarrassed. Or something. I don't do this casually. I don't really like the idea of casual sex. I'm a prude, deep down."

"Ha! That's the funniest thing I've ever heard.

"Funny as you being a villain?"

"See how you feel in the morning. Or an hour. Maybe it won't be so funny."

She squirmed, twisting until she unlocked their hold on each other and she could face him. He threw a leg over her hip and snugged them tightly together again.

"You will still be my good guy in a black hat." She traced his shoulder. "You do all these good things—making love is just one more that shouldn't have surprised me. If you had kids of your own, you'd be a perfect father. You'd kill to protect them. You'd be amazing."

He reacted like a man zapped by electricity, pulling from her arms, and rolling like a felled tree trunk onto his back.

"What?" She scrabbled to him and leaned across his chest. "What's wrong?"

"Weren't you listening when I told you about my marriage? Talk of kids might be nothing to you, but they aren't in my future, Rose. I cannot have children."

He couldn't give her children. She'd heard him say it. She hadn't thought more than twice about it, and only to wonder what he'd meant. To her shame, she realized she'd forgotten.

He shifted from beneath her and tried to roll away, out of the bed.

"Stop," she said. "Where are you going?"

"Look. I've made my peace with this. I've had to. But no woman wants to know she might be involved with a guy who's . . . well . . . I get that. I thought, maybe, since you knew, you were okay with it."

"What do you mean?"

"I can see your face. It's the look of every woman who's ever found out."

"Not fair. You don't know what I'm thinking."

"I know what you're thinking."

"I'm thinking this made such an impression on me that I completely forgot, and I'm feeling awful because I was just very insensitive and hurt you."

"No."

"Bullcrap, Dewey. It doesn't sound to me like you've made peace with this at all. I get it. Not having another baby is a sad thought for me, too, but having you leave me right now after what we shared is much worse. Don't you dare run off."

He relaxed back into the bed, his face a confusion of emotion. "What do you expect now?"

"I expect that if we both liked this as much as I think we did, we'll talk about everything over time—you, me, feelings and sensitivity—whenever you're willing. I know it's heavy stuff, but it doesn't turn me off. Far from it." She drew lines along the planes of his high cheekbones, traced over his ear and into his hair. "And it brings up a question. Why did you worry about a condom?"

He stared for a moment as if she were insane. "Really? *That's* your question?"

"Sorry, that was supposed to break the tension, but when it came out it wasn't funny. I'm sorry, Dewey."

She waited out his moment of silence and then his smile returned. "They do protect from other things, right? You don't really know if I'm a good guy."

"Oh?" She stroked his face again. "I do, though."

His sudden growl and surge to flip their positions took her breath away, and even though she could see the glistening spot of an unshed tear in the corner of one eye, his laughter drove straight into her heart.

DEWEY PICKED A female pup. Jill and Chase expressed delight at having one of the homeless little rescues go to him. They were equally excited to hold the male Jesse had

chosen in reserve for two weeks—to give Dewey a chance
to talk Rose into him.

The idea was more than presumptuous, and he had
no plans to force it or mention it to the boy if Rose stuck
to her "no dogs" guns. However, something deep in his
gut convinced him after his week with Jesse at football
practice that the kid needed more normal stimulation
in his life. Rose couldn't have been a more fabulous
mother. He saw it in Jesse's overall politeness and good
nature. But Jesse also had a lack of flexibility and something missing when it came to understanding relationships. Dewey was positive the uncomplicated adoration
of a dog would help reach the little stuck parts of Jesse's
brain.

Wednesday morning, he sat at his usual table in the
Loon Feather, his new puppy, Sandy, safe in a large kennel
cage at the station where Elle was more than happy to
keep an eye on her. He'd only had her one night, and tonight he'd invited Rose and Jesse to his place for dinner
so they could meet her. The anticipation excited him far
more than it should have. Because of Rose, life in general
excited him far more than it had in a long time. Just the
thought of seeing her made his body and his emotions
hum like the cars he turned into mechanical works of art.
The memory of their night together only fired his blood
into desperately wanting the next time.

His confidence when it came to her soared, and even
though the slight smugness when it came to her son
didn't soar—he knew he had an easy bond with Jesse. For
the first time since Rachel had left, Dewey was starting to

believe, maybe, he had some*one* rather than some*thing* he could help.

Not to mention that *someone* was a good and beautiful woman

"Well, Dewey, Dewey, Dewey. I was hoping I'd find you here."

He looked up from his coffee, and his heart leapt with relief to see Gladdie Hanson, as robust and smiley as ever. Her sister Claudia stood beside her, long gray hair braided as always and hanging over her shoulder. He hadn't seen either sister since Gladdie had been in the hospital. He stood rapidly and found his arms around the crazy old girls before he realized it.

"I'm so glad to see you," he said. "Come sit with me. How are you?"

"Much better. Sick to death of being sick. Let me tell you, hospitals are for the birds. Or the dead."

He laughed.

"That's my sister," Claudia said. "Won't drive the ding-dang car on the freeway, but is perfectly able to drive everyone around her crazy. She's a horrible patient."

Gladdie didn't argue. She did, indeed, have the reputation of being the coolest, most with-it nearly-seventy-year-old who wouldn't drive more than the five miles around town, and she made no bones or apologies. She took a chair next to Dewey and patted his arm.

"Had no time to be a patient. Too much to do. I missed the big city council meeting, as it was. Poor Rose—how's she doing with all those protestors? That library board of ours, I don't know what to do about them."

Dewey's heart stuck in his throat at the secret he kept. The one imperfect thing about his life at the moment was Taylor Dunn. He'd gotten his mother's permission to come to practice. He was quiet and obedient enough, but had spoken no more about the rock throwing or what he intended to do. He simply rode Jason's coattails into the safety zone Dewey had created for him.

Dewey had determined to give the boy until the end of the week before forcing his hand, but as he sat listening to Gladdie muse on the next board meeting coming up Friday night, the idea hit him. When she said the magic words, he knew exactly what to do.

"I wish they could find the person who damaged that window. I know the worry that it'll happen again weighs on Rose and everyone. And even though they aren't going to fire Rose over something this stupid, they're still talking about it. I know she hates it."

"Gladdie? Claudia? I need your help," he said. "I have someone you should meet—a boy who will definitely surprise you. But please, will you promise that what I'm about to tell you will go no further until you talk to him?"

It was a wonderful thing that the Sisters loved intrigue. Their eyes lit with concern, yes, but more so with anticipation as Dewey told his story.

SANDY THE PUP was a bigger success than Dewey had hoped. Even Rose softened, watching Jesse tumbling around the floor, squealing with the delight of a boy playing with a dog.

"They still have the one he picked out the other day."
He nuzzled Rose's neck, moving behind her ear, touching
his tongue to the goose bumps he raised on her skin.

"Be quiet, Dewey," she said, closing her eyes in pleasure.

"Okay."

"We'll come and borrow your dog. Like this."

"That's good, too."

"I like your house. It's all rustic and manly. Fun to see
after knowing how your sister decorates."

"Sorry it took so long to get you here."

He lived four miles from downtown Kennison Falls,
on twenty acres he'd purchased after returning to take
over the mill. He'd intended to build a house for himself
and Rachel but hadn't had time to start it until after she'd
left. She'd never wanted a log home, but something more
suburban and less woodsy. Over the years, he'd come to
see how few things he and Rachel had wanted matched.

Other than children.

He pushed that out of his mind—with more ease than
he ever had before. There was a child in front of him now
that he could concentrate on helping. Maybe Jesse wasn't
the legacy Dewey had always pictured, but that was starting to hurt less.

"Jesse," he called. "I have something for us to do on
Sunday. Did you hear what's going on at the fire station?"

That pulled Jesse straight out of his wrestling match
with Sandy. "What?"

"The Minneapolis Fire Department is bringing its
brand-new urban-search-and-rescue rig down to show it
off. We can go get a tour of it. Even sit in it."

"What kind is it?"

"I don't know—that's your area of expertise. Bet you can't wait to find out."

"When is it coming?"

"Sometime this weekend. Gladdie told me about it. I thought you'd be excited."

"We can go, right, Mom?"

"Of course."

"And maybe we can go visit the horses, too.," Jesse added. "And Hotshot. Maybe we could bring Hotshot and Sandy to see Loki at the fire station."

"Sweetheart, Hotshot doesn't belong to us, and I doubt the firefighters would let strange dogs into the station. That's what Loki is there for, to protect his house."

"Well, we could go visit him, then."

"What did you do to him?" She whispered in Dewey's ear. "Since when is anything more interesting than a fire engine?"

"Since he figured out how much fun animals that love you are."

"I'm serious, do you two talk about this now? Are you in his evil employ or something? I feel very ganged-up on."

"I have never mentioned that dog to him. I swear. This is all happening organically."

"Yeah, sure it is." She kissed his ear. "I don't trust either of you. I think I'll be glad to have him back at the fire station with the truck. I can handle the trucks."

"You can trust me. Watch how I magically find a way to ravish you without traumatizing your son."

"This I gotta see."

"Hey, Jess. Time to take Sandy out and see if she'll pee outside. Bring her out to that spot we used before, and wait until she does something. After she does, bring her back in and we'll eat pizza."

Jesse disappeared with the puppy in less than a flash. Dewey turned to her, his heart racing with joy to see the welcoming heat in her eyes. He pushed her onto her back along the sofa cushions and shifted so he could lie fully on top of her. She arched into him and took his mouth with hers like a hungry tigress.

He rubbed her breast gently through the soft purple sweater she wore.

"I've really missed you," she said against his lips. "Last Friday seems like eons ago."

"I'm really glad to hear you say that. I'm running out of cold water."

"Well, we can't do it here and now," she whispered.

"Friday. After the library board meeting. I have a feeling you'll be ready to celebrate."

"You're ever the optimist."

"I am. And I'll bet I can find someone to watch Jesse and the dog while we"—he suckled her bottom lip—"go, um, out to dinner again."

He pressed into her, his body hardening swiftly and a little painfully. He was insane to tease her like this when Jesse would be back any second. "Don't move like that," she whispered, her voice hoarse. "I'm almost to the edge already. Been there since you left Saturday morning."

"You should not have told me that," he replied and pushed off her. As rapidly as he could, he pulled her up and nestled in behind her. Eagerly, he pressed his fingers at the junction of her thighs. "Maybe he'll stay out there long enough . . ."

She moaned and lifted her hips. "Dewey, no, there's not . . ."

Sure enough, the back door slammed. Dewey groaned as Rose scrambled away.

"She peed and pooped!" Jesse called before he reached the living room.

"Thanks for teaching him that," Rose whispered. "So crass. Just like you. Now, how am I supposed to wait for Friday?"

"Maybe you won't have to. I'm pretty creative. Let's eat pizza."

"That's not much of a consolation prize."

He grinned at her as Jesse entered the room, the pup in his arms.

"You told." Dewey faced the irate eyes of Taylor Dunn with calm patience. "I can't believe I trusted you. You're as big a fake as everyone else around this stupid school and this whole stupid town."

"Take it easy. We're going to have a little chat," Dewey said.

"I'm not chatting with you or anyone. I'm in so much trouble."

"I had nothing to do with that."

Taylor glared. He'd come charging at Dewey like an angry elephant, with Jason behind him, early on Thursday just as they'd been early to help set up every day that week. Now Jason stood helplessly by, looking like he thought this was his fault. But Dewey had not come unprepared.

"Jason, see Jesse over there? He's been in a cranky mood since school let out, and I think you could help him. He claims to hate football. Didn't you tell me once you felt that way when you were a kid?"

"I did."

"Do you think maybe you could show him some of the things you learned when you were young? You're a pretty good teacher."

"Sure," he said slowly. "I wouldn't mind. Do you need me here?"

"Nope. Taylor and I are going to work some things out."

Jason nodded and headed for Jesse, who was, indeed, in a crappy mood. He'd had a fight with his mom about dogs again. He thought it would be cool to have Sandy's brother so they could stay friends their whole entire lives. Rose remained unbending. And today, for the first time in over a week, he'd apparently acted out in gym class again even though they were on to basketball. He evidently hated basketball more than football.

Dewey watched long enough to see that he didn't run or turn away when Jason reached him, then he turned to the slight boy waiting sullenly by his side.

"So, Mr. Dunn. Things can't be too bad if you're here."

"My mother said I had to come and tell you I wouldn't be here after school anymore."

"That's fine. The deal was you had to stay until you told what happened."

"I didn't tell! You told."

"I told Mrs. Hanson. I know her and I knew she'd help take care of this. She must have talked to your mom."

"They're making me go to the library board meeting on Friday and tell the story."

"And you'll go. I'll come with you if you like."

"Why would I want that?"

"Because I can tell what a good job you did for me this week. That I think you should have to pay for the window but that you should also get help from your mom. Mrs. Hanson is talking to her about that. And about your dad. We want you to get some help, Taylor."

"I don't want any help! My dad will kill me."

"He won't. That's what Mrs. Hanson will help your mom prevent—your dad getting too angry. She's worked in all kinds of places and helped all kinds of people. Trust me, she's a better go-between than I am. Tell me the truth. You weren't going to tell your mom anything until I forced you to, were you?"

He didn't meet Dewey's eyes.

"This is just starting, and it's going to be hard. But there are people to help you, and if you're strong, you'll fix this."

"It can't be fixed."

"Sure, it can. Anything can be fixed. Now, you can stay here today or go on home—either is fine. I will plan to see you Friday night. I'll sit in the back and say what

I have to say, and you don't have to talk to me. But I care what happens. You came to me for help. This is the best I can do."

Taylor kicked at the grass. Thirteen and so confused. Dewey placed a hand on his shoulder, and even though the boy shrugged away, he walked toward Jason rather than away toward the parking lot.

And at that moment Dewey heard Jason call, "Okay, you got this." And he tossed a football about ten feet to Jesse, who caught it and started laughing loudly enough to carry down the field.

Dewey stood thunderstruck, understanding clearly the weird gut feelings he'd been experiencing the past three weeks. He'd seen their needs and put all these kids together. The satisfaction of watching Jason pass on his skill and Jesse succeed squeezed at his heart and spread satisfaction like an a warm embrace through his soul. The heat made him want to keep this day going despite Taylor's anger and troubles, despite the work waiting for him at his real job, despite the fact that Jesse dropped the next pass. He *was* good at kids, just as people said. And he'd been ignoring the emotions of that talent for the past fifteen years.

Chapter Twenty-Three

GLADDIE CALLED AN impromptu planning meeting at Dewey's Loon Feather table Friday morning. She brought two of the library board members with her—Brian Duncan, who'd been a supporter of Pat Dunn's, and Abby Stadtler-Covey, a staunch supporter of Rose's.

"Hey, Abby." Dewey greeted her warmly, and she threw her arms around his neck in a friendly bear hug. "How are you feeling?" he asked quietly. "Do we still have a secret?"

"If you're talking about that amazing baby we can't wait to meet, no," Gladdie called across the table. "It's definitely not a secret."

Abby flushed. "I'm feeling great, Dewey. Hit three months, and the morning sickness disappeared like magic."

"I'm glad. When's the baby due?"

"February, sometime around Valentine's Day."

If that wasn't perfect for Abby and Gray. He kissed her on the forehead. "That's terrific. I'm very happy for you."

"Aw, thanks. Now we're battening the hatches for a media storm when everyone finds out."

"Hey, could be kind of fun running off reporters again."

The whole town had rallied to keep the media away from Gray when he'd first settled in Kennison Falls with Abby. It would certainly rally again to protect their baby.

"I'm counting on you," she said.

For the first time, Dewey was purely happy for a friend's baby news. No strings attached.

"Now then," Gladdie said, when they were all seated. "I believe Brian's been persuaded to join our side. He and Abby have been talking. Is that right?"

"Brian called me last night after he'd spoken to Pat," Abby said. "When Brian heard Taylor's story, he asked if there was any way the board would consider not pressing charges. I felt we had to sound out the members who've been on the board longest. Gladdie thinks we can work something out. I would like to as well. But what about Rose? Dewey, have you mentioned any of this to her?"

"I haven't. It's probably wrong not to. I thought it would be a wonderful surprise for her to get to the meeting tonight and learn the mystery has been solved."

"Do you think she'll go along if the board comes up with its own form of discipline for young Taylor?" Abby asked. "It sounds like he's going through a lot, although I'm anxious to hear Pat's version."

"Pat is devastated," Brian said. "She won't be active in the protests anymore. She says she's got to concentrate on her son's issues."

"The smartest move she's made in a while," Dewey said.

"Be nice," Gladdie reprimanded.

"How boring." He grinned. "As for Rose, I have no doubt she'll be all for a creative solution. I won't speak for her, but retribution isn't her style."

"Then we're agreed," Gladdie said. "Abby, you'll call for all the charges to be dropped if Taylor agrees to some sort of agreed-upon punishment? Rose will have to be involved in that, as we said."

"I will."

"Brian, you'll announce that the petitions to challenge the list of books presented to the town council are being withdrawn?"

"Yes, I will."

"Okay. Now all that remains is to get together with Rose and decide what to do with young Mr. Dunn. And the entire board must vote on the suggestion tabled last time to renegotiate Rose's contract."

Dewey's phone buzzed in his pocket, and he pushed back from the table to check it. "Speaking of head librarians." He smiled, stood, and stepped away.

"Hey. This is a surprise," he said into the phone.

"Dewey?" He recognized the panic in her voice immediately. And without another word, he knew Jesse was in trouble again.

"What's wrong? What do you need me to do?"

"He's missing this time. Oh God, Dewey, they're telling me Jesse actually ran away from school. And nobody has been able to find him."

What the . . . ? What on Earth was going on with this kid?

"Was he upset this morning?"

"He's been upset since we were at your house, and I told him we wouldn't be getting Sandy's puppy brother. This morning he wanted me . . ." She hesitated, and her voice actually lightened slightly. "He wanted me to get you to move in with us."

"Is that right?"

"I told him it wasn't possible, and he huffed out the door."

"Wait. You didn't ask *me* if it wasn't possible."

"This is not funny."

"Of course not. Well, it's a little funny."

"Oh, Dewey, it can be funny after I find him. The school thinks he's been missing almost two hours. Joyce Middleburg assumed he was out sick because he wasn't in class. And his regular classroom teacher didn't notice for about ten minutes that he hadn't come back from gym. They spent some time looking for him at school, and then they called me."

"He's fine," Dewey promised, despite a wave of concern. "He probably walked home. Or maybe to the station to try and see Sandy."

"Would you check? Please?"

"Of course."

"The only other idea they had was that Josh Cassidy actually was home sick today. Since Jesse has latched on to him, they wondered if he might have gone there. I'll try calling Liz. If he's not there, I'll go home."

"I'll check the station, see if Elle has seen him."

"Thank you. I don't know what I'd do without you."

"You'd be fine, Rose."

But he did like hearing those words.

Jesse wasn't at the Gas 'n' Garage, and Elle hadn't seen him. Rose texted that he hadn't been to Liz's house, and she was heading home. "Please pray he hasn't been abducted," she'd finished.

Dewey wanted to call her right up and reassure her that kids didn't get abducted in Kennison Falls. Everyone knew everyone. But that wasn't necessarily true. They'd never *had* an abduction, but plenty of other small towns had. If Jesse had followed the main road into town from school . . .

He shoved away the thoughts that followed. Jesse was quick and resourceful, and he didn't like strangers. He was fine. But where? Dewey racked his brain for ideas. His own house was too far out of town, as was Jill and Chase's. The only other place Jesse had ever been was the fire station . . .

Relief rushed over him like cool, soothing water.

He called Rose, but she didn't answer. He left a message, and three minutes later he was at the Kennison Falls Fire Department. Sure enough, outside the fire garage stood an enormous truck with "Minneapolis USAR #1" emblazoned on the door and the sides. Several men in dark blue uniforms stood around a pair of opened doors. What he didn't see was a short, obnoxious kid.

"Hey, Dewey!" Chief Severson stood among the representatives of the MFD and stepped forward when Dewey approached. "Come to check out the amazing apparatus?"

"Actually, I'm hoping maybe you've seen the little Hanrehan boy. Jesse. He walked out of school today, and nobody knows where he is. I was almost positive he would have come by here. You know how he loves fire trucks."

"Man, Dewey, I haven't seen him."

His heart plummeted. There was no place else to look.

"Well, if he does show up, you'll let us know?"

"Of course."

Then another thought struck him. "Is there anyone in the fire station?"

"Not at the moment. Just the dog."

Aha. "Do you mind if I stick my head in and look around?"

"Not at all."

It took only two minutes to find him. He sat on the floor in the kitchen, his back against a cabinet door next to Loki, jabbering as if he conversed with a human.

"I looked it up. It's got a Gladiator cab and chassis and a Cummins ISL 550 horsepower engine. And I saw when they opened it, it has a hydraulic lift-up rear staircase, a 35,000-watt generator, and a two-bottle SCBA fill station."

Loki periodically licked Jesse's hand, and Dewey felt for the kid. Here, with this dog, he could go on about details to his heart's delight. Nobody got bored. Nobody asked him to please stop.

Nonetheless.

"Jesse Loren Hanrehan?" Dewey's big voice echoed through the kitchen, and Jesse jumped. "What are you doing here?"

Jesse's eyes went saucer-shaped, and he turned back to the dog. "I came to see the truck."

"You have no business coming anywhere when you're supposed to be in school."

"I hate school."

"I don't care if you hate school. You don't walk out without telling anyone. Your mom is worried to death. She thinks you got kidnapped. And I'm not too happy with you either."

With the suddenness of an exploding grenade, Jesse slammed his hand against the cabinet door and glared. "I'm not happy either. With you or with my mom. You guys suck, and you don't care if I hate school and you don't care if I want a dog. Everybody has a fucking dog."

By this time, Loki had slipped away, unnerved by the outburst. Dewey couldn't blame him. He had no idea what to say.

"Go away," Jesse continued. "I want to stay here."

"You can't stay here. Your mom is on her way."

"I don't *want* her." He banged the cupboard again.

"Then come with me."

"No! No, no, no. I don't have to go anywhere with you. Not to football, not to riding. You're not my dad. You're nobody's dad. Go get your own kid."

Jesse was only ten years old, and Dewey had been warned about this moment, no matter how much he'd thought Rose had been exaggerating. Nonetheless, the vicious words laid him low like nothing anyone had ever said. Even Rachel's leaving had felt kinder.

"It's time to go," he said, his voice thick in spite of himself. *Ten. He's ten. Don't get sucked into taking this personally.*

"I'm not going."

"Well, you are if I have to haul you out kicking and screaming."

"No. No. No. No. No." Jesse pounded rhythmically on the cupboards and screeched the words. He looked frighteningly like he belonged in a horror movie.

"This is ridiculous," Dewey said. "Come on, Jesse James. Calm down, now." With that, he bent over and scooped his arm around Jesse's midsection, the way he'd done the very first time he'd seen him climbing on a fire truck.

The boy screamed like he was being hacked to pieces.

"Be quiet, Jesse."

"No!"

He carried him outside and set him on the lawn, far from the firefighters. Jesse broke for the truck, and Dewey grabbed him.

"Knock it off," he demanded.

"Let me go!"

"Not until you behave yourself."

"You suck! You suck, Dewey. You're not the boss of me. You're not the dad of me."

Again the words tore at him. Stupidly, he took Jesse by the shoulders and drew him nose to nose. "What's gotten into you? Stop!"

"No, Dewey, you stop!"

He looked up to see Rose running toward them. She glared at him, and took Jesse from his grasp. Without another word, she walked Jesse six feet away and knelt in front of him.

"Jesse. Honey? Take a deep breath. Come on, you're upset again. Remember what you're supposed to do?"

"I want to see the truck."

"Absolutely not until you're calmer. Now, breathe. What did you say to Dewey? He's very upset."

"He sucks. He told me I was bad for leaving school."

"It was wrong to leave school. Now, look at me. Jesse? Look at me. What do you say when you've said something rude?"

"I'm sorry."

"Now, say it to Dewey."

Dewey could hardly look at the boy, but he managed it. Something was breaking inside, and he had no idea what was happening. Jesse was just a boy. There was no need to react like he was one himself. But the ideal world of half an hour before was imploding.

"I'm sorry, Dewey."

"It's okay, Jesse."

Neither of them meant it.

Slowly, Rose calmed the boy. The light of crazed frustration left Jesse's eyes, and he started to droop. Tears slid down his cheeks, but he didn't bawl.

"What happened today?" Rose asked.

"The sixth-grade class got to come and see the engine this morning. Our teacher said the fourth-grade class wasn't going because we had other field trips planned. I wanted to see it."

"But you can see it tomorrow or Sunday."

"I wanted to see it today. It's not fair."

Dewey stared in amazement and distress. What had turned adoring Jesse into the child from hell?

"When something like this happens and you want to do something, what should you do?"

"Talk to you. But you'd say no."

"Maybe I would. We all have to hear *no* sometimes. You understand that."

"Everything okay here?" Chief Severson strolled to them and raised a concerned brow. "I see Mr. Jesse really was here."

"I'm sorry," Rose said. "He got a little overexcited about seeing the search-and-rescue engine, and walked here from school."

"We had a group from school here earlier this morning."

"Sixth grade," Jesse mumbled.

"Would you like to come and get a personal tour of the apparatus?"

Jesse's eyes awoke from their dark anger, and he transformed instantly into Excited Angelic Child. Dewey nearly choked on his astonishment. He'd run from school, caused panic and searching, thrown a temper tantrum worthy of *The Exorcist*, and now he was getting a prize? He stared at Rose.

"Go ahead, sweetheart," she said softly.

When he'd gone with the chief, Rose turned to Dewey, fuming. Before he could get a word off, she lit into him.

"Haven't you learned by now that you can't grab him and get into his space?"

"No. I've wrestled with the kid, what the heck? And what's with rewarding him for the worst behavior I've ever seen?"

"You didn't believe me, did you?"

He hadn't believed her.

"That's beside the point. How does he get away with this?"

"His brain doesn't work the way ours do, Dewey. Can't you get that through your own head? If you don't short-circuit a problem before it starts, he can't stop it himself. He's learning, but it's a long-term training exercise, and when he blows, it's ugly."

"I'll say."

Her features froze, and she straightened, her explanations over. "Well, thanks for your understanding."

"I don't understand, it's true." He looked across the station yard to Jesse, laughing as one of the Minneapolis firefighters dressed him in a giant jacket. "If I'd have acted like this, I'd have had a mouth full of soap and a week in my room."

"You wouldn't have acted this way."

"Whatever, Rose. I obviously have no idea what I'm doing. I'm nobody's dad. Ask your son."

"Wait. He said that?"

"Yeah, he did."

"Well, but it's true, isn't it? Is this about hurt feelings?"

"Don't be ridiculous." His own anger flared at her callousness. "Look. Clearly, I need to back away for now. At least he's safe, and he'll do better alone with you. He was pretty mad at me."

"And vice versa."

"Okay. In the interest of honesty."

"It'll be over for him next time you talk to him."

"Sure. He got what he wanted."

"He doesn't think like that. He falls apart because he doesn't get what he wants, not because he's scheming to get it. The difference is subtle but it's real. He doesn't plan his meltdowns."

"Maybe not, but don't think for one second he doesn't know what will happen when he pulls something like this. He knew if he got in trouble at school, you'd come running. Better yet, we'd both come running. He likes us together, Rose. He manipulates things to make it happen."

"Don't be ridiculous."

"Think about it."

"Excuse me? I've had nearly eleven years to think about it."

"With nobody else's input. That's your fallback, Rose. You're the only expert on the kid. But other people have eyes, too."

She looked slapped.

His heart raced with the adrenaline of anger.

"That was a little bit unfair. And that's the nicest thing I can say about it." She bit her bottom lip.

"It was," he said. "I'm sorry. But I also am going to leave now. It won't do Jesse any good to see us like this. We have a problem, Rose. I think it's mostly mine, but even so, it's better if I'm not here."

"That's your solution when there's a problem, whoever has it? Walk away?"

"Sometimes walking away is the smartest, best thing to do while you figure out the fix. I'll see you tonight."

"Tonight?"

"I'll be at the library board meeting."

"What in the world for?"

"Maybe I have a vested interest in a lot of things around here."

He left her gaping, her eyes boring into his back as he strode to his car. Numbness kept confusion and anger pinned to the background of his mind, but they hovered there, waiting for him to come out of shock to pounce.

He lasted until he got back to the gas station. Then he sat in his car, afraid to face Elle or anyone else who might see something was wrong. And something was definitely wrong.

It wasn't Jesse's meltdown, it wasn't his swearing or inadvertent cruel words. It wasn't Jesse at all.

He'd fallen into the trap he'd sworn never to go near again. He'd begun to believe that he could fix his biggest problem—the problem of never being a father. He'd had it by the tail, damn it. He'd all but believed he'd been sent, by God above, even, into Rose's life to love her and help with her son. He'd thought he had it all figured out.

As it turned out, he had nothing figured out.

The bottom line was, cruel and simple, he was helping Jesse not out of love but out of arrogance, and he had fallen for Rose out of selfishness. The kid drove him crazy, and he and Rose couldn't have a civil conversation about him to save themselves.

They were not living a relationship. They were living a frickin' life lesson.

Well, he'd had far too many of those—that's why he'd built his life the way he had. In a backward kind of way, he understood Jesse. Dewey didn't melt down the same way, but he did know how to withdraw and protect himself from things getting out of hand.

He didn't know, however, how to protect himself from the emotions that now cried for attention. The picture of Rose in her bed, the promise of lovemaking to come, the hot sweet desire nobody else had awakened in him for so long—all of that was moot. She came with precious baggage—and Dewey didn't want responsibility for the baggage in the long term. It made him a shallow, awful person, but it was the truth.

If Elle noticed anything that afternoon, she didn't say. She was nearly ready to start her Camaro, which she'd worked on faithfully the past several weeks. Dewey focused on the U-joint he had to replace in a local farmer's pickup and then dragged himself to football practice.

Not surprisingly, neither Jesse nor Taylor showed up. It was too expected, Dewey thought, his mood spreading to encompass annoyance and depression. He and Rose had agreed Jesse would come to practice through today. He supposed the boy didn't want anything to do with him either, but still—it was one more thing he was escaping and getting to blame on his "different brain chemistry."

Only Jason was his cheerful self, and the rest of the squad worked out with no inkling Dewey was scraping the bottom of his emotional barrel to appear normal. All because two messed-up kids hadn't shown up to do what he'd told them to do.

He really must be some kind of egotistical jerk.

The board meeting that night, held on Rose's turf in the library conference room, put the capper on his excruciating day. The worst moment came when Pat Dunn walked in, subdued and embarrassed, without Taylor. As if Dewey needed any more proof that his ego had led the way in trying to help these kids, Taylor's no-show was salt in the wound. Pat apologized profusely on her son's behalf and claimed he'd run off to his grandmother's in Faribault because of fear.

Another convenient excuse.

Dewey said his promised piece about Taylor's work ethic when he'd been helping with the team, but his praise felt like fraud. Especially when Rose stared at him throughout the entire speech as if he were Brutus to her Caesar for knowing about Taylor at all. Afterward, she refused to look at him as the board decided the boy's punishment: paying for half the cost of the window's $1200 repair and donating it to the library fund, and volunteering three hours a week for six months.

Gladdie announced that Reverend Nathanial was backing down because he couldn't fight the book fight on his own.

Finally, Rose sat with back straight and face calm as the board then voted, with one dissention from Wilma

Nesrud who felt none of the problems would have happened at all if Rose had simply acquiesced to the board's wishes, to suspend any talk of reneging on Rose's contract. Only when Abby made a formal statement reiterating the board's confidence in her, did Rose finally let emotional tears fall.

Such a quick end to a drawn-out emotional issue. Dewey was almost thankful for Taylor's angry, rock-throwing prowess. He'd accomplished in his blind delinquency a solution that had proven too difficult for a town full of angry adults to find.

"You knew about Pat's son?"

He'd tried to leave the meeting unseen, but Rose accosted him in the library foyer. His heart pounded. A confrontation over the Taylor issue was the last thing he wanted. "He came to me and begged me to help him."

"And you didn't think I'd like to know?"

"I swore I wouldn't. It was the only way to gain his trust. As it was, I broke it when I told Gladdie. Only last minute, by the way. She's got influence with Pat, and I hoped she could bring this to an end. She did."

"And you thought I couldn't handle it?"

"You couldn't be part of it at first, Rose. Besides, I thought I'd like to surprise you with a done deal. It's that simple. Don't take it personally."

"You got it wrong," she said. "It's not simple at all. The fact that you hid this information for a week is not okay with me."

"It has to be. It's done."

"Do you take anything seriously?"

He held his temper. He took things so seriously he'd be drummed from the laid-back, good ol' boys' club if anyone knew. "If you have to ask, then it makes what I was going to tell you once this settles all the easier. You and I aren't a good idea, Rose. Attraction isn't enough to get us through these things that are important. You said the one thing you always needed to know was if a man didn't have it within himself to accept your son. Clearly, I don't."

The shock on her face truly surprised him. He'd been certain she'd have said the words first but, instead, her chest moved in and out like a runner finishing a race.

"You're really going to do this?" she asked. "You're going to walk out? You make love to me—make me break all the promises I've made to myself about loving someone and being loved. You make Jesse love you. And then you back out? Of all the arrogant, selfish things, Dewey."

"I can't build a life with Jesse on just the fun stuff. You've said that yourself. And as for us? I was almost fooled, too. But look what happens to *us* when it comes to family. We fall short of what each other needs."

"Don't do this."

"We've already done it." He leaned in and kissed her on the corner of the mouth. "You're an amazing woman and an even more amazing mother. And you're more than fine without me. We'll have to see each other, even be friends, in a town this small. But I've done that before, too."

"Dewey, I can't be—"

He touched the spot he'd kissed. "I promise, Rose. It's really not that hard."

Chapter Twenty-Four

FOR THE TENTH time in the six short weeks of this school year, Rose sat in Linda Verum's office and rubbed her eyes, both to clear the headache pounding there and to hide the burning that threatened to spill tears. All she could say about this meeting was that Jesse hadn't done anything wrong today. The accumulated demerits, however, had come home to roost.

"Jesse is simply not happy here," Mrs. Verum said. "We don't believe even creating an IEP for him at this point will help."

Joyce Middleburg also sat in the small office, as did Jesse's classroom teacher.

"That's why we honestly believe Prairie Path would be a wonderful fit for both of you," Joyce said. "The staff there works almost exclusively with kids that have special interests."

For all that Joyce was Dewey's old friend, Rose didn't

like her very much. She'd been less than helpful with Jesse's problems, certainly not innovative, and now she looked pleased and smug that she'd been the one to suggest the entire idea. Including the euphemistic language. Kids with special interests her ass. Prairie Path, was a private school specializing in students with learning and discipline problems.

"I really don't feel private school is the answer," Rose said. "I still have faith in public education. In addition, I simply don't have a lot of money to spend on tuition. Unless you'd like to take up my salary with the library board."

Which she'd never let them do. The library had enough budget issues.

"We can't force you to send Jesse to a private school," Mrs. Verum said. "But if Jesse can't learn in this environment, we think you should consider a different district. We only want what's best for Jesse."

They were giving her doublespeak and platitudes, but she hadn't come to this town fighting for independence for no reason. Even though she didn't feel a bit of the confidence she turned on them, she faced them with squared shoulders.

"I will consider your suggestions," she said. "But I'm also telling you that I don't believe you've done much at all in Jesse's best interests. You won't give him special consideration unless he's tested for the tenth time in his life, and you won't admit he does not have problems with his schoolwork but with his socializing. He requires a little creativity that apparently stretches the limits of the teachers at this school. That's not impressive to me. If I decide to leave him here, I'll expect better. If I decide to move, it will be because *I* decide to move."

She stood, leaving the three educators ruffled—she hoped.

But once she exited the school, her nerves failed, and the tears she'd successfully held back blurred her path to Miss Scarlet waiting in the parking lot. The move from Boston had been going to free her, give her independence and strength away from her suffocating parents.

Instead, she was suffocating in the rigidity of a small-minded town and a smaller-minded school. It was too bad Gladdie, or Liz, or even Dewey had no say in the education system. Something needed revamping.

Dewey.

She still couldn't fathom what had happened. She'd seen him shouting at Jesse at the fire station last week, and she'd panicked. Jesse's body language had given away the severity of his tantrum, and she'd never heard Dewey so much as correct her son with more than a few words. She hadn't known what to do, so she'd lashed out at the adult rather than the child. And the adult had flipped out. There was no other phrase for it.

She'd been furious at him for walking away. Hurt beyond words. And Jesse was beside himself, asking if Dewey was ever coming to visit again. Dewey had torn apart two hearts. And yet, she didn't hate him. She was angry. Hurt. But she missed him. Missed the laconic voice, his big, beautiful hands, his body next to hers.

She wanted him now. Crying in his arms would not

fix her problem, but that had been Dewey's magic. He could fix without fixing. He gave her the tools to sort life out herself.

With effort, she pushed thoughts of him aside. They'd surface again when Jesse got home anyway, since her son hadn't gone a single day in six without talking about Dewey. She started for the library but couldn't make herself go back there. Her emotions swirled. What would happen if Jesse had to move schools again? He'd lose Josh. He'd lose the familiar bus ride. He'd start all over again with a new set of problems.

She had to talk this out. She needed perspective. Her mother? That would garner a lecture. Gladdie? She'd soothe, which would be nice but not helpful. Liz was on a deadline. She'd become a good friend, and Rose would call her later that night. But she wasn't a good enough friend to interrupt her writing time.

Elle.

Elle was one of the sweetest, strongest people Rose knew. It sometimes frustrated her that Dewey didn't know what he had in his sister. Elle could run the entire shop. Rose believed it with her whole heart.

They weren't that close, but always chatted like long-lost friends when they were together. Maybe if Rose talked to her, used her as a sounding board, like one might use a bartender, Elle would get incensed but still be levelheaded. Elle would listen.

But she'd have to face Dewey in order to get to his sister.

Tears coursed down her cheeks when she closed the

Mustang door behind her and sat in the silence. She couldn't go anywhere like this.

Maybe the café. She'd go to the Loon Feather and sit by herself, sort out her brain, talk to Lester and Cotton.

Neither Dewey's car nor the tow truck was at the Gas 'n' Garage. She tried to drive by, but at the last minute, she had to take a chance that Elle was the one working. She pulled up to the pumps and sat, trembling, for long seconds. Finally she extracted herself from the low-slung car.

"Rose?" Elle walked from the garage, wiping her hands on a rag. "Oh my gosh, I thought I'd lost you forever because of my dumbass of a brother. It's wonderful to see you."

"Hey, Elle. Yeah. You too."

"Whoa, what's wrong? You look like you've been crying."

"Is Dewey here?"

Elle looked furtively behind her. "Ah. Do you want him to be?"

"No, actually, it's you I'm looking for. Do you have a minute? I need a shoulder to cry on."

"Of course I do. Come on, there's coffee in the office."

Rose had been right. Elle listened with growing anger as Rose told about the principal's "suggestion." And she ranted on Jesse's behalf for a satisfying minute before huffing into a chair and propping her chin in her hands.

"I'm sorry," she said. "What can I do?"

"Tell me I'm not crazy for wanting Jesse to stay in a school where he isn't wanted." Rose wiped her eyes, feeling utterly foolish, and yet better, as she'd hoped, after voicing her worry.

"Of course you aren't crazy. The school's job is to help kids like Jesse. He's such a cool little dude, why are they singling him out?"

"I don't know. I'm pretty sure the gym teacher has taken a dislike to me, and she seems to have the principal's ear. I know she and Dewey are friends, but . . ."

"That's neither here nor there." Elle shot to her feet unexpectedly. "I'm sorry, Rose, I'll be right back, I just remembered something I left not-quite done in back. Sit, I promise this'll only take half a minute."

"I don't have to stay. I just needed to tell someone."

"No, no, finish your coffee. I'm glad you came."

She disappeared. Rose heard the radio in the garage and Elle moving something around. She returned after a few minutes, her face set in frustration.

"Everything okay?" Rose asked.

"Sure. I just have a stupid customer who wants things done a certain way."

"You seem happy here, Elle. Good for you."

"Yeah. Dewey's coming around. Giving me more responsibility. I guess I wore him down. But I'm more worried about Jesse. Will you tell him about the new-school idea?"

"I don't know. Not until I have a chance to think about this a bit."

"You're amazing, Rose. You have so much love and patience for Jesse. This will work out."

"And that's what I needed you to say!" Rose stood, truly feeling better.

"Please come back and visit again. Or better yet, let's get together sometime. I know I'm a kid, basically, but I have more in common with you than I do with my own sister."

"Of course. And thank you. I knew you'd be a great shoulder."

It was nearly four when Rose left the station. Elle had talked her off the ledge, but she still didn't know what to do. About anything. Maybe it would be easiest simply to go back to Boston.

The thought made her ill.

"You can come out now." Elle's voice, stern and sharp, pulled Dewey from his spot at the office door.

"Thanks," he said, slinking sheepishly into the room. Elle had begged him to come and talk to Rose, but he'd refused, choosing instead to eavesdrop like the Sisters at the Loon Feather.

"You are the dumbest ass of all dumbasses, Duane Mitchell. She's the best thing that ever happened to you."

There wasn't any doubt of that. He sat heavily on his desktop and inspected the floor morosely. "Maybe. But I'm certainly not the same for her. That's the trouble."

"Did you hear what she said?"

"I did." His stomach was still in the process of tying itself in knots over Jesse. "Joyce Middleburg needs her complacent-teacher's ass kicked."

"Yes. And Rose needs you." Elle leaned beside him on the big desk, her fingers splayed like Donald Trump about to fire someone.

"She doesn't. Not this way."

What he meant was not with his head still this screwed up, but Elle actually nailed it better.

"What way? As the town wimp? Yeah, I don't blame you."

"You're a little big for your britches again lately."

"You're not big enough for yours. You idiot. Don't you see the look in her eyes when she says your name? Raw pain, bro. Stop being a dick and go talk to her."

"You have to clean up your language, sister, if you're going to be a businesswoman."

"I've had to hone my swearing so these antiquated farmers around here will even do business with me. I have four brothers who taught me well. Quit acting all sanctimonious and pitiful."

"I'm leaving," he replied.

"Now where?"

"Rose won't take any help from me. Well, fine. But maybe I can help Jesse instead. I'm going to have a little chat with my old friend Joyce."

"Whoa, whoa. What on Earth are you going to say to her? You aren't going to change her mind with emotion. You need facts. You might be Mr. Know-it-All when it comes to motors and engines, but you've proven you know nothing about Jesse's problem. I'd stay away from Joyce Middleburg, brother of mine. Don't make things worse."

"You little . . ." Dewey clenched his teeth over the remaining words threatening to snap like a whip tail across Elle's intractable glare.

The desire to defend himself was so strong he could

barely contain it. He'd done everything he could to befriend the child, to help him, to guide him. To understand . . .

Anger drained from him like hot air from a balloon. More like hot air from a pompous . . . again Elle had said it best, *dumbass*. He'd been through the self-chastisement, but he'd even missed the point with himself. The point *was*, he'd done nothing to understand Jesse. Not truly. Not from Rose's point of view. The school administration was frustrated enough with the boy it was trying to get rid of him. Get rid of, no, *give up* on a ten-year-old child. What hell on Rose's part had he been ignoring? What had happened to education in the past fifteen years?

"Dewey? Dewey, I'm sorry."

He looked down when Elle gripped the sides of his face with strong hands. He must have been staring like a madman since he felt a little mad. His fingers covered hers and he bent forward to peck her on the forehead.

"Don't be sorry." A little effervescent bubble from inside turned into a harsh laugh. "I admit, for a second I wanted to punch you like I'd punch Glen or Bart if they pissed me off."

"I could see that."

He kissed her again, this time on top of her head. The excitement that had steamrollered him back when he'd been working with Jason, Jesse, and Taylor blossomed again. He didn't know everything. Hell, he knew very little. But he'd been selfish to keep himself from getting educated about kids all this time. Maybe he plain needed to stop crying in his motor oil.

"You want more hours here, right?"

"Ah . . . yeah?"

"Want to start right now?" He backed away, waiting for an answer.

"Dewey? Where are you going? I was sorry but serious—"

"Too late! I'm going to school."

"Duane! Don't you dare!"

He ignored her.

DEWEY REMEMBERED THE corridors of Peik Hall at the University of Minnesota well even after nearly sixteen years. He found the office door he wanted easily and knocked, pushing it open before the jovial "come in" rang from inside.

"Duane Mitchell, as I live and breathe!" Professor Thomas Hanson, his thick black hair only slightly grayer, and his jowls only slightly saggier than they'd been all those years ago, stood and met Dewey halfway across his bright, yellow-painted office in the College of Education's department of Curriculum and Instruction.

"Professor Hanson."

"Good heavens, after all this time call me Tom," he said. "I can't tell you how great it is to see you looking well. You were a student I'll never forget."

Dewey ran a hand self-consciously through his hair and laughed. "Sorry to hear that."

"Not at all! I only remember the gifted ones. Come. Sit. And explain yourself. Our phone conversation earlier this week was low on details."

"Very simply I want to re-certify my teaching certificate."

"Fantastic, my boy!"

"And, while I was researching how to do that and looking into a new area of interest, your name came up." Dewey set three books on his old teacher's desk and smiled. "You are an expert in autism spectrum disorder. I had no idea."

Tom Hanson nodded self-deprecatingly at his writings. "As much as anyone is an expert. It's equivalent to exploring outer space in some ways. What's your interest in autism?"

"At this point it's more precisely Asperger's. Do you have time for the story of a boy I've gotten to know?"

"I always have time for a story."

Two hours later, Tom leaned back in a chair at the work table in Burton Hall where he'd taken Dewey for what he'd called some in depth research. Dewey rubbed his eyes and stretched. It hadn't been as much research as a glossed-over crash course in everything experts knew and didn't know about Asperger's, now officially referred to as one of many autism spectrum disorders.

He couldn't help himself; his mind had drifted continuously to Rose and what she lived with every day. She'd have been more supported, more understood if Jesse had been born with full-on autism. Having a child with difficult symptoms but no real cognitive or learning impairments, which characterized Asperger's, made the disorder nearly impossible to deal with. No wonder she'd shunned so-called professional help and educational plans in a school that didn't want to accommodate her son in the first place. And Jesse wasn't severely Asperger's. He didn't talk robotically, or completely shun others, or inappropriately hug or touch them. He just didn't get some things about social skills.

But the biggest thing Dewey now understood completely was that the problem was real. He couldn't make it go away by treating Jesse like a normal kid. Rose had been right. It had to be dealt with slowly, over time.

The knowledge made the memory of Jesse's hugs and true trust ache like a wound in Dewey's mind. It made the memory of his last angry interaction with the boy burn like acid in his heart. And it made him want to scoop Jesse Loren Hanrehan up and protect him from every last hurt and mean thing anyone could ever say to him.

It made him want to hold Rose Hanrehan and keep her safe and strong until the end of time.

"I think I've saturated your brain enough for one meeting," Tom said, clapping Dewey on one arm.

"I agree. I'm overwhelmed. But I'm excited."

"It's just knowledge, however. Don't forget that. Your Jesse is one child. Remember—"

" 'If you meet one person with autism, you've met one person with autism. He's a unique person with unique symptoms. Got it."

And, Tom had also walked him through all the requirements he'd need to fulfill to get his teaching certificate re-certified. He knew now it would take him six months or so. A lifetime for someone in as sudden a hurry as Dewey was, and yet, it was no time. Whether

Rose would ever take another chance on him or not, Dewey had just made the biggest change in his life's plan since giving up professional football.

"I can't thank you enough for this," he said.

"You go get that girl." Tom knew the whole story now. Dewey had seen no point in trying to hide his motivations. He'd hidden enough things the past decade and a half. "She'll be lucky to have you."

"Don't bet the house on her taking me back." Dewey offered a rueful shrug. "But I at least have to try."

Chapter Twenty-Five

"Mom, can we have popcorn?"

"Are you done with that homework?" Rose put away the last of the dishes from the dishwasher.

"Yeah."

"Then we can have a little for your bedtime snack. But it's still only Thursday, so you can't stay up late. We'll find a movie tomorrow night. Maybe we can go to one."

"Maybe Dewey can come."

"I don't think so, honey." Her heart thudded to the bottom of her chest.

"Maybe we could go see Sandy."

As if her heart could take any more hits. The stupid dog had caused more grief, yet she missed it. She was three heartbeats away from picking up the brother pup. Especially if Jesse ended up leaving this school, which, after the past weeks of research, talking, arguing and head-against-wall banging, Rose was almost ready to agree he would, he'd need a friend.

She'd just put the popcorn in the microwave when the phone rang. The instant she recognized Liz's phone number, she answered immediately.

"Hey! Everything okay?"

"Rose! Yes, yes, of course. I'm heading out to a meeting, but I had to call first and find out what you thought when you saw Dewey."

Again her heart splayed like a deflated ball against her ribcage. "I haven't seen him in three weeks, Liz. We're, uh, not . . ."

"I know, I know. Everyone is bummed about that. And I'm sorry. I assumed you'd have seen him at work or something. Well, it's nothing. Just thought you'd have an opinion. Let's get the boys together this weekend."

"Sure." Rose frowned.

"Gotta run. I'll call tomorrow."

"Uh, Liz . . . ?"

She was gone. It had to be one of the strangest phone call she'd ever received. What was the big deal?

She popped the corn, dumped it into a bowl, and settled in with Jesse to watch his favorite show, *The Big Bang Theory*. She prescreened them for the most blatant sexual content, and for the most part, innuendo went way over his head. She explained what few things he asked about by telling him outright there were things grown-ups got to do that kids didn't.

Which only brought her thoughts directly back to Dewey.

The phone rang again. This time, it was Gladdie.

"I heard you're taking Saturday off and letting Kate handle story time. I'm proud of you. You're working so hard for us."

"That's nice of you to say. Thanks, Gladdie."

"I want you to know how proud I am of you for weathering the first storm. I knew we'd chosen the right girl for the job."

"Well, really, thank you. But it's what I was hired to do."

"It was. By the way, did you see Dewey today? Wasn't that something?"

Okay, this was now officially weird. "Gladdie, what the heck is up with Dewey? You all know this is cruel, right?"

"All who? I thought you might have the strongest opinion of anyone, but if you haven't seen him yet then mine is a moot question. Okay, dear, I'll see you tomorrow. Kiss that young man of yours. Bye-bye."

"Gladdie, wait!" But she was gone, too.

All through Jesse's bedtime routine, the two bizarre calls weighed on Rose's mind. Both Liz and Gladdie knew she was still raw about Dewey. Why would they do such a thing?

At last she'd tucked Jesse into bed, and the only sound in the house was the low hum of a television drama serving as company. Rose puttered around the kitchen, cleaning up the popcorn bowls, half fearing more strangeness. Sure enough, not ten seconds after she finally picked up a book to read, the phone rang a third time. She read the name on the screen and scowled.

"Elle? What the heck is going on?"

"Huh?"

"Are you calling about Dewey, too?"

"Well, yeah. I thought I'd see if you were as freaked out as I was."

"I do not know what you're talking about."

"Oh. Well, okay then, it's no big deal."

"Elle, don't you dare hang up on me. What's going on?"

She didn't get a chance to answer. The doorbell buzzed, something neither Rose nor her pounding heart found funny in the least. Her friends were going to guarantee she ran away from home—screaming.

"Sounds like you have company." She could hear Elle's smile over the cell. "I'll catch you tomorrow."

"Don't you—" Rose growled into the dead phone and smacked it onto a couch cushion.

A soft knock followed the bell. Rose threw open the door, a hot reprimand on her lips, and she stopped—speechless and frozen in her tracks.

"Hi," he said, the deep sable of his hair skimming the shearling jacket collar. "I wondered if you'd seen that Dewey Mitchell idiot around anywhere."

It was gone. The mustache. The iconic brush of hair she'd grown to love touching, love feeling on her skin, had been shorn away. Her heart nearly pounded through her chest wall. He looked naked, young, so . . .

"Gorgeous." She clapped a hand over her mouth and the unintentional outburst.

If Dewey Mitchell had been handsome and distinguished before, he was now *GQ* hot. It took every ounce of willpower not to throw open the screen door and feel the bare textured skin above his lip to make sure she wasn't dreaming the sight of his full, perfectly shaped, sexy upper lip.

"Dewey Mitchell?" she managed. "No. I'm not sure he's in town at all."

"Gorgeous?" He cocked his head.

"Don't get big headed." She bit back the smile that wanted desperately to escape.

"Can I come in for a minute? I have something to tell you," he said. She opened the door. "Is Jesse asleep?"

"Just barely. This might be worth waking him up for."

"No. Not yet. Not until we talk."

"Okay." She couldn't quit staring. "You know, an old picture would have been fine. You didn't have to do this."

"I did. I needed a big change. Needed to change an old, stubborn, arrogant persona, in fact. Plus, I don't want to look like an old fart going back to school."

She felt the cool night breeze fill her open mouth. "Going back to what?"

"It's been an eventful three weeks."

"Umm, okay. You'd better tell me."

"First, though, is Jesse all right? Are you? Elle told me about what the school wanted you to do. Rose, it's unconscionable. Have you made the decision to move him?"

"I haven't. I haven't even mentioned it to him. I . . . don't really know how. Honestly? I'm scared to."

It felt amazing to tell him that. Whatever he said or did next, at least he knew her world was as messy as ever. It had always made her feel better to tell him so.

"You don't have to be afraid. You're the toughest mom I know. And the toughest woman. You don't need white-hat heroes."

"I don't know about that—"

"I have a confession."

"Oh?"

"I was at the station the day you talked to Elle. That was the day *I* wimped out, even though Elle tried to get me to see you. But even though I'm a dumbass—Elle's name, but she's right—the idea of Jesse being forced to change schools hit me like an atom bomb. And, it forced me to do some research. Into several things. I wanted . . . I needed a chance to see if you'd let me tell you about it, but I didn't know how to come back after this long."

Her jaw dropped again. "Hold on. Did you set up this whole did-you-see-Dewey-today phone-tree thing? You weirdo."

"I needed someone to grease my way. First of all, I thought you might run me off with, I don't know, whatever librarians use for weapons. Second, I wanted you to have a little warning. People stare something awful."

"As they should. My Lord, you could turn angels' heads."

"All right. Stop *that*."

"I'd touch that bare lip if we weren't enemies."

He groaned and reached for her before she realized what he was doing.

"I hereby declare that we're no longer enemies. I don't know what we *are*, but I can't stand this. It's been a horrible three weeks. When I heard what was happening to

Jesse, I thought my heart was going to break for him. And then I thought it was going to break for you. That's when I knew everything I thought I felt for you two was wrong, and I had to figure out what the hell my problem was."

"Wrong?"

"I wanted Jesse to be a fun-project kid. That was safe. That was fixable. But he's not a project. He never was, but I wouldn't admit it. He's part of my life now. I don't just care about him, I'm crazy about the annoying twerp. And then there's you. I thought I'd lost a limb in the last three weeks. How can that be when I'd only known you for six weeks before that?"

"Well, how can it be that all I wanted after getting talked to by the school principal was for you to help us? Talk about Sweet Polly Pureheart tied to the railroad tracks. I was pathetic."

He kissed her. She kissed him back. On the mouth. On the bottom lip. On the smooth, mustache-less upper lip that made him look like every movie star and every man to pop up in a fantasy ever in the history of the world.

He sighed. "That feels strange. Like I'm missing half my clothes."

"I would like to arrange that, as well."

"First things first," he whispered. His mouth covered hers again, and this time it didn't matter whether the mustache was gone or not—she didn't notice.

"I'm so sorry, Rose," he said after he pulled away, and she reluctantly let him. "I was out of line at the fire station. You *are* the expert when it comes to your son. I'm not just saying that, I mean it. It's going to take me a long time to earn my way into fatherhood, but I'd like to start."

"Fatherhood means coming running when they need you, Dewey. You've mastered that a hundred times over since we've met you. And it's being intuitive and creative with solutions. I was unfair, too. You're right. I've been isolated with Jesse, and I'm stuck in my ways. I need your insight. You do have wisdom.

"I know the fact that you can't have biological babies hurts you. But it doesn't define you to me. There are lots of paths to fatherhood. There are kids out there who need help. They need dads. Jesse is one of them."

"And there are men who need smart, strong women to haul them through life and make it worth living. I would be one of those."

"Okay, as long as we're playing one-up, there are women who are tired of trying to know everything on their own. We need—"

"Fix-it men?"

"Lovers."

"I like that better."

"Actually, we need mates," she said. "I think that's the natural order of things."

"Mates who argue with each other? We seem to like to argue."

"How else do you work things out? We simply have to learn not to walk away from a fight."

"If you say you'll give me another chance, I'll make that promise. But be warned: then you're stuck with me. So think carefully."

"There's one more thing I have to know." She traced the smooth skin beneath his handsome, sexy nose. What's this going-back-to-school thing you mentioned, as if in passing?"

"Yeah." He scratched the back of his head, tipping his black hat forward slightly. "I sold half interest in the garage to Elle. I'm signed up to start the continuing education credits I need to get re-certified for teaching. I go back to class in January. It'll mean I'm not the town handyman anymore. At least not full time. But I'll make good on any jobs you have for me. A perk of taking a chance on a guy with a black Stetson."

"Are you kidding me?"

"I am not. Although I still think my sister is insane. Why anyone would want such a thing is beyond me."

Rose squealed and leaped into his arms, unsure he could hold her along with all the feelings bursting from her heart. "That's the most wonderful thing I've ever heard."

"Better than 'Will you marry me, Rose Hanrehan?'"

She pulled back, and he braced his hands beneath her seat. "Dewey?"

"I warned you."

"Then yeah, *that's* the most wonderful thing I've ever heard."

"So it's a yes?"

"Yes! Yes, it's ten yeses."

"Mom?" The uncertain voice of the boy who never got out of bed stopped them just as the kiss would have deepened. Surprised, Rose rubbed Dewey's nose with hers and took time to run her thumb yet again across the smooth skin of his lip. She uncrossed her legs from around his hips and slid to her feet.

"Thought he always stayed in bed." Dewey grinned.

"Must be a special occasion or something," she whispered, and turned. "Hey, sweetheart."

"Dewey?" Jesse's little brow puckered.

"Hi, Jesse James."

"Where's your mustache?"

Dewey laughed from his belly. "The bad guys took it."

"Oh. Okay. What's going on?"

Rose joined in the laughter, amazed as always at how she couldn't predict what her son would do—ever—around this man.

"Well," she said slowly and shrugged for Dewey's benefit. "How'd you like to get a puppy?"

"What?!" Jesse James Loren Hanrehan screeched in disbelief and broke into a run from his dead standstill. When he jumped at full speed, four very strong, loving arms caught him and twirled him until he was dizzy.

"Me *and* a puppy?" Dewey whispered in her ear. "Madam Librarian, I'm not sure what to say."

"It was a pretty crappy three weeks here, too. That does something to a woman's resolve."

"Jesse?" Dewey said without looking at him. "I'm putting you down now. And I'm going to kiss your mom, so no "yucks" out of you, got it?"

Jessie wriggled to the floor on his own. Dewey claimed Rose's mouth—hot, slick, knee-weakening.

"Yuck!" Jesse covered his eyes and slumped to the floor, giggling.

Rose closed her eyes, her sigh uneven, desirous. She shoved the Stetson off Dewey's head and delved her fingers into his hair. "I love you," she murmured against his lips. "And there's an awful lot stored up. Can you handle it?"

"Hey, can I wear your hat?" Jesse crowed.

"For the rest of your life," Dewey murmured back, and as far as Rose was concerned, it didn't matter in the least which of them he was answering.

"No!" Jesse covered her eyes and slumped to the floor, giggling.

Rose closed her eyes, her chin uneven, desperate. She moved the ribbon off Dewey's head and slicked her fingers into his hair. "I love you," she murmured against his lips. And there, it's awful he stood up, can you handle it?

"They can't hear you, hon," Jesse crowed.

"Yes, the rest of your life." Dewey murmured back, and as far as Rose was concerned, it didn't matter to the least what of them he was answering.

Continue reading for excerpts from

THE RANCHER AND THE ROCK STAR,

RESCUED BY A STRANGER,

and

BEAUTY AND THE BRIT

Available now from Avon Impulse!

An Excerpt from

THE RANCHER AND THE ROCK STAR

FATE WAS A nasty flirt.

Gray Covey dropped his forehead to the steering wheel of his rented Chevy Malibu and sighed, a plaintive release of breath, like a balloon with a pinhole leak. He had no idea what he'd done to her, but Fate had been after him for months. After this last wrong turn in her twisted maze, he knew she'd finally trapped him.

The long, pitted road before him wasn't described in the useless directions scribbled on the slip of paper in his hand. Neither were the two branches fanning left and right fifty yards away. And being lost wasn't enough. Oh-ho, no. On top of everything, Fate had hung an angry, bruise-colored sky about to unleash enough water to terrify Noah.

He lifted his eyes, rubbing the creases above his brow. As he prepared to admit defeat, the edge of a small sign to the left caught his eye, and his first small hope sparked.

Inching the Malibu over the washboard road, he pulled up to the hand-lettered sign he'd been told to look for. Hope flared into gratitude.

Hallelujah. *Jabberwicki Ranch.*

Still unable to believe someone would give a piece of property such a stupid-ass name, he stopped short of laughing. Half an hour ago, a dour attendant named Dewey at the only gas station in Kennison Falls, Minnesota, had made it clear nobody in the town of eight hundred souls laughed at anything Abby Stadtler–related. The woman Gray sought was no less than revered.

And yet . . .

The saintly Abby Stadtler was harboring a missing child.

His.

He rolled past the Jibberjabber sign, stopping at side-by-side black mailboxes. *A. Stadtler—Jabberwicki* and *E. Mertz.* Ethel Mertz. What?

Alice in Wonderland meets *I Love Lucy*?

"You've got to be kidding me." He spoke out loud without meaning to. Out of habit he checked over his shoulder to make sure he hadn't been followed and overheard.

This explained why Dawson had been so hard to find—he'd fallen down a friggin' rabbit hole. The sophomoric humor helped him remember he was only half serious about throttling his runaway son to within an inch of his life. And it kept him distanced from emotions that had been scraped raw in the past weeks. His current jinxed concert tour aside, between his mother's worsening illness, moving her to the care facility, and Dawson's disappearance within days of that, life lately had been sorely lacking in humor.

Except, maybe, for Ariel. In his ex-wife's case, all he could do was laugh. "They've found Dawson," she'd announced on the phone the night before in her clipped British accent. "But unless you want the authorities to fetch him, you'll have to pick him up, darling. I can't leave Europe with the baby."

Of course not. After all, only six weeks had passed since their son's disappearance—nobody could make arrangements for a two-year-old on such short notice.

Gray had not been about to let the police "fetch" his son, nor had he wanted to alert Dawson and send the boy running again. So here he was in Jabbitybobbits, Minnesota, despite the monumental nightmare he'd caused by leaving his manager, his baffled band members, and eighteen thousand fans in the lurch.

Well, what the hell? It was just Fate adding another hilarious disaster to the worst tour in rock history. Re-focusing, he looked left toward a homey log house, then right into a thick stand of pine and oak. Which fork led to Ethel Mertz and which to The Jabberwock's ranch?

Eeny, meeny, miny . . . He couldn't get lost if he stayed right. Slowly he drove toward the trees and didn't see the diminutive, elderly woman staring at him until he'd drawn even with where she stood in an opulent flower garden near the road. For a moment he considered stopping, but her assessing glower and the stern set to her square-jowled face convinced him to settle for an impersonal wave and continue around the gentle curve through the woods. He hoped the dour watchwoman wasn't the much-adored Abby Stadtler.

The house he *hoped* belonged to Jabberwocket ... *Ranch?* didn't appear until he was in its front yard—an old, two-story farmhouse painted non-traditional Guinness brown with windows and doors trimmed in blue and white. A disheveled patch of shaggy, colorful wildflowers, much less immaculate than the garden he'd just passed, stretched along one side.

The growl of thunder greeted Gray as he exited the car, and he looked with concern at smoke-bellied thunderheads piling high. The end-of-May breeze smelled wet and thick. In front of a small garage stood an older, red Explorer, and on his left a short stone path led to a porch wrapping two sides of the house.

After mounting two loose steps, he faced a pair of dusty saddles, the kind with big, sturdy horns in front, sitting on sawhorses, and several flowerpots in various stages of being planted. A small square of black electrical tape covered the doorbell. He knocked, got no answer, then knocked again. Several minutes later he returned to the driveway, searching his surroundings. Down another gravel slope, a couple hundred yards away, stood a vintage barn, its white paint worn and the haymow window boarded up from the inside. He sighed and climbed back into his car.

Heady scents of hay, sawdust, and animals hung in the heavy air when he left the Malibu once again. To his delight, a golden retriever loped toward him with lolling tongue and giant doggy smile. "Hey, fella." Gray scratched the dog's ears. "Got a boss around here somewhere?"

A muffled *thunk* answered. Ahead, backed up against the open door of the barn, stood a flatbed trailer loaded high with spring-green hay. The golden led him to the wagon front, and a pair of small, gloved hands emerged from inside the barn, grabbed the twine on one bale, and yanked it out of sight. Intrigued, he watched until the owner of the hands popped from the dim barn interior. She placed her palms on the flatbed and, in one graceful movement, hoisted her long-legged body to a stand. Reaching for a top-tier bale, she dragged on it, toppling the entire stack. Gray's brows lifted in appreciation.

"Afternoon," he called.

Her startled cry rang more like a bell than a screech of fear, but she stared at him with her mouth in a pretty *oh* and her chest heaving. "Jeez Louise!" she said at last. "You scared me half to death!"

Flawless skin was flushed with exertion, and her round, bright eyes flashed uncertainty. A thick, soft pile of chestnut made a haphazard bun atop her head, but long wisps of hair had escaped and swung to her shoulders. Her face stopped Gray's thoughts dead. It was not the toughened visage he'd have expected of a woman who chucked hay bales like a longshoreman. The elegant, doe-eyed face belonged in a magazine, not a barn.

"I'm really sorry," he said.

A rumpled, hay-flecked flannel shirt hung loose over body-hugging, faded jeans that had suffered one nicely placed rip across her left thigh. He braced for the inevitable squeal of recognition.

"Can I help you with something?" She squinted at him for a few seconds, but rather than squeal, she shook her head and pulled down another stack of hay.

"Are you Abby Stadtler?"

"Yes." She continued dragging bales, and he sighed in relief.

"I'm looking for my son."

That stopped her. "Son?" Her eyes took on a glint of protectiveness. "Who are you?"

That stopped him. For an instant his vanity stung, but the freedom of unaccustomed anonymity hit, and he allowed a private grin. "David Graham." He used his official alias. "Pleased to meet you."

"Likewise," she said. "Excuse my rudeness, but this hay has to get in that barn before the storm hits. I can't help you with your son. I don't know anybody named Graham."

Abby Stadtler hopped to the ground. The plaid shirt swung open to reveal a bright blue tank top hugging a curvy hip. "My boy isn't Graham," he said, meeting her eyes, which were unlike anything he'd ever seen. Greenish? Bluish? "He's Dawson. Dawson Covey."

"I know a Dawson. His last name is Cooper."

He tamped down a flicker of irritation, as she grabbed twine, swung a bale, and took two steps to dump it in the barn. There was not a single sound of exertion—or any hint she was taking him seriously.

"Yes, that would be my devious son." He held on to a pleasant tone. "Cooper is his grandmother's name."

"And why would he use a different name?"

As she turned the interrogation on him, a rope of tension twisting down his neck knotted between his shoulder blades and threatened to stiffen him top to toe. He willed his fingers to uncurl, one-by-one. "Because he's sixteen years old, he's pissed off at his mother and is hiding from me. He's also sharp as a knife blade, so it's taken us a while to find him. You've obviously never had teenagers."

An immediate illusion of height accompanied the steeling of her spine, and the soft, nameless color of her eyes turned to stormy aquamarine. "You shouldn't make assumptions." She tossed another hay bale, and Gray took a step backward.

"I apologize. I only meant you don't look old enough to have teenagers." That was true.

"If that was an attempt at getting yourself off the hook, it was smooth but ineffective." The sharpest prickles left her voice.

Finally, she stopped tossing and crossed her arms. The rolled-up sleeves on her overshirt exposed slender forearms with sexy lines of definition curved along the muscle.

Gray produced his best version of a devilish grin. "Dang. I usually have better luck with a silver tongue."

"I'll just bet. Look, Mr. Graham." She hesitated. "Wait a minute. Did you say sixteen?"

"Yup. My Dawson is sixteen. How old is yours?"

She didn't respond to the humor. "Eighteen. We definitely have some confusion here. I hired a young man six weeks ago to help around the farm. He'll be leaving for home in another month. Colorado."

Gray snorted. "He'll be leaving for Colorado over my dead body."

"Mr. Graham." Her voice flashed with annoyance to match her eyes. "I think you have the wrong Dawson. People must have mixed up the information they gave you."

"I do not have the wrong Dawson." Slamming his palm on the wooden bed of the hay wagon hard enough to cause flakes of alfalfa, and Abby Stadtler, to jump, the humor Gray had been using so desperately as a shield disintegrated. His make-nice smiles hardened into anger lines he could feel. "Look, Madam Jabberingwickets, or whatever the hell this place is called. You've got my son." He jabbed his fingers into a back pocket, yanked out his wallet, and flipped through the three pictures that were part of its meager contents. "Tell me this isn't the little con artist you call Dawson Cooper."

The photo was two years old, but it did the trick. Abby leaned over it with skepticism, and then her shoulders sagged. "Oh no."

"Oh yes."

"I-I'm sorry."

He gave her points for the apology, although she looked for all the world as if she didn't want to give it. "It's all right." He calmed his voice. "All I want is to find my son."

"I've never heard Dawson mention a father. He's talked about his mother in New York."

In a stinging sort of way that made sense, Dawson wouldn't want to mention his dad's notoriety. He jammed the wallet back into his pocket. "She's not in New York. They live in London, and he packed up and left his private school just after Easter last month. Didn't you check him out before letting him move in?"

Anger flared in her face again. For some reason, Gray found the rising and falling storms in her seawater eyes knee-weakening. "You *really* need to stop making judgments. What you just said was condescending and insulting."

She turned her back and grabbed another hay bale, tossing it willy-nilly into a pile along with the others already in the barn. This one went a fair distance with the steam of her anger behind it. He couldn't help but grin in admiration. Abby Stadtler was soft and enticing as a chocolate éclair on the outside, with TNT instead of custard beneath the surface.

"Look, I don't know you . . ."

"That's right." Her fuse obviously still sparked, she clambered onto the wagon again. "For your information, your son had a New York driver's license, references from a past employer, and a personal reference. No, I didn't do an FBI background check on him. Up until now, I've had no reason to suspect I needed to. I don't know where you come from, but around here we try our hardest to believe the best of people."

Gray scarcely heard beyond the fact Dawson had come up with faked reference documents. He didn't know whether to be horrified or impressed as hell.

"I . . . That's amazing." He tried finding some amusement in her face, but she kept yanking hay bales from the pile, her back flexing, captivating him. He wondered where Mr. Stadtler was. "Abby . . . Mrs. Stadtler." He struggled not to anger her again. "I told you my son is smart. I forgot how smart. He's pulled off a professional-level scam here, and I can't tell you how grateful I am he came to a safe place like this."

She threw a glance over her shoulder, her eyes no longer sizzling. "He's a good boy, Mr. Graham, even now that I know the truth. Not that he won't get a proper lecture."

The very first hint of humor tinged her voice, and Gray grinned back, relief sweet in his chest. "You'd be justified. So where is he?" Realization struck him. "Why isn't he helping?"

"He isn't here."

His attention snapped back to her. "Excuse me?"

"He and Kim are gone for the weekend."

"Gone! Gone?" Gray balled his fists and wanted to hurl a hay bale across the barn himself. "Gone where? And who the—" He took a deep breath. "Who is Kim?"

"The teenager you thought it obvious I never had." This time her eyes danced with a hint of laughter, and if her newfound cheerfulness hadn't come at his expense he'd have found the crinkled corners of her eyes appealing.

"When will he be back from wherever he went? With your teenage daughter." He forced his voice to stay modulated and pleasant.

"They've been on a retreat with the church youth group all week. They'll be back tomorrow late morning."

"Tomorrow?" *Another day?* Gray lost his hold on calm. "Damn it!"

He stalked from the hay wagon. The cloying air pressed heavier with every step, and the clouds encroached, purple and black. Thunder reverberated, close, angry. He had another show in Chicago tomorrow night. No way could he miss it, too. What would Chris do when he found out tonight's gig hadn't needed to be canceled at all?

Slipping his hand into the pocket of his leather blazer, he fumbled for a pack of cigarettes. He hated them. He was down to half a pack a day, but times like this he despaired of ever kicking the habit. With automatic skill he drew one out, flicked his lighter flame against the end of the cigarette, and took a drag.

The idea of Chris Boyle on a rant made Gray swear under his breath again. Everything came down to money for his manager. Sometimes Gray felt like no more than a windup monkey who waddled onstage, banged its cymbals together, made the crowd screech, and raked in the dough. He dug his fingers through his hair and started a vicious second drag—

Thwack!

The cigarette flew from his lips as if a bullwhip had snatched it, and he choked on air and smoke.

"Are you really this phenomenally stupid?" Abby, her face florid, her posture like a boxer ready to jab, ground her boot toe into the smoldering cigarette until shattered pulp remained.

"What the . . . ?" He stared at the ruins, then into her furious eyes.

"This is a barn. Fifty feet away is a wagon loaded with hay. Do you have any idea what a gust of wind could do with one of your stupid ashes?"

"Oh, damn, Abby, Mrs. . . . Abby. I'm sorry." Contrition twisted his gut.

He *hadn't* considered the danger before lighting up. Her gaze drilled into his, and regret gave way to a slow roll of deep, unexpected attraction. Earlier they'd been separated by hay and irritation, but now they were separated by nothing but five inches of steamy, sultry air. An asinine string of thoughts ran through his brain: how smooth her cheek was up close; how the middle of her pupil was soft and calm like the eye of a hurricane; how much he wished he had a breath mint.

"It won't happen again."

Along with his sudden, inappropriate desire came an image of Fate laughing as he got pummeled by Mr. Abby Stadtler—who probably always carried breath mints. Then, without warning, Abby's face drained of color. Slowly, she covered her mouth with one slender hand.

ABBY PRESSED SO hard against her lips she could almost feel pulses in her fingertips—ten runaway jackhammers. Every clue, every suspicion, crashed over her as she stared at the earnest-eyed man before her. How in the world had she missed it? What was he doing in her farmyard?

When he said, "It won't happen again," his thick

brows furrowed in honest apology, his rich baritone was suddenly, obviously, as familiar as her daughter's voice. And his pale blue eyes were ones she'd seen as many times as she'd entered her child's bedroom, only this time they mesmerized in person, not from a dozen posters on Kim's walls.

He'd given it away himself. "Dawson Covey."

Oh, Lord, she'd slapped a cigarette from Gray Covey's mouth.

Strangled laughter caught at her throat. This was far from the meeting fantasized by ten thousand adoring women at any given time. What did you say to a rock legend after you'd called him a liar? She dropped her hands from her mouth. "You—"

His face changed. The instant before she'd recognized him, he'd shown honest contrition. Now his mouth slipped into a strange, plastic smile, automatic, a little self-satisfied. Her annoyance sparked. It reminded her why, despite his knee-weakening looks, he'd irritated her with his assumptions and attitude. All at once, she didn't want to give him the satisfaction of fawning over his identity.

"SORRY." SHE FORCED herself to spin away and pull off a fib. "I just got a mental picture of my barn going up in flames. I accept your apology. But know this. If it *does* happen again, I won't be knocking the cigarette out of your mouth. I'll be drowning it with you attached."

Ignoring his celebrity left her uplifted, as if she was

going against nature—something her practical streak rarely allowed. She half-expected him to protest with wounded pride but, in fact, he remained silent until she was back at the hay wagon.

"You're funny even when you're mad," he said. "I guess I consider myself lucky."

"My daughter wouldn't say I'm funny." She half-grinned, although her back was to him.

"Speaking of your daughter and, by association it seems, my son. I don't suppose there's any way of getting them home early? I was hoping to take him with me tonight."

Irritation seized her again, and she glared over her shoulder. Her breath caught now that she recognized who he was, but she shook it off. "Dawson's been living here for almost six weeks. Won't it be kinder to give him time to adjust?"

"You do understand he's a runaway, right?" His voice lifted a notch in irritation. "You have no claim to him. Not to mention, a lot of people have been put out by your . . . employee."

"Put out? How about worried? Has anyone been worried in all the time it took to locate him?" Immediately Abby regretted the thoughtless words. Gray's features stilled, and his eyes iced. "I'm sorry. That was rude of me . . ."

The first plop of rain hit her dead on the nose, followed by a second on her head. Her heart sank. She'd let herself get distracted, and now she risked losing the eighty bales of hay still on the rack if they got soaked.

"Crap, crap, crap." For half a second she waffled between Gray and the hay wagon. She groaned and chose the hay. "I'm sorry. Can you finish this discussion from the barn?"

Two more fat drops left splotches on her shoulders, and she hoisted herself back up onto the wagon. Normally, she didn't mind stacking hay. It taxed her body while anesthetizing her brain. But even if she threw as hard as she could she wouldn't beat this storm.

"I worried about him." Gray's voice held as much promise of thunder as the storm.

"I didn't mean that." She pulled two stacks of bales into heaps with one movement, and they banged into her legs, nearly knocking her off balance. More rain splashed her cheeks. "At least, I didn't mean it to sound so harsh."

"Let's just call us even for assumptions. The point is, I flew from Chicago and am missing work to be here. I'm sure this will sound even crasser to you, but I have appointments I can't miss. My job involves more than just me and a boss."

Two bales. Three. Four.

"So you thought you'd simply grab your son and, what, take him to work with you?"

"As a matter of fact, that's exactly what I thought. I'm his father. I have considered what's best for him."

Five. Six. Seven. Abby heaved the hay just far enough to get it into the barn door. She could stack it later. Her arms started to sting from their exaggerated motions, but she knew how to ignore the discomfort.

"I'm sure that's true." She grunted with exertion. "But

wouldn't you like to know why he ran away in the first place, before you haul him off again?"

"Lady." His taut voice caused her to look into his angry face. "I don't know if you think you're some sort of pop psychiatrist, but I'm not the sixteen-year-old here. I know why my son ran and, frankly, I don't blame him. But, it's not your business, and I don't have the freedom to hang around waiting for him to come back."

The drops fell faster, and the breeze picked up. An eerie twilight settled over the farm.

"Seems to me you do what you have to do where your children are concerned. Sacrifice. Ask yourself what your priorities are." She tossed harder. The tender alfalfa leaves in the fragrant bundles glistened with moisture. In ten minutes the bales would be soaked deep. The rain saturated her shirt, and the tendrils escaping her loose chignon clung to her cheeks.

"You're something, you know that? You warn me about making assumptions then tell me my priorities are screwed up. Who the hell do you think you are?"

The knife-blade edge to his voice made her stop and blink. She'd concentrated so hard on fighting the rain that she'd forgotten her actual fight with the person next to her. Lecture mode always seemed to slip out when she multi-tasked, but Gray's glare of unequivocal anger told her she'd stepped over the line. Although the water beating into her hay made her cringe, she looked him in the eye.

"I'm sorry," she began, but something fluttered in her chest, and she caught her breath in surprise. He didn't look exactly like any picture of him she'd ever seen—and Kim had scrapbooks full of clippings and magazine photos. Three dimensions served him incredibly well. "You're right." She reined in her emotions. "I've grown fond of your son, Mr. . . . Graham. But I don't have the right to be protective of him."

The anger drained from his eyes, but his body remained a study of sculpted seriousness. Cocoa-colored hair feathered back from his forehead and framed his high cheekbones with thick locks that kissed his collar. A chiseled Adam's apple bobbed when he swallowed, and Abby's stomach fluttered again. If the rock-and-roll lifestyle was supposed to ravage a body, Gray Covey's hadn't paid attention to the rule.

Unable to ignore her hay any longer, she pulled her gaze from Gray's, jumped off the wagon, and began dragging bales. This time her back muscles whined with every surge.

"I don't suppose you could wait to finish until this passes?" he asked. He held up his palm to show he knew the answer. The rain on the old barn roof drummed like the backbeat on one of his songs. A flash of lightning slashed the dark sky, and thunder followed mere seconds later. He shucked off his leather jacket. "Aw, hell."

An Excerpt from

RESCUED BY A STRANGER

THE DOG IN the middle of the road was all legs and mottled black patches. It stood still beside the yellow centerline, a good fifty feet away but too close to ignore, and Jill Carpenter eased off the accelerator of her Chevy Suburban.

"Get out of the way, sweetie," she murmured, switching her foot to the brake.

Because she'd worked at the only vet clinic in Kennison Falls since junior high school, she knew most of the dogs in the area. This one, however, was shabbily unfamiliar. And stubbornly unmoving. It stared at her with a mutt-in-the-headlights look that didn't bode well.

Finally, twenty feet from the unblinking animal, Jill blared her horn and stomped her brakes until the anti-lock system grabbed, and loose pebbles pinged the chassis like buckshot. At the very last moment the dog leaped—directly in front of her.

Accidents supposedly happened in slow motion, but no leisurely parade of her life played before her eyes. The jerk of her steering wheel, her shriek, a blur of darting, raggedy fur, and the boulder of dread dropping into the pit of her stomach all happened in something under five nanoseconds.

Then her stomach dropped again as it followed the nose of her truck across the narrow county road and down a six-foot ditch. The Suburban gave a carnival-ride fishtail, its rear axle grinding in protest. Something warm spurted into her face, and she came to rest parallel to the road on the steep ditch bank, wedged in precarious place against a slender maple sapling.

For a moment, all she noticed was her own wheezing breath—her lungs forcing twice as much carbon dioxide out as they sucked oxygen in.

Had she missed the dog? She was sure she had. Please let her have missed the dog. Her heart pounded in concern until she peered out her windshield, shifted to see better, and the Suburban rocked. The dog's fate was forgotten in a gasp.

The world was sideways.

Something sticky ran down one cheek, and an old Counting Crows song filled the truck interior. The turn signal *ploink-ploink*ed to the music like a metronome. Through the windshield and up to her right she could see the edge of the road. To her left through her driver's window lay the bottom of the ditch three feet below. All she'd have to do was shift the wrong way, and she'd be roof down, hanging from her seat belt.

A flurry of sailor-approved words charged through her mind, but her frantic heartbeat choked them off before they turned into sound—almost certainly a good thing, since the air stream caused by swearing would probably be enough to roll her. She pressed her lips together and tried to slow her respiration. Her shoulder, jammed against the door, ached slightly, her seat belt effectively throttled her, but as far as she could tell, she hadn't hit her head.

The Creature, her un-pet name for the vehicle she'd detested since buying it, growled as if angry its spinning back tire wasn't getting anywhere. "Crap!" Jill shot her arm forward, ignoring the pinch of her seat belt, and turned the key.

The truck rocked again, the Crows quit Counting, and the turn signal halted its irritating pinging. At last time stopped whizzing past like an old Super 8 movie, and her thoughts careened into each other with a little less force.

This was definitely going to wreck an already no-good, very bad day.

Sudden pounding startled her, rocking the SUV again. She swiveled her head to the passenger window and let loose a terrified scream. Pressed to the glass was a smoosh-nosed, flattened-featured face. Jill squeezed her eyes shut.

"Ma'am? Ma'am? Can you hear me?" The window-pane muffled the gargoyle's voice.

Slowly Jill forced her eyes open, and the face pulled back. Her panic dissipated as the nose unflattened, lengthening into straightness with perfect oval flares at its tip, and divided a strong, masculine face into two flawless halves. Inky, disheveled bangs fell across deep furrows in his forehead. For an instant Jill forgot her straits, and her mouth went dry. A brilliant sculptor somewhere was missing his masterwork.

"Can you get the window down?" he shouted, refocusing her attention on the phone in his hand. "I'm calling 911. Can you tell me where you're hurt?"

Intense navy-blue eyes pierced her for answers, her pulse accelerated, and embarrassed heat infused her face. "No!" she called. Shaking off her adrenaline-fueled hormones and forcing her brain to function, Jill turned her key once more to activate the accessory system and twisted to punch the window button, jostling The Creature. "No!" she gasped again, as the glass whirred into the door frame. "No calls. I'm fine."

"You are not fine, honey. Stay still now." His drawl was comforting and sing-songy—born of the South.

Truly confused, Jill watched him swipe the face of his phone. He might be the best-looking Samaritan between her predicament and the Iowa border, but although she *was* balanced pretty precariously, his intensity was a tick past overreactive.

"Honestly. All I need is to get out of this murderous truck without rolling it on top of me."

His eyes switched from worry to the kind of sympathy a person used when about to impart bad news. "I'm afraid your face and the front of your shirt tell a different story. You're in shock."

She peered down at herself. At first she gasped at the bright red splotches staining her white tank top. She touched her cheek and brought a red fingertip away. Strangled laughter replaced her shock. He reached for her and made the Suburban wobble.

"Don't lean!" She choked. "Seriously, don't! I'm not bleeding to death, I swear."

His eyes narrowed. "Are you bleeding not to death?"

"No." She stuck her red-coated finger into her mouth and, with the other hand, scooped up a half-dozen French fries caught between her hip and the door. She'd picked them up not ten minutes ago from The Loon Feather Café in town, and Effie had put three little paper cups of ketchup in the take-out tray. Eating fries while driving—another of her vices, along with owning too many horses, flightiness in all things, and swerving to avoid dumb dogs in the road. Gingerly she held up the flat, empty, red-checkered box. "It's only Type A Heinz," she said. "See? No 911 needed. Besides, this is rural Rice County, and it'd take the rescue guys twenty minutes to find me. Is the dog all right?"

"Dog?"

"The one I swerved to miss. You didn't see an injured dog?"

His indigo eyes performed a laser scan from her head to her toes. They settled on her face and softened. "It must have disappeared. I wasn't watching it since I was prayin' to all the angels while you barreled down this ditch."

"But it didn't get hit?"

"I'm pretty sure it didn't get hit," he repeated gently. "You really all right? The dog isn't exactly important at the moment. Nothing hurts? Did you black out?"

Jill let out a breath of relief. This morning, the docs at Southwater Vet Clinic had put down two families' beloved dogs and a young client's show horse. Knowing the stray in the road had survived didn't balance the scales, but it helped a little.

"I just didn't want the dog to be dead. Nothing hurts. I didn't black out. All I want is to get out of my homicidal truck."

"Homicidal?" He laughed and took a step back. "Are you blaming your poor stuck truck for this?"

"Poor truck?" Jill glanced around her seat to see how she dared start extricating herself. The first thing she did was unlatch the seat belt, and the pressure on her arm eased. "This is The Creature. She's a diva. Any other vehicle would *not* have kept going left after I cranked the wheel back to the right." She looked at the man. "She'd kill me outright, but who else would pour college loan money into her like I do?"

The right side of his upper lip, as perfectly sculpted as the rest of his features, lifted in an Elvis-y half grin— a cute-on-handsome action that made Jill's mouth go parched again.

"Sounds like we'd best get you out before Lizzie Borden the truck here changes her mind." His warm, humor-filled voice calmed with its hypnotic Southern cadence.

"I'd be very, very good with that," she replied.

"Let's try the door." He reached for the handle.

"No! Wait. Don't! Whenever I move the whole thing rocks. I—"

"Okay, it's okay." He held up his hands. "I'll look first and see how solid she's sitting."

He stepped away and walked slowly around the front of the Suburban. Jill took the time to regroup. She wasn't a wimp, dang it. This was stupid. The man already believed she was half-baked. She needed to stop whining and simply crawl out. And she had to get the stupid truck out of this stupid ditch or she'd miss the most important riding lesson of her life. Maybe if she could see how to straighten her wheels she could just drive—

"She isn't hanging on by a lot, you're right." He returned to the window. "But you should be able to ease out this way. I'll open the door very carefully. Trust me."

Trust him? For all she knew he had a handgun in his pocket, a twelve-page rap sheet, and a mug shot at the post office. "Fine." She grimaced. "Just don't mug me until I'm fully out. One crisis at a time."

His slightly nasal laugh flowed between them, as musical as his voice. "Gotta love a woman who's funny in the face of adversity."

Funny? This merely kept her from weeping. In addition to causing expense for which there was no money, this accident was messing up two appointments she couldn't afford to miss.

"I'm not being funny." She wriggled out from behind the steering wheel. "On the other hand, if you murder me right here I'll have a great excuse for being late." She edged to the passenger side and glanced at her watch. "Make that very late."

"Lizzie here didn't murder you, and I'm not going to either."

He tugged on the door and it hit the slope, barely opening ten inches. Jill was small, but not that small.

"Great. Just awesome." She eyed the stranger dubiously.

"I'm afraid it's out the window for you." He shrugged.

"Well, this gets better and better." She simply wanted out, and she reached for the oversized tote she used as purse, clothing bag, and carry-all. "Would you toss this on the ground? I hope that stupid dog appreciates its life."

"It's on its knees thanking—"

"All the angels?" she teased.

"Yes, ma'am." The return of his Elvis grin sent a flutter through her belly. He hefted her striped, leather-handled bag and grunted. "Lord love a monkey, what have you got in here? Car parts?"

"Riding boots." She reached for the top of the window opening and suddenly heard what he'd said. "*What?*"

"Sorry, my granddaddy's saying. Gotta admit"—he grunted—"didn't expect you to say boots."

"Only because you don't know me," she muttered.

"Let's go then. We can do getting-to-know-you once you're free."

The easiest way out was headfirst, since it caused the least amount of wiggling. But halfway out, with her torso flopped over the door frame and her knees hovering above the passenger seat, The Creature slowly swung its nose downward. She shrieked.

"Got you!" Strong hands caught her beneath the armpits.

The Creature spun left and spit her from the window.

The momentum squirted her out and propelled the stranger backward. One second Jill's shoe toes skimmed the window frame, the next she sprawled atop a very long, very hard male body. He grabbed her and held the back of her head expertly, as if people fell on him all the time and he knew precisely what to do.

"Sorry. Sorry. I'm okay. Are you okay?" Her words were muffled in his shoulder.

She should move.

He should move.

Instead, his chest rose and fell beneath her, and his breath warmed the top of her head. His fingers formed a firm brace at the base of her neck, and he lay like a stone beneath her. When she finally made the tiniest effort to roll away, his free hand planted itself on her hip.

"No," he commanded in a hoarse whisper.

No?

"Relax. Make sure you're all in one piece."

She certainly didn't know this guy well enough to relax in a reverse missionary position with him . . . but the pleasant musk of masculine perspiration prickled her nose and mingled with the redolent scent of his leather jacket. Her eyelids floated closed in spite of herself, and she went all but limp with relief. When he relaxed, too, however, she couldn't ignore his long, lean form beneath her or the intense pressure gathering low in her body. She tried to concentrate on the fact that nothing bad was happening while he held her—no accidents, no animals dying, no worry she was late for—

"Oh my gosh!" She jerked hard against his hold.

Immediately he released her, gave her shoulder a squeeze, and a mini-explosion of sparks raced for every nerve ending in her body. She pushed onto her hands and stared into eyes as calm as a waveless lake.

"Hi," he said, his mouth only inches from hers. "I'm Chase Preston. Nice to meet you."

She rolled off him laughing and sat up on the incline. "Hi, back. I'm Jill Carpenter. How can I thank you for rescuing me?"

He waved dismissively. "You'd have figured out how to escape, Jill Carpenter, but glad I could help."

He sat up, too, and stuck out his hand, but Jill was almost afraid to take it. Her stomach dipped in anticipation at the sight of his long, clever-looking fingers and knuckles flanked by prominent tendons. At last, she let his grip engulf hers, as warm and comforting as his full-body hold had been. When he rocked to a stand he pulled her along, and her body rose with no more effort than surfacing from buoyant water.

She tried to smile—to thank him by holding their clasped hands a second longer, but after a final, slow squeeze, he let his fingers slide free.

"Now that you're safe, it's time to find you a way out of this ditch. Is there anyone you can call way out here in rural whatever county?"

Jill took her first good look at The Creature, and her heart sank. She'd harbored the ghostly hope that, once free, she'd see how to drive it from the ditch. It hadn't been a very strong hope, but now it was dashed beyond any stretch of imagination. The Creature's grille touched the bottom of the ditch, one rear tire had spun a bald patch into the grass, and the passenger side corner hovered six inches off the ground. It wasn't going anywhere under its own power. Anger at her predicament started a slow burn.

Jill grabbed the bag Chase had set on the hillside, the anger heating up as reality smacked her in the face. How was this fair? For once it had seemed her dream would have a fighting chance, but oh no. With short, angry stomps she marched up the steep slope, and when she reached the road after working up to full-fledged fury, she nearly crashed into a gleaming, silver-and-red motorcycle. She glimpsed the intricate Triumph logo on the gas tank and jumped back. Motorcycles were not her thing.

"So who can you call?"

She stopped short of snapping at him, dropped her bag, and pressed her fingertips against her eyes to hide her frustration. "Dewey's Garage 'n' Gas in town." She sighed.

"Can I take you there? Or call for you?"

"No. I have my phone, and you've helped too much already. Believe me, Dewey knows this truck. He won't be at all surprised he has to tow her out of a ditch."

"Then give him a call. I'll wait with you."

She started to object. Being rescued was far out of her realm of experience, but the man's presence had a calming, spell-like effect on her worry and her anger. She found Dewey's number and punched the call button. A familiar voice answered. "Dewey Mitchell."

She explained her problem and waited for Dewey to calculate his ETA.

"I'm out delivering some fuel, and it'll take forty-five minutes or so to get back to the tow truck. Sorry I'm not closer."

Disappointment spread through her like chills. "I'll take you as soon as I can get you, Dewey. Thanks." She described where she was and hung up.

"He could be an hour." She tried desperately to hide her rekindled anger. Of all the days for disaster to hit . . . "All he said was he'll hurry."

She plopped to her seat in the grass beside the road. Her consultation with a brand-new riding student was supposed to start in five minutes, but the bigger issue was Colin Pitts-Matherson. The visiting coach of the U.S. Equestrian Eventing Team was not known for magnanimity. As a talent scout would for any sport, he'd asked for one chance to see her perform. He'd expect to see her ride. In forty-five minutes. With no sob-story excuse about a dog in the road. Her shot at an Olympic dream could well be resting in the ditch along with The Creature's hood ornament.

A mellow rustling of clothing distracted her, and something heavy draped across her shoulders, steeping the air in a scent she recognized as his, even after this short time. Chase squatted in front of her and drew the jacket securely around her body. She stared at him, mesmerized and annoyed in equal measure.

"What the heck?"

"You're shivering. I don't want to see you go into shock."

Chase now wore only a soft, heathery-gray Henley, fitted to his broad pecs like superhero Lycra. A smear of ketchup marred the front, and she couldn't stop her fingers from brushing at it. The juxtaposition of fur-soft brushed cotton over the hard wall of muscle behind it made her quiver.

Oh brother.

She shoved at him with all her strength. He barely moved.

"For crying out loud!" She tried to fling the jacket off, but he held it firmly in place. "I'm missing two important appointments while I'm sitting here on my ass, and I can't get help for an hour. I'm not in shock. I'm majorly pissed off."

When she quit struggling, he released his hold on the jacket, grasped her chin gently, and studied her face.

"I'm sorry." His voice tightened. "First-responder training from an old job. It's habit." He released her chin. An odd emptiness replaced his touch. "Let me take you to your appointment. You'll get there safely and on time. The truck's not going anywhere until it's towed."

"But I'm going six miles in the opposite direction of where you were going. I can call my boss to come get me."

"Heck, six miles? That's barely spittin' distance after what I've done the last two days."

A swirl of nervousness circled through her chest. She wouldn't climb aboard a motorcycle with someone she knew, much less a random stranger—despite the fact that he'd rescued her butt and had a phenomenal body.

"That's very nice of you," she said. "You've gone above and beyond, but I'll give David a call."

"You sure? I can have you there in ten minutes."

Or he could have her splatted like a dead raccoon on the asphalt in thirty seconds.

"Oh, I'm pretty sure." She nodded emphatically.

A eureka-moment smile blossomed on his lips. "Hey. You aren't afraid of a little ol' motorcycle?"

Over her shoulder, she took in the Triumph with a serious eye. Its crimson gas tank and chrome fenders shone in the sunshine, and although she knew next to nothing about motorcycles—except that when someone wiped out at fifty miles per hour he wound up half-mangled and in casts in the hospital, scaring his kids half to death—she could tell this one was not new.

"It's a good-looking machine," she allowed. "It's gotta be an older model?"

"Vintage is what the bike geeks call it. It's a '75 Bonneville. Belongs to my grandfather actually, his pride and joy. Would you believe he bought it right here in Minnesota? When I decided to come this way, he thought the old girl should have a road trip home."

"Ooo-kay, there's not much of a story in *that* teaser." She lifted her eyes and got a wink.

"Hop on and I'll tell it to you."

"Now, that sounds like a bad biker boy's version of 'come see my etchings.'"

"I'll have to remember that." His laugh added to the warmth emanating from his jacket.

"How far *have* you come in two days?"

"From Memphis."

She let out a low, appreciative whistle. "How much farther are you going?"

"I'm not entirely sure. I'm heading for a town somewhere around here called Northfield."

"Oh, it's *close*. Maybe fifteen miles once you go through Kennison Falls."

His Elvis smile enchanted her as always. "That's very, very good news."

He stood and held out his hand to pull her to her feet. Jill brushed away a smudge of dust on her thigh. She wasn't wary by nature, and strangers weren't rare. Kennison Falls, Minnesota, got enough through-traffic to keep the local merchants in good business. But leather-jacketed bikers with gorgeous, penetrating eyes were not the norm.

She wished she could control the sudden pounding of her pulse, but tangled as she was in his eyes, his accent, and her ridiculous fear, containing her heartbeat was a lost cause.

"My mama warned me about taking rides from strangers."

"I won't let the big, bad Triumph hurt you, you know."

She closed her eyes and took another deep breath. "This is nuts."

He peered at her. "You really are scared."

"Always was." She forced herself not to look embarrassed. "Even when my father had one."

He didn't tease or even comment. From the seat, he picked up a black, shiny-visored helmet and held it out to her. "You can wear this. It possesses the power to keep you safe. Put your arms into the jacket, too, that's more protection."

Twice, now, he'd promised to protect her. Something primitive finally calmed her nerves, if only slightly. With resignation she pulled the helmet over her head. It fit like a fishbowl and dimmed the light like three pairs of sunglasses.

Chase rapped on the hard shell while she snapped the chinstrap.

"Where's your bag of boots?" He chuckled.

She grabbed it from the grass, and he plopped it atop a small duffel, pushing them to the metal tail behind the seat and stretching a bungee cord around both bags. He flipped down the passenger foot pegs and swung his leg over the seat.

"Squeeze on," he said blithely, and she did. The padded seat cushioned her better than her best riding saddle did, but there was no life beneath her, no living thing to partner with. "Put your feet on the rests here over the pipes. Don't let them dangle—the metal gets good and hot. Hang on to me or hold that strap on the seat. And don't worry."

She flipped up the visor. "I ride horses not Hogs. You can reason with a horse. And they're smart enough to keep from doing stupid things because they don't want to die any more than I do." She snapped the visor back in place.

"Well, this isn't a Hog, it's a Triumph. And, honey, I'm smart enough to know I don't want to die either." He laughed and shifted one hip to bring a boot heel down on the kick-starter.

The bike answered with a grumpy rumble but didn't catch. He stomped again. The Bonneville sprang to life, vibrating beneath Jill like a purring lion. The pulsations went through her like electrical current.

"One more thing," he called, twisting over his shoulder. "Lean with me into the turns. It won't be your instinct, but it'll be safer. Ready?"

She clutched the seat strap, and the motorcycle rolled forward a foot. Chase let out the clutch. With a slight jolt, and a tilt to the right, the bike roared onto the road.

They picked up speed like a launched rocket, and Jill swayed from side to side, her wimpy grip on the leather seat strap not nearly secure enough to keep her stable. As they followed a curve to the left and the bike leaned, she held in a screech, squeezed her eyes shut, and threw her arms around Chase's waist. Immediately her torso quit swaying.

Don't crash. Don't crash. Don't crash. The mantra played through her mind until, finally, they'd been underway long enough that the silliness of her fear hit home. She opened her eyes and watched familiar sights flash past in an unfamiliar way. The wind whipped at Chase's jacket, but sheltered in its folds she felt no chill. Beneath her hands, Chase's stomach muscles contracted and flexed as he moved as one with the motorcycle. Hanging on to him was like pressing up against a safe, brick wall. It took a second for her to comprehend when his fingers pried gently at hers, wiggling and loosening her grip.

"Relax!" he called over his shoulder, the word barely audible as it whizzed past her helmeted ear with the wind.

She hadn't realized how tightly she'd been squeezing. With effort, she pulled her hands apart and let go, grasping for a hold on the leather again, but he caught one hand and tugged her arm forward, patting it when the hold was just right. A hard shiver rolled through her body and then, for the first time, Jill found the ability to relax as he'd commanded. Beneath her hold, he came to life, not a brick wall at all but a supple, tensile lifeline.

"Be ready to tell me where to turn," he shouted again. "I've got you. Trust me."

An Excerpt from

BEAUTY AND THE BRIT

"I CAN'T BELIEVE you've been in this country ten years and this is your first game of hoops. Sad, man. How'd they even grant you citizenship?"

David Pitts-Matherson ignored the jibe and crouched in front of his friend. Dr. Chase Preston looked very little like a physician at the moment. He dribbled the ball slowly, intense as Kevin Love, the bounce echoing through the cavernous gymnasium.

"Chatter on, mate," David replied with a practiced sneer. "I'm a fast study."

"Sure y'are. I'll go easy on you anyhow, Limey, so you understand what you're studyin'."

David feinted left and then right, his shoes squeaking on the polished wood floor. The fake worked. He batted the ball from Chase's hand and headed down the court, his dribble admittedly sloppy. When Chase reached him in three long strides, David stopped, took hurried aim, and let the ball fly. It missed the basket and the backboard by a foot, careened off a caged clock, took a hearty bounce, and skittered into a wall.

Chase doubled over in laughter.

"What was *that*?" he crowed. "Thing had about as much control as a fart in a fan factory."

David choked, his own laughter wheezing free in a fit of coughing. He might have a noticeable accent, but as far as he was concerned nothing took the prize for sheer outlandishness like Chase's Southern drawl and resulting phrases of lunacy.

"Nice steal, though." Chase wiped his eyes. "We'll work on the shooting."

David retrieved the ball, dribbled three or four times, and took a jump shot. The ball banked off the backboard and swished neatly through the net.

"No need."

"Did I ever tell you how much I hate British arrogance?" Chase grinned and captured the ball, dribbled it to the free-throw line, turned, and sank the shot. "Nothin' but net."

"Did I ever tell you how much I hate Americans showing off?"

"Yup. You have."

David laughed again and clapped Chase on the arm. Not quite a year before, Chase had married David's good friend and colleague Jill Carpenter, and this was the second time David had overnighted with Chase at Crossroads youth and community center in Minneapolis. He was grateful for the camaraderie, and for the free lodging on his supply runs to the city, but mostly for the distraction from life at the stable back home in Kennison Falls. Here there were no bills staring up at him from his desk, no finances to finagle, no colicky horses. Here he could forget he was one disaster away from . . . well, disaster.

It also boggled his mind that he and Chase had an entire converted middle school to themselves.

"All right, play to thirty," Chase said, tossing him the ball. "Oughta take me no more'n three minutes to hang your limey ass out to dry."

"Bring it on, Nancy-boy."

A loud buzzer halted the game before it started.

"Isn't that the front door?" David asked.

"Yeah." Deep lines formed between Chase's brows.

The center had officially closed an hour before at nine o'clock. Members with ID pass cards could enter until eleven—but only did so for emergencies. David followed Chase toward the gymnasium doors. Voices echoed down the hallway.

"Stop pulling, Rio, you're worse than Hector. He's not going to follow us in here."

"It's Bonnie and Rio Montoya." Surprise colored Chase's voice. "Rio's one of the really good ones. Sane. Hardworking. I can't imagine why she's here."

Rio? David searched his memory but could only recall ever hearing the name in the Duran Duran song.

"Don't be an idiot." A second voice, filled with firm, angry notes, rang out clearly as David neared the source. "Of course they're following us. They might not come inside, but they'll be waiting, and you cannot handle either of them no matter how much you think you can. Dr. Preston's on duty tonight. He might be able to run interference."

"They won't listen to him. To them he's just a pretty face. Let me talk to Heco. You never gave me the chance."

"And I won't, even if I have to lock you in juvie for a year."

"God, Rio, you just don't get it."

"You're right, Bonnie Marie. I don't. What in God's name possessed you to meet Hector Black after curfew? Do you know what almost went down in that parking lot? Do you know who that other dude *was*?"

Chase hustled through the doorway. "Rio? Bonnie? Something happen?"

David followed five feet behind him. The hallway outside the gym glowed with harsh fluorescent lighting. Chase had the attention of both girls, but when David moved into view, one of them turned. A force field slammed him out of nowhere—a force field made up of amber-red hair and blazing blue eyes.

Frozen to the spot, he stared and she stared back. Her hair shone the color of new pennies on fire, and her complexion, more olive and exotic than a typical pale redhead's, captivated him. Her lips, parted and uncertain, were pinup-girl full. Her body, beneath a worn-to-softness plaid flannel shirt, was molded into the kind of feminine curves that got a shallow-thinking man in trouble. David normally prided himself on having left such loutishness behind in his university days, but he was rapidly reverting.

"Rio? You all right?" Chase called, and she broke the staring contest first.

David blinked.

"Fine," she said. "I'm sorry to come in so late. I needed a safe place for this one."

The teenage girl with her couldn't have been more her opposite. Model slender and taller than Rio, a pair of dark eyes and a fall of glossy black hair showed a rich Latina heritage.

"Very funny," the teen said, her lip curled in disgust.

Chase gave an easy chuckle. "Not our sweet-tempered little Bonita." The teasing in his drawl coaxed a smile from the girl. "All right, now. You both look terrified as june bugs in a twister. What's goin' on?"

"About five minutes ago I broke up a transaction that included this one here. Paul and his asshat *amigo,* Hector, are beyond pissed off. I don't think we should go home, at least for a few minutes."

Chase folded his arms. "It was smart to come. Do you want a place to stay for the night?"

"No, no." Rio dismissed the question. "Once we're home we'll be fine. They just need some time, a chance for everyone to cool off."

Chase nodded. "Let's sit here awhile, then, and I'll be glad to take you home. But I'd feel better knowing what's really going on."

"What's going on is that Rio came busting in on my date with Hector like Buffy the Vampire Slayer." Bonnie's laugh was half a step from hysterical. "She clawed at him so hard she left scratch marks that will definitely leave scars down Heco's face. That's what made him furious."

"And what does Paul have to do with this?" Chase asked.

"He was there," Rio said. "He ran off with Hector after Boyfriend's car drove away."

"Boyfriend?" Chase's features transformed instantaneously from concerned to fully alarmed. "*He* was part of this 'transaction'? Is that what you meant?"

Rio nodded.

"That's it. I have to have a talk with your brother."

David listened to the exchange, amazed. He already knew how effective Chase's people skills were from his reputation back in Kennison Falls. He'd heard the stories about his work with inner-city kids two days a week, but he'd never seen the calm, serious community leader in action.

A crash, like a chair clattering across the floor, made all four of them jump. It reverberated from the lobby, followed by a foul expletive and the quick beat of running feet. Seconds later a handsome Latino man hurtled around the corner, eyes half-crazed.

"Rio, where the hell are you?" He caught sight of them and slowed to a walk, jabbing his finger through the air as he approached. "Damn it, *Manita*, I could kill you. Do you know what kind of a mess you caused out there?" He spoke with a slightly exaggerated Mexican accent.

"Don't you 'little sister' me in your fake Spanish. This is a mess you started, assh—" Rio cut herself off. "At least your real little sister is safe. No thanks to you."

"I was handling it."

"Handling it? Bonnie was in the car with him. Do you have some *special* kind of shit for brains? Get lost, *Inigo*. I'm starting to think *Paul* is dead to us."

Rage twisted his features, and he lunged forward. David tensed instinctively, recognizing the look of a man momentarily unhinged. Paul made it two steps, and David slid sideways into his path, throwing one arm straight out, clotheslining the young man midleap. Paul's feet shot out from under him, and he landed on his back, but not before hooking David behind the knees. David slammed the deck flat-backed, and the air left his lungs in one sharp exhale. Paul flailed around, attempting to right himself.

David forced himself upright, coughing as his lungs reinflated. Rio reached out a hand to her brother. Paul slapped it away and scrambled to his feet. To David's shock, she offered her hand to him next. With only the slightest hesitation, he took it.

If he'd expected her grasp to be light and feminine, he'd been quite mistaken. She clasped his hand firmly, planted her feet, and pulled him up, keeping her eyes on his as he rose. Her head reached the bottom of his lip.

"Thanks."

To his further shock she smiled. "Nice tackle. Are you all right?"

Behind her, Chase held the wriggling, still cursing brother by both shoulders.

"Brilliant," David said. "Dusted the floor, but none the worse."

Her mouth gaped. The accent caused that all too frequently, something he found slightly ridiculous.

Paul pulled toward Bonnie, and Chase spun him away. "That's enough, Mr. Montoya. Lead the way to my office. Ladies, let's get this straightened out."

Rio ignored the directive. "You're Br—"

"Bruised up?" David cut her off with a teasing wink. "I'm not, though. Honestly. Please don't worry."

"Worry?" She scoffed although her eyes remained wide. "I'm trying to figure out what the Duke of Edinburgh is doing in a place like this."

"I see. Well, since the Duke of Edinburgh is Philip, husband to Queen Elizabeth, I'd say you don't need to worry about that either. But I appreciate the mistaken identity."

She wanted to laugh. He could see it in the quiver of her lower lip and the sparkle trying to overtake the anger in her eyes. Even the weak little smile she'd offered seconds ago had transformed her face; he'd have loved seeing the full-blown version. Instead she battled back the forces of mirth and tightened her lips.

"You Not-Duke-of-Edinburghs all look the same to me." She shrugged. The joke in the middle of her crisis touched him. That took strength. "Thank you, whoever you are, for stopping Paul. He wouldn't have hurt us on purpose, but he'd have knocked me down."

"Glad I could be of service."

She slapped one hand over her mouth—to hold in the laughter, as evidenced from the return of the sparkle to her eyes. When she got control she shook her head.

"I don't believe for one minute you aren't a duke. Nobody talks like that."

"Evidently I do." He stuck out his hand in a proper greeting. "David," he said. "Not to be confused with Philip."

"Rio, short for Arionna," she replied. This time her fingers slipped like satin into his handshake, trailing tiny jolts of pleasure across his palm. "And now I need to go see what the doc thinks I have to do."

He had a suggestion. Stay away from her brother, stand there, and keep talking to him.

Rio slipped into Chase's spartan, yellow-painted office, mostly unadorned except for a bookcase full of books—Crossroads' bare-bones lending library. Although not many books found their ways back once lent. Chairs had been pilfered from other rooms, and everyone had a seat except Doc Preston, who perched on the edge of an old, black metal desk. Bonnie sat several feet away from Paul, who slouched sullenly on a metal folding chair. Rio sat beside Bonnie, far too aware of David-Not-Philip taking up a post by the door.

"First of all," Chase said. "The extra person back there is David Pitts-Matherson, a good friend from Kennison Falls."

The small town in southern Minnesota where Doc lived. Rio spun to look again at the duke. The stuffy, hyphenated name fit the first image Rio had had of him—a little stiff, a lot extremely hot man. But now that she'd glimpsed his inner laughing-eyed joker, she couldn't reconcile anything hoity-toity with him.

"I think you need a better class of friends, Doc." Paul practically spat the words.

Rio glared at him. He'd dropped the fake accent he used on the street, something that drove her insane.

"I'm sorry to have met on such violent terms," David said.

Rio wasn't sorry. Few people took Paul Montoya down anymore because he was the gang leader's right-hand man. David had done it as easily as stepping off a curb.

And his voice made her see, a little bit, why women dragged their drooling tongues on the ground over British accents. They wreaked havoc on a person's nervous system.

On the other hand, she'd lost her self-control a couple of times now over the accent, and losing control annoyed her. She took in her brother and sister, the former tight as a time bomb, the latter slumped into her folding chair. She had no time to slobber over men from a different league and class.

"Tell me where you were going tonight, Bonnie." Doc's perpetually kind voice eased some of the rigidity from Bonnie's posture.

"Hector said we were going to meet a friend of his. Said the guy was totally cool and had a sick collection of albums. He knows I love new music. But we didn't go to Heco's place. We met his friend in the school parking lot. We were just starting to talk about favorite groups and stuff, and we were sitting in the back of his friend's car because he had an expensive new sound system in it. That's when Rio showed up."

"That's when Rio saved your little ass," Rio replied.

"Whatever."

"Paul." Chase turned to him. "Were you part of this?"

"No, man. I just found out Hector was dealing with Boyfriend. I went to tell him to leave Bonnie alone. But my stupid idiot of a sister had to bust in and humiliate everyone. Now we're all in trouble."

"How's that?"

"Aside from getting a fist in my face after she left?"

"What?" Rio stared more closely at her brother. Sure enough, she could see the faint outline of a lump blossoming beneath his right eye.

He sneered. "They punched me out when they thought I'd narked to my sister. But that's the least of it. You had to get into a damn physical fight with Hector, and now he's vowed to pay you back."

"Oh, what's he going to do, Inigo?" She used his street name derisively. "Come and scratch my face, too?"

"You underestimate him. He's real mad."

"I've lived here for twenty-six years. I know how to handle a threat from Hector Black."

"Not this time."

Paul bore the same olive-skinned Mexican beauty Bonnie did. Both had inherited the dark hair, eyes, and classic bone structure from their mother, her papa's second wife. Rio had missed out on that beautiful mix of chromosomes and gotten instead a set of spliced genes from her Irish mother's family. She literally *was* the redheaded stepchild.

But Irish or Mexican, stubbornness ran rampant through the Montoyas' bloodstreams. If Paul, obstinate since birth, thought this mess was her fault, it would take lightning and a voice from the Almighty Himself to change his mind. Losing his mother seven years before hadn't helped, but age had done nothing to soften him. She turned to Chase.

"When I realized Bonnie had defied the rules and gone out, I had to follow. In all honesty, that's something she doesn't normally do. Then, when I saw her actually get into that car, I don't know whether I was more angry or panicked. Hector, who isn't the freshest tortilla in the pack, is the one who let slip who was in the car, and I know girls who go off with Boyfriend don't come back."

Chase turned stern eyes on Bonnie. "What do you think?"

"I think I could have taken care of myself." Bonnie's defensiveness was trying to turn to defiance. She crossed one leg over the other and shook her foot in frustration, slapping her rhinestoned flip-flop against her sole like a castanet.

"Bonnie, I'm not sure I would want to try and take care of myself in a locked car with a guy like that." Chase raised his brows.

"She didn't have to attack Heco. I would have gotten out."

"But you wouldn't have." Rio kept her voice calm with effort. She needed to be the parent right now, not get drawn into a pissing contest. "Hector was physically blocking me from getting to you and blocking you from getting out so, yes, I absolutely fought him. If he's mad as hell, so be it. I'd do it again."

She turned finally to her brother. "And you can protest all you want, but you were not going to stand up to Hector."

"You'll never know that, will you?"

She held her tongue with difficulty.

"Are you positive you three don't want a place to stay tonight?" Chase looked from Paul to Rio.

"I'm positive." She had faith in her locks, one of the few things she'd splurged on in the old house she'd inherited from her mother's meager estate. She also had faith—she had to—that Paul carried enough street cred to get them through this. She sighed, burying her pride with effort to ask for one more thing. "If I could just be sure she gets home safely," she said, inclining her head toward Bonnie, "we'll be fine after that."

"Is your car nearby?" Chase asked.

"No, it's at the house. It was faster to run the three blocks."

"Will Hector retaliate?" Chase turned to Paul.

"He could. Send his boys to threaten her."

"Aren't *you* one of his boys?" Bonnie leveled her gaze at Paul, showing anger with her brother for the first time. "If Heco loves me like he says he does, he won't hurt you or Rio."

Paul sank even more deeply into his chair, his features swimming in sour annoyance. "I'll handle it."

"I can get you home," Chase said. "I'm still not convinced I should leave you there."

"It'll be fine." Rio sat on the edge of her chair. "I'll take Bonnie to school tomorrow before work. *You*, Inigo, will make sure she gets home afterward. Safely. Do you hear me?"

"I don't know. I doubt I can be trusted." He glowered.

"You might be an idiot." She glowered back. "But I know you love your sister. Just keep her away from that scumbag Hector for one hour tomorrow. Can you do that?"

"I'm right here, dumbasses." Bonnie straightened in her chair. "Quit making plans for me like I'm a kindergartner or I'll leave and take care of myself."

Weariness fell on Rio like a thick, suffocating blanket. Her lungs wanted one minute of simple, stress-free breathing, but she couldn't get one *breath* that didn't contain the stifling, gang-ridden, fear-scented air of Minneapolis.

"Fine." She threw up her hands. "You're right. We can't do this without your cooperation, so if you want to go trust your future to Hector, we'll back off. I don't want to pull you out of any more cars, rooms, or God forbid, a drawer in a morgue, so let me know as soon as possible and I'll get on with my life, too."

Bonnie snapped her mouth shut.

"That's enough." Chase stood from his seat on the desk. "Paul, take Bonnie and get something to drink from the kitchen. Rio, hang on a second."

When the two had shuffled from the room, Chase knelt in front of her chair.

"I'm sorry." Exhaustion sent her head into her palms.

"No apologizing. We've focused completely on Bonnie and Paul, but it's you I worry about. This is not a small gang scuffle, honey, this is serious. Maybe it's time for you to get some help."

She popped her head up, adrenaline surging. She'd worked her butt off the past seven years at every restaurant or dive that would hire her, and she'd never had to ask for assistance, steal to get by, or sell herself.

Over Chase's head, she caught the eyes of David-Not-Philip. The warm-cocoa gaze shone with sympathy, and her face flamed, knowing how he was seeing her and her family. Despite his kind eyes and her schoolgirl attraction, his cool, quiet demeanor aggravated her. She was holding her world together with sheer will and sarcasm, and he was observing from the corner like a visitor at the zoo.

She forced her attention back to Chase. "I appreciate your concern, but I can handle things."

"Don't stretch yourself too thin." He placed one hand on her knee. "You've been mom, sister, truant officer, and rescuer for a lot of years. You're too special around here to lose to burnout—or something worse."

"Thank you." His words warmed a cold spot in her heart. "I've dealt with Paul's friends a long time."

"I know better than to argue with you." He stood. "I have to be here another forty-five minutes. Can you hang tight? I'll take you home then."

"Whatever we need to do."

David moved from the corner for the first time. "I have my car out back," he said. "Why don't I just run you home?"

Rio turned back to him, her pulse rising one tiny,

excited half beat. The man shocked her every time he opened his mouth. "I couldn't make you do that."

"I understand if you're not comfortable with a stranger after what you've been through. But I'm certainly happy to help. You said you have to work in the morning, that's all."

She could think of ten reasons having this man drive down Lake Street to her neighborhood at this time of night was a bad idea. Aside from the fact he'd show up like a spotlight in a coal mine, he could get lost, he could get his car keyed, he could find Hector lying in wait and get his English ass handed to him . . . and she'd have to rescue him right along with everyone else.

"It's not a bad idea," Chase said. "Less time for Paul to get antsy and leave to go solve things on his own."

That point was worth considering.

"I'd be honored to do more than stand around gawping."

Honored? She sighed. She didn't want to be responsible for him out on the streets, but when that patient smile slipped onto his lips, her brain tilted off balance yet again.

"All right," she said, before she could stop herself. "But let me warn you, where we're going isn't an English garden. It's about as un-pretty as it gets."

"It's quite all right." He nodded, unperturbed. "I'm sure I've seen worse."

She remembered her manners just in time to stop a snort of disbelief.

About the Author

LIZBETH SELVIG writes fun, heartwarming contemporary romantic fiction. Her debut novel, *The Rancher and the Rock Star,* was released in 2012. Her second, *Rescued by a Stranger,* is a 2014 RWA RITA® Award nominee. Lizbeth lives in Minnesota with her best friend (aka her husband), a hyperactive border collie, and a gray Arabian gelding. After working as a newspaper journalist and magazine editor, and raising an equine veterinarian daughter and a talented musician son, Lizbeth entered Romance Writers of America's Golden Heart® contest in 2010 with *The Rancher and the Rock Star* (then titled *Songbird*) and won the Single Title Contemporary category. In her spare time, she loves to hike, quilt, read, horseback ride, and spend time with her new granddaughter. She also has four-legged grandchildren—more than twenty—including a wallaby, two alpacas, a donkey, a pig, three sugar gliders, and many dogs, cats, and horses (pics of all appear on her website www.lizbethselvig. com). She loves connecting with all her readers.

Give in to your impulses . . .
Read on for a sneak peek at six brand-new
e-book original tales of romance
from Avon Impulse.
Available now wherever e-books are sold.

BEAUTY AND THE BRIT
By Lizbeth Selvig

THE GOVERNESS CLUB: SARA
By Ellie Macdonald

CAUGHT IN THE ACT
BOOK TWO: INDEPENDENCE FALLS
By Sara Jane Stone

SINFUL REWARDS 1
A BILLIONAIRES AND BIKERS NOVELLA
By Cynthia Sax

WHEN THE RANCHER CAME TO TOWN
A VALENTINE VALLEY NOVELLA
By Emma Cane

LEARNING THE ROPES
By T. J. Kline

An Excerpt from

BEAUTY AND THE BRIT
by Lizbeth Selvig

Tough and self-reliant Rio Montoya has looked after her two siblings for most of their lives. But when a gang leader makes threats against her sister Bonnie, even Rio isn't prepared for the storm that could destroy her family. Rio seeks refuge for them all at a peaceful horse farm in the small town of Kennison Falls, Minnesota, but her budding romance with the stable's owner, handsome British ex-pat David Pitts-Matherson, feels as dangerous as her past.

"Did I ever tell you how much I hate British arrogance?" Chase grinned and captured the ball, dribbled it to the free-throw line, turned, and sank the shot. "Nothin' but net."

"Did I ever tell you how much I hate Americans showing off?"

"Yup. You have."

David laughed again and clapped Chase on the arm. Not quite a year before, Chase had married David's good friend and colleague Jill Carpenter, and this was the second time David had overnighted with Chase at Crossroads Youth and Community Center in Minneapolis. He was grateful for the camaraderie, and for the free lodging on his supply runs to the city, but mostly for the distraction from life at the stable back home in Kennison Falls. Here there were no bills staring up at him from his desk, no finances to finagle, no colicky horses. Here he could forget he was one disaster away from . . . well, disaster.

It also boggled his mind that he and Chase had an entire converted middle school to themselves.

"All right, play to thirty," Chase said, tossing him the ball. "Oughta take me no more'n three minutes to hang your limey ass out to dry."

"Bring it on, Nancy-boy."

A loud buzzer halted the game before it started.

"Isn't that the front door?" David asked.

"Yeah." Deep lines formed between Chase's brows.

The center had officially closed an hour before at nine o'clock. Members with I.D. pass cards could enter until eleven—but only did so for emergencies. David followed Chase toward the gymnasium doors. Voices echoed down the hallway.

"Stop pulling, Rio, you're worse than Hector. He's not going to follow us in here."

"It's Bonnie and Rio Montoya." Surprise colored Chase's voice. "Rio's one of the really good ones. Sane. Hardworking. I can't imagine why she's here."

Rio? David searched his memory but could only recall ever hearing the name in the Duran Duran song.

"Don't be an idiot." A second voice, filled with firm, angry notes, rang out clearly as David neared the source. "Of course they're following us. They may not come inside, but they'll be waiting, and you cannot handle either of them no matter how much you think you can. Dr. Preston's on duty tonight. He might be able to run interference."

"They won't listen to him. To them he's just a pretty face. Let me talk to Heco. You never gave me the chance."

"And I won't, even if I have to lock you in juvie for a year."

"God, Rio, you just don't get it."

"You're right, Bonnie Marie. I don't. What in God's name possessed you to meet Hector Black after curfew? Do you know what almost went down in that parking lot? Do you know who that other dude *was?*"

Chase hustled through the doorway. "Rio? Bonnie? Something happen?"

David followed five feet behind him. The hallway outside the gym glowed with harsh fluorescent lighting. Chase had the attention of both girls, but when David moved into view, one of them turned. A force field slammed him out of nowhere—a force field made up of amber-red hair and blazing blue eyes.

Frozen to the spot, he stared and she stared back. Her hair shone the color of new pennies on fire, and her complexion, more olive and exotic than a typical pale redhead's, captivated him. Her lips, parted and uncertain, were pinup-girl full. Her body, beneath a worn-to-softness plaid flannel shirt, was molded into the kind of feminine curves that got a shallow-thinking man in trouble. David normally prided himself on having left such loutishness behind in his university days, but he was rapidly reverting.

"Rio? You all right?" Chase called, and she broke the staring contest first.

David blinked.

"Fine," she said. "I'm sorry to come in so late. I needed a safe place for this one."

An Excerpt from

THE GOVERNESS CLUB: SARA
by Ellie Macdonald

Sweet Sara Collins is one of the founding members of the Governess Club. But she has a secret: She doesn't love teaching. She'd much prefer to be a vicar's wife and help the local community. Nathan Grant is the embodiment of everything that frightens her. When Sara decides it's time to take a chance and experience *all* that life has to offer, Nathan is the first person she thinks of. Will Sara's walk on the wild side ruin her chances at a simple, happy life? Or has she just opened the door to a once-in-a-lifetime chance at passion?

Mr. Pomeroy helped her down from the gig, and Sara took a long look at Windent Hall. Curtains covering the windows shielded the interior from a visitor's view, lending the building a cold and unwelcoming front. Rotted trees and dead grass lined the driveway, and cracks were visible along the red brickwork. Piles of crumbled mortar littered the edge of the manor house, and even the front portico was listing to the side, on the verge of toppling over.

The place reeked of neglect, which was to be expected after thirty years of vacancy. What Sara hadn't expected was the blanket of loneliness that shrouded the house, adding to the chilly ambiance. She couldn't help feeling that it had been calling out to be noticed, only to be ignored that much longer.

She couldn't suppress the shiver that ran down her body.

Sara turned to Mr. Pomeroy as he offered his arm. "Are you certain we should be here? We are uninvited."

He led her gingerly up the front steps. "Even so, I feel it is my duty to welcome him to the community. One can see that taking on this place is a task of great proportions. He needs to know that he is welcomed here and be informed of the local tradesmen and laborers available."

His logic was sound. But she couldn't keep from wincing

when the door protested his banging with a loud crack down the middle. Mr. Pomeroy and Sara shared a glance. He grimaced apologetically.

The door creaked open, only to stop partway. A muffled curse was heard from the other side, and eight fingers appeared in the opening. Grunting started as whoever was on the far side started to pull. Mr. Pomeroy shrugged and added his efforts in pushing. With a loud squeal, the door inched open until Sara and the vicar were able to pass through.

They stepped into a dark foyer, dustcovers over everything, including a large chandelier and all the wall sconces. The man who had opened the door was walking away down a corridor on one side of the main staircase. "I don't get paid enuff fer this," they could hear him muttering. He pushed open a door and pointed into the room. "Youse wait in there." He disappeared farther down the corridor.

Sara stared. Mr. Pomeroy stared. They looked at each other. With another shrug, Mr. Pomeroy started down the corridor, and she had little choice but to follow.

It was a parlor, as far as Sara could tell, underneath all the dust. The pale green walls were faded and damaged, giving the impression of sickness. No paintings adorned them, and none of the other small pieces one expected in a room such as this were evident. The furniture that was not hidden by dustcovers was torn and did not appear strong enough to hold any weight whatsoever. She sat on the sofa gingerly, hoping it would not give out underneath her.

"Perhaps we should not have come today," she whispered to Mr. Pomeroy. "It does not appear Mr. Grant is prepared to receive visitors of any sort."

The vicar acknowledged her point with an incline of his head. "We are here now, however. We will not stay long, simply offer our welcome and depart."

They had been waiting in the sparse room for nearly twenty-five minutes before she heard a tapping out in the corridor. It drew closer, and Sara turned her head to the door, wondering what was causing the sound. A gold tip struck the floor at the threshold, and Sara's eyes followed a black shaft upward to a matching gold top shaped into the form of a wolf's head. The head was loosely grasped by lean fingers, confident of their ability to control the cane.

Her eyes continued to rise, taking in the brown coat, striped waistcoat, and snowy white cravat before reaching the gentleman's face. Her eyes widened in recognition, and her breath caught in her throat when she realized that the man was none other than the stranded traveler from a few days prior.

Up close and stationary, his icy blue eyes were even paler, and at this moment, the bloodshot orbs exuded barely concealed disdain that made her even more aware of their lack of an invitation to visit. She barely registered the ants in her throat, for she was too riveted by his face.

An Excerpt from

CAUGHT IN THE ACT
Book Two: Independence Falls
by Sara Jane Stone

For Liam Trulane, failure is not an option. He is determined to win a place in Katie Summers' life before she leaves Independence Falls for good. First, he needs to make amends for the last time they got down and dirty. But falling for his rivals' little sister could cost him everything in the second installment of a hot new series from contemporary romance writer Sara Jane Stone.

"**W**hat are you going to do with it?" Katie asked, drawing him back to the present and the piece of land that proved he was walking down the path marked success. The equity stake in Moore Timber his best friend had offered Liam in exchange for help running the company was one more milestone on that road—and one he had yet to prove he deserved.

"Thinking about building a home here someday," Liam said.

"A house? I would have thought you'd want to forget about this place. About us. After the way you ended it." Katie raised her hand to her mouth as if she couldn't believe she'd said those words out loud.

Liam stopped beside her, losing his grip on the goat's lead and allowing the animal to graze. "I messed up, Katie. I think we both know that. But I panicked when I realized how young you were, and how—"

"I was eighteen," she snapped.

"By a few weeks. You were so innocent. And I felt all kinds of guilt for not realizing it sooner."

"Not anymore," she said, her voice firm. Defiant. "I'm not innocent anymore."

"No." Liam knew every line, every angle of her face. There

were days he woke up dreaming about the soft feel of her skin. But it was the way Katie had looked at him after he'd gone too far, taken too much, that haunted his nightmares. In that moment, her green eyes had shone with hope and love.

Back then, when he was fresh out of college, returning home to build the life he'd dreamed about, that one look had sent him running scared. He wasn't ready for the weight of her emotions.

And he sure as hell wasn't ready now. Eric had given Liam one job since handing over part of the company—buy Summers Family Trucking. Liam couldn't let his best friend, now his business partner, down. Whatever lingering feelings he had for Katie needed to wait on the sidelines until after Liam finished negotiating with her brothers. There was too much at stake—including his vision of a secure future—to blow this deal over the girl who haunted his fantasies.

He drew the goat away from the overgrown grass and started toward the wooded area on the other side of the clearing. "We should go. Get you home before too late."

But Katie didn't follow. She marched down to the fir trees. "I'm twenty-five, Liam. I don't have a curfew. My brothers don't sit around waiting for me to come home."

"I know."

Brody, Chad, and Josh were waiting for him. Liam had been on his way to see her brothers when he'd spotted her car on the side of the road. They'd reluctantly agreed to an informal meeting to discuss selling to Moore Timber.

She spun to face him, hands on her hips. "I think you wanted to take a walk down memory lane."

"Katie—"

"Back then, you never held back." She closed the gap between them, the toes of her sandal-clad feet touching his boots. "So tell me, Liam, what are we doing here?"

He fought the urge to reach for her. He had no right. Not to mention bringing her here had confirmed one thing: After seven years, Katie Summers still held his mistakes against him.

She raised one hand, pressing her index finger to his chest. Damn, he wished he'd kept his leather jacket on. Her touch ignited years of flat-out need. No, he hadn't lived like a saint for seven years, but no one else turned him on like Katie Summers.

An Excerpt from

SINFUL REWARDS 1
A Billionaires and Bikers Novella
by Cynthia Sax

Belinda "Bee" Carter is a good girl; at least, that's
what she tells herself. And a good girl deserves
a nice guy—just like the gorgeous and moody
billionaire Nicolas Rainer. Or so she thinks,
until she takes a look through her telescope
and sees a naked, tattooed man on the balcony
across the courtyard. He has been watching
her, and that makes him all the more enticing.
But when a mysterious and anonymous text
message dares her to do something bad, she
must decide if she is really the good girl she has
always claimed to be, or if she's willing to risk
everything for her secret fantasy of being watched.

An Avon Red Novella

An Excerpt from

SINFUL REWARDS 1
A Billionaires and Bikers Novella
by Cynthia Sax

Belinda "Bee" Carter is a good girl, isn't she? She thinks she is, until she meets a sexy, tattooed, motorcycle-riding hunk like Hawke at the worst possible time. A billionaire businessman like Nicolas could have his choice of women, so why is he interested in plain-speaking, unfashionable Bee? And why are all these eligible, gorgeous men suddenly pursuing her? This smart, fun, sexy, emotional, and wholly satisfying erotic romance from the pen of Cynthia Sax will fill your coffers with sinful rewards!

I'd told Cyndi I'd never use it, that it was an instrument purchased by perverts to spy on their neighbors. She'd laughed and called me a prude, not knowing that I was one of those perverts, that I secretly yearned to watch and be watched, to care and be cared for.

If I'm cautious, and I'm always cautious, she'll never realize I used her telescope this morning. I swing the tube toward the bench and adjust the knob, bringing the mysterious object into focus.

It's a phone. Nicolas's phone. I bounce on the balls of my feet. This is a sign, another declaration from fate that we belong together. I'll return Nicolas's much-needed device to him. As a thank you, he'll invite me to dinner. We'll talk. He'll realize how perfect I am for him, fall in love with me, marry me.

Cyndi will find a fiancé also—everyone loves her—and we'll have a double wedding, as sisters of the heart often do. It'll be the first wedding my family has had in generations.

Everyone will watch us as we walk down the aisle. I'll wear a strapless white Vera Wang mermaid gown with organza and lace details, crystal and pearl embroidery accents, the bodice fitted, and the skirt hemmed for my shorter height. My hair will be swept up. My shoes—

Voices murmur outside the condo's door, the sound piercing my delightful daydream. I swing the telescope upward, not wanting to be caught using it. The snippets of conversation drift away.

I don't relax. If the telescope isn't positioned in the same way as it was last night, Cyndi will realize I've been using it. She'll tease me about being a fellow pervert, sharing the story, embellished for dramatic effect, with her stern, serious dad— or, worse, with Angel, that snobby friend of hers.

I'll die. It'll be worse than being the butt of jokes in high school because that ridicule was about my clothes and this will center on the part of my soul I've always kept hidden. It'll also be the truth, and I won't be able to deny it. I am a pervert.

I have to return the telescope to its original position. This is the only acceptable solution. I tap the metal tube.

Last night, my man-crazy roommate was giggling over the new guy in three-eleven north. The previous occupant was a gray-haired, bowtie-wearing tax auditor, his luxurious accommodations supplied by Nicolas. The most exciting thing he ever did was drink his tea on the balcony.

According to Cyndi, the new occupant is a delicious piece of man candy—tattooed, buff, and head-to-toe lickable. He was completing armcurls outside, and she enthusiastically counted his reps, oohing and aahing over his bulging biceps, calling to me to take a look.

I resisted that temptation, focusing on making macaroni and cheese for the two of us, the recipe snagged from the diner my mom works in. After we scarfed down dinner, Cyndi licking her plate clean, she left for the club and hasn't returned.

Three-eleven north is the mirror condo to ours. I

straighten the telescope. That position looks about right, but then, the imitation UGGs I bought in my second year of college looked about right also. The first time I wore the boots in the rain, the sheepskin fell apart, leaving me barefoot in Economics 201.

Unwilling to risk Cyndi's friendship on "about right," I gaze through the eyepiece. The view consists of rippling golden planes, almost like . . .

Tanned skin pulled over defined abs.

I blink. It can't be. I take another look. A perfect pearl of perspiration clings to a puckered scar. The drop elongates more and more, stretching, snapping. It trickles downward, navigating the swells and valleys of a man's honed torso.

No. I straighten. This is wrong. I shouldn't watch our sexy neighbor as he stands on his balcony. If anyone catches me . . .

Parts 1, 2, and 3 available now!

An Excerpt from

WHEN THE RANCHER CAME TO TOWN
A Valentine Valley Novella
by *Emma Cane*

Welcome to Valentine Valley! Emma Cane
returns to the amazing and romantic town for
the latest installment in her sparkling series.
When an ex-rodeo star falls in love with an
agoraphobic B&B owner, he must pull out
all the stops to get her out of her shell.

With the pie in the oven, Amanda set the timer on her phone, changed into old clothes suitable for gardening, smeared on sunscreen, and headed outside. The grounds of the B&B took just as much work as the inside. She'd hired a landscaper for some of the major stuff like lawn and tree care, but the flowers, shrubs, and design work were all hers. She felt at peace in her garden, with the high bushes that formed walls on either side. The terraced lawn sloped down amidst rock gardens to Silver Creek, where she kept kayaks, canoes, and paddleboards for her guests. She had little hidden walkways between tall shrubs, where unusual fountains greeted visitors as a reward for their curiosity. She'd strung lights between the trees, and at night, her garden was like her own private fairy world.

One she had to share with guests, of course.

As she headed across the deck that was partially covered by an arbor, she glanced toward the hot tub beneath the gazebo—and did a double take. Mason Lopez sat alone on the edge of the tub, his jeans rolled up to his knees, his feet immersed. Though he was staring at the bubbling water, he seemed to be looking inward.

She must have made a sound, because he suddenly turned

his head. For a moment, she was pinned by his gaze, aware of him as a man in a way she hadn't felt about anyone in a long time.

She shook it off and said, "Sorry to disturb you." She was about to leave him in peace, but found herself saying instead, "Is everything all right?"

He smiled, white teeth gleaming out of the shadows of the gazebo, but it was a tired smile that quickly died.

"Sure, everything's fine. My meeting just didn't go as expected."

She felt frozen, unable to simply leave him when he'd said something so personal. "I bet you'll be able to work it out."

A corner of his mouth quirked upward. "I'm glad you're sure of that."

"You're not?" Where had that come from? And then she walked toward him, when she should have been giving him his privacy. But he looked so alone.

"Will you join me?" he asked.

She was surprised to hear a thread of hope in his voice. As a person who *enjoyed* being alone, this felt foreign to her, but the need to help a guest overruled that. She sat down cross-legged beside him. They didn't talk at first, and she watched him rub his shoulder.

He noticed her stare and gave a chagrinned smile. "I injured it years ago. It still occasionally aches."

"I imagine the hard work of ranching contributes to that."

"Yeah, it does, but it's worth it. I love working the land that's been in my family for almost seventy-five years. But we've been going through a tough time, and it's been pretty obvious we need a championship bull to invigorate our breeding program. I thought if I met with some of the ranchers here, we could find some investment partners."

"That was what your meeting today was about?"

"Yeah. But the Sweetheart Ranch is a large operation, and it's all they want to handle right now."

"We have other ranches around here."

He glanced at her and grinned. "Yeah, I have more meetings tomorrow."

"I'm sure you'll be successful." She looked away from him, the magnetism of his smile making her feel overheated though she was sitting in the shade. Or maybe it was the proximity of the hot tub, she told herself.

An Excerpt from

LEARNING THE ROPES
by T. J. Kline

From author T. J. Kline comes the stunning
follow-up to *Rodeo Queen*. When former
rodeo queen Alicia falls for perpetual playboy
Chris, she must find a way to tame him.

Alicia Kanani slapped the reins against her horse's rump as he stretched out, practically flying between the barrels down the length of the rodeo arena, dirt clods rising behind them as the paint gelding ate up the ground with his long stride. She glanced at the clock as she pulled him up, circling to slow him to a jog as a cowboy opened the back gate, allowing her to exit. 14.45. It was only good enough for second place right now. If only she'd been able to cut the first barrel closer, it might have taken another tenth of a second off her time.

She walked her favorite gelding, Beast, back to the trailer and hooked his halter around his neck before loosening his cinch. She heard the twitter of female laughter before she actually recognized the pair of women behind her trailer and cringed. Delilah had been a thorn in her side ever since high school, when Alicia had first arrived in West Hills. There'd never been a lack of competition between them, but it seemed, years later, only one of them had matured at all.

"Look, Dallas, there's Miss Runner-Up." Delilah jerked her chin at Alicia's trailer. "Came in second again, huh?" She flipped her long blonde waves over her shoulder. "I guess you can't win them all . . . oh, wait." She giggled. "You don't seem to win any, do you? That would be me." The pair laughed as if it were the funniest joke ever.

"Isn't it hard to ride a broom *and* a horse at the same time, Delilah?" Alicia tipped her head to the side innocently as Delilah glared at her and stormed away, pulling Dallas with her.

Alicia snidely imitated Delilah's laugh to her horse as she pulled the saddle from his back and put it into the trailer. "She thinks she's so funny. 'You haven't won. I have,'" she mimicked in a nasally voice. "Witch," she muttered as she rubbed the curry comb over Beast's neck and back.

"I sure hope you don't kiss your mother with that mouth."

Alicia spun to see Chris Thomas, her best friend Sydney's brother, walking toward her trailer. She'd rodeoed with Chris and Sydney for years, until Chris had gone pro with his team roping partner. For the last few years, they'd all been pursuing the same goal, the National Finals Rodeo, in their respective events. So far their paths hadn't crossed since Sydney's wedding nearly two years before. She'd suspected she might see him here since they were so close to home and this rodeo boasted a huge purse for team ropers.

"Chris!" She hurried over and gave him a bear hug. "Did you rope already?"

"Tonight during the slack." Most of the team ropers would be competing tonight before the barbecue and dance. "I see Delilah's still giving you a hard time."

She shrugged and smirked. "She's still mad I beat her out for rodeo queen when Sydney gave up the title."

"That was a long time ago. You'd think she'd let it go." Chris stuffed his hands into his pockets and leaned against the side of her trailer, patting Beast's neck. "Maybe you should put Nair in her shampoo like she did to you."

Alicia cringed at the memory. "It was a good thing I smelled it before I put it on my head. That could've been traumatizing, but I got her back."

"That's right. Didn't you put liniment in her lip gloss?" She smiled at the reminder of the prank, and Chris laughed. They'd had some good times together in the past. She wondered how they'd managed to drift apart over the past few years. She missed his laugh and the way he always seemed to bring the playful side of her personality to the surface.

"So, how'd you do?"

"Second—so far," she clarified. "Again."

He chuckled and crossed his arms over his chest. His biceps bulged against the material of his Western shirt, and she couldn't help but notice how much he'd filled out since she'd last seen him. And in all the right places. "Second's nothing to complain about."

"It's nothing to brag about either," she pointed out, tearing her eyes away from his broad chest. She finished brushing down the horse, feeling slightly uncomfortable with the way he continued to silently watch her, as if he wanted to say something but wasn't sure how to bring it up. Finally she turned and faced him. "What?"